To Free the
Dragonqueen . . .

An impossible, improbable quest to some, certain death to most. Dragonmaw clan would forever retain its hold on Khaz Modan unless Alexstrasza was freed, and so long as the orcs there continued the work of the Horde, they remained a possible rallying point for those in the guarded enclaves.

A brief rumble of thunder disturbed Rhonin's contemplations. He looked up but saw only a few cottony clouds.

A second, more menacing rumble set every muscle taut as a massive shadow covered their surroundings.

An ear-shattering roar shook the vicinity and a force akin to a tornado ripped at the landscape. Rhonin twisted around so as to see the heavens—and saw instead a hellish sight.

A dragon the color of raging fire filled the sky above and in its forepaws it held what remained of his horse and his costly and carefully chosen supplies. The crimson leviathan consumed in one gulp the rest of the carcass, eyes already fixed on the tiny, pathetic figures below.

And seated atop the shoulders of the beast, a grotesque, greenish figure with tusks and a battle-ax barked orders in some harsh tongue and pointed directly at Rhonin.

Maw gaping and talons bared, the dragon dove toward him.

For information regarding special discounts for bulk purchases, please contact Simon & Schuster Special Sales at 1-800-456-6798 or business@simonandschuster.com

WARCRAFT®

DAY OF THE DRAGON

RICHARD A. KNAAK

POCKET BOOKS

New York   London   Toronto   Sydney

This book is a work of fiction. Names, characters, places and incidents are products of the author's imagination or are used fictitiously. Any resemblance to actual events or locales or persons living or dead is entirely coincidental.

An *Original* Publication of POCKET BOOKS

POCKET BOOKS, a division of Simon & Schuster, Inc.
1230 Avenue of the Americas, New York, NY 10020

ISBN 13: 978-0-671-04152-6
ISBN 10:   0-671-04152-5

First Pocket Books printing February 2001

19 18 17 16 15 14

POCKET and colophon are registered trademarks of Simon & Schuster, Inc.

Cover art by Sam Didier

Printed in the U.S.A.

ONE

War.

It had once seemed to some of the Kirin Tor, the magical conclave that ruled the small nation of Dalaran, that the world of Azeroth had never known anything but constant bloodshed. There had been the trolls, before the forming of the Alliance of Lordaeron, and when at last humanity had dealt with that foul menace, the first wave of orcs had descended upon the lands, appearing out of a horrific rip in the very fabric of the universe. At first, nothing had seemed able to stop these grotesque invaders, but gradually what had looked to be a horrible slaughter had turned instead into an agonizing stalemate. Battles had been won by attrition. Hundreds had died on both sides, all seemingly for no good reason. For years, the Kirin Tor had foreseen no end.

But that had finally changed. The Alliance had at last managed to push back the Horde, eventually routing them entirely. Even the orcs' great chieftain, the legendary Orgrim Doomhammer, had been unable to stem the advancing armies and had finally capitulated. With the exception of a few renegade clans, the surviving invaders had been rounded up into enclaves and kept under secure watch by military units led personally by members of the Knights of the Silver Hand. For the first time in many, many years, lasting peace looked to be a promise, not a faint wish.

And yet . . . a sense of unease still touched the senior council of the Kirin Tor. Thus it was that the highest of the high met in the Chamber of the Air, so-called because it seemed a room without walls, only a vast, ever-changing sky with clouds, light, and darkness, racing past the master wizards as if the time of the world had sped up. Only the gray, stone floor with its gleaming diamond symbol, representing the four elements, gave any solidity to the scene.

Certainly the wizards themselves did nothing in that regard, for they, clad in their dark cloaks that covered not only face but form, seemed to waver with the movements of the sky, almost as if they, too, were but illusion. Although their numbers included both men and women, the only sign of that was whenever one of them spoke, at which point a face would become partially visible, if somewhat indistinct in detail.

There were six this meeting, the six most senior, although not necessarily the most gifted. The leaders of the Kirin Tor were chosen by several means, magic but one of them.

"Something is happening in Khaz Modan," announced the first in a stentorian voice, the vague image of a bearded face briefly visible. A myriad pattern of stars floated through his body. "Near or in the caverns held by the Dragonmaw clan."

"Tell us something we don't already know," rasped the second, a woman likely of elder years but still strong of will. A moon briefly shone through her cowl. "The orcs there remain one of the few holdouts, now that Doomhammer's warriors have surrendered and the chieftain's gone missing."

The first mage clearly took some umbrage, but he kept himself calm as he replied. "Very well! Perhaps this will interest you more. . . . I believe Deathwing is on the move again."

This startled the rest, the elder woman included. Night suddenly changed into day, but the wizards ignored what, for them, was a common thing in this chamber. Clouds drifted past the head of the third of their number, who clearly did not believe this statement.

"Deathwing is dead!" the third declared, his form the only one hinting at corpulence. "He plunged into the sea months ago after this very council and a gathering of our strongest struck the mortal blow! No dragon, even him, could withstand such might!"

Some of the others nodded, but the first went on. "And where was the corpse? Deathwing was like no other dragon. Even before the goblins sealed the adamantium plates to his scaly hide, he offered a threat with the potential to dwarf that of the Horde. . . ."

"But what proof do you have of his continued existence?" This from a young woman clearly in the bloom of youth. Not as experienced as the others, but still powerful enough to be one of the council. "What?"

"The death of two red dragons, two of Alexstrasza's get. Torn asunder in a manner only one of their own kind— one of gargantuan proportions—could have managed."

"There are other large dragons."

A storm began to rage, the lightning and rain falling

upon the wizards and yet touching neither them nor the floor. The storm passed in the blink of an eye, a blazing sun once more appearing overhead. The first of the Kirin Tor gave this latest display not even the least of his interest. "You have obviously never seen the work of Deathwing, or you'd never make that statement."

"It may be as you say," interjected the fifth, the outline of a vaguely elven visage appearing and disappearing faster than the storm. "And, if so, a matter of import. But we hardly can concern ourselves with it for now. If Deathwing lives and now strikes out at his greatest rival's kind, then it only benefits us. After all, Alexstrasza is still the captive of Dragonmaw clan, and it is her offspring that those orcs have used for years to wreak bloodshed and havoc all over the Alliance. Have we all so soon forgotten the tragedy of the Third Fleet of Kul Tiras? I suspect that Lord Admiral Daelin Proudmoore never will. After all, he lost his eldest son and everyone else aboard those six great ships when the monstrous red leviathans fell upon them. Proudmoore would likely honor Deathwing with a medal if it proved true that the black beast was responsible for these two deaths."

No one argued that point, not even the first mage. Of the mighty vessels, only splinters of wood and a few torn corpses had been left to mark the utter destruction. It had been to Lord Admiral Proudmoore's credit that he had not faltered in his resolve, immediately ordering the building of new warships to replace those destroyed and pushing on with the war.

"And, as I stated earlier, we can hardly concern ourselves with that situation now, not with so many more immediate issues with which to deal."

"You're referring to the Alterac crisis, aren't you?"

rumbled the bearded mage. "Why should the continued sniping of Lordaeron and Stromgarde worry us more than Deathwing's possible return?"

"Because now Gilneas has thrown its weight into the situation."

Again the other mages stirred, even the unspeaking sixth. The slightly corpulent shade moved a step toward the elven form. "Of what interest is the bickering of the other two kingdoms over that sorry piece of land to Genn Greymane? Gilneas is at the tip of the southern peninsula, as far away in the Alliance as any other kingdom is from Alterac!"

"You have to ask? Greymane has always sought the leadership of the Alliance, even though he held back his armies until the orcs finally attacked his own borders. The only reason he ever encouraged King Terenas of Lordaeron to action was to weaken Lordaeron's military might. Now Terenas maintains his hold on the Alliance leadership mostly because of our work and Admiral Proudmoore's open support."

Alterac and Stromgarde were neighboring kingdoms that had been at odds since the first days of the war. Thoras Trollbane had thrown the full might of Stromgarde behind the Lordaeron Alliance. With Khaz Modan as its neighbor, it had only made sense for the mountainous kingdom to support a united action. None could argue with the determination of Trollbane's warriors, either. If not for them, the orcs would have overrun much of the Alliance during the first weeks of the war, certainly promising a different and highly grim outcome overall.

Alterac, on the other hand, while speaking much of the courage and righteousness of the cause, had not been so forthcoming with its own troops. Like Gilneas, it had provided only token support; but, where Genn Greymane had held back out of ambition, Lord Perenolde, so it had been rumored, had done so because of fear. Even among the Kirin Tor it had early on been asked whether Perenolde had thought to perhaps make a deal with Doomhammer, should the Alliance crumble under the Horde's unceasing onslaught.

That fear had proven to have merit. Perenolde had indeed betrayed the Alliance, but his dastardly act had, fortunately, been short-lived. Terenas, hearing of it, had quickly moved Lordaeron troops in and declared martial law in Alterac. With the war in progress, no one had, at the time, seen fit to complain over such an action, especially Stromgarde. Now that peace had come, Thoras Trollbane had begun to demand that, for its sacrifices, Stromgarde should receive as just due the entire eastern portion of its treacherous former neighbor.

Terenas did not see it so. He still debated the merits of either annexing Alterac to his own kingdom or setting upon its throne a new and more reasonable monarch . . . presumably with a sympathetic ear for Lordaeron causes. Still, Stromgarde had been a loyal, steadfast ally in the struggle, and all knew of Thoras Trollbane's and Terenas's admiration for one another. It made the political situation that had come between the pair all the more sad.

Gilneas, meanwhile, had no such ties to any of the lands involved; it had always remained separate from the other nations of the western world. Both the Kirin Tor and King Terenas knew that Genn Greymane sought to intervene not only to raise his own prestige, but to perhaps further his dreams of expansion. One of Lord Perenolde's nephews had fled to that land after the treachery, and rumor had it that Greymane supported his claim as successor. A base in Alterac would give Gilneas access to resources the southern kingdom did not have, and the excuse to send its mighty ships across the Great Sea. That, in turn, would draw Kul Tiras into the equation, the maritime nation being very protective of its naval sovereignty.

"This will tear the Alliance apart. . . ." muttered the young mage with the accent.

"It has not come to that point yet," pointed out the elven wizard, "but it may soon. And so we have no time to deal with dragons. If Deathwing lives and has chosen to renew his vendetta against Alexstrasza, I, for one, will not oppose him. The fewer dragons in this world the better. Their day is done, after all."

"I have heard," came a voice with no inflection, no identifiable gender, "that once the elves and dragons were allies, even respected friends."

The elven form turned to the last of the mages, a slim, lanky shape little more than shadow. "Tales only, I can assure you. We would not deign to traffic with such monstrous beasts."

Clouds and sun gave way to stars and moon. The sixth mage bowed slightly, as if in apology. "I appear to have heard wrong. My mistake."

"You're right about the importance of calming this political situation down," the bearded wizard rumbled to the fifth. "And I agree it must take priority. Still, we can't afford to ignore what is happening around Khaz Modan! Whether or not I'm wrong about Deathwing, so long as the orcs there hold the Dragonqueen captive, they're a threat to the stability of the land!"

"We need an observer, then," interjected the elder female. "Someone to maintain watch on matters and only alert us if the situation there becomes critical."

"But who? We can spare no one now!"

"There is one." The sixth mage glided a step forward. The face remained in shadow even when the figure spoke. "There is Rhonin. . . ."

"Rhonin?!?" burst out the bearded mage. "Rhonin! After his last debacle? He isn't even fit to wear the robes of a wizard! He's more of a danger than a hope!"

"He's unstable," agreed the elder woman.

"A maverick," muttered the corpulent one.

"Untrustworthy . . ."

"Criminal!"

The sixth waited until all had spoken, then slowly nodded. "And the only skilled wizard we can afford to be without at this juncture. Besides, this is simply a mission of observance. He will be nowhere near any potential crisis. His duty will be to monitor matters and report back, that is all." When no more protests arose, the dark mage added, "I am certain that he has learned his lesson."

"Let us hope so," muttered the older of the women. "He may have accomplished his last mission, but it cost most of his companions their lives!"

"This time, he will go alone, with only a guide to bring him to the edge of Alliance-controlled lands. He shall not even enter Khaz Modan. A sphere of seeing will enable him to watch from a distance."

"It seems simple enough," the younger female responded. "Even for Rhonin."

The elven figure nodded brusquely. "Then let us agree on this and be done with the topic. Perhaps if we are fortunate, Deathwing will swallow Rhonin, then choke to death, thus finishing forever the matters of both." He surveyed the others, then added, "And now I must demand that we finally concentrate on Gilneas's entry into the Alterac situation and what role we may play to diffuse it. . . ."

He stood as he had for the past two hours, head down, eyes closed in concentration. Around him, only a dim light with no source gave any illumination to the chamber, not that there was much to see. A chair he had left unused stood to the side, and behind him on the thick, stone wall hung a tapestry upon which had been sewn an intricate, knowing eye of gold on a field of violet. Below the eye, three daggers, also gold, darted earthward. The flag and symbols of Dalaran had stood tall in their guardianship of the Alliance during the war, even if not every member of the Kirin Tor had performed their duties with complete honor.

"Rhonin . . ." came a voice without inflection, from everywhere and nowhere in the chamber.

From under thick, fiery hair, he looked up into the darkness with eyes a startling green. His nose had been broken once by a fellow apprentice, but despite his skills, Rhonin had never bothered to have it fixed. Still, he was not unhandsome, with a strong, clean jaw and angular features. One permanently arched brow ever gave him a sardonic, questioning look that had more than once gotten him in trouble with his masters, and matters were not helped by his attitude, which matched his expression.

Tall, slim, and clad in an elegant robe of midnight blue, he made for quite a sight, even to other wizards. Rhonin hardly appeared recalcitrant, even though his last mission had cost the lives of five good men. He stood straight and eyed the murk, waiting to see from which direction the other wizard would speak to him.

"You summoned. I've waited," the crimson-tressed spellcaster whispered, not without some impatience.

"It could not be helped. I myself had to wait until the matter was brought up by someone else." A tall cloaked and hooded figure half-emerged from the gloom—the sixth member of the Kirin Tor inner council. "It was."

For the first time, some eagerness shone in the eyes of Rhonin. "And my penance? Is my probation over?"

"Yes. You have been granted your return to our ranks . . . under the provision that you accede to taking on a task of import immediately."

"They've that much faith left in me?" Bitterness returned to the young mage's voice. "After the others died?"

"You are the only one they have left."

"That sounds more realistic. I should've known."

"Take these." The shadowy wizard held out a slim, gloved hand, palm up. Above the hand there suddenly flashed into existence two glittering objects—a tiny sphere of emerald and a ring of gold with a single black jewel.

Rhonin held out his own hand in the same manner . . . and the two items appeared above it. He seized both and inspected them. "I recognize the sphere of seeing, but not this other. It feels powerful, but not, I'm guessing, in an aggressive manner."

"You are astute, which is why I took up your cause in the first place, Rhonin. The sphere's purpose you know;

the ring will serve as protection. You go into a realm where orc warlocks still exist. This ring will help shield you from their own devices of detection. Regrettably, it will also make it difficult for us to monitor you."

"So I'll be on my own." Rhonin gave his sponsor a sardonic smile. "Less chance of me causing any extra deaths, anyway. . . ."

"In that regard, you will not be alone, at least as far as the journey to the port. A ranger will escort you."

Rhonin nodded, although he clearly did not care for any escort, especially a ranger. Rhonin and elves did not get along well together. "You've not told me my mission."

The shadowed wizard propped back, as if sitting in an immense chair the younger spellcaster could not see. Gloved hands steepled as the figure seemed to consider the proper choice of words. "They have not been easy on you, Rhonin. Some in the council even considered forever dismissing you from our ranks. You must earn your way back, and to do that, you will have to fulfill this mission to the letter."

"You make it sound like no easy task."

"It involves dragons . . . and something they believe only one of your *aptitude* can manage to accomplish."

"Dragons . . ." Rhonin's eyes had widened at first mention of the leviathans and, despite his tendency toward arrogance at most times, he knew he sounded more like an apprentice at the moment.

Dragons . . . Simply the mention of them instilled awe in most younger mages.

"Yes, dragons." His sponsor leaned forward. "Make no mistake about this, Rhonin. No one else must know of this mission outside of the council and yourself. Not even the ranger who guides you nor the captain of the Alliance ship who drops you on the shores of Khaz Modan. If word got out what we hope from you, it could set all the plans in jeopardy."

"But what is it?" Rhonin's green eyes flared bright. This would be a quest of tremendous danger, but the rewards were clear enough. A return to the ranks and obvious added prestige to his reputation. Nothing advanced a wizard in the Kirin Tor quicker than reputation, although none of the senior council would have ever admitted to that base fact.

"You are to go to Khaz Modan," the other said with some hesitation, "and, once there, set into motion the steps necessary to free from her orc captors the Dragonqueen, *Alexstrasza*. . . ."

TWO

Vereesa did not like waiting. Most people thought that elves had the patience of glaciers, but younger ones such as herself, just a year out of her apprenticeship in the rangers, were very much like humans in that one regard. She had been waiting three days for this wizard she was supposed to escort to one of the eastern ports serving the Great Sea. For the most part, she respected wizards as much as any elf respected a human, but this one had earned nothing but her ire. Vereesa wanted to join her sisters and brothers, help hunt down each and every remaining orc still fighting, and send the murderous beasts to their well-deserved deaths. The ranger had not expected her first major assignment to be playing nursemaid to some doddering and clearly forgetful old mage.

"One more hour," she muttered. "One more hour, and then I leave."

Her sleek, chestnut-brown, elven mare snorted ever so slightly. Generations of breeding had created an animal far superior to its mundane cousins, or so Vereesa's people believed. The mare was in tune with her rider, and what would have seemed to most nothing more than a simple grunt from the horse immediately sent the ranger to her feet, a long shaft already notched in her bow.

Yet the woods around her spoke only of quiet, not treachery, and this deep within the Lordaeron Alliance she could hardly expect an attack by either orcs or trolls. She glanced in the direction of the small inn that had been designated the meeting place, but other than a stable boy carrying hay, Vereesa saw no one. Still, the elf did not lower her bow. Her mount rarely made a sound unless some trouble lurked nearby. Bandits, perhaps?

Slowly the ranger turned in a circle. The wind whipped some of the long, silver-white hair across her face, but not enough to obscure her sharp sight. Almond-shaped eyes the color of purest sky blue drank in even the most minute shift of foliage, and the lengthy, pointed ears that rose from her thick hair could pick up even the sound of a butterfly landing on a nearby flower.

And still she could find no reason for the mare's warning.

Perhaps she had frightened away whatever supposed menace had been nearby. Like all elves, Vereesa knew she made an impressive appearance. Taller than most humans, the ranger stood clad in knee-high leather boots, forest-green pants and blouse, and an oak-brown travel cloak. Gloves that stretched nearly to her elbows protected her hands while yet enabling her to use her bow or the sword hanging at her side with ease. Over her blouse she wore a sturdy breastplate fashioned to her slim but still curved form. One of the locals in the inn had made the mistake of admiring the feminine aspects of her appearance while entirely ignoring the military ones. Because he had been drunk and possibly would have held back his rude suggestions otherwise, Vereesa had only left him with a few broken fingers.

The mare snorted again. The ranger glared at her mount, words of reprimand forming on her lips.

"You would be Vereesa Windrunner, I presume," a low, arresting voice on her blind side suddenly commented.

She had the tip of the shaft directly at his throat before he could say more. Had Vereesa let the arrow loose, it would have shot completely through the newcomer's neck, exiting through the other side.

Curiously, he seemed unimpressed by this deadly fact. The elf stared him up and down—not an entirely unpleasant task, she had to admit—and realized that her sudden intruder could only be the wizard for whom she had been waiting. Certainly that would explain her mount's peculiar actions and her own inability to sense his presence before this.

"You are Rhonin?" the ranger finally asked.

"Not what you're expecting?" he returned with just the hint of a sardonic smile.

She lowered the bow, relaxing slightly. "They said a wizard; that was all, human."

"And they told me an elven ranger, nothing more." He gave her a glance that almost made Vereesa raise the bow again. "So we find ourselves even in this matter."

"Not quite. I have waited here for three days! Three valuable days wasted!"

"It couldn't be helped. Preparations needed to be made." The wizard said nothing more.

Vereesa gave up. Like most humans, this one cared nothing for anyone but himself. She considered herself fortunate that she had not had to wait longer. It amazed her that the Alliance could have ever triumphed against the Horde with so many like this Rhonin in their ranks.

"Well, if you wish to make your passage to Khaz Modan, then it would be best if we left immediately." The elf peered behind him. "Where is your mount?"

She half-expected him to tell her that he had none, that he had used his formidable powers to transport himself all the way here . . . but if that had been the case, Rhonin would not have needed her to guide him to the ship. As a wizard, he no doubt had impressive abilities, but he also had his limits. Besides, from what little she knew of his mission, she suspected that Rhonin would need everything he had just to survive. Khaz Modan was not a land welcoming to outsiders. The skulls of many brave warriors decorated the orc tents there, so she had heard, and dragons constantly patrolled the skies. No, not a place even Vereesa would have gone without an army at her side. She was no coward, but she was also no fool.

"Tied near a trough by the inn, so that he can get some water. I've already ridden long today, milady."

His use of the title for her might have flattered Vereesa, if not for the slight touch of sarcasm she thought she noted in his tone. Fighting down her irritation with the human, she turned to her own horse, replaced the bow and shaft, then proceeded to ready her animal for the ride.

"My horse could do with a few more minutes' rest," the wizard suggested, "and so could I."

"You will learn to sleep in the saddle quickly enough . . . and the pace I set at first will enable your steed to recoup. We have waited far too long. Few ships, even those of Kul Tiras, are endeared to the thought of sailing to Khaz Modan simply for a wizard on observation duty. If you do not reach port soon, they may decide that they have more worthy and less suicidal matters with which to deal."

To her relief, Rhonin did not argue. Instead, with a frown, he turned and headed back toward the inn. Vereesa watched him depart, hoping that she would not find herself tempted to run him through before they managed to part company.

She wondered about his mission. True, Khaz Modan remained a threat because of the dragons and their orc masters there, but the Alliance already had other, more well-trained observers in and around the land. Vereesa suspected that Rhonin's mission concerned a very serious matter, or else the Kirin Tor would have never risked so much for this arrogant mage. Still, had they considered the matter well enough when they had chosen him? Surely there had to have been someone more able—and trustworthy? This wizard had a look to him, one that spoke of a streak of unpredictability that might lead to disaster.

The elf tried to shrug off her doubts. The Kirin Tor had made up their minds in this matter, and Alliance command had clearly agreed with them or else she would not have been sent along to guide him. Best she put aside any concerns. All she had to do was deliver her charge to his vessel, and then Vereesa could be on her way. What Rhonin might or might not do after their separation did not concern her in the least.

For four days they journeyed, never once threatened by anything more dangerous than a few annoying insects. Had circumstances been different, the trek might have seemed almost idyllic, if not for the fact that Rhonin and his guide had barely spoken with one another all that time. For the most part, the wizard had not been bothered much by that fact, his thoughts focused on the dangerous task ahead. Once the Alliance ship brought him to the shores of Khaz Modan, he would be on his own in a realm still overrun not only with orcs but patrolled from the sky by their captive dragons. While no coward, Rhonin had little desire to face torture and slow, agonizing death. For that alone, his benefactor in the council had provided him with the latest known movements of the Dragonmaw clan. Dragonmaw would be most on the watch now, especially if, as Rhonin had been told, the black leviathan Deathwing did indeed live.

Yet, as dangerous as the mage's quest appeared, Rhonin would not have turned back. He had been given an opportunity to not only redeem himself but to advance among the Kirin Tor. For that he would forever be most grateful to his patron, whom he only knew by the name *Krasus*. The title was surely a false one, not an uncommon practice among those in the ruling council. The masters of Dalaron were chosen in secret, their ascension known only to their fellows, not even their loved ones. The voice of Rhonin's benefactor could be nothing like his true voice . . . if male was even the correct gender.

It was possible to guess the identities of some of the inner circle, but Krasus remained an enigma even to his clever agent. In truth, though, Rhonin barely even cared about Krasus's identity anymore, only that through him the younger wizard could achieve his own dreams.

But those dreams would remain distant ones if he never made his ship. Leaning forward in the saddle, he asked, "How much farther to Hasic?"

Without turning, Vereesa blandly replied, "Three more days at least. Do not worry; our pace will now get us to the port on time."

Rhonin leaned back again. So much for their latest conversation, only the second of today. The only thing possibly worse than riding with an elf would have been traveling with one of the dour Knights of the Silver Hand. Despite their ever-present courtesy, the paladins generally made it clear that they considered magic an occasional, necessary evil, one with which they would do without at all other times. The last one that Rhonin had encountered had quite clearly indicated that he believed that, after death, the mage's soul would be condemned to the same pit of darkness shared by the mythical demons of old. This no matter how pure Rhonin's soul might have been otherwise.

The late afternoon sun began to sink among the treetops, creating contrasting areas of brightness and dark shadow among the trees. Rhonin had hoped to reach the edge of the woods before dark, but clearly they would not do so. Not for the first time, he ran through his mental maps, trying not only to place their present location but verify what his companion had said about still making the ship. His delay in meeting with Vereesa had been unavoidable, the product of trying to find necessary supplies and components. He only hoped it would still not prove to jeopardize his entire mission.

To free the Dragonqueen . . .

An impossible, improbable quest to some, certain death to most. Yet, even during the war, Rhonin had proposed such. Clearly, if the Dragonqueen were freed, it would at the very least strip from the remaining orcs one of their greatest weapons. However, circumstance had never enabled such a monumental quest to come to fruition.

Rhonin knew most of the council hoped he would fail. To be rid of him would be to erase what they considered a black mark from the history of their order. This mission had a double edge to it; they would be astounded if he succeeded, but relieved if he failed.

At least he could trust in Krasus. The wizard had first come to him, asking if his younger counterpart still believed he could do the impossible. Dragonmaw clan would forever retain its hold on Khaz Modan unless Alexstrasza was freed, and so long as the orcs there continued the work of the Horde, they remained a possible rallying point for those in the guarded enclaves. No one wanted the war renewed. The Alliance had enough strife within its own ranks to keep it busy.

A brief rumble of thunder disturbed Rhonin's contemplations. He looked up but saw only a few cottony clouds. Frowning, the fiery-haired spellcaster turned his gaze toward the elf, intending to ask her if she, too, had heard the thunder.

A second, more menacing rumble set every muscle taut.

At the same time, Vereesa *leapt* at him, the ranger somehow having managed to turn in the saddle and push herself in his direction.

A massive shadow covered their surroundings.

The ranger and the wizard collided, the elf's armored weight shoving both off the back of Rhonin's own mount.

An ear-shattering roar shook the vicinity, and a force akin to a tornado ripped at the landscape. As the wizard struck the hard ground, through the shock of pain he heard the brief whinny of his mount—a sound cut off the next moment.

"Keep down!" Vereesa called above the wind and roaring. "Keep down!"

Rhonin, though, twisted around so as to see the heavens—and saw instead a hellish sight.

A dragon the color of raging fire filled the sky above. In its forepaws it held what remained of his horse and his costly and carefully chosen supplies. The crimson leviathan consumed in one gulp the rest of the carcass, eyes already fixed on the tiny, pathetic figures below.

And seated atop the shoulders of the beast, a grotesque, greenish figure with tusks and a battle-ax that looked nearly as large as the mage barked orders in some harsh tongue and pointed directly at Rhonin.

Maw gaping and talons bared, the dragon dove toward him.

"I thank you again for your time, Your Majesty," the tall, black-haired noble said in a voice full of strength and understanding. "Perhaps we can yet keep this crisis from tearing your good work asunder."

"If so," returned the older, bearded figure clad in the elegant white and gold robes of state, "Lordaeron and the Alliance will have much to thank you for, Lord Prestor. It's only because of your work that I feel Gilneas and Stromgarde might yet see reason." Although no slight man himself, King Terenas felt a little overwhelmed by his larger companion.

The younger man smiled, revealing perfect teeth. If Terenas could have found a more regal-looking man than

Lord Prestor, he would have been surprised. With his short, well-groomed black hair, clean-shaven hawklike features that had set many of the women of the court atwitter, quick mind, and a bearing more princely than any prince in the Alliance, it was not at all surprising that everyone involved in the Alterac situation had taken to him, Genn Greymane included. Prestor had an engaging manner that had actually made the ruler of Gilneas smile on a rare occasion, so Terenas's marveling diplomats had informed him.

For a young noble whom no one had even heard of prior to five years before, the king's guest had made quite a reputation for himself. Prestor came from the most mountainous, most obscure region of Lordaeron, but could claim bloodlines in the royal house of Alterac as well. His tiny domain had been destroyed during the war by a dragon attack and he had come to the capital on foot, without even one servant to dress him. His plight and what he had made of himself since his arrival had become the thing of storybook tales. More important, his advice had aided the king many times, including during the dark days when the graying monarch had debated on what to do about Lord Perenolde. Prestor had, in fact, been the swaying factor. He had given Terenas the encouragement needed to seize power in Alterac, then solidify martial law there. Stromgarde and the other kingdoms had understood the need for action against the traitorous Perenolde, but not Lordaeron's continued holding of that kingdom for its own purposes after the war had ended. Now at last, Prestor appeared to be the one who could explain it all to them and make them accept any final decision.

Which had, of late, made the aging, broad-featured monarch mull over a possible solution that would stun even the clever man before him. Terenas refused to turn over Alterac to Perenolde's nephew, whom Gilneas had tried to support. Nor did he think it wise to divide the kingdom in question between Lordaeron and Stromgarde. That would surely earn the wrath of not only Gilneas, but Kul Tiras even. Annexing Alterac completely was also out of the question.

What if, though, he placed the region in the capable hands of one admired by all, one who had shown he wanted nothing but peace and unity? An able administrator, too, if King Terenas were any judge, not to mention someone certain to remain a true ally and friend to Lordaeron. . . .

"No, indeed, Prestor!" The king reached up to pat the much taller lord on the shoulder. Prestor had to be nearly seven feet in height, but while slim, he could hardly be called lanky. Prestor well fit his blue and black dress uniform, looking every inch the martial hero. "You've much to be proud about . . . and much to be rewarded for! I'll not soon forget your part in this, believe me!"

Prestor fairly beamed, likely believing he would soon have his tiny realm restored to him. Terenas decided to let the boy keep that little dream; when the ruler of Lordaeron proposed him as new monarch of Alterac, the expression on Prestor's face would be that much more entertaining. It was not every day that someone became king . . . unless they inherited the position, of course.

Terenas's honored guest saluted him, then, bowing gracefully, retreated from the imperial chamber. The elder man frowned after Prestor left, thinking that the silken curtains, the golden chandeliers, and even the pure white marble floor could not brighten the room enough now that the young noble had departed. Truly Lord Prestor stood out among the many odious courtiers flocking to the palace. Here was a man anyone could believe in, a man worthy of trust and respect in all matters. Terenas wished his own son could have been more like Prestor.

The king rubbed his bearded chin. Yes, the perfect man to rebuild the honor of a land and at the same time restore harmony between the members of the Alliance. New and strong blood.

Considering the matter further, Terenas thought of his daughter, Calia. Still a child, but certainly soon to be a beauty. Perhaps one day, if matters went well, he and Prestor could strengthen their friendship and alliance with a royal marriage, too.

Yes, he would go talk to his advisors now, relate to them his royal opinion. Terenas felt certain that they would agree with him on this decision. He had met no one yet who disliked the young noble.

King Prestor of Alterac. Terenas could just imagine the look on his friend's face when he learned the extent of his reward. . . .

"You've the shadow of a smile on your face—did someone die a horrible, grisly, bloody death, o venomous one?"

"Spare me your witticisms, Kryll," Lord Prestor replied as he shut the great iron door behind him. Above, in the old chalet given over to him by his host, King Terenas, servants specifically chosen by Prestor stood guard to see that no unwarranted visitors dropped in. Their master had work to do, and even if none of the servants truly knew what went on in the chambers below-ground, they had been made to know that it would be their lives if he was disturbed.

Prestor expected no interruptions and trusted that those lackeys would obey to the death. The spell upon them, a variation of the one that caused the king and his court to so admire the dashing refugee, allowed no room for second thoughts. He had honed its effectiveness quite well over time.

"Most humble apologies, o prince of duplicity!" rasped the smaller, wiry figure before him. The tone in the other's voice held hints of mischief and madness and an inhuman quality—not surprising, as Prestor's companion was a goblin.

His head barely reaching above the noble's belt buckle, some might have taken the slight, emerald-green creature for weak and simple. The madcap grin, however, revealed long teeth so very sharp and a tongue blood-red and almost forked. Narrow, yellow eyes with no visible pupils sparkled with merriment, but the sort of merriment that came from pulling the wings off flies or the arms off experimental subjects. A ridge of dull brown fur rose up from behind the goblin's neck, finishing as a wild crest above the hideous creature's squat forehead.

"Still, there is reason to celebrate." The lower chamber had once been used to house supplies. In those days, the coolness of the earth had kept wine rack after wine rack at just the right temperature. Now, however, thanks to a little engineering on the part of Kryll, the vast room felt as if it sat in the middle of a raging volcano.

For Lord Prestor, it felt just like home.

"Celebrate, o master of deceit?" Kryll giggled. Kryll giggled a lot, especially when foul work was afoot. The emerald creature's two chief passions were experimentation and mayhem, and whenever possible he combined the two. The back half of the chamber was, in fact, filled with benches, flasks, powders, curious mechanisms, and macabre collections all gathered by the goblin.

"Yesss, celebrate, Kryll." Prestor's penetrating, ebony eyes fixed unblinkingly on the goblin, who suddenly lost his smile and all semblance of mockery. "You would like to be around to join in that celebration, wouldn't you?"

"Yes . . . Master."

The uniformed noble took a moment to breathe in the stifling air. An expression of relief crossed his angular features. "Aaah, how I miss it . . ." His face hardened. "But I must wait. Go only when necessary, eh, Kryll?"

"As you say, Master."

The smile, now so very sinister, returned to Prestor's expression. "You are likely looking at the next king of Alterac, you know."

The goblin bent his narrow but muscular body nearly to the ground. "All hail his royal majesty, King D—"

A clatter made both glance to the right. From a metal grate leading to an old ventilation shaft emerged a smaller goblin. Nimbly, the tiny figure pulled itself through the opening and rushed over to Kryll. The newcomer wore a fiendishly amused look on his ugly face, a look that quickly faded under Prestor's intense gaze.

The second goblin whispered something into Kryll's large, pointed ear. Kryll hissed, then dismissed the other creature with a negligent wave of the hand. The newcomer vanished back through the open grate.

"What is it?" Although the words came calmly and smoothly from the lips of the aristocrat, they also clearly demanded no hesitation on the part of the goblin to answer.

"Aaah, gracious one," Kryll began, the madcap smile once more upon his bestial face. "Luck is with you this day, it seems! Perhaps you should consider making a wager somewhere? The stars must truly favor—"

"*What is it?*"

"Someone . . . someone is attempting to free Alexstrasza. . . ."

Prestor stared. He stared so long and with such intensity that Kryll fairly shriveled up before him. Surely now, the goblin imagined, surely now death would come. A pity that. There had been so many more experiments he had wanted to try, so many more explosives to test . . .

At that moment, the tall, black figure before him broke out laughing, a laugh deep, dark, and not entirely natural.

"Perfect . . ." Lord Prestor managed to utter between bouts of mirth. He stretched his arms out as if seeking to capture the very air. His fingers seemed impossibly long and almost clawed. "So perfect!"

He continued to laugh and, as he did, the goblin Kryll settled back, marveling at the odd sight and shaking his head ever so slightly.

"And they call *me* mad," he muttered under his breath.

THREE

The world became fire.

Vereesa cursed as she and the wizard scattered under the inferno suddenly exhaled by the crimson behemoth as it descended. If Rhonin had not delayed the start of their journey, this would have never happened. They would have arrived in Hasic by now, and she would have parted from his company. Now, it seemed very likely both of them would be parting with their lives. . . .

She had known that the orcs of Khaz Modan still sent out occasional dragon flights to wreak terror on the otherwise peaceful lands of their enemies, but why had she and her companion had the misfortune to be found by one? Dragons were fewer these days, and the realms of Lordaeron immense.

She glanced at Rhonin, who had thrown himself deeper into the woods. Of course. Somehow it had to do with the fact that her companion was a wizard. Dragons had senses far above those of even elves; some said they could, within limitations, even smell magic. Somehow this disastrous turn of events had to be the wizard's fault. The orc and his dragon had to have come for him.

Rhonin evidently thought something similar, for he hurried from her sight as quickly as he could, darting into the woods in the opposite direction from her. The ranger snorted. Wizards were never good in the front line; it was easy to attack someone from a distance or behind his back, but when they had to actually face a foe . . .

Of course, it *was* a dragon.

The dragon veered toward the vanishing human. Despite what she might personally think of him, Vereesa did not want to see the spellcaster dead. Yet, peering around, the silver-haired ranger saw no manner by which she could aid him. Her mount had been taken along with his, and with it had gone her favored bow. All that remained with her was her sword, hardly a weapon to be used against such a rampaging titan. Vereesa looked around for something else she could use, but nothing suited.

That left her with little choice. As a ranger, she could not let even the wizard fall to harm if she could help it. Vereesa had to do the only thing she could think of in order to possibly save his life.

The elf leapt up from her hiding place, waved her hands in the air, and shouted, "Here! Over here, spawn of a lizard! Here!"

However, the dragon did not hear her, his—Vereesa had finally managed to identify it as a male—attention on the burning woods below him. Somewhere in that inferno Rhonin struggled to survive. The dragon sought to make certain that he did not.

Cursing, the elven warrior looked around and found a heavy rock. For a human, what she sought to do would have been nigh unto impossible, but for her it still remained in the realm of probability. Vereesa only hoped her arm was as good as it had been a few short years back.

Stretching back, she threw the rock directly at the head of the crimson leviathan.

She had the distance, but the dragon suddenly moved, and for a moment Vereesa expected her rock to miss. However, although it did not hit the head, the projectile did bounce off the tip of the nearest of the webbed wings. Vereesa did not even expect to injure the beast— a mere rock against hard dragonscale a laughable weapon—but what she had hoped for was to attract the behemoth's attention.

And so she did.

The massive head immediately swerved her way, the dragon roaring in annoyance at this interruption. The orc shouted something unintelligible at his mount.

The great winged form abruptly banked, steering toward her. She had succeeded in taking his attention from the hapless mage.

And now what? the ranger chided herself.

The elf turned and ran, already knowing she had no chance of outpacing her monstrous pursuer.

The treetops above her burst into flames as the dragon coated the landscape. Burning foliage dropped before her, cutting off Vereesa's intended route. Without hesitation, the ranger shifted to the left, diving among trees that had not yet become a part of the inferno.

You are going to die! she informed herself. *All for that useless wizard!*

An ear-splitting roar made her look over her shoulder. The red dragon had reached her, and even now one taloned paw stretched down to seize the fleeing ranger.

Vereesa imagined that paw crushing her or, worse fate, dragging her into the behemoth's horrific maw, where she would be chewed up or swallowed whole.

Yet, just as death came within inches of her, the dragon suddenly pulled back his claws and began squirming in midair. The claws raked against his own torso. In fact, every set of claws was trying to scratch somewhere, anywhere, as if—as if the leviathan suffered an incredibly painful itch. Atop him, the orc struggled for control, but he might as well have been the very flea that seemed to trouble the dragon for all the beast obeyed him now.

Vereesa stopped and stared, never having witnessed so startling a sight. The dragon twisted and turned as he tried to relieve his agony, his actions growing more and more frantic. His orc handler could barely hold on. What, the elf wondered, could have caused the monster so much—

The answer came out as a whisper. "Rhonin?"

And, as if by saying his name she had summoned him like some ghost, the mage stood before her. His fiery hair hung disheveled and his dark robe had become muddy and torn, but he looked undeterred by what he had so far suffered.

"I think it'd be better if we left while we could, eh, elf?"

She did not need him to offer again. This time, Rhonin led the way, using some skill, some magical ability, to guide them through the blazing forest. As a ranger, Vereesa could not have done better herself. Rhonin led her along paths the elf could not even see until they were upon them.

All the while, the dragon soared overhead, tearing at its hide. Once Vereesa glanced up and saw that he had even managed to draw blood, his own claws one of the few things capable of ripping through his armored skin.

Of the orc she saw no more sign; at some point the tusked warrior must have lost his grip and fallen. Vereesa felt no remorse for him.

"What did you do to the dragon?" she finally managed to gasp.

Rhonin, intent on finding the end of the blaze, did not even look back at her. "Something that didn't turn out the way I planned! He should've suffered more than an intense irritation!"

He actually sounded annoyed with himself, but the ranger, for once, found herself impressed by him. He had turned certain death into possible safety—provided they found their way out.

Behind them, the dragon roared his frustration at the world.

"How long will it last?"

Now he finally paused to eye her, and what she saw in that gaze unsettled her greatly. "Not nearly long enough. . . ."

They redoubled their efforts. Fire surrounded them wherever they turned, but at last they reached its very edge, racing past the flames and out into a region where only deadly smoke assailed them. Both choking, the pair stumbled on, searching for a path that would keep the wind blowing at them from the front and, consequently, help to slow the fire and smoke behind.

And then another roar shook them, for it did not speak of agony, but rather fury and revenge. Wizard and ranger turned about, glanced at the crimson form in the distance.

"The spell's worn off," Rhonin muttered unnecessarily.

It had indeed worn off, and Vereesa could see that the dragon knew exactly who had been responsible for his pain. With an almost unerring aim, the dragon pushed toward them with his massive, leathery wings, clearly intent on making them pay.

"Do you have another spell for this?" Vereesa called as they ran.

"Perhaps! But I'd rather not use it here! It could take us with it!"

As if the dragon would not do that anyway. The elf hoped that Rhonin would see his way to unleashing this deadly spell before they both ended up as fare for the behemoth.

"How far—" The wizard had to catch his breath. "How far to Hasic?"

"Too far."

"Any other settlement between here and there?"

She tried to think. One place came to mind, but she could not recall either its name or its purpose. Only that it lay about a day's journey from here. "There is something, but—"

The dragon's roar shook them both again. A shadow passed overhead.

"If you do have another spell that might work, I would suggest using it now." Vereesa wished again for her bow. With it she could have at least tried for the eyes with some hope of success. The shock and agony might have been enough to send the monster flying off.

They nearly collided as Rhonin came to an unexpected halt and turned to face the dire threat. He took hold of her arms with surprisingly strong hands, for a wizard, then shifted the ranger aside. His eyes literally glowed, something Vereesa had heard could happen with powerful mages but had never in her life seen.

"Pray that this doesn't backfire on us," he muttered.

His arms went up straight, hands pointed in the direction of the red dragon.

He started to mutter words in a language that Vereesa did not recognize, but which somehow sent shivers up and down her spine.

Rhonin brought his hands together, started to speak again—

Through the clouds came three more winged forms.

Vereesa gasped and the tall wizard held his tongue, stalling the spell. He looked ready to curse the heavens, but then the elf recognized what had emerged just above their horrific foe.

Gryphons . . . massive, eagle-headed, leonine-bodied, winged gryphons . . . with riders.

She tugged at Rhonin's arm. "Do not do anything!"

He glared at her, but nodded. They both looked up as the dragon filled their view.

The three gryphons suddenly darted around the dragon, catching him by surprise. Now Vereesa could identify the riders, not that she had really needed to do so. Only the dwarves of the distant Aerie Peaks, a foreboding, mountainous region beyond even the elven realm of Quel'thalas, rode the wild gryphons . . . and only these skilled warriors and their mounts could face dragons in the air.

Although much smaller than the crimson giant, the gryphons made up for the size difference with huge, razor-sharp talons that could tear off dragonscale and beaks that could rip into the flesh beneath. In addition, they could move more swiftly and abruptly through the sky, turning at angles a dragon could never match.

The dwarves themselves did not simply manage their

mounts, either. Slightly taller and leaner than their earthier cousins, the mountain dwarves were no less muscled. Although their favored weapons when patrolling the skies were the legendary Stormhammers, this trio carried great double-edged battle-axes with lengthy handles that the warriors manipulated with ease. Made of a metal akin to adamantium, the blades could cut through even the bony, scaled heads of the behemoths. Rumor had it that the great gryphon-rider Kurdran had struck down a dragon more immense than this one with just one well-aimed blow from an ax like these.

The winged animals circled their foe, forcing him to constantly turn from side to side to see which one threatened most. The orcs had early on learned to be wary of the gryphons, but without his own rider, this particular monster appeared somewhat lost as to what to do. The dwarves immediately took advantage of that fact, making their mounts dart in and out, much to the dragon's growing frustration. The long beards and ponytails of the wild dwarves fluttered in the wind as they literally laughed in the face of the giant menace. The bellowing laughter only served to antagonize the dragon more, and he slashed about madly, accompanying his futile attacks with spurts of flame.

"They are completely disorienting him," Vereesa commented, impressed by the tactics. "They know he is young and that his temper will keep him from attacking with strategy!"

"Which makes it a good time for us to leave," Rhonin replied.

"They might need our help!"

"I've a mission to fulfill," he said ominously. "And they've got matters well in hand."

True enough. The battle seemed to belong to the gryphon-riders, even though they had yet to strike a blow. The trio kept flying around and around the red dragon, so much so that he nearly looked dizzy. He tried his best to keep his eyes on one, but ever the others would distract him. Only once did flame come close to touching one of his winged opponents.

One of the dwarves suddenly began hefting his mighty ax, the head of it gleaming in the late-day sun. He and his mount flew once more about the dragon, then, as they neared the back of the behemoth's skull, the gryphon suddenly darted in.

Claws sank into the neck, ripping away scale. Even as the pain registered in the dragon's mind, the dwarf brought the mighty ax around and swung hard.

The blade sank deep. Not enough to kill, but more than enough to make the dragon shriek in agony.

Out of sheer reflex, he turned. His wing caught the dwarf and the gryphon by surprise, sending them spiraling out of control. The rider managed to hold on, but his ax flew out of his grip, falling earthward.

Vereesa instinctively started in the direction of the weapon, but Rhonin blocked her path with his arm. "I said that we need to leave!"

She would have argued, but one more glance at the combatants revealed that the ranger could be of no use. The wounded dragon had flown higher into the air, still harassed by the gryphon-riders. Even with the ax, all Vereesa could have done was wave it futilely.

"All right," the elf finally muttered.

Together they hurried from the struggle, relying now on Vereesa's knowledge of where their ultimate destination lay. Behind them, the dragon and the gryphons shrank to tiny specks in the heavens, in part because the battle itself had moved in the opposite direction of the elf and her companion.

"Curious . . ." she heard the wizard whisper.

"What is?"

He started. "Those ears aren't just for show, then, are they?"

Vereesa bristled at the insult, even though she had heard far worse. Humans and dwarves, quite jealous of the natural superiority of the elven race, often chose the long, tapering ears as the focus of their ridicule. At times, her ears had been compared to those of donkeys, swine, and, worst of all, *goblins*. While Vereesa had never drawn a weapon on anyone because of such comments, more often than not she had still left them much regretting their choice of words.

The emerald eyes of the mage narrowed. "I'm sorry; you took that as an insult. Didn't mean it that way."

She doubted the veracity of his statement, but knew she had to accept his weak attempt at an apology. Forcing down her anger, she asked again, "What do you find so curious?"

"That this dragon should appear in so timely a fashion."

"If you think like that, you might as well ask where the gryphons came from. After all, they chased it off."

He shook his head. "Someone saw him and reported the situation. The riders merely did their duties." He considered. "I know Dragonmaw clan's supposed to be desperate, supposed to be trying to rally both the other rebel clans and the ones in the enclaves, but this wouldn't be the way to go about it."

"Who can say what an orc thinks? This was clearly a

random marauder. This was not the first such attack in the Alliance, human."

"No, but I wonder if—" Rhonin got no further, for suddenly they both became aware of movement in the forest . . . movement from every direction.

With practiced ease, the ranger slid her blade free from its sheath. Beside her, Rhonin's hands disappeared into the deep folds of his wizard's robes, no doubt in preparation for a spell. Vereesa said nothing, but she wondered how much aid he would be in close combat. Better he stand back and let her take on the first attackers.

Too late. Six massive figures on horseback suddenly broke through the woods, surrounding them. Even in the dimming sunlight their silver armor gleamed sharp. The elf found a lance pointing at her chest. Rhonin not only had one touching his breast, but another between his shoulder blades.

Helmed visors with a leonine head for a crest hid the features of their captors. As a ranger, Vereesa wondered how anyone could move in such suits, let alone wage war, but the six maneuvered in the saddle as if completely unencumbered. Their huge, gray war-horses, also armored on top, seemed unperturbed by the extra weight foisted upon them.

The newcomers carried no banner, and the only sign of their identities appeared to be the image of a stylized hand reaching to the heavens embossed on the breastplate. Vereesa thought she knew who they were from this alone, but did not relax. The last time the elf had met such men, they had worn different armor, with horns atop the helm and the lettered symbol of Lordaeron on both their breastplate and shield.

And then a seventh rider slowly emerged from the forest, this one in the more traditional armor that Vereesa had first been expecting. Within the shadowy, visorless helm, she could see a strong and—for a human—older and wiser face with a trim, graying beard. The symbols of both Lordaeron and his own religious order marked not only his shield and breastplate, but also his helm. A silver lion's-head buckle linked together the belt in which hung one of the mighty, pointed warhammers used by such as him.

"An elf," he murmured as he inspected her. "Your strong arm is welcome." The apparent leader then eyed Rhonin, finally commenting with open disdain, "And a *damned soul*. Keep your hands where we can see them and we won't be tempted to cut them off."

As Rhonin clearly fought to keep his fury down, Vereesa found herself caught between relief and uncertainty. They had been captured by paladins of Lordaeron—the fabled Knights of the Silver Hand.

The two met in a place of shadow, a place reachable only by a few, even among their own kind. It was a place where dreams of the past played over and over, murky forms moving about in the fog of the mind's history. Not even the two who met here knew how much of this realm existed in reality and how much of it existed only in their thoughts, but they knew that here no one would be able to eavesdrop.

Supposedly.

Both were tall and slim, their faces covered by cowls. One could be identified as the wizard Rhonin knew as Krasus; the other, but for the greenish tinge of the otherwise gray robes, might as well have been the wizard's twin. Only when words were spoken did it become clear that, unlike the councilor of the Kirin Tor, this figure was definitely male.

"I do not know why I've even come," he commented to Krasus.

"Because you had to. You needed to."

The other let loose with an audible hiss. "True, but now that I'm here, I can choose to leave any time I desire."

Krasus raised a slim, gloved hand. "At least hear me out."

"For what reason? So that you can repeat what you have repeated so many times before?"

"So that for once what I am saying might actually register!" Krasus's unexpected vehemence startled both.

His companion shook his head. "You've been around them much too long. Your shields, both magical and personal, are beginning to break down. It's time you abandoned this hopeless task . . . just as we did."

"I do not believe it hopeless." For the first time, a hint of gender, a voice far deeper than any of the other members of the Kirin Tor's inner circle would have believed possible. "I cannot, so long as she is held."

"What she means to you is understandable, Korialstrasz; what she means to us is that of the memory of a time past."

"If that time is past, then why do you and yours still stand your posts?" Krasus calmly retorted, his emotions once more under control.

"Because we would see our final years calm ones, peaceful ones. . . ."

"All the more reason to join with me in this."

Again the other hissed. "Korialstrasz, will you never give in to the inevitable? Your plan does not surprise us, who know you so well! We've seen your little puppet on his fruitless quest—do you think he can possibly accomplish his task?"

Krasus paused for a moment before replying. "He has the potential . . . but he is not all I have. No, I think he will fail. In doing so, however, I hope that his sacrifice will aid in my final success . . . and if you would join with me, that success would be more likely."

"I was right." Krasus's companion sounded immensely disappointed. "The same rhetoric. The same pleading. I only came because of the alliance, once strong, between our two factions, but clearly I should not have even bothered because of that. You are without backing, without force. There is only you now, and you must hide in the shadows—" he gestured at the mists surrounding them "—in places such as this, rather than show your true nature."

"I do what I must. . . . What is it that you do, anymore?" An edge once more arose in Krasus's voice. "What purpose do you exist for, my old friend?"

The other figure started at this penetrating question, then abruptly turned away. He took a few steps toward the embracing mists, then paused and looked back at the wizard. Krasus's companion sounded resigned. "I wish you the very best on this, Korialstrasz; I really do. I—*we*—just don't believe that there can be any return to the past. Those days are done, and we with them."

"That is your choice, then." They almost parted company, but Krasus suddenly called out. "One request, though, before you return to the others."

"And what is that?"

The mage's entire form seemed to darken, and a hiss

escaped him. "Do not ever call me by that name again. *Ever.* It must not be spoken, even here."

"No one could possibly—"

"*Even here.*"

Something in Krasus's tone made his companion nod. The second figure then hurriedly departed, vanishing into the emptiness.

The wizard stared at the place where the other had stood, thinking of the repercussions of this futile conversation. If only they could have seen sense! Together, they had hope. Divided, they could do little . . . and that would play into their foe's hands.

"Fools . . ." Krasus muttered. *"Abysmal fools . . ."*

FOUR

The paladins brought them back to a keep that had to have been the unnamed settlement of which Vereesa had earlier spoken. Rhonin was unimpressed by it. Its high stone walls surrounded a functional, unadorned establishment where the holy knights, squires, and a small population of common folk attempted to live in relative frugality. The banners of the brotherhood flew side-by-side with those of the Lordaeron Alliance, of which the Knights of the Silver Hand were the most staunch supporters. If not for the townsfolk, Rhonin would have taken the settlement for a completely military operation, for the rule of the holy order clearly had control over all matters here.

The paladins had treated the elf with courtesy, some of the younger knights adding extra charm whenever Vereesa spoke with them, but with the wizard they would not traffic any more than necessity demanded, not even when, at one point, he asked how far they still had to go to reach Hasic. Vereesa had to repeat the question in order for him to find out. Despite initial impressions, the pair were not, of course, prisoners, but Rhonin certainly felt like an outcast among them. They treated him with minimal civility only because their oath to King Terenas demanded it of them, but otherwise he remained a pariah.

"We saw both the dragon and the gryphons," their leader, one Duncan Senturus, boomed. "Our duty and honor demanded we ride out immediately to see what aid we might be."

The fact that the combat had been entirely aerial and, therefore, far out of their reach apparently had not dampened their holy enthusiasm nor struck a chord with their common sense, Rhonin thought wryly. They and the ranger made for good company in that. Curiously, though, the wizard felt a twinge of possessiveness now that he did not have to deal with Vereesa on his own. *After all, she was appointed my guide. She should remain true to her duty until Hasic.*

Unfortunately, as for Hasic, Duncan Senturus had intentions for that, too. As they dismounted, the broad-shouldered senior knight offered his arm to the elf, saying, "Of course, it would be remiss of us to not see you along the safest and quickest route to the port. I know it's a task you've been given, milady, but clearly it was chosen by a higher power that your paths would lead you to us. We know well the way to Hasic, and so a small party, led by myself, will journey with you come the morrow."

This seemed to please the ranger, but hardly encouraged Rhonin any. Everyone in the keep eyed him as if he had been transformed into a goblin or orc. He had suffered enough disdain around his fellow spellcasters and felt no need to have the paladins add further to his troubles.

"It's very kind of you," Rhonin interjected from behind them. "But Vereesa is a capable ranger. We'll reach Hasic in time."

Senturus's nostrils flared as if he had just smelled something noxious. Keeping his smile fixed, the senior paladin said to the elf, "Allow me to personally escort you to your quarters." He glanced at one of his subordinates. "Meric! Find a place to put the wizard. . . ."

"This way," grumbled a hulking young knight with a full mustache. He looked ready to take Rhonin by the arm even if it meant breaking the limb in question. Rhonin could have taught him the folly of doing that, but for the sake of his mission and peace between the various elements of the Alliance, he simply took a quick step forward, coming up beside his guide and not saying a word through the entire journey.

He had expected to be led to the most dank, most foul place in which they could honestly let him bed down for the night, but instead Rhonin found himself with a room likely no more austere than those used by the dour warriors themselves. Dry, clean, and with stone walls that surrounded him on all sides save where the wooden door stood, it certainly served Rhonin better than some of the places he had stayed in the past. A single, neatly kept wooden bed and a tiny table made up the decor. A well-used oil lamp appeared to be the only means of illumination, not even the tiniest of windows evident. Rhonin thought of at least requesting a window, but suspected the knights had nothing better to offer. Besides, this would better serve to keep curious eyes from him.

"This will do," he finally said, but the young warrior who had brought Rhonin here had already begun to depart, closing the door as he left. The wizard tried to recall if the outside handle had a bolt or some sort of lock, but the paladins would surely not go that far. Damned soul

Rhonin might be to them, but he was still one of their allies. The thought of the mental discomfort that last put the knights through cheered him a bit. He had always found the Knights of the Silver Hand a sanctimonious lot.

His reluctant hosts left him alone until evening meal. He found himself seated far from Vereesa, who seemed to have the commander's ear whether she wanted it or not. No one but the elf spoke more than a few words to the wizard throughout the entire repast, and Rhonin would have left shortly after that if the subject of dragons had not been brought up by none other than Senturus.

"The flights have grown more common the last few weeks," the bearded knight informed them. "More common and more desperate. The orcs know that their time is short, and so they seek to wreak what havoc they can before the day of their final judgment." He took a sip of wine. "The settlement of Juroon was set aflame by two dragons just three days ago, more than half its population dead in the ungodly incident. That time, the beasts and their masters fled before the gryphon riders could reach the site."

"Horrible," Vereesa murmured.

Duncan nodded, a glint of almost fanatical determination in his deep brown eyes. "But soon a thing past! Soon we shall march on the interior of Khaz Modan, on Grim Batol itself, and end the threat of the last fragments of the Horde! Orc blood will flow!"

"And good men'll die," Rhonin added under his breath.

Apparently the commander had hearing as good as that of the elf, for his gaze immediately shifted to the mage. "Good men will die, aye! But we have sworn to see Lordaeron and all other lands free of the orc menace and so we shall, no matter what the cost!"

Unimpressed, the wizard returned, "But first you need to do something about the dragons, don't you?"

"They will be vanquished, spellcaster; sent to the underworld where they belong. If your devilish kind—"

Vereesa softly touched the commander's hand, giving him a smile that made even Rhonin a bit jealous. "How long have you been a paladin, Lord Senturus?"

Rhonin watched with some amazement as the ranger transformed into an enchanted and enchanting young woman, akin to those he had met in the royal court of Lordaeron. Her transformation in turn changed Duncan Senturus. She teased and toyed with the graying knight, seeming to hang on his every word. Her personality had altered so much that the observing wizard could scarce believe this was the same female who had ridden as his guide and his guard for the past several days.

Duncan went into great detail about his not-so-humble humble beginnings, as the son of a wealthy lord who chose the order to make his name. Although surely the other knights had heard the story before, they listened with rapt attention, no doubt seeing their leader as a shining example to their own careers. Rhonin studied each briefly, noticing with some unease that these other paladins barely blinked, barely even breathed, as they drank in the tale.

Vereesa commented on various parts of his story, making even the most mundane accomplishments of the elder man seem wondrous and brave. She downplayed her own deeds when Lord Senturus asked her of her past training, although the mage felt certain that, in many skills, his ranger readily surpassed their host.

The paladin seemed enamored by her act and went on at tremendous length, but Rhonin finally had enough. He excused himself—an announcement that drew the attention of no one—and hurried outside, seeking air and solitude.

Night had settled over the keep, a moonless dark that enveloped the tall wizard like a comforting blanket. He looked forward to reaching Hasic and setting forth on his voyage to Khaz Modan. Only then would he be done with paladins, rangers, and other useless fools who did nothing but interfere with his true quest. Rhonin worked best alone, a point he had tried to make before the last debacle. No one had listened to him then, and he had been forced to do what he had to in order to succeed. The others on that mission had not heeded his warnings, nor understood the necessity of his dangerous work. With the typical contempt of the nontalented, they had gone charging directly into the path of his grand spell . . . and thus most had perished along with the true targets—a band of orc warlocks intent on raising from the dead what some believed had been one of the demons of legend.

Rhonin regretted each and every one of those deaths more than he had ever let on to his masters in the Kirin Tor. They haunted him, urged him on to more risky feats . . . and what could be more risky than attempting, all by himself, to free the Dragonqueen from her captors? He had to do it all by himself, not only for the glory it would bring him, but also, Rhonin hoped, to appease the spirits of his former comrades, spirits who never left him even a moment's rest. Even Krasus did not know about those troubling specters—likely a good thing, as it might have made him question Rhonin's sanity *and* worth.

The wind picked up as he made his way to the top of the keep's surrounding wall. A few knights stood sentry duty, but word of his presence in the settlement had evidently traveled swiftly, and after the first guard identified him by way of inspection by lantern, Rhonin once again became shunned. That suited him well; he cared as little for the warriors as they did for him.

Beyond the keep, the vague shapes of trees turned the murky landscape into something magical. Rhonin found himself half-tempted to leave the questionable hospitality of his hosts and find a place to sleep under an oak. At least then he would not have to listen to the pious words of Duncan Senturus, who, in the mage's mind, seemed far more interested in Vereesa than a knight of the holy order should have been. True, she had arresting eyes and her garments suited her form well—

Rhonin snorted, eradicating the image of the ranger from his thoughts. His forced seclusion during his penance had clearly had more of an effect on him than he had realized. Magic was his mistress, first and foremost, and if Rhonin *did* decide to seek the company of a female, he much preferred a more malleable type, such as the well-pampered young ladies of the courts, or even the impressionable serving girls he found occasionally during his travels. Certainly not an arrogant, elven ranger . . .

Best to turn his attention to more important matters. Along with his unfortunate mount, Rhonin had also lost the items Krasus had given him. He had to do his best to make contact with the other wizard, inform him as to what had happened. The young mage regretted the necessity of doing so, but he owed too much to Krasus to not try. By no means did Rhonin consider turning back; that would have ended his hopes of ever regaining face not only among his peers but also with himself.

He surveyed his present surroundings. Eyes that saw

slightly better than average in the night detected no sentries in the near vicinity. A watchtower wall shielded him from the sight of the last man he had passed. What better place than here to begin? His room might have served, too, but Rhonin favored the open, the better to clear the cobwebs from his thoughts.

From a pocket deep within his robe he removed a small, dark crystal. Not the best choice for trying to create communication across miles, but the only one left to him.

Rhonin held the crystal up to the brightest of the faint stars overhead and began to mutter words of power. A faint glimmer arose within the heart of the stone, a glimmer that increased slowly in intensity as he continued to speak. The mystical words rolled from his tongue—

And at that moment, the stars abruptly *vanished*. . . .

Cutting off the spell in mid-sentence, Rhonin stared. No, the stars he had fixed on had not vanished; he could see them now. Yet . . . yet for a brief moment, no more than the blink of an eye, the mage could have sworn . . .

A trick of the imagination and his own weariness. Considering the trials of the day, Rhonin should have gone to bed immediately after dining, but he had first wanted to attempt this spell. The sooner he finished, then, the better. He wanted to be fully rejuvenated come the morrow, for Lord Senturus would certainly set an arduous pace.

Once more Rhonin raised the crystal high and once more he began muttering the words of power. This time, no trick of the eye would—

"What do you do there, spellcaster?" a deep voice demanded.

Rhonin swore, furious at this second delay. He turned

to the knight who had come across him and snapped, "Nothing to—"

An explosion rocked the wall.

The crystal slipped from Rhonin's hand. He had no time to reach for it, more concerned with keeping himself from tumbling over the wall to his death.

The sentry had no such hope. As the wall shook, he fell backward, first collapsing against the battlements, then toppling over. His cry shook Rhonin until its very abrupt end.

The explosion subsided, but not the damage caused by it. No sooner had the desperate wizard regained his footing when a portion of the wall itself began to collapse inward. Rhonin leapt toward the watchtower, thinking it more secure. He landed near the doorway and started inside—just as the tower itself began to teeter dangerously.

Rhonin tried to exit, but the doorway crumbled, trapping him within.

He started a spell, certain that it was already too late. The ceiling fell upon him—

And with it came something akin to a gigantic hand that seized the wizard in such a smothering grip Rhonin completely lost his breath . . . and all consciousness.

Nekros Skullcrusher brooded over the fate that the bones had rolled for him long, long ago. The grizzled orc toyed with one yellowed tusk as he studied the golden disk in the meaty palm of his other hand, wondering how one who had learned to wield such power could have been sentenced to playing nursemaid and jailer to a brooding female whose only purpose was to produce progeny after progeny. Of course, the fact that she was the greatest of dragons might have had something to do with that role—that and the fact that with but one good leg Nekros could never hope to achieve and hold onto the role of clan chieftain.

The golden disk seemed to mock him. It always seemed to mock him, but the crippled orc never once considered throwing it away. With it he had achieved a position that still kept him respected among his fellow warriors . . . even if he had lost all respect for himself the day the human knight had hacked off the bottom half of his left leg. Nekros had slain the human, but could not bring himself to do the honorable thing. Instead, he had let others drag him from the field, cauterize the wound, and help build for Nekros the support he needed for his maimed appendage.

His eyes flickered to what remained of the knee and the wooden peg attached there. No more glorious combat, no more legacy of blood and death. Other warriors had slain themselves for less grievous injuries, but Nekros *could* not. The very thought of bringing the blade to his own throat or chest filled him with a chill he dared not mention to any of the others. Nekros Skullcrusher very much wanted to live, no matter what the cost.

There were those in Dragonmaw clan who might have already sent him on his way to the glorious battlefields of the afterlife if not for his skills as a warlock. Early on, his talent for the arts had been noticed, and he had received training from some of the greatest. However, the way of the warlock had demanded from him other choices that Nekros had not wanted to make, dark choices that he felt did not serve the Horde, but rather worked to undermine it. He had fled their ranks, returned to his warrior ways, but from time to time his chieftain, the great Shaman, Zuluhed, had demanded the use of his other talents—especially in what even most orcs had believed impossible, the capturing of the Dragonqueen, Alexstrasza.

Zuluhed wielded the ritualistic magicks of the ancient shaman belief as few had done since first the Horde had been formed, but for this task, he had also needed to call upon the more sinister powers in which Nekros had been trained. Through resources the wizened orc had never revealed to his crippled companion, Zuluhed had uncovered an ancient talisman said to be capable of tremendous wonders. The only trouble had been that it had not responded to shamanistic spellwork no matter how great the effort put in by the chieftain. That had led Zuluhed to turn to the only warlock he felt he could trust, a warrior loyal to Dragonmaw clan.

And so Nekros had inherited the *Demon Soul*.

Zuluhed had so named the featureless gold disk, although at first the other orc had not known why. Nekros turned it over and over, not for the first time marveling at its impressive yet simplistic appearance. Pure gold, yes, and shaped like a huge coin with a rounded edge. It gleamed in even the lowest light, and nothing could tarnish its look. Oil, mud, blood . . . everything slipped off.

"This is older than either shaman or warlock magic, Nekros," Zuluhed had told him. *"I can do nothing with it, but perhaps you can. . . ."*

Trained though he was, the peg-legged orc had doubted that he, who had sworn off the dark arts, could do better than his legendary chieftain. Still, he had taken the talisman and tried to sense its purpose, its use.

Two days later, thanks to his astonishing success and Zuluhed's firm guidance, they had done what no one would have imagined possible, especially the Dragon-queen herself.

Nekros grunted, slowly raising himself to a standing position. His leg ached where the knee met the peg, an ache intensified by the great girth of the orc. Nekros had no illusions about his ability to lead. He could scarcely get around the caves as it was.

Time to visit her highness. Make certain that she knew she had a schedule to maintain. Zuluhed and the few other clan leaders left free still had dreams of revitalizing the Horde, stirring those abandoned by the weakling Doomhammer into a revolt. Nekros doubted these dreams, but he was a loyal orc, and as a loyal orc he would obey his chieftain's commands to the letter.

The *Demon Soul* clutched in one hand, the orc trundled through the dank cavern corridors. Dragonmaw clan had worked hard to lengthen the system already running through these mountains. The complex series of corridors enabled the orcs to deal more readily with the burdensome task of raising and training dragons for the glory of the Horde. Dragons filled up a lot of space and so needed separate facilities, each of which had to be dug out.

Of course, there were fewer dragons these days, a point Zuluhed and others had made with Nekros quite often lately. They needed dragons if their desperate campaign had any hope of succeeding.

"And how'm I supposed to make her breed faster?" Nekros grunted to himself.

A pair of younger, massive warriors strode by. Nearly seven feet tall, each as wide as two of their human adversaries, the tusked fighters dipped their heads briefly in recognition of his rank. Huge battle-axes hung from harnesses on their backs. Both were dragon-riders, new ones. Riders had a death ratio about twice that of their mounts, generally due to an unfortunate loss of grip. There had been times when Nekros had wondered whether the clan would run out of able warriors before it ran out of dragons, but he never broached the subject with Zuluhed.

Hobbling along, the aging orc soon began to hear the telltale signs of the Dragonqueen's presence. He noted labored breathing that echoed through the immediate area as if some steam vent from the depths of the earth had worked its way up. Nekros knew what that labored breathing meant. He had arrived just in time.

No guards stood at the carved-out entrance to the dragon's great chamber, but still Nekros paused. Attempts had been made in the past to free or slay the gargantuan red dragon within, but all those attempts had ended in grisly death. Not from the dragon, of course, for she would have embraced such assassins with relief, but rather from an unexpected aspect of the talisman Nekros held.

The orc squinted at what seemed nothing but an open passage. "Come!"

Instantly, the very air around the entrance flared. Tiny balls of flame burst into being, then immediately merged. A humanoid form began to fill, then overflow, the entrance.

Something vaguely resembling a burning skull formed where the head should have been. Armor that appeared to be flaming bone shaped itself into the body of a monstrous warrior that dwarfed even the enormous orcs. Nekros felt no heat from the hellish flames, but he knew that if the creature before him touched the orc even lightly, pain such as even a seasoned fighter could not imagine would rake him.

Among the other orcs it had been whispered that Nekros Skullcrusher had summoned one of the demons of lore. He did not discourage that rumor, although Zuluhed knew better. The monstrous creature guarding the dragon had no sense of independent thought. In attempting to harness the abilities of the mysterious artifact, Nekros had unleashed something else. Zuluhed called it a golem of fire—perhaps of the essence of demon power, but certainly not one of the supposedly mythical beings.

Whatever its origins or its previous use, the golem served as the perfect sentry. Even the fiercest warriors steered clear of it. Only Nekros could command it. Zuluhed had tried, but the artifact from which the golem had emerged seemed now tied to the one-legged orc.

"I enter," he told the fiery creature.

The golem stiffened . . . then shattered in a wild shower of dying sparks. Despite having witnessed this departure time and time again, Nekros still backed up some, not daring to move forward until the last of the sparks had faded away.

The moment the orc stepped inside, a voice remarked, "I . . . knew . . . you would be . . . here soon. . . ."

The disdain with which the shackled dragon spoke affected her jailer not in the least. He had heard far worse from her over the years. Clutching the artifact, he made his way toward her head, which, by necessity, had been clamped down. They had lost one handler to her mighty jaws; they would not lose another.

By rights the iron chains and clamps should not have been sufficient to hold such a magnificent leviathan, but they had been enhanced by the power of the disk. Struggle all she might, Alexstrasza would never be able to free herself. That, of course, did not mean that she did not try.

"Do you need anything?" Nekros did not ask out of any concern for her. He only wanted to keep her alive for the Horde's desires.

Once the crimson dragon's scales had gleamed like metal. She still filled the vast cavern tail to head, yet these days her rib bones showed slightly underneath the skin and her words came out more beleaguered. Despite her dire condition, though, the hatred in those vast, golden eyes had not faded, and the orc knew that if the Dragonqueen ever *did* escape, he would be the first one down her gullet or fried to a crisp. Of course, since the odds of that were so very minor, even one-legged Nekros did not worry.

"Death would be nice. . . ."

He grunted, turning away from this useless conversation. At one point during her lengthy incarceration, she had tried to starve herself, but the simple tactic of taking her next clutch of eggs and breaking one of them before her horrified eyes had been enough to end that threat. Despite knowing that each hatchling would be trained to terrorize the Horde's enemies and likely die because of that, Alexstrasza clearly held out hope that someday they would be free. Shattering the egg had been like shattering a part of that hope. One less dragon with the potential to be his own master.

As he always did, Nekros inspected her latest clutch. Five eggs this time. A fair number, but most were a bit smaller than usual. That bothered him. His chieftain had already remarked on the runts produced in the last batch, although even a runt of a dragon stood several times higher than an orc.

Dropping the disk into a secure pouch at his waist, Nekros bent to lift up one of the eggs. The loss of his leg had not yet weakened his arms, and so the massive orc had little trouble hefting the object in question. A good weight, he noted. If the other eggs were this heavy, then at least they would produce healthy young. Best to get them down to the incubator chamber as soon as possible. The volcanic heat there would keep them at just the right temperature for hatching.

As Nekros lowered the egg, the dragon muttered, "This is all useless, mortal. Your little war is all but over."

"You may be right," he grunted, no doubt surprising her with his candor. The grizzled orc turned back to his gargantuan captive. "But we'll fight to the end, lizard."

"Then you shall do so without us. My last consort is dying, you know that. Without him, there will be no more eggs." Her voice, already low, became barely audible. The Dragonqueen exhaled with effort, as if the conversation had taxed her already weakening strength too much.

He squinted at her, studying those reptilian orbs. Nekros knew that Alexstrasza's last consort was indeed dying. They'd started out with three, but one had perished trying to escape over the sea and another had died of injuries when the rogue dragon Deathwing had caught him by surprise. The third, the eldest of the lot, had remained by his queen's side, but he had been centuries older than even Alexstrasza, and now those centuries, coupled with past near-mortal injuries, had taken their toll.

"We'll find another, then."

She managed to snort. Her words barely came out as a whisper. "And how . . . would you go about doing that?"

"We'll find one . . ." He had no other answer for her, but

Nekros would be damned if he would give the lizard that satisfaction. Frustration and anger long held in began to boil over. He hobbled toward her. "And as for you, lizard—"

Nekros had dared come within a few yards of the Dragonqueen's head, aware that, thanks to the enchanted bonds, she would be unable to flame or eat him. Thus it was to his tremendous dismay that suddenly Alexstrasza's head, brace and all, suddenly twisted toward him, filling his gaze. The dragon's maw opened wide, and the orc had the distinctive displeasure of gazing deep into the gullet of the creature who was about to make a snack of him.

Or would have, if not for Nekros's quick reaction. Clutching the pouch in which he carried the *Demon Soul*, the warlock muttered a single word, thought a single command.

A pained roar shook the chamber, sending chunks of rock falling from the ceiling. The crimson behemoth pulled back her head as best she could. The brace around her throat glowed with such power that the orc had to shield his eyes.

Near him, the fiery servant of the disk materialized in a flash, dark eye sockets looking to Nekros for command. The warlock, however, had no need for the creature, the artifact itself having dealt with the nearly disastrous situation.

"Leave," he commanded the fire golem. As the creature departed in an explosive display, the crippled orc dared walk before the dragon. A scowl spread across his ugly features, and the frustration of knowing that he served a cause lost urged Nekros to greater anger at the leviathan's latest attempt on his life.

"Still full of tricks, eh, lizard?" He glared at the brace, which Alexstrasza had clearly worked long to loosen from the wall. The enchantment affecting her bonds did not extend to the stone upon which they were fastened, Nekros realized. That mistake had nearly cost him.

But failing to achieve his death would now cost her. Nekros fixed his heavily browed gaze on the now truly injured dragon.

"A daring trick . . ." he snarled. "A daring trick, but a foolish one." He held up the golden disk for her widening eyes to see. "Zuluhed commanded I keep you as healthy as possible, but my chieftain also commanded me to punish whenever I thought necessary." Nekros tightened his grip on the artifact, which now glowed bright. "Now is—"

"Excuse this pitiful one's interruption, o gracious master," came a jarring voice from within the cavern. "but word's come you must hear, oh, you must!"

Nekros nearly dropped the artifact. Whirling about as best he could with one good leg, the huge orc stared down at a pitifully tiny figure with batlike ears and a vast set of sharp teeth set in a mad grin. Nekros did not know what bothered him more, the creature himself or the fact that the goblin had somehow managed to infiltrate the dragon's cavern without being stopped by the golem.

"You! How'd you get in here?" Reaching down, he grasped the tiny form by the throat and lifted him upward. All thought of punishing the dragon vanished. "How?"

Even though he spoke words half-choked, the foul little creature still smiled. "J-just walked in, o gracious m-master! Just w-walked in!"

Nekros considered. The goblin must have entered when the fire golem had come to its master's aid. Goblins were tricky and often found their way into places thought secure, but even this clever rogue could not have worked his way inside otherwise.

He let the beast drop to the ground. "All right! Why come? What news do you bring?"

The goblin rubbed his throat. "Only the most important, only the most important, I assure you!" The toothy smile broadened. "Have I ever let you down, wondrous master?"

Despite the fact that, deep down, Nekros felt that goblins had less of a sense of honor than a ground slug, the orc had to admit that this one had never steered him wrong. Questionable allies at best, the goblins played many games of their own, but always fulfilled the missions set upon them by Doomhammer and, before him, the great Blackhand. "Speak, then, and be quick about it!"

The devilish imp nodded several times. "Yes, Nekros, yes! I come to tell you that there is a plan under way, more than one, actually, to free—" He hesitated, then cocked his head toward weary Alexstrasza, "—that is, to cause great disaster to Dragonmaw clan's dreams!"

An uncomfortable sensation coursed down the orc's spine. "What do you mean?"

Again the goblin cocked his head toward the dragon. "Perhaps elsewhere, gracious master?"

The creature had the right of it. Nekros glanced at his captive, who appeared to be unconscious from pain and exhaustion. Still, better to be wary around her for now. If his spy brought him the news he suspected, the orc warlock hardly wanted the Dragonqueen to hear the details.

"Very well," he grunted. Nekros hobbled toward the cavern entrance, already mulling over the likely news. The goblin hopped beside him, grinning from ear to ear.

Nekros felt tempted to wipe that annoying smile off the other's face, but needed the creature for now. Still, for the slightest excuse . . . "This'd better be good, Kryll! You understand?"

Kryll nodded as he hurried to keep up, his head bobbing up and down like a broken toy. "Trust me, Master Nekros! Just *trust* me. . . ."

FIVE

He had nothing to do with the explosion," Vereesa insisted. "Why would he do something like that?"

"He is a wizard," Duncan returned flatly, as if that answered any and all questions. "They care nothing about the lives and livelihoods of others."

Well aware of the prejudices of the holy order toward magic, Vereesa did not try to argue that point. As an elf, she had grown up around magic, even could perform some slight bit herself, and so did not see Rhonin in the terrible light that the paladin did. While Rhonin struck her as reckless, he did not seem to her so monstrous as to not care about the lives of others. Had he not helped her during their flight from the dragon? Why bother to risk himself? He could still have gotten to Hasic on his own.

"And if he is not to blame," Lord Senturus continued, "then where has he gone? Why is there no trace of him in the rubble? If he is innocent of this, his body should be there along with the two of our brothers who perished during his spell. . . ." The man stroked his beard slightly. "No, this foul work is the fault of his, mark me."

And so you would hunt him down like an animal, she thought. Why else had Duncan summoned ten of his best to ride with them in search of the missing spellcaster? What Vereesa had originally seen as a rescue mission had quickly revealed itself as otherwise. When she and the rest had heard the explosion, discovered the ruin, the elf had felt a twinge inside her heart. Not only had she failed to keep her companion alive, but he and two other men had perished for no good reason. However, Duncan had clearly from the first seen it otherwise, especially when a search had revealed no trace of Rhonin's corpse among the rubble.

Her first thought had been of goblin sappers, well-versed in sneaking up to a fortress and setting off deadly charges, but the senior paladin had insisted that his region had been swept clean of any trace of the elements of the Horde, goblins especially. While the foul little creatures did possess a few fantastic and utterly improbable flying machines, none had been reported. Besides, such an airship would have had to move with lightning speed to avoid detection, something not possible for the cumbersome devices.

Which, of course, left Rhonin as the most likely source of the destruction.

Vereesa did not believe it possible of him, especially since he had been so dedicated to fulfilling his mission. She only hoped that if they found the young wizard she would be able to keep Duncan and the others from running him through before they had a chance to find out the truth.

They had scoured the nearby countryside and were now headed toward the actual direction of Hasic. Although it had been suggested by more than one of the younger knights that Rhonin had likely used his magic to spirit himself away to his destination, Duncan Senturus had evidently not thought enough of the wizard's abilities in that respect to take it to heart. He fervently believed that they would be able to track down the rogue mage and bring him to justice.

And as the day aged and the sun began its downward climb, even Vereesa began to question Rhonin's innocence. *Had* he caused the disaster, then fled the murderous scene?

"We shall have to make camp soon," Lord Senturus announced some time later. He studied the thickening woods. "While I do not expect trouble, it would serve us little good to go wandering through the dark, possibly missing our quarry at our very feet."

Her own eyesight superior to that of her companions, Vereesa considered continuing on by herself, but thought better of it. If the Knights of the Silver Hand discovered Rhonin without her, the wizard stood little chance of surviving.

They rode on a bit farther, but spotted nothing. The sun slipped below the horizon, leaving only a faint glow of light to illuminate their way. As he had promised, Duncan called a reluctant halt to the search, ordering his knights to immediately set up camp. Vereesa dismounted, but her eyes continued to sweep over the surrounding territory, hoping against hope that the fiery wizard would make himself known.

"He is nowhere about, Lady Vereesa."

She turned to look up at the lead paladin, the only man among the searchers tall enough to force her to such an action. "I cannot help looking, my lord."

"We will find the scoundrel soon enough."

"We should hear his story first, Lord Senturus. Surely that is fair enough."

The armored figure shrugged as if it did not make a difference either way to him. "He will be given his chance to make his penance, of course."

After which they would either take Rhonin back in chains or execute him on the spot. The Knights of the Silver Hand might be a holy order, but they were also known for their expedience in meting out justice.

Vereesa excused herself from the senior paladin, not trusting her tongue to keep her from infuriating him at this point. She led her horse to a tree at the edge of the campsite, then slipped in among the trees. Behind her, the sounds of the camp muted as the elf moved farther into her own element.

Again she felt the temptation to continue with the search on her own. So very easy for her to move lithely through the forest, seek out those crevices and areas of thick foliage that might hide a corpse.

"Always so eager to go rushing off, handling matters in your own inimitable style, eh, Vereesa?" her first tutor had asked one day shortly after her induction into the select training program of the rangers. Only the best were chosen for their ranks. *"With such impatience, you might as well have been born a human. Keep this up and you will not be among the rangers for very long. . . ."*

Yet despite the skepticism of more than one of her tutors, Vereesa had prevailed and risen to among the best of her select group. She could not now fail that training by turning reckless.

Promising herself that she would return to the others after a few minutes' relaxation in the forest, the silver-haired ranger leaned against one of the trees and exhaled. Such a simple assignment, and already it had nearly fallen apart not once but twice. If they never found Rhonin, she would have to think of something to say to her masters, not to mention even the Kirin Tor of Dalaran. None of the fault in this lay with her, but—

A sudden gust of wind nearly threw Vereesa from the tree. The elf managed to cling to it at the last moment, but in the distance she could hear the frustrated calls of the knights and the wild clattering of loose objects tossed about.

As quickly as the wind struck, it suddenly died away. Vereesa pushed her disheveled hair from her face and hurried back to camp, fearful that Duncan and the others had been attacked by some terrible force akin to the dragon earlier that day. Fortunately, even as she approached, the ranger heard the paladins already discussing the repair of their camp, and as she entered the area, Vereesa saw that, other than bedrolls and other objects lying strewn about, no one seemed much out of sorts.

Lord Senturus strode toward her, eyes filled with concern. "You are well, milady? No harm has come to you?"

"Nothing. The wind surprised me, that is all."

"Surprised everyone." He rubbed his bearded jaw, gazing into the darkened forest. "It strikes me that no normal wind blows in such a manner. . . ." He turned to one of his men. "Roland! Double the guard! This may not be the end of this particular storm!"

"Aye, milord!" a slim, pale knight called back. "Christoff! Jakob! Get—"

His voice cut off with such abruptness that both Duncan, who had turned back to the elf, and Vereesa looked to see if the man had suddenly been struck down by an arrow or crossbow bolt. Instead, they found him staring at a dark bundle lying amidst the bedrolls, a dark bundle with legs stretched together and arms crossed over the chest, almost as if in deathly repose.

A dark bundle gradually recognizable as Rhonin.

Vereesa and the knights gathered around him, one of the men holding a torch near. The elf bent down to investigate the body. In the flickering light of the torch, Rhonin looked pale and still, and at first she could not tell whether he breathed or not. Vereesa reached for his cheek—

And the eyes of the mage opened wide, startling everyone.

"Ranger . . . how nice . . . to see you again. . . ."

With that, his eyes closed once more and Rhonin fell asleep.

"Fool of a wizard!" Duncan Senturus snapped. "You'll not up and vanish after good men have died, then think you can simply reappear in our midst and go to sleep!" He reached for the spellcaster's arm, intending to shake Rhonin awake, but let out a startled cry the moment his fingers touched the dark garments. The paladin gazed at his gauntleted hand as if he had been bitten, snarling, "Some sort of devilish, unseen fire surrounds him! Even through the glove it felt like seizing hold of a burning ember!"

Despite his warning, Vereesa had to see for herself. Sure enough, she felt some discomfort when her fingers touched Rhonin's clothes, but nothing of the intensity that Lord Senturus had described. Nevertheless, the ranger pulled back her hand and nodded agreement. She saw no reason at the moment why she should inform the senior paladin of the difference.

Behind her Vereesa heard the scrape of steel as it slid from its sheath. She quickly glanced up at Duncan, who had already begun shaking his head at the knight in question. "No, Wexford, a Knight of the Silver Hand cannot slay any foe who cannot defend himself. The stain would be too great to our oaths. I think we must post guards for the evening, then see what happens with our spellcaster here in the morning." Lord Senturus's weathered visage took on a grim aspect. "And, one way or another, justice *will* be served once he awakes."

"I will stand by him," Vereesa interjected. "No one else need do so."

"Forgive me, milady, but your association with—"

She straightened, staring the senior paladin in the eye as best she could. "You question the word of a ranger, Lord Senturus? You question my word? Do you assume that I will help him flee again?"

"Of course not!" Duncan finally shrugged. "If that is what you want, then that is what you want. You have my permission. Yet to do so all night with no relief—"

"That is my choice. Would you do any less with one left in your charge?"

Vereesa had him there. Lord Senturus finally shook his head, then turned to the other warriors and began giving orders. In seconds, the ranger and the wizard were alone in the center of camp. Rhonin had been left atop two of the bedrolls, the knights not certain as to how to remove them without getting burned.

She examined the sleeping form as best she could without touching him again. Rhonin's robes appeared torn in places and the face of the wizard bore tiny scars and bruises, but otherwise he seemed to be unharmed. His expression looked drained, however, as if he had suffered great exhaustion.

Perhaps it was the near darkness through which she inspected him, but Vereesa thought that the human looked so much more vulnerable now, even sympathetic. She also had to admit that he had fair looks, although the elf quickly eliminated any other thoughts along that line. Vereesa tried to see if there was any method by which she could make the unconscious mage's position more comfortable, but the only way to do so would have meant revealing that she could tolerate touching him. That, in turn, might have encouraged Lord Senturus to try to use her to better secure Rhonin, which went against the elf's bond to the mage.

With no other recourse, Vereesa settled near the prone body and looked around, eyeing the area for any possible threat. She still found Rhonin's sudden reappearance very questionable and, although he had said little about it, clearly so did Duncan. Rhonin hardly seemed capable of having transported himself to the midst of their camp. True, such an effort would explain why he now lay almost comatose, but it still did not ring true. Rather, Vereesa felt as if she looked at a man who had been kidnapped, then tossed back after the kidnapper had done with him what he would.

The only question that remained—who could have done such a fantastic thing . . . and why?

He woke knowing that they were all against him.

Well, not all of them, perhaps. Rhonin did not know exactly where he stood—providing he could stand at all—with the elven ranger. By rights, her oath to see him safely to Hasic should have meant she would defend him even against the pious knights, but one never knew. There had been an elf in the party from his last mission, an older ranger much like Vereesa. That ranger, however, had treated the wizard much the same way as Duncan Senturus did, and without the elder paladin's level of tact.

Rhonin exhaled lightly so as not to alert anyone just yet to his consciousness. He had only one way of finding out where he stood with everyone, but he needed a few more moments to collect his thoughts. Among the initial questions he would be asked would be his part in the disaster and what had happened to him afterward. Some bit of the first half the weary wizard could answer. As for the second, they likely knew as much as he.

He could delay no longer. Rhonin took another breath, then purposely stretched, as if waking.

Beside him, he heard slight movement.

With planned casualness, the mage opened his eyes and looked about. To his relief and—surprisingly—some pleasure, Vereesa's concerned countenance filled his immediate field of vision. The ranger leaned forward, striking sky-blue eyes studying him close. Those eyes suited her well, he thought for a moment . . . then quickly dismissed the thought as the sound of clanking metal warned him that the others knew he had awakened.

"Back among the living, is he?" Lord Senturus rumbled. "We shall see how that lasts—"

The slim elf immediately leapt to her feet, blocking the paladin's path. "He has only just opened his eyes! Give him time to recoup and eat at least before you question him!"

"I will deny him no basic right, milady, but he shall answer questions *while* he has his breakfast, not after."

Rhonin had propped himself up by his elbows just enough to be able to see Duncan's scowling visage, and knew that the Knights of the Silver Hand believed him to be some sort of traitor, possibly even a murderer. The weakened mage recalled the one unfortunate sentry who had plummeted to his death and suspected that there might have been more such victims. Someone had no doubt reported Rhonin's presence on the wall, and the natural prejudices of the holy order had added up the facts and gotten the wrong answer, as usual.

He did not want to fight them, doubted that at this point he could even cast more than one or two light spells, but if they tried to condemn him for what had happened at the keep, Rhonin would not hold back to defend himself.

"I'll answer as best I can," the wizard replied, declining any aid from Vereesa as he struggled to his feet. "But, yes, only with some food and water in my stomach."

The normally bland rations of the knights tasted sweet and delicious to Rhonin from the moment of the first bite. Even the tepid water from one of the flasks seemed more like wine. Rhonin suddenly realized that his body felt as if it had been forcibly starved for nearly a week. He ate with gusto, with passion, with little care for manners. Some of the knights watched him with amusement, others, especially Duncan, with distaste.

Just as his hunger and thirst at last began to level off, the questioning began. Lord Senturus sat down before him, eyes already judging the spellcaster, and growled, "The time for confession is at hand, Rhonin Redhair! You have filled your belly, now empty the burden of sin from your soul! Tell us the truth about your misdeed on the keep wall. . . ."

Vereesa stood beside the recuperating mage, her hand by the hilt of her sword. She clearly had positioned herself so as to act as his defender in this informal court, and not, Rhonin liked to think, simply because of her oath. Certainly, after their experience with the dragon, she knew him better than these oafs.

"I'll tell you what I know, which is to say not much at all, my lord. I stood atop the keep wall, but the fault of the destruction isn't mine. I heard an explosion, the wall shook, and one of your tin warriors had the misfortune to fall over the side, for which you've my sympathy—"

Duncan had not yet put on his helmet, and so now ran a hand through his graying, thinning hair. He looked as if he fought the valiant struggle to maintain control of his temper. "Your story already has holes as wide as the chasm in your heart, wizard, and you have barely even started! There are those who live, despite your efforts, who saw you casting magic just before the devastation! Your lies condemn you!"

"No, *you* condemn me, just as you condemn all my kind for merely existing," Rhonin quietly returned. He took another bite of hard biscuit, then added, "Yes, my lord, I cast a spell, but one only designed to communicate along the distances. I sought advice from one of my seniors on how to proceed on a mission that has been sanctioned by the highest powers in the Alliance . . . as the honorable ranger here'll vouch, I'd say."

Vereesa spoke even as the knight's eyes shifted to her. "His words bear truth, Duncan. I see no reason why he would cause such damage—" She held up a hand as the elder warrior started to protest, no doubt again pressing the point that all wizards became damned souls the moment they took up the art. "—and I will meet any man, including you, in combat, if that is what it takes to restore his rights and freedom."

Lord Senturus looked disgruntled at the thought of having to face the elf in battle. He glared at Rhonin, but finally nodded slowly. "Very well. You have a staunch defender, wizard, and on her word and bond I will accept that you are not responsible for what happened." Yet the moment he finished the statement, the paladin thrust a finger at the mage. "But I would hear more about your own experience during that time and, if you can dredge it from your memories, how you come to be dropped in our midst like a leaf fallen from a high tree. . . ."

Rhonin sighed, knowing he could not escape the telling. "As you wish. I'll try to tell you all I know."

It was not much more than he had related prior. Once more the weary mage spoke to them of his trek to the wall, his decision to try to contact his patron, and the sudden explosion that had rocked the entire section.

"You are certain of what you heard?" Duncan Senturus immediately asked him.

"Yes. While I can't prove it beyond doubt, it sounded like a charge being set off."

The explosion did not mean that goblins were responsible, but of course, years of war had ingrained such thoughts into even the head of the wizard. No one had reported goblins in this part of Lordaeron, but Vereesa came up with a suggestion. "Duncan, perhaps the dragon that pursued us earlier also carried with it one or two goblins. They are small, wiry, and certainly capable of hiding at least for a day or two. That would explain much."

"It would indeed," he agreed with reluctance. "And if so, we must be doubly vigilant. Goblins know no other pastimes than mischief and destruction. They would certainly strike again."

Rhonin went on with his story, telling next how he fled to the dubious safety of the tower, only to have it collapse about him. Here, though, he hesitated, knowing for certain that Senturus would find his next words questionable, at the very least.

"And then—*something*—seized me, my lord. I don't know what it was, but it took me up as if I was a toy and whisked me away from the devastation. Unfortunately, I couldn't breathe because I was held so tight, and when I next opened my eyes—" The wizard looked at Vereesa. "It was to see her face."

Duncan waited for more, but when it became clear that his wait would be fruitless, he slapped one hand against his armored knee and shouted, "And that is it? That is all you know?"

"That's all."

"By the spirit of Alonsus Faol!" the paladin snapped, calling upon the name of the archbishop whose legacy had led, through his apprentice, Uther Lightbringer, to the creation of the holy order. "You have told us nothing, *nothing* of worth! If I thought for one moment—" A slight shift by Vereesa made him pause. "But I have given my word and taken that of another. I will abide by my previous decision." He rose, clearly no longer interested in remaining in the company of the wizard. "I also make another decision here and now. We are already on route to Hasic. I see no reason why we should not move on as quickly as possible and get you to your ship. Let them deal with your situation as they see fit! We leave in one hour. Be prepared, wizard!"

With that, Lord Duncan Senturus turned and marched

off, his loyal knights following immediately thereafter. Rhonin found himself alone save for the ranger, who walked to a spot before him and sat down. Her eyes settled on his. "Will you be well enough to ride?"

"Other than exhaustion and a few bruises, I seem in one piece, elf." Rhonin realized that his words had come out a little sharper than he had intended. "I'm sorry. Yes, I'll be able to ride. Anything to get me to the port on time."

She rose again. "I will prepare the animals. Duncan brought an extra mount, just in case we did find you. I will see to it that it is waiting when you finish."

As the ranger turned, an unfamiliar emotion rose within the tired spellcaster. "Thank you, Vereesa Windrunner."

Vereesa looked over her shoulder. "Taking care of the horses is part of my duty as your guide."

"I meant about standing with me during what might have turned into an inquisition."

"*That,* too, was part of my duty. I took an oath to my masters that I would see you to your destination." Despite her words, however, the corners of her mouth twitched upward for a moment in what might have been a smile. "Better ready yourself, Master Rhonin. This will be no canter. We have much time to make up."

She left him to his own devices. Rhonin stared at the dying campfire, thinking about all that had happened. Vereesa did not know how close to the truth she had been with her simple statements. The journey to Hasic would be no easy gallop, but not just for the sake of time.

He had not been entirely truthful with them, not even the elf. True, Rhonin had not left out any part of his story, but he had left out some of his conclusions. He felt no guilt where the paladins were concerned, but Vereesa's dedication to their journey and his safety stirred some feelings of remorse.

Rhonin did not know who had set the charge. Goblins likely. He really did not care. What did concern him was what he had quickly passed over, even misdirected. When he had talked of being seized from the crumbling tower, he had not told them about having felt as if a giant hand had done so. They probably would not have believed him or, in the case of Senturus, pointed at it as proof of his communing with demons.

A giant hand *had* saved Rhonin, but no human one. Even his brief moment of consciousness had been enough to recognize the scaly skin, the wicked, curved talons greater in length than his entire body.

A *dragon* had rescued the wizard from certain death . . . and Rhonin had no idea why.

SIX

"So where is he? I've little time to waste pacing around in these decadent halls!"

For what seemed the thousandth time, King Terenas silently counted to ten before responding to Genn Greymane's latest outburst. "Lord Prestor will be here before long, Genn. You know he wants to bring us all together on this matter."

"I don't know anything of the sort," the huge man in black and gray armor grumbled. Genn Greymane reminded the king of nothing less than a bear who had learned to clothe himself, albeit somewhat crudely. He seemed fairly ready to burst through his armor, and if the ruler of Gilneas downed one more flagon of good ale or devoured one more of the thick Lordaeron pastries Terenas's chefs had prepared, surely that would happen.

Despite Greymane's ursine appearance and his arrogant, outspoken manner, the king did not underestimate the warrior from the south. Greymane's political manipulations had been legendary, this latest no less so. How he had managed to give Gilneas a voice in a situation that should not have even concerned the faraway kingdom still amazed Terenas.

"You might as well tell the wind to stop howling," came a more cultured voice from the opposite end of the great hall. "You'll have more success there than getting that creature to quiet even for a moment!"

They had all agreed to meet in the imperial hall, a place where, in times past, the most significant treaties in all Lordaeron had been agreed to and signed. With its rich history and ancient but stately decor, the hall cast an aura of tremendous significance upon any discussion taking place here . . . and certainly the matter of Alterac was of significance to the continued life of the Alliance.

"If you don't like the sound of my voice, Lord Admiral," Greymane snarled, "good steel can always make certain you never hear it—or anything else—again."

Lord Admiral Daelin Proudmoore rose to his feet in one smooth, practiced sweep. The slim, weathered seaman reached for the sword generally hanging at the side of his green naval uniform, but the sheath there rattled empty. So, too, did the sheath of Genn Greymane. The one thing reluctantly agreed upon from the first had been that none of the heads of state could carry arms into the discussions. They had even agreed—even *Genn Greymane*—to having themselves searched by selected sentries from the Knights of the Silver Hand, the only military unit they all trusted despite its outward allegiance to Terenas.

Prestor, of course, was the reason that this incredible summit had managed to reach even this point. Rarely did the monarchs of the major realms come together. Generally, they spoke through couriers and diplomats, with the occasional state visit thrown in as well. Only the amazing Prestor could have convinced Terenas's uneasy allies to abandon their staffs and personal guard outside and join together to discuss matters face-to-face.

Now, if only the young noble would himself arrive. . . .

"My lords! Gentlemen!" Desperate for assistance, the king looked to a stern figure standing near the window, a figure clad in leather and fur despite the relative warmth of the region. A fierce beard and jagged nose were all Terenas could make out of Thoras Trollbane's gruff visage, but he knew that, despite Thoras's intense interest in whatever view lay outside, the lord of Stromgarde had digested every word and tone of his counterparts. That he did nothing to aid Terenas in this present crisis only served to remind the latter of the gulf that had opened up between them since the start of this maddening situation.

Damn Lord Perenolde! the king of Lordaeron thought. *If only he had not forced us into all of this!*

Although knights from the holy order stood by in case any of the monarchs came to actual blows, Terenas did not fear physical violence so much as he did the shattering of any hope of keeping the human kingdoms allied. Not for a moment did he feel that the orc menace had been forever eradicated. The humans had to remain allied at this crucial moment. He wished Anduin Lothar, regent lord of the refugees from the lost kingdom of Azeroth, could have been here, but that was not possible, and without Lothar, that left only—

"My lords! Come, come! Surely this isn't seemly behavior for any of us!"

"Prestor!" Terenas gasped. "Praise be!"

The others turned as the tall, immaculate figure entered the great hall. *Amazing the effect the man had on his el-*

ders, so the king thought. *He walks into a room and quarrels cease! Bitter rivals lay down their weapons and talk of peace!*

Yes, definitely the choice to replace Perenolde.

Terenas watched as his friend went about the chamber, greeting each monarch in turn and treating all as if they were his best friends. Perhaps they were, for Prestor seemed not to have an arrogant bone in his body. Whether dealing with the rough-edged Thoras or the conniving Greymane, Prestor seemed to know how best to speak with each of them. The only ones who had never seemed to fully appreciate him had been the wizards from Dalaran, but then, they were wizards.

"Forgive my belated arrival," the young aristocrat began. "I'd ridden out into the countryside this morning and not realized just how long it would take me to get back."

"No need for apologies," Thoras Trollbane kindly returned.

Yet another example of Prestor's almost magical manner. While a friend and respected ally, Thoras Trollbane never spoke kindly to anyone without much effort. He tended to speak in short, precise sentences, then lapse into silence. The silences were not intended as insults, as Terenas had gradually learned. Instead, the truth was that Thoras simply did not feel comfortable with long conversations. A native of cold, mountainous Stromgarde, he much preferred action over talk.

Which made the king of Lordaeron even more pleased that Prestor had finally arrived.

Prestor surveyed the room, meeting each gaze for a moment before saying, "How good it is to see all of you again! I hope that this time we can resolve our differences so that our future meetings will be as good friends and sword-mates. . . ."

Greymane nodded almost enthusiastically. Proud-moore wore a satisfied expression, as if the noble's coming had been the answer to his prayers. Terenas said nothing, allowing his talented friend to take control of the meeting. The more the others saw of Prestor, the easier it would be for the king to present his proposal.

They gathered around the elaborately decorated ivory table that Terenas's grandfather had received as a gift from his northern vassals, after his successful negotiations with the elves of Quel'Thalas over the borders there. As he always did, the king planted both hands firmly on the tabletop, seeking to draw guidance from his predecessor. Across the table, Prestor's eyes met his for a moment. Looking into those strong, ebony orbs, the robed monarch relaxed. Prestor would handle any matters of dispute.

And so the talks began, first with stiff opening words, then more heated, blunt ones. Yet, under the guidance of Prestor, never did any threat of violence arise. More than once he had to take one or another of the participants in hand and engage in private conversation with them, but each time those intimate dialogues ended with a smile on Prestor's hawklike visage and great advancement toward the mending of Alliance ties.

As the summit tapered to a close, Terenas himself held such an exchange. While Greymane, Thoras, and Lord Admiral Proudmoore drank from the finest of the king's brandy, Prestor and the monarch huddled near the window overlooking the city. Terenas had always enjoyed this view, for from it he could see the health of his people. Even now, even with the summit going on, his subjects went about their duties, pushed on with their lives. Their faith in him bolstered his weary mind, and he knew that they would understand the decision he would make this day.

"I don't know how you did it, my boy," he whispered to his companion. "You've made the others see the truth, the need! They're actually sitting in this chamber, acting civilly with not only each other, but me! I thought Genn and Thoras would demand my hide at one point!"

"I merely did what I could to assuage them, my lord, but thank you for your kind words."

Terenas shook his head. "Kind words? Hardly! Prestor, my lad, you've single-handedly kept the Alliance from crumbling to bits! What did you tell them all?"

A conspiratorial look crossed his companion's handsome features. He leaned close to the monarch, eyes fixed on Terenas's. "A little of this, a little of that. Promises to the admiral about his continued sovereignty of the seas, even if it meant sending in a force to take control of Gilneas; to Greymane about future naval colonies near the coastal edge of Alterac; and Thoras Trollbane thinks that he'll be ceded the eastern half of that region . . . all when I become its legitimate ruler."

For a moment, the king simply gaped, not certain that he had heard right. He stared into Prestor's mesmerizing eyes, waiting for the punch line to the awful joke. When it did not come, though, Terenas finally blurted in a quiet voice, "Have you taken leave of your senses, my boy? Even jesting about such matters is highly outrageous and—"

"And you will not remember a thing about it, regardless, you know." Lord Prestor leaned forward, his eyes seizing Terenas's own gaze and refusing to release it. "Just as none of them will remember what I truly told them.

All you need to recall, my pompous little puppet, is that I have guaranteed a political advantage for you, but one that demands for its culmination and success my appointment as ruler of Alterac. Do you understand that?"

Terenas understood nothing else. Prestor had to be chosen new monarch of the battered realm. The security of Lordaeron and the stability of the Alliance demanded it.

"I see that you do. Good. Now you will go back and, just as the conference comes to an end, you will make your bold decision. Greymane already knows he will act the most reticent, but in a few days, he will agree. Proudmoore will follow your lead and, after mulling the situation a bit, Thoras Trollbane will also acquiesce to my ascension."

Something nudged at the robed king's memory, a notion he felt compelled to express. "No . . . no ruler may be chosen without . . . without the agreement of Dalaran and the Kirin Tor. . . ." He struggled to complete his thought. "They are members of the Alliance, too. . . ."

"But who can trust a wizard?" Prestor reminded him. "Who can know their agenda? That's why I had you leave them out of this situation in the first place, is it not? Wizards cannot be trusted . . . and eventually they must be dealt with."

"Dealt with . . . you're right, of course."

Prestor's smile widened, revealing what seemed far more teeth than normal. "I always am." He put a companionable arm around Terenas. "Now, it is time we returned to the others. You are very satisfied with my progress. In a few minutes, you will make your suggestion . . . and we shall move on from there."

"Yes . . ."

The slim figure steered the king back to the other

monarchs, and as he did, Terenas's thoughts returned to the business at hand. Prestor's more dire statements now lay buried deep in the king's subconscious, where the ebony-clad noble desired them.

"Enjoying the brandy, my friends?" Terenas asked the others. After they nodded, he smiled and said, "A case will go back with each of you, my gift for your visit."

"A splendid show of friendship, wouldn't you say?" Prestor urged Terenas's counterparts.

They nodded, Proudmoore even toasting the monarch of Lordaeron.

Terenas clasped his hands together. "And thanks to our young associate here, I think we'll all leave even closer in heart than we were before."

"We've not signed any agreement yet," Genn Greymane reminded him. "We've not even agreed what to do about the situation."

Terenas blinked. The perfect opening. Why wait any longer to make his grand suggestion?

"As to that, my friends," the king said, taking Lord Prestor's arm and guiding him toward the head of the table. "I think I've hit upon the solution that will appeal to us all. . . ."

King Terenas of Lordaeron smiled briefly at his young companion, who could not possibly have any idea of the great reward he was about to receive. Yes, the perfect man for the role. With Prestor in charge of Alterac, the future of the Alliance would be assured.

And then they could begin to deal with those treacherous wizards in Dalaran. . . .

*   *   *

"This is not right!" the heavyset mage burst out. "They've no cause to leave us out of this!"

"No, they don't," returned the elder woman. "But they have."

The mages who had met earlier in the Chamber of the Air now met there again, only this time there were five. The one that Rhonin would have known as Krasus had not taken his position in this magical place, but the others were too concerned with the events of the outside world to wait. The lords of the untalented had met in seclusion, discussing a major situation without the general guidance of the Kirin Tor. While most among this council respected King Terenas and some of the other monarchs, it disturbed them that the ruler of Lordaeron would put together such an unprecedented summit. One of the inner council of the Kirin Tor had ever been present at such past events. It had only been fair, as Dalaran had always stood at the forefront of the Alliance's defense.

Times, though, appeared to be changing.

"The Alterac dilemma could have been resolved long ago," pointed out the elven mage. "We should have insisted on our proper part in the proceedings."

"And started another incident?" retorted the bearded man in stentorian tones. "Haven't you noticed of late how the other realms have been pulling back from us? It's almost as if they fear us now that the orcs've been pushed to Grim Batol!"

"Absurd! The untalented have always been suspicious of magic, but our faith to the cause is without question!"

The elder woman shook her head. "When has that mattered to those who fear our abilities? Now that the orcs have been battered, the people begin to notice that

we're not like them; that we are superior in every
way. . . ."

"A dangerous way to think, even for us," came the
calm voice of Krasus. The faceless wizard stood in his
chosen spot.

"About time you got here!" The bearded wizard turned
toward the newcomer. "Did you find out anything?"

"Very little. The meeting was unshielded . . . yet all we
could read were surface thoughts. Those told us nothing
we did not know before. I finally had to resort to other
methods to garner even some success."

The younger female dared speak. "Have they made a
decision?"

Krasus hesitated, then raised a gloved hand. "Be-
hold . . ."

In the center of the chamber, directly over the symbol
etched in the floor, materialized a tall, human figure. In
every way, he looked as real, if not more so, than the
gathered wizards. Majestic of frame, clad in elegant, dark
clothing and with features avian and handsome, he
brought a moment of silence to the six.

"Who is he?" the same woman asked.

Krasus surveyed his companions before answering,
"All hail the new ruler of Alterac, *King Prestor the First.*"

"*What?*"

"This is outrageous!"

"They can't do this without us—can they?"

"Who is this Prestor?"

Rhonin's patron shrugged. "A minor noble from the
north, dispossessed, without backing. Yet, he seems to
have ingratiated himself not only to Terenas, but even the
rest, Genn Greymane included."

"But to make him *king*?" snapped the bearded spell-caster.

"On the surface, not a terrible choice. It places Alterac as once more an independent kingdom. The other monarchs find much about him they respect, so I gather. He seems to have single-handedly kept the Alliance from falling apart."

"So you approve of him?" the elder female asked.

In reply, Krasus added, "He also seems to have no history, apparently is the reason we have not been included in these talks, and—most curious of all—appears as a void when touched by magic."

The others muttered among themselves about this strange news. Then the elven wizard, clearly as puzzled as the rest, inquired, "What do you mean by the last?"

"I mean that any attempt to study him through magic reveals *nothing*. Absolutely *nothing*. It is as if Lord Prestor does not exist . . . and yet he must. Approve of him? I think I fear him."

Coming from this eldest of the wizards assembled, the words sank deep. For a time the clouds flew overhead, the storms raged, and the day turned into night, but the masters of the Kirin Tor simply stood in silence, each digesting the facts in his or her own way.

The youthful male broke the silence first. "He's a wizard then, is he?"

"That would seem most logical." Krasus returned, dipping his head slightly to accent his agreement.

"A powerful one," muttered the elf.

"Also logical."

"Then, if so," continued the elven mage, "who? One among us? A renegade? Surely a wizard of this ability would be known to us!" -

The younger woman leaned toward the image. "I don't recognize his face."

"Hardly surprising," retorted her elder counterpart. "When each of us could wear a thousand masks ourselves . . ."

Lightning flashed through Krasus, going unnoticed by him. "A formal announcement will take place in two weeks. After that, unless one of the other monarchs changes his mind, this Lord Prestor will be crowned king a month later."

"We should lodge a protest."

"A start. However, what we really need to do, I think, is to find out the truth about this Lord Prestor, search into every crevice and tomb and discover his past, his true calling. We dare not confront him openly until then, for he surely has the backing of every member of the Alliance but us."

The elder woman nodded. "And even we cannot face the combined might of the other kingdoms, should they find us too much of a nuisance."

"No, we cannot."

Krasus dismissed the image of Prestor with a wave of his hand, but the young noble's countenance had already been burned into the minds of each of the Kirin Tor. Through silence, they agreed on the importance of this quest.

"I must depart again," Krasus said. "I suggest all of you do as I and think hard on this dire matter. Follow all trails, no matter how obscure and impossible, but follow them swiftly. If the throne of Alterac is filled by this enigma, I suspect that the Alliance will not long stand firm, however of one mind its rulers presently are." He took a breath. "And I fear that Dalaran may fall with the rest if that happens."

"Because of this one man?" the bearded wizard spouted.

"Because of him, yes."

And as the rest pondered his words, Krasus vanished again—

—to rematerialize in his sanctum, still shaken by what he had discovered. Guilt wracked him, for Krasus had not been entirely truthful with his counterparts. He knew— or rather *suspected*—far more about this mysterious Lord Prestor than he had let on to the others. He wished that he could have told them everything, yet not only would they have questioned his sanity, but even if they had believed him, it might only have served to reveal too much about himself and his methods.

He could ill afford to do that at this desperate juncture.

May they act as I hope they will. Alone in his darkened sanctum, Krasus dared at last pull back his hood. A single dim light with no visible source offered the only illumination in the chamber, and in its soft glow stood revealed a handsome, graying man with angular features treading near the cadaverous. Black, glittering eyes hinted of even more age and weariness than the rest of the visage. Three long scars traveled side by side down the right cheek, scars that, despite their age, still throbbed with some pain.

The master wizard turned his left hand over, revealing the gloved palm. Atop that palm suddenly materialized a sphere of light blue. Krasus passed his other hand over the sphere and immediately images formed within. He leaned back to observe those images, a high stone chair sliding into place behind him.

Once more Krasus observed the palace of King Terenas. The regal stone structure had served the monarchs of the realm for generations. Twin turrets rising several stories flanked the main edifice, a gray, stately structure like a miniature fortress. The banners of Lordaeron flew prominently not only from the turrets, but the gated entrance as well. Soldiers clad in the uniforms of the King's Guard stood station outside the gates, with several members of the Knights of the Silver Hand on duty within. Under normal conditions, the paladins would not have been a part of the defense of the palace, but with some minor matters still to be discussed by the various monarchs visiting, clearly the trustworthy warriors were needed now.

Again the wizard passed his other hand over the sphere. To the left of the vision of the palace emerged the picture of an inner chamber. Staring at it, the wizard brought the chamber into better view.

Terenas and his youthful protégé. So, despite the end of the summit and the other rulers' imminent departures, Lord Prestor still remained with the king. Krasus felt a great temptation to try to probe the mind of the ebony-clad aristocrat, but thought better of it. Let the others attempt that likely impossible feat. One such as Prestor would no doubt expect such incursions and deal with them promptly. Krasus did not want to reveal his hand just yet.

However, if he dared not probe the thoughts of the man, at least he could research his background . . . and where better to start that than at the chateau where the regal refugee had taken up residence under the king's protection? Krasus waved one hand over the sphere and a new image formed, that of the building in question, as viewed from far away. The wizard studied it for a moment, seeing and detecting nothing of consequence, then sent his magical probe closer.

As his probe neared the high wall surrounding the building, a minor spell, much minor than he had expected, briefly prevented his entry. Krasus readily sidestepped the spell without setting it off. Now his view revealed the very exterior of the chateau, a rather morbid place despite its elegant facade. Prestor evidently believed in keeping a neat house, but not necessarily a pleasant one. Not at all a surprise to the mage.

A quick search revealed yet another defensive spell, this one more elaborate yet still nothing Krasus could not circumnavigate. With one deft gesture, the angular figure once more bypassed Prestor's handiwork. Another moment and Krasus would be inside, where he could—

His sphere blackened.

The blackness spread beyond the edges of the sphere.

The blackness *reached* for the wizard.

Krasus threw himself from the chair. Tentacles of purest night enveloped the stone seat, pouring over it as they would have the mage himself. As Krasus came to his feet, he watched the tentacles pull away—leaving no trace of the chair behind.

Even as the first tentacles reached for him, more sprouted from what remained of the magical orb. The mage stumbled back, for one of the few times in his life momentarily startled into inaction. Then, recalling himself, Krasus muttered words not heard by another living soul in several lifetimes, words he himself had never uttered, only read with fascination.

A cloud sparkled into life before him, a cloud that thickened like cotton. It immediately flowed toward the seeking tentacles, meeting them in midair.

The first tentacles to touch the soft cloud crumbled, turning to ash that faded even as it touched the floor. Krasus let out an exhalation of relief—then watched in horror as the second set of tentacles enshrouded his counterspell.

"It cannot be . . ." he muttered, eyes wide. "It cannot be!"

As the others had done to the chair, these ebony limbs now took in the cloud, absorbed it, *devoured* it.

Krasus knew what he faced. Only the *Endless Hunger*, a spell forbidden, acted so. He had never witnessed its casting before, but any who had studied the arts as long as he had would have recognized its foul presence. Yet, something had been changed, for the counterspell he had chosen should have been the one to end the threat. For a minute it had seemed to . . . and then a sinister transformation had occurred, a shifting in the dark spell's essence. Now the second set of tentacles came at him, and Krasus did not immediately know how to stop them from adding him to their meal.

He considered fleeing the chamber, but knew that the monstrous thing would simply continue after him no matter where in the world Krasus might hide. That had been part of the *Endless Hunger's* special horror; its relentless pursuit generally wore the victim down until he simply gave up.

No, Krasus had to put a stop to it here and now.

One incantation remained that might do the work. It would drain him, leave him useless for days, but it did have the potential to rid Krasus of this dire threat.

Of course, it also could kill him as readily as Lord Prestor's trap would.

He threw himself aside as one tentacle reached out. No more time to weigh matters. Krasus had only seconds to formulate the spell. Even now the *Hunger* moved to cut him off, to envelop him whole.

The words which the elder mage whispered would have sounded to the ordinary person like the language of Lordaeron spoken backwards, with the wrong syllables emphasized. Krasus carefully pronounced each, knowing that even one slip due to his predicament meant utter oblivion for him. He thrust out his left hand toward the reaching blackness, trying to focus on the very midst of the expanding horror.

The shadows moved swifter than he had thought possible. As the last few words fell from his tongue, the *Hunger* caught him. A single, slim tentacle wrapped itself around the third and fourth fingers of his outstretched hand. Krasus felt no pain at first, but before his eyes those fingers simply faded, leaving open, bleeding wounds.

He spat out the last syllable just as agony suddenly coursed through his body.

The sun exploded within his tiny sanctum.

Tentacles melted away like ice caught in a furnace. Light so brilliant it blinded Krasus even with his eyes shut tight filled every corner and crack. The wizard gasped and fell to the floor clutching his maimed hand.

A hissing sound assailed his ears, sending his already heightened pulse racing more. Heat, incredible heat, seared his skin. Krasus found himself praying for a swift end.

The hiss became a roar that rose and rose in intensity,

almost as if a volcanic eruption were about to take place in the very midst of the chamber. Krasus tried to look, but the light remained too overwhelming. He pulled himself into a fetal position and prepared for the inevitable.

And then . . . the light simply ceased, plunging the chamber into a still darkness.

The master mage could not at first move. If the *Hunger* had come for him now, it would have found him without the ability to resist. He lay there for several minutes, trying to regain his sense of reality and, when he finally recalled it, stem the flow of blood from his terrible wound.

Krasus passed his good hand over the injured one, sealing the bloody gap. He would not be able to repair the damage. Nothing touched by the dark spell could ever be regenerated.

He finally dared open his eyes. Even the unlit room initially appeared too bright, but, gradually, his eyes adjusted. Krasus made out a couple of shadowed forms—furniture, he believed—but nothing more.

"*Light . . .*" the battered spellcaster muttered.

A small emerald sphere burst into being near the ceiling, shedding dim illumination across the chamber. Krasus scanned his surroundings. Sure enough, the shapes he had seen were his remaining bits of furniture. Only the chair had not survived. As for the *Hunger,* it had been completely eradicated. The cost had been great, but Krasus had triumphed.

Or perhaps not. So much catastrophe in the space of a few seconds, and he did not even have anything to show for it. His attempt to probe the chateau of Lord Prestor had ended in defeat.

And yet . . . and yet . . .

Krasus dragged himself to his feet, summoned a new chair identical to the first. He fell into the chair gasping. After a momentary glance at his ruined appendages to assure himself that the bleeding had indeed stopped, the wizard summoned a blue crystal with which to once more view the noble's abode. A horrific notion had just occurred to him, one that, after all that had happened, he believed he could now verify with but a short, safe glimpse.

There! The traces of magic were evident. Krasus followed the traces further, watched their intertwining. He had to be careful, lest he reawaken the foulness he had just escaped.

Verification came. The skill with which the *Endless Hunger* had been cast, the complexity with which its essence had been altered so as to make his first counterattack unsuccessful—both pointed to knowledge and technique beyond even that of the Kirin Tor, the best mages humanity and even the elves could offer.

But there was another race whose trafficking in magic went farther back than the elves.

"I know you now. . . ." Krasus gasped, summoning a view of Prestor's proud visage. "I know you now, despite the form you wear!" He coughed, had to catch his breath. The ordeal had taken much out of Krasus, but the realization of just whose power he had confronted in many ways struck him deeper than any spell could have. "I know you—*Deathwing!*"

SEVEN

Duncan reined his horse to a halt. "Something is wrong here."

Rhonin, too, had that feeling, and coupled with his suspicions over what had happened to him at the keep, he could not help wondering if what they observed now somehow related to his journey.

Hasic lay in the distance, but a subdued, silent Hasic. The wizard could hear nothing, no sound of activity. A port such as this should have been bustling with noise loud enough to reach even their party. Yet, other than a few birds, he could make out no sound of life.

"We received no word of trouble," the senior paladin informed Vereesa. "If we had, we would have ridden here immediately."

"Maybe we are just overanxious because of the trek." Yet even the ranger spoke in low, cautious tones.

They sat there for so long that Rhonin finally had to take matters into his own hands. To the surprise of the others, he urged his mount forward, determined to reach Hasic with or without the rest.

Vereesa quickly followed, and Lord Senturus naturally

hurried after her. Rhonin held back any expression of amusement as the Knights of the Silver Hand pushed forward to take the lead from him. He could tolerate their arrogance and pomposity for a little longer. One way or another, the wizard and his undesired companions would depart company in the port.

That is . . . if anything was left of the port.

Even their mounts reacted to the silence, growing more and more tentative. At one point, Rhonin had to prod his animal to move on. None of the knights made jests over his difficulty, though.

To their relief, as the party drew nearer, they did begin to hear some sounds of life from the direction of the port. Hammering. A few voices raised. Wagon movement. Not much, but at least proof that Hasic had not become a place of ghosts.

Still, they approached cautiously, aware that something did not sit well. Vereesa and the knights kept one hand by their sword hilts, while Rhonin began running through his spells in his mind. No one knew what to expect, but they all clearly expected it soon.

And just as they rode within sight of the town gate, Rhonin spotted three ominous forms rising into the sky.

The wizard's horse shied. Vereesa grabbed hold of the reins for Rhonin and brought the animal under control. Some of the knights began to draw their swords, but Duncan immediately signaled them to return the weapons to their sheaths.

Moments later, a trio of gigantic gryphons descended before the group, two alighting onto the tops of the mightiest trees, the third landing directly in their path.

"Who rides toward Hasic?" demanded its rider, a

bronze-skinned, bearded warrior who, despite likely not even coming up to the mage's shoulder, looked capable of lifting not only him, but his horse as well.

Duncan immediately rode forward. "Hail to you, gryphon-rider! I am Lord Duncan Senturus of the order of the Knights of the Silver Hand, and I lead this party to the port! If you will permit a question, has some misfortune befallen Hasic?"

The dwarf gave a harsh laugh. He had none of the stout look of his more earthbound cousins, instead seeming more like a barbarian warrior who had been taken by a dragon and crushed to half-size. This one had shoulders even wider than those of the strongest knight and muscles that rippled of their own accord. A wild mane of hair fluttered behind the stocky, unyielding face.

"If you can call a pair of dragons just a misfortune, then, yes, Hasic suffered one! They came three days ago, tearing apart and burning anything they could! If not for my flight here having arrived that very morning, you'd find none of your precious port intact, human! They had barely begun when we took them in the sky! A glorious battle it was, though we lost Glodin that day!" The dwarves slapped a fist over their hearts. "May his spirit fight proud through eternity!"

"We saw a dragon," Rhonin interjected, fearful for a moment that the trio would break into one of the epic mourning songs he had heard about. "About that time. With an orc handler. Three of you came and fought it—"

The lead rider had scowled at him as soon as his mouth had opened, but at mention of the other struggle, the dwarf's eyes had lit up and a wide smile had returned to his face. "Aye, that was us as well, human! Tracked down the cowardly reptile and took him in the sky! A good and dangerous fight that was, too! Molok up there—" He indicated a fuller, slightly bald dwarf atop the tree to Rhonin's right. "—lost a fine ax, but at least he still has his hammer, eh, Molok?"

"Would rather shave off my beard than lose my hammer, Falstad!"

"Aye, 'tis the hammer that impresses the ladies most, 'tisn't it?" Falstad replied with a chuckle. The dwarf seemed to notice Vereesa for the first time. Brown eyes glittered bright. "And here's a fine elven lady now!" He made a bad attempt at a bow while still atop the gryphon. "Falstad Dragonreaver at your service, elven lady!"

Rhonin belatedly recalled that the elves of Quel-'Thalas had been the only other people whom the wild dwarves of the Aeries truly trusted. That, of course, did not look to be the entire reason why Falstad now focused on Vereesa; like Senturus, the gryphon-rider clearly found her very attractive.

"My greetings, Falstad," the silver-haired ranger solemnly returned. "And my congratulations on a victory well fought. Two dragons are much for any flight group to claim."

"All a day's task for mine, all a day's task!" He leaned as near as he could. "We've not been graced with any of your folk in this area, though, especially not so fine a lady as yourself! In what way can this poor warrior serve you best?"

Rhonin felt the hair on the nape of his neck bristle. The dwarf's tone, if not his words, offered more than simple assistance. Such things should not have disturbed the wizard, yet for some reason they did at this moment.

Perhaps Duncan Senturus felt the same way, for he answered before anyone else could. "Your offer of aid is appreciated, but likely not necessary. We have but to reach the ship that awaits this wizard so that he may be on his way from our shores."

The paladin's response made it sound as if Rhonin had been exiled from Lordaeron. Gritting his teeth, the frustrated mage added, "I am on an observation mission for the Alliance."

Falstad appeared unimpressed. "We've no cause to stop you from entering Hasic and searching for your vessel, human, but you'll find that not so many remain after the dragons attacked. Likely yours is flotsam on the sea!"

The thought had already occurred to Rhonin, but hearing it from the dwarf made the point sink home. However, he could not be defeated this early in his quest. "I have to find out."

"Then we'll be out of your way." Falstad urged his mount forward. He took one last long glance at Vereesa and grinned. "A definite pleasure, my elven lady!"

As the ranger nodded, the dwarf and his mount rose up into the air. The massive wings created a wind that blew dust into the eyes of the party, and the sudden nearness of the gryphon as it left the ground made even the most hardened of the horses step back. The other riders joined Falstad, the three gryphons quickly dwindling in the heavens. Rhonin watched the already faint forms bank toward Hasic, then fly off at an incredible rate of speed.

Duncan spat dust from his mouth; from his expression, his opinion of the dwarves was clearly not that much higher than what he thought of wizards. "Let us ride. We may still find fortune on our side."

Without another word they rode toward the port. It did not take long for them to see that Hasic had suffered even more than Falstad had let on. The first buildings they came across stood more or less intact, but with each passing moment the visible damage intensified. Crop fields in the outer lands had been scorched, the landowners' domiciles reduced to splinters. Stronger structures with stone bases had withstood the onslaught much better, but now and then they saw one that had been completely demolished, as if one of the dragons had chosen that place to alight.

The stench of burnt matter especially touched the wizard's heightened senses. Not everything the two leviathans had charred had been made of wood. How many of Hasic's inhabitants had perished in this desperate raid? On the one hand, Rhonin could actually appreciate the desperation of the orcs, who certainly had to know by now that their chances of winning the war had dropped to nil, but on the other hand . . . deaths such as these demanded justice.

Curiously, several areas near the very harbor itself looked entirely intact. Rhonin would have expected these to be in the worst condition, but other than a sullenness among the workers they saw, everything here looked as if Hasic had never been attacked.

"Perhaps the ship survived after all," he muttered to Vereesa.

"I do not think so. Not if that is any sign."

He looked out into the harbor itself, to the place at which the ranger pointed. The wizard squinted, trying to identify what exactly he saw.

"The mast of a ship, spellcaster," Duncan gruffly informed him. "The rest of the vessel and her valiant crew no doubt reside in the water below."

Rhonin bit back a curse. Surveying the harbor, he now saw that bits and pieces of wood and other material dotted the surface, flotsam from more than a dozen ships, the mage suspected. Now he realized in part why the port itself had survived; the orcs must have directed their mounts to attack the Alliance vessels first, not wanting them to escape. It did not explain why the outer reaches of Hasic had suffered worse than the interior, but perhaps most of that damage had taken place after the coming of the gryphon-riders. Not the first time that a settlement had found itself caught in the midst of a violent struggle and suffered for it. Still, the devastation would have been a lot worse if the dwarves had not come along. The orcs would have had their dragons level the port and try to slay everyone within sight.

Speculation, however, did not help with the problem at hand, namely the fact that now he had no ship on which to travel to Khaz Modan.

"Your quest is ended, wizard," Lord Senturus announced for no good reason that Rhonin could see. "You have failed."

"There may yet be a boat. I've the funds to hire one—"

"And who here will sail to Khaz Modan for your silver? These poor wretches have suffered through enough trials. Do you expect some of them to sail willingly to a land still held by the very orcs who did this?"

"I can only try to find out. I thank you for your time, my lord, and wish you well." Turning to the elf, Rhonin added, "And you as well, rang—Vereesa. You're a credit to your calling."

She looked startled. "I'm not leaving you yet."

"But your task—"

"Is incomplete. I cannot in good conscience leave you here with nowhere to go. If you still seek a way to Khaz Modan, I shall do what I can to help you—Rhonin."

Duncan suddenly straightened in the saddle. "And certainly we cannot leave matters so, either! By our honor, if you believe this task still worthy of continuation, then I and my fellows will also do what we can to seek transport for you!"

Vereesa's decision to remain for the time being had pleased Rhonin, but he could have done without the Knights of the Silver Hand. "I thank you, my lord, but there're many in need here. Wouldn't it be best if your order helped the good people of Hasic to recover?"

For the space of a breath, he actually thought that he had rid himself of the elder warrior, but after some clear deliberation with himself, Duncan finally announced, "Your words have some merit for once, wizard, yet I think we can arrange that both your mission and Hasic can benefit from our presence. My men will aid the citizens in recovery efforts while I take a personal hand in seeing if we can find a craft for you! That should settle the matter rightly, eh?"

Defeated, Rhonin simply nodded. At his side, Vereesa reacted with more grace. "Your assistance will no doubt prove invaluable, Duncan. Thank you."

After the senior paladin had sent the other knights on their way, he, Rhonin, and the ranger briefly discussed how best to go about their search. They soon agreed that separate paths would cover more ground, with all three returning at evening meal to discuss any possibilities. Lord Senturus clearly doubted that any of them would have success, but his duty to Lordaeron and the

Alliance—and possibly his infatuation with Vereesa—demanded he do his part.

Rhonin scoured the northern area of the port, seeking out any craft larger than a dinghy. The dragons had been thorough, however, and as the day waned, he found himself with nothing yet to report. It gradually got to the point where he remained uncertain as to which bothered him more—being unable to find transport, or fearing that the so-grand lord knight would be the one to present them with the answer to Rhonin's predicament.

There were methods by which a wizard could span such long distances, but only those like the both legendary and cursed Medivh had ever used them with confidence. Even if Rhonin did successfully cast the spell, he risked not only possible detection by any orc warlock in the area, but also unexpected changes in his destination due to the emanations from the region where the Dark Portal lay. Rhonin did not want to find himself materializing over an active volcano. Yet, by what other method could he make his journey?

While he struggled to find an answer, the recovery of Hasic took place around him. Women and children gathered what wreckage they found floating in from the harbor, scavenging whatever still seemed of use and piling the rest to one side for later disposal. A special unit of the town guard went along the shoreline, searching for the waterlogged corpses of any of the mariners who had gone down with their ships. A few of the people stared at the somber, dark-clad mage as he walked among them, some of the parents pulling their children to them as he passed. Now and then Rhonin read expressions that hinted of blame, as if somehow he had been responsible for this terrible assault.

Even under such dire conditions the common folk could not forget their prejudices and fears concerning his kind.

Above him, a pair of the gryphons flew past, the dwarves maintaining watch for any new attack. Rhonin doubted the region would be seeing any dragon strikes soon, the last one having cost the orcs far too much. Falstad and his companions would have better served the port by landing and helping those left, but the wary spellcaster suspected that the dwarves, not the most friendly of Lordaeron's allies, preferred to stay aloft and aloof. Given any good reason, they no doubt would have even abandoned Hasic entirely rather than—

Another reason?

"Of course . . ." Rhonin muttered. He watched the two creatures and their riders descend to the southwest. Who else but the dwarves might find his offer tempting? Who else was insane enough?

Disregarding the spectacle he might be making of himself, Rhonin ran after the dwindling figures.

Vereesa left the southernmost edge of the docks in total disgust. Not only had she met with no success, but of all the human settlements she had visited, Hasic ranked among the highest in stench. It had little to do with the disaster or even the smell of fish. Hasic just stank. Most humans had little enough sense of smell; the people here clearly had none.

The ranger wanted to be rid of this place, to return to her own kind so that she could be appointed to a more critical role, but until Vereesa could satisfy herself that she had done all she could for Rhonin, the ranger could not, in good conscience, depart. Yet there seemed no method by which the wizard might continue with his journey, one she now remained positive had to do with more than simply observation. Rhonin had revealed himself far too determined to be simply going on such a minor mission. No, he had something else in mind.

If only she knew what it might be . . .

The time for evening meal fast approached. With no sign of hope, the ranger headed inland, utilizing the most direct streets and alleys available despite the sometimes overwhelming scents. Hasic also maintained land routes to its neighbors, especially the major realms of Hillsbrad and Southshore. Although it would take more than a week to reach either one, perhaps that remained the only chance.

"Well . . . my beautiful elven lady!"

She looked the wrong way at first, thinking one of the humans spoke so with her, but then Vereesa recalled who had last used such terms. The ranger turned to her right and shifted her gaze more earthward . . . there to see Falstad in all his half-sized glory, the wild dwarf's eyes bright and his mouth open in a wide, knowing grin. He carried a sack over one shoulder and had his great hammer slung over the other. The weight of either would have left many an elf or human slumping from effort, but Falstad carried both with the ease of his kind.

"Master Falstad. Greetings to you."

"Please! I am Falstad to my friends! I am master of nothing save my own wondrous fate!"

"And I am simply Vereesa to my friends." Although the dwarf seemed to have a high opinion of himself, something in his manner made it hard not to like him, albeit not as much as Falstad possibly hoped. He did little to hide his interest in her, even allowing his eyes now and then to wander below her face. The ranger decided she had to deal with that situation immediately. "And they remain my friends only so long as they treat me with the respect with which I in turn treat them."

The dark orbs shot back up to meet her own, but otherwise Falstad pretended innocence. "How goes your quest to set the wizard on the water, my elven lady? Not good, I'd say, not good at all!"

"No, not good. It seems that the only vessels not damaged took to the sea as soon as they could for safer climes. Hasic is a port without function. . . ."

"A pity, a pity! We should discuss this further over a good flagon of spirits! What say you?"

She held back the slight smile his jovial persistence stirred. "Another time, perhaps. I still have a task to fulfill and you—" Vereesa indicated the sack "—seem to have one of your own."

"This little pouch?" He swung the heavy sack around with ease. "Some small bit of supplies, enough to last us until we leave this human place. All I need do is give them to Molok and you and I can be on our way to—"

The polite yet more blunt refusal forming on the ranger's lips died away as the angry squawk of a gryphon some short distance away—followed by voices rising in argument—set both her and Falstad to full alertness. Without a word the dwarf turned from her, sack dropped to the ground and stormhammer already unslung. He moved with such incredible swiftness for one of his build and size that even though Vereesa immediately followed after, Falstad had already vanished halfway down the street.

Vereesa unsheathed her own weapon, picking up her

pace. The voices grew stronger, more strident, and she had the uncomfortable feeling that one of them belonged to Rhonin.

The street quickly gave way to one of the open areas caused by the devastation. Here some of the gryphonriders awaited their leader, and here the wizard had apparently decided to accost them for some inexplicable reason. Wizards had often been called mad, but surely Rhonin had to be one of the most insane if he thought himself safe in arguing with wild dwarves.

And, in fact, one of them already had the mage by the clasp of his robe and had lifted the human up more than a foot off the ground.

"I said leave us be, foul one! If your ears don't be working, then I might as well tear them off!"

"Molok!" Falstad shouted. "What's this spellcaster done that's so enraged you?"

Still holding Rhonin in the air, the other dwarf, who could have been Falstad's twin save for a scar across his nose and a less humorous cast to his features, turned to his leader. "This one's followed Tupan and the others, first to the base camp, then, even after Tupan turned him away and flew off, here to where we all agreed to meet! Told him thrice to clear off, but the human just won't see good sense! Thought maybe he'd see clearer if I gave him a higher point from which to think about things!"

"Spellcasters . . ." the flight leader muttered. "You've my lasting sympathy, my elven lady!"

"Tell your companion to put him down, or I shall be forced to show him the superiority of a good elven sword over his hammer."

Falstad turned, blinking. He stared at the ranger as if

seeing her for the first time. His gaze briefly shifted to the sleek, gleaming blade, then back to the narrowed, determined eyes.

"You'd do that, wouldn't you? You'd defend this creature from those who've been the good friends of your people since before these humans even existed!"

"She has no need to defend me," came Rhonin's voice. The dangling mage seemed more annoyed by his predicament than rightfully fearful. Perhaps he did not realize that Molok could easily break his back in two. "Thus far, I've held my temper in check, but—"

Anything he said from this point on would only ensure that a struggle would develop. Vereesa moved swiftly, cutting off Rhonin with a wave of her hand and setting herself between Falstad and Molok. "This is utterly reprehensible! The Horde has not even been completely destroyed, and already we are at each other's throat. Is this how allies are to act? Have your warrior release him, Falstad, and we shall see if we cannot resolve this with reason, not fury."

" 'Tis only a spellcaster . . ." the lead gryphon rider muttered, but he nonetheless nodded, signaling Molok to release Rhonin.

With some reluctance, the other dwarf did just that. Rhonin straightened his robe and pushed his hair back in place, his expression guarded. Vereesa prayed that he would maintain his calm.

"What happened here?" she demanded of him.

"I came to them with a simple proposal, that was all. That they chose to react the way they did shows their barbaric—"

"He wanted us to fly him to Khaz Modan!" snapped Molok.

"The gryphon-riders?" Vereesa could not help but admire Rhonin's audacity, if not his recklessness. Fly across the sea on the back of one of the beasts—and not even as the principal rider, but someone forced to hold on to the dwarf in control? Truly Rhonin's mission had to be of more importance than he had let on for the wizard to attempt to convince Molok and the others to do this! Small wonder they thought him mad.

"I thought them capable and daring enough . . . but evidently I was wrong about that."

Falstad took umbrage. "If there's a hint at all in your words that we're cowards, human, I'll do to you what I kept Molok from doing! There's no more bold people, no mightier warriors, than the dwarves of the Aerie Peaks! 'Tisn't that we fear the orcs or dragons of Grim Batol; 'tis more that we care not to suffer the touch of your kind any more than necessary!"

Vereesa expected fury from her charge, but Rhonin only pursed his lips, as if he had expected Falstad's response to be so. Thinking of her own past thoughts and comments concerning wizards, the ranger realized that Rhonin must have lived most his life with such condemnations.

"I am on a mission for Lordaeron," the mage replied. "That's all that should matter . . . but I see it doesn't." He turned his back on the dwarves and started off.

Sword still gripped tight, Vereesa came to a swift and desperate decision, born from her suspicions concerning Rhonin's so-called observation mission. "Wait, mage!" He paused, no doubt somewhat surprised by her abrupt call. The ranger, however, did not speak to him, but rather faced the lead gryphon-rider again. "Falstad, is there no hope at all that you might take us as close as possible to Grim Batol? If not, then Rhonin and I are surely defeated!"

The dwarf's expression grew troubled. "I thought the wizard was traveling alone."

She gave him a knowing look, hoping that Rhonin, who watched her carefully, would not misunderstand. "And what would his chances be the first time he faced a strong orc ax? He might handle one or two with his spells, but if they came close, he would need a good sword arm."

Falstad watched her brandish the blade, the troubled look fading. "Aye, and a good arm it is, with or without the sword!" The dwarf glanced at Rhonin, then his men. He tugged on his lengthy beard, his gaze returning to Vereesa. "For him, I'd do very little, but for you—and the Lordaeron Alliance, of course—I'd be more than willing. Molok!"

"Falstad! You can't be serious—"

The lead dwarf went to his friend's side, putting a companionable arm around the shoulder of a dismayed Molok. "'Tis for the good of the war, brother! Think of the daring you can boast about! We may even slay a dragon or two along the way to add to our glorious annals, eh?"

Only slightly mollified, Molok finally nodded, muttering, "And I suppose you'll be carrying the lady behind you?"

"As the elves are our eldest allies and I'm flight leader, aye! My rank demands it, doesn't it, brother?"

This time Molok only nodded. His glowering expression said all else.

"Wonderful!" roared Falstad. He turned back to Vereesa. "Once more the dwarves of the Aerie Peaks come to the rescue! This calls for a drink, a flagon of ale or two, eh?"

The other dwarves, even Molok, lit up at this suggestion. The ranger saw that Rhonin would have preferred to take his leave at this point, but chose not to say such. Vereesa had given him his transport to the shores of Khaz Modan, and possibly even near to Grim Batol, and so it behooved him to show his gratitude to all involved. True, Falstad and his fellows would also have been glad to be rid of Rhonin, but Vereesa gave silent thanks that she would have someone other than the gryphon-riders with whom to talk.

"We shall be happy to join you," she finally replied. "Is that not so, Rhonin?"

"Very much so." His words came out with all the enthusiasm of one who had just discovered something odorous in the shoe he had just put on.

"Excellent!" Falstad's gaze never once shifted to the wizard. To Vereesa he said, "The Sea Boar is still intact and much appreciative of our fine business in the past! They should be able to scrounge up a few more casks of ale! Come!"

He would have insisted on escorting her himself, but the ranger expertly maneuvered away from his reach. Falstad, perhaps more eager for ale than elves at the moment, seemed not to take any notice of her slight. Waving to his men, he led them off in the direction of their favored inn.

Rhonin joined her, but as she attempted to follow after the dwarves, he suddenly pulled her aside, his expression dark.

"What were you thinking?" the flame-haired mage whispered. "Only *I* am heading to Khaz Modan!"

"And you would never have the chance to get there if I had not mentioned my going with you. You saw how the dwarves reacted earlier."

"You don't know what you're trying to get yourself into, Vereesa!"

She pushed her face within scant inches of his own, daring him. "And what is it? More than simply observation of Grim Batol. You plan something, do you not?"

Rhonin almost seemed ready to answer her, but at that moment another figure called out. They both looked back to see Duncan Senturus coming toward them.

Somthing struck the elf. She had not thought of the paladin when she had been trying to convince Falstad to carry Rhonin and her across the sea. Knowing the knight as she already did, Vereesa had the horrible feeling that he would insist on going with them, too.

That thought had not likely occurred yet to the wizard, whose fury still centered around the ranger. "We'll talk of this when we've more privacy, Vereesa, but know this already—when we reach the shores of Khaz Modan, I and *only* I will continue on! You'll be returning with our good friend Falstad . . . and if you think of going any farther—"

His eyes flared. Literally flared. Even the stalwart elf could not help but lean back in astonishment.

"—I'll send you back here myself!"

EIGHT

They were closing in on Grim Batol.

Nekros had known this day would come. Since the catastrophic defeat of Doomhammer and the bulk of the Horde, he had begun counting the days until the triumphant humans and their allies would come marching toward what remained of the orcs' domain in Khaz Modan. True, the Lordaeron Alliance had had to fight tooth and nail every inch of the way, but they had finally made it. Nekros could almost envision the armies amassing on the borders.

But before those armies struck, they hoped to weaken the orcs much further. If he could trust the word of Kryll, who had no reason to lie this time, then a plot was afoot to either release or destroy the Dragonqueen. Exactly how many had been sent, the goblin had not been able to say, but Nekros envisioned an operation as significant as this, combined with reports of increased military activity to the northwest, to require at least a regiment of hand-picked knights and rangers. There would also certainly be wizards, powerful ones.

The orc hefted his talisman. Not even the *Demon Soul*

would enable him to defend the lair sufficiently, and he could expect no help from his chieftain at this point. Zuluhed had his followers preparing for the expected onslaught to the north. A few lesser acolytes watched the southern and western borders, but Nekros had as much faith in them as he did the mental stability of Kryll. No, as usual, everything hinged on the maimed orc himself and the decisions he made.

He hobbled through the stone passage until he came to where the dragon-riders berthed. Few remained of the veterans, but one Nekros trusted well still rode at the forefront of every battle.

Most of the massive warriors were huddled around the central table in the room, the place where they discussed battle, ate, drank, and played the bones. By the rattling coming from within the gathered throng, someone had a good game going on even now. The riders would not appreciate his interruption, but Nekros had no other choice.

"Torgus! Where's Torgus?"

Some of the warriors looked his way, angry grunts warning him that his intrusion had better be of some import. The peg-legged orc bared his teeth, his heavy brow furrowing. Despite his loss of limb, he had been chosen leader here and no one, not even dragon-riders, would treat him as less.

"Well? One of you lot say something, or I'll start feeding body parts to the Dragonqueen!"

"Here, Nekros . . ." A great form emerged from within the group, rising until it stood a head taller than any of the other orcs. A countenance ugly even by the standards of his own race glared back at Nekros. One tusk had been broken off and scars graced both sides of the squat, ursine face. Shoulders half again as wide as that of the elder warrior connected to muscular arms as thick as Nekros's one good leg. "I'm here . . ."

Torgus moved toward his superior, the other riders making a quick, respectful retreat from his path. Torgus walked with all the bristling confidence of an orc champion, and with every right, for under his guidance his dragon had wreaked more havoc, sent to death more gryphon-riders, and caused more routing of human forces than any of his brethren. Markers and medallions from Doomhammer and Blackhand, not to mention various clan leaders such as Zuluhed, dangled from the ax harness around his chest.

"What do you want, old one? Another seven and I'd have cleaned out everyone! This better be good!"

"It's what you've been trained for!" Nekros snapped, determined not to be humiliated by even this one. "Unless you only fight the battles of wagering now?"

Some of the other riders muttered, but Torgus looked intrigued. "A special mission? Something better than scorching a few worthless human peasants?"

"Something maybe including soldiers and a wizard or two! Is that more your game?"

Brutish red orbs narrowed. "Tell me more, old one. . . ."

Rhonin had his transport to Khaz Modan. The thought should have pleased him much, but the cost that transport demanded seemed far too high to the wizard. Bad enough that he had to deal with the dwarves, who clearly disliked him as much as he did them, but Vereesa's claim that she needed to come along, too—granted, a necessary subterfuge in order to actually gain Falstad's permission—had turned his plans upside down. It had been paramount that he journey to Grim Batol alone—no useless comrades, no risk of a second catastrophe.

No more deaths.

And, as if to make matters worse, he had just discovered that Lord Duncan Senturus had somehow convinced the unconvincible Falstad to take the paladin along as well.

"This is insanity!" Rhonin repeated, not for the first time. "There's no need for anyone else!"

Yet, even now, even as the gryphon-riders prepared to fly them to the other side of the sea, no one listened. No one cared to hear his words. He even suspected that, if he protested much more, Rhonin might actually find himself the only one *not* going, as nonsensical as that seemed. The way Falstad had been looking at him of late . . .

Duncan had met with his men, giving Roland command and passing on his orders. The bearded knight turned over to his younger second what seemed a medallion or something similar. Rhonin almost thought nothing of it—the Knights of the Silver Hand seeming to have a thousand different rites for every minor occasion—but Vereesa, who had come up to his side, chose then to whisper, "Duncan has handed Roland the seal of his command. If something happens to the elder paladin, Roland will permanently ascend to his place in the rolls. The Knights of the Silver Hand take no chances."

He turned to ask her a question, but she had already stepped away again. Her mood had been much more formal since his whispered threat to her. Rhonin did not want to be forced to do something to make the ranger return, but he also did not want anything to befall her because of his mission. He even did not want anything dire to happen to Duncan Senturus, although likely the paladin had far more chance of surviving in the interior of Khaz Modan than Rhonin himself.

"'Tis time for flight!" Falstad shouted. "The sun's already up and even old ones have risen and begun their day's chores! Are we all ready at last?"

"I am prepared," Duncan replied with practiced solemnity.

"So am I," the anxious spellcaster quickly answered after, not wanting anyone to think that he might be the reason for any delay. Had he had his way, he and one of the riders would have departed the night before, but Falstad had insisted that the animals needed their full night's rest after the activities of the day . . . and what Falstad said was law among the dwarves.

"Then let us mount!" The jovial elf smiled at Vereesa, then extended his hand. "My elven lady?"

Smiling, she joined him by his gryphon. Rhonin fought to maintain an expression of indifference. He would have rather she had ridden with any of the dwarves other than Falstad, but to comment so would only make him look like an absolute fool. Besides, what did it matter to him with whom the ranger rode?

"Hurry up, wizard!" grumbled Molok. "I'd just as soon get this journey over with!"

Clad more lightly, Duncan mounted behind one of the remaining riders. As a fellow warrior, the dwarves respected, if not liked the paladin. They knew the prowess of the holy order in battle, which had apparently been why it had been easier for Lord Senturus to convince them of the necessity of bringing him along.

"Hold tight!" Molok commanded Rhonin. "Or you may end up as fish bait along the way!"

With that, the dwarf urged the gryphon forward . . . and into the air. The wizard held on as best he could, the unnatural sensation of feeling his heart jump into his throat giving him no assurance as to the safety of the journey. Rhonin had never ridden a gryphon, and as the vast wings of the animal beat up and down, up and down, he decided quickly that, should he survive, he would never do so again. With each heavy flap of the part avian, part leonine creature's wings, the wizard's stomach went up and down with it. Had there been *any* other way, Rhonin would have eagerly chosen it.

He had to admit, though, that the creatures flew with incredible swiftness. In minutes, the group had flown out of sight of not only Hasic, but the entire coast. Surely even dragons could not match their speed, although the race would have been close. Rhonin recalled how three of the smaller beasts had darted around the head of the red leviathan. A dangerous feat, even for the gryphons, and likely capable by few other animals alive.

Below, the sea shifted violently, waves rising threateningly high, then sinking so very, very low. The wind tore at Rhonin's face, wet spray forcing him to pull the hood of his robe tight in order to at least partially protect himself. Molok seemed unaffected by the harsh elements and, in fact, appeared to revel in them.

"How—how long do you think before we reach Khaz Modan?"

The dwarf shrugged. "Several hours, human! Couldn't say better than that!"

Keeping his darkening thoughts to himself, the wizard

huddled closer and tried to ignore the journey as much as possible. The thought of so much water underneath him bothered Rhonin more than he had thought. Between Hasic and the shores of Khaz Modan only the ravaged island kingdom of Tol Barad brought any change to the endless waves, and Falstad had previously indicated that the party would not be landing there. Overwhelmed early in the war by the orcs, no life more complex than a few hardy weeds and insects had survived the Horde's bloody victory. An aura of death seemed to radiate from the island, one so intense that even the wizard did not argue with the dwarf's decision.

On and on they flew. Rhonin dared an occasional glimpse at his companions. Duncan, of course, faced the elements with a typically stalwart pose, evidently oblivious to the moisture splattering his bearded countenance. Vereesa, at least, showed some effects of having to travel in this insane manner. Like the mage, she kept her head low for the most part, her lengthy silver hair tucked under the hood of her travel cloak. She leaned close to Falstad, who seemed, to Rhonin, to be enjoying her discomfort.

His stomach eventually settled to something near tolerable. Rhonin peered at the sun, calculated that they had now been in the air some five hours or more. At the rate of speed with which the gryphon traveled the skies, surely they had to be past the midway point. He finally broke the silence between Molok and himself, asking if this would be so.

"Midway?" The dwarf laughed. "Two more hours and I think we'll see the crags of western Khaz Modan in the distance! Midway? Ha!"

The news more than his companion's sudden good

humor made Rhonin smile. He had survived nearly three-fourths of the journey already. Just a little over a couple of hours and his feet would at last be planted firmly on the ground again. For once, he had made progress without some dire calamity to slow him down.

"Do you know a place to land once we get there?"

"Plenty of places, wizard! Have no fear! We'll be rid of you soon enough! Just hope that it doesn't pour before we get to them!"

Peering up, Rhonin inspected the clouds that had formed over the period of the last half-hour. Possible rain clouds, but he suspected that, if so, they would hold off more than long enough for the party to reach their destination. All he need worry about now was how best to make his way to Grim Batol once the others returned to Lordaeron.

Rhonin well knew how audacious his plan might look to the rest should they discover the truth. Again he thought of the ghosts that haunted him, the specters of the past. They were his true companions on this mad quest, the furies that drove him on. They would watch him succeed or die trying.

Die trying. Not for the first time since the deaths of his previous companions did he wonder if perhaps that would be the best conclusion to all of this. Perhaps then Rhonin would truly redeem himself in his own eyes, much less the ghosts of his imagination.

But first he had to reach Grim Batol.

"Look there, wizard!"

He started, not realizing that, at some point, he had drifted off. Rhonin stared past Molok's shoulder in the direction the dwarf now pointed. At first the wizard could see nothing, the ocean mists still splattering his eyes. After clearing his gaze, however, he saw two dark specks on the horizon. Two stationary specks. "Is that land?"

"Aye, wizard! The first signs of Khaz Modan!"

So near! New life and enthusiasm arose within Rhonin as he realized that he had managed to sleep through the remainder of the flight. Khaz Modan! No matter how dangerous the trek from here on, he had at least made it this far. At the rate at which the gryphons soared, it would only be a short time before they touched down on—

Two new specks caught his attention, two specks in the sky that *moved*, growing larger and larger, as if they closed in on the party.

"What are those? What's coming toward us?"

Molok leaned forward, squinting. "By the jagged ice cliffs of Northeron! Dragons! Two of them!"

Dragons . . .

"Red?"

"Does the color of the sky matter, wizard? A dragon is a dragon and, by my beard, they're coming fast for us!"

Glancing in the direction of the other gryphon-riders, Rhonin saw that Falstad and the rest had also spotted the dragons. The dwarves immediately began adjusting their formation, spreading out so as to present smaller, more difficult targets. The wizard noted Falstad steering more to the rear, likely due to the fact that Vereesa rode with him. On the other hand, the gryphon upon which Duncan Senturus traveled raced ahead, nearly outpacing the rest of the group.

The dragons, too, moved with strategy in mind. The larger of the pair rose to a higher altitude, then broke away from its companion. Rhonin instantly recognized that the two leviathans intended to force the gryphons into an area between them, where they could better pick off the smaller creatures and their riders.

Hulking forms atop each dragon coalesced into two of the largest, most brutish orcs the wary mage had ever seen. The one atop the greater behemoth looked to be the leader. He waved his ax toward the other orc, whose beast instantly veered farther to the opposite direction.

"Well-skilled riders, these!" shouted Molok with much too much eagerness. "The one on the right most of all! This will be a glorious battle!"

And one in which Rhonin might very well lose his life, just as it seemed he might have a chance to go on with his mission. "We can't fight them! I need to get to the shore!"

He heard Molok grunt in frustration. "My place is in the battle, wizard!"

"My mission must come first!"

For a moment he thought that the dwarf might actually throw him off their mount. Then, with much reluctance, Molok nodded his head, calling, "I'll do what I can, wizard! If an opening presents itself, we'll try for the shore! I'll drop you off and that'll be the end of it between us!"

"Agreed!"

They spoke no more, for at that point, the two opposing forces reached one another.

The swifter, much more agile gryphons darted about the dragons, quickly frustrating the lesser one. However, burdened as they were by extra weight, the animals ridden by Rhonin and the others could not maneuver quite so fast as usual. A massive paw with razor talons nearly swiped Falstad and Vereesa, and a wing barely missed clipping Duncan and the dwarf with him. The paladin and his companion continued to fly much too close, as if they sought to take on the one dragon in some bizarre sort of hand-to-hand combat.

With some effort, Molok removed his stormhammer, waving it about and shouting like someone who had just had his hair set on fire. Rhonin hoped that the dwarf would not forget his promise in the heat of battle.

The second dragon came down, unfortunately choosing Falstad and Vereesa for his main target. Falstad urged his gryphon on, but the wings could not beat fast enough with the elf in tow. The huge orc urged his reptilian partner on with murderous cries and mad swings of his monstrous battle-ax.

Rhonin gritted his teeth. He could not just let them perish, especially the ranger.

"Molok! Go after that larger one! We've got to help them!"

Eager as he was to obey, the scarred dwarf recalled Rhonin's earlier demand. "What about your precious mission?"

"Just go!"

A huge grin spread over Molok's visage. He gave a yell that sent every nerve in the mage's body into shock, then steered the gryphon toward the dragon.

Behind him, Rhonin readied a spell. They had only moments before the crimson leviathan would reach Vereesa. . . .

Falstad brought his mount around in a sudden arc that startled the dragon rider. The great behemoth soared past, unable to match the maneuverability of its smaller rival.

"Hold tight, wizard!"

Molok's gryphon dove almost straight down. Trying

not to let base fears overwhelm him, Rhonin went over the last segment of his spell. Now if he could manage enough breath to cast it—

The dwarf let out a war cry that brought the attention of the orc. Brow furrowing, the grotesque figure twisted around so as to meet his new foe.

Stormhammer briefly met battle-ax.

A shower of sparks nearly caused the wizard to lose his grip. The gryphon squawked in surprise and pain. Molok nearly toppled from his seat.

Their mount reacted quickest, racing higher into the sky, nearly into the thickening clouds above. Molok readjusted his seating. "By the Aerie! Did you see that? Few weapons or their wielders can stand against a stormhammer! This'll be a fascinating match!"

"Let me try something first!"

The dwarf's expression darkened. "Magic? Where's the honor and courage in that?"

"How can you battle the orc if the dragon won't let you near again? We got lucky once!"

"All right! So long as you don't steal the battle!"

Rhonin made no promises, mostly because he hoped to do just that. He stared at the dragon, which had quickly followed them up, muttering the words of power. At the last moment, the wizard glanced at the clouds above.

A single bolt of lightning shot down, striking at the pursuing giant.

It hit the dragon full on, but the effects were not what Rhonin had hoped. The creature's entire form shimmered from wing tip to wing tip and the beast let out a furious shriek, but the beast did not plummet from the heavens. In fact, even the orc, who no doubt suffered great, did nothing more than slump forward momentarily in his seat.

Disappointed, the wizard had to console himself that at least he had stunned the massive creature. It also occurred to him that now neither he nor Vereesa were in any immediate danger. The dragon struggled just to keep itself aloft.

Rhonin put a hand on Molok's shoulder. "To the shore! Quickly now!"

"Are you daft, wizard? What about the battle that you just told me to—"

"Now!"

More likely because he wanted to be rid of his exasperating cargo than because he believed in any authority on the mage's part, Molok reluctantly steered his gryphon away again.

Searching around, the anxious spellcaster sought any sign of Vereesa. Neither she nor Falstad were to be found. Rhonin thought of countermanding his order again, but he knew he *had* to reach Khaz Modan. Surely the dwarves could handle this pair of monsters. . . .

Surely they could.

Molok's gryphon had already begun to pull them away from their former adversary. Rhonin again contemplated sending them back.

A vast shadow covered them.

Both man and dwarf looked up in astonishment and consternation.

The second dragon had come up on them while they had been preoccupied.

The gryphon tried to dive out of reach. The brave beast almost made it, but talons ripped through the right wing. The leonine beast roared out its agony and tried desperately to stay aloft. Rhonin looked up to see the maw of the dragon opening. The gargantuan horror intended to swallow them whole.

From behind the dragon soared a second gryphon, Duncan and his dwarf companion. The paladin had positioned himself in an awkward manner and seemed to be trying to direct the dwarf to do something. Rhonin had no idea what the knight intended, only that the dragon would be upon the wizard and Molok before he could cast a suitable spell.

Duncan Senturus leapt.

"Gods and demons!" Molok shouted, for once even the wild dwarf astounded by the courage and insanity of another being.

Only belatedly did Rhonin understand what the paladin sought to do. In a move that would have left anyone else falling to their doom, the skilled knight landed with astonishing accuracy on the neck of the dragon. He clutched the thick neck and adjusted his position even as both the beast and its orc handler finally registered exactly what had happened.

The orc raised his ax and tried to catch Lord Senturus in the back, just barely missing. Duncan took one look at him, then seemed to forget his barbaric opponent from there on. Instead he inched himself forward, avoiding the awkward attempts by the dragon to snap at him.

"He must be mad!" Rhonin shouted.

"No, wizard—he's a *warrior.*"

Rhonin did not understand the dwarf's subdued, respectful tone until he saw Duncan, legs and one arm wrapped tight around the reptilian neck, draw his gleaming blade. Behind the paladin, the orc slowly crawled forward, a murderous red glare in his eyes.

"We've got to do something! Get me nearer!" Rhonin demanded.

"Too late, human! There are some epic songs meant to be. . . ."

The dragon did not try to shake Duncan free, no doubt in order to avoid doing the same to its handler. The orc moved with more assurance than the knight, quickly coming within range of a strike.

Duncan sat nearly at the back of the beast's head. He raised his long sword up, clearly intending to plunge it in at the base, where the spine met the skull.

The orc swung first.

The ax bit into Lord Senturus's back, cutting through the thinner chain mail the man had chosen for the journey. Duncan did not cry out, but he fell forward, nearly losing his sword. Only at the last did he retain his hold. The knight managed to press the point against the spot intended, but his strength clearly began to give out.

The orc raised his ax again.

Rhonin cast the first spell to come to mind.

A flash of light as intense as the sun burst before the eyes of the orc. With a startled cry, he fell back, losing both his grip on his weapon and his seating. The desperate warrior fumbled for some sort of hold, failed, and dropped over the side of the dragon's neck, screaming.

The wizard immediately turned his worried gaze back to the paladin—who stared back at him with what Rhonin almost thought a mixture of gratitude and respect. His back a spreading stain of deep red, Duncan yet managed to straighten, lifting his sword hilt up as high as he could.

The dragon, realizing at last that he had no reason to remain still any longer, began to dip.

Lord Duncan Senturus rammed the blade deep into the soft area between the neck and skull, burying his blade halfway into the leviathan.

The red beast twitched uncontrollably. Ichor shot forth from the wound, so hot it scalded the paladin. He slipped back, lost hold.

"To him, damn it!" Rhonin demanded of Molok. "To him!"

The dwarf obeyed, but Rhonin knew they would never reach Duncan in time. From across the way he saw another gryphon soar near. Falstad and Vereesa. Even with so much weight already upon his mount, the lead rider hoped to somehow rescue the paladin.

For a moment, it seemed as if they would. Falstad's gryphon neared the teetering warrior. Duncan looked up, first at Rhonin, then at Falstad and Vereesa.

He shook his head . . . and slumped forward, rolling off the shrieking dragon.

"No!" Rhonin stretched a hand toward the distant figure. He knew that Lord Senturus had already died, that only a corpse had fallen, but the sight stirred up all the misgivings and failures of the wizard's last mission. His fear had come to pass; now he had already lost one of those with him, even if Duncan had invited himself along.

"Look out!"

Molok's sudden warning stirred him from his reverie. He looked up to see the dragon, still aloft despite its death throes, spinning wildly about. The gargantuan wings fluttered everywhere, moving almost at random. Falstad barely got his own beast out of range of one, and too late Rhonin realized that this time he and Molok would not escape a blow by the other.

"Pull up, you blasted beast!" roared Molok. "Pull—"

The wing struck them full force, ripping the mage from his seat. He heard the dwarf scream and the gryphon squawk. Stunned, Rhonin barely realized that, for a moment at least, he flew higher into the sky. Then, gravity took over and the half-conscious wizard began to descend . . . rapidly.

He needed to cast a spell. *Some* spell. Try as he might, however, Rhonin could not concentrate enough to even recall the first words. A part of him knew that this time he would surely die.

Darkness overwhelmed him, but an unnatural darkness. Rhonin wondered if perhaps he was blacking out. However, from the darkness suddenly came a booming voice, one that struck a distant chord in his memory.

"I have you again, little one! Never fear, never fear!"

A reptilian paw so great that Rhonin did not even fill the palm enveloped the wizard.

NINE

D uncan!"

"'Tis too late, my elven lady!" Falstad called. "Your man's already dead—but what a glorious tale to leave behind!"

Vereesa cared nothing about glorious tales nor the incorrect assumption that she had admired Lord Senturus more than she actually did. All that mattered to her was that a brave man whom she had come to know all too briefly had perished. True, like Falstad, the elf had immediately realized that it had only been Duncan's shell that had fallen earthward, but the horror of his tragic death had still struck her deep.

Yet, Vereesa took some comfort in the knowledge that Duncan had managed the near-impossible. The dragon had been struck a mortal blow, one that caused it to continue to thrash about madly. The dying leviathan sought to pull the blade from the base of its skull, but its efforts grew weaker and weaker. It was only a matter of time before the giant joined its slayer in the depths of the sea.

However, even in dying the dragon remained a threat. A wing nearly caught the dwarf and her. Falstad had the gryphon dive in order to avoid the wild movements of the behemoth. Vereesa held on for dear life, no longer able to concern herself with Duncan's fate.

As for the second dragon, it, too, still menaced the gryphons. Falstad brought his mount up again, rising above the other monster in order to prevent them being seized by the horrific talons. Another rider narrowly escaped the snapping jaws.

They could no longer remain here. The orc guiding this second beast clearly had vast experience in aerial combat with gryphons. Sooner or later his mount would catch one of the dwarves. Vereesa wanted no more deaths. "Falstad! We have to get away!"

"For you I would do that, my elven lady, but the scaly beast and its handler seem to have other ideas!"

True enough, the dragon now appeared fixated on Vereesa and her companion, most likely at the orc's behest. Perhaps he had noted the second rider, and possibly thought her of some importance. In fact, the very presence of the two crimson behemoths brought many questions to the ranger's mind—specifically whether or not they had come because of Rhonin's mission. If so, then he more than she should have been the likely target. . . .

And where was Rhonin? As Falstad urged the gryphon to greater speed and the dragon closed behind them, the elf quickly glanced around, but again found no sign of him. Disturbed, she took a second look. Not only did Vereesa not see the mage, but she could not even locate the gryphon he had been riding.

"Falstad! I do not see Rhonin—"

"A worry for another time! 'Tis more important that you hold tight!"

She obeyed . . . and just in time. Suddenly the gryphon arced at such a severe angle that, had Vereesa hesitated, she might have been tossed off.

Talons slashed at the spot she and the dwarf had most recently occupied. The dragon roared its frustration and banked.

"Prepare for battle, my elven lady! It appears we are not to have any other choice!"

As he unslung his stormhammer, Vereesa cursed again the loss of her bow. True, she had a sword, but unlike Duncan, the ranger could not yet bring herself to commit such a sacrifice. Besides, she still needed to find out what had happened to Rhonin, who remained her first priority.

The orc had his own long battle-ax out, and now waved it around his head, shouting some barbaric war cry. Falstad responded with a guttural cry of his own, clearly eager for combat despite his earlier concern for Vereesa. With nothing left for her to do, the ranger held on, hoping that the dwarf's aim would be true.

A titanic form the color of night dropped in among the combatants, falling upon the crimson dragon and sending both beast and handler into a state of confusion.

"What in the name of—" was all Falstad managed.

The elf found herself speechless.

Black wings twice the span of those of the red filled Vereesa's vision, metallic glints from those wings almost blinding her. A tremendous roar shook the sky like thunder, sending the gryphons scattering.

A dragon of immense proportions snapped at the smaller red one. Dark, narrow orbs eyed the lesser leviathan with contempt. The orc's dragon roared back, but clearly it did not find this new foe to its liking.

"We may be done for now, my elven lady! 'Tis none other than the dark one himself!"

The black goliath spread his wings wide, and the sound that escaped his mighty jaws reminded Vereesa of harsh, mocking laughter. Again she caught sight of metal—*plates* of metal—spread across much of the newcomer's vast body. The natural armor of a dragon proved difficult enough to pierce; what metal would a creature such as this wear to protect its hard scales?

The answer came quick. *Adamantium.* Only it truly outshone the nearly impenetrable scale . . . and only one great leviathan had ever put himself through such agony in the name of power and ego.

"Deathwing . . ." she whispered. "Deathwing . . ."

Among the elves, it had been said long ago that there were five great dragons, five leviathans who represented arcane and natural forces. Some claimed that Alexstrasza the red represented the essence of life itself. Of the others, little was known, for even before the coming of humans the dragons had lived sheltered, hermitic existences. The elves had felt their influence, had even dealt with them on various occasions, but never had the elder creatures truly revealed their secrets.

Yet, among the dragons, there *had* been one who had made himself known to all, who ever reminded the world that, before all other races, *his* kind had ruled. Although originally bearing another name, he himself had long ago chosen *Deathwing* as his title, the better to show his contempt and intentions for the lesser creatures around him. Even the elders of Vereesa's race could not claim to know what drove the ebony giant, but throughout the years he had done what he could to destroy the world built by the elves, dwarves, and humans.

The elves had another name for him, spoken only in whispers and only in the elder tongue almost forgotten. *Xaxas.* A short title with many meanings, all dire. Chaos. Fury. The embodiment of elemental rage, such as found in erupting volcanoes or shattering earthquakes. If Alexstrasza represented the elements of life that bound the world together, then Deathwing exemplified the destructive forces that constantly sought to rip it apart.

Yet now he hovered before them, attempting, it seemed, to defend them from one of his own kind. Of course, Deathwing likely did not see it that way. This was a foe with scale of crimson, the color of his greatest rival. Deathwing hated dragons of all other colors and did his best to see that each he confronted perished, but those bearing the mantle of Alexstrasza the ebony behemoth despised most.

" 'Tis an impossible sight, eh?" murmured Falstad, for once subdued. "And yet I thought the foul monster dead!"

So had the ranger. The Kirin Tor had combined the might of the best of their human wizards with those of their elven counterparts to finally, so they had claimed, bring an end to the threat of the black fury. Even the metallic plates that Deathwing had long ago convinced the mad goblins to literally weld to his body had not protected him from those sorcerous strikes. He had fallen, fallen . . .

But now, apparently, flew triumphant again.

The war against the orcs had suddenly become a very minute thing. What were all the remnants of the Horde in Khaz Modan compared to this single, sinister giant?

The lesser dragon, also evidently a male, snapped angrily at Deathwing. The snout came near enough that the black beast could have swatted it with his left forepaw, but for some reason Deathwing held that paw closed and near to his body. Instead, he whipped his tail at his adversary, sending the red reeling back. As the black dragon moved, under the shifting metal plates what seemed to be a vast series of veins filled with molten fire radiated along both his throat and torso, flaring with each roar from the titan. Legend had it that to touch those veins of fire was to risk truly being burned. Some said this was due to an acidic secretion by the dragon, but other tales took it as literal flame.

Either way, it meant death.

"The orc is either brave beyond compare, a fool, or without any control over his beast!" Falstad shook his head. "Even I would not remain in such a fray if it could be helped!"

The other gryphons neared. Tearing her gaze away from the posturing dragons, Vereesa inspected the newcomers, but saw no sign of either Molok or Rhonin. In fact, their little group now numbered only her and four dwarves.

"Where is the wizard?" she called to the others. "Where is he?"

"Molok is dead," one of them proclaimed to Falstad. "His mount lies drifting in the sea!"

For their small stature, dwarves had incredibly muscular, dense bodies and so did not float well. Falstad and the others chose to take the discovery of the dead gryphon as proof enough of the warrior's fate.

But Rhonin was human and, therefore, whether dead or alive, stood a better chance of floating for a time. Vereesa seized on that slight hope. "And the wizard? Did you see the wizard?"

"I think 'tis obvious, my elven lady," Falstad returned, glancing back at her.

She clamped her mouth shut, knowing he spoke truth. At least with the incident at the keep, there had been enough question. Here, however, matters seemed final. Even Rhonin's magic certainly could not have saved him up here and from this height, striking the water below would have been like striking solid rock. . . .

Unable to keep from glancing down, Vereesa made out the half-sunken form of the other red dragon. Death must have come to Rhonin and Molok from one of the creature's mad turns during its final fit. She only hoped the end had been swift for both.

"What should we do, Falstad?" called out one of the other dwarves.

He rubbed his chin. "Deathwing is no warrior's friend! He'll no doubt come after us after he deals with this lesser beast! Facing him is no proper battle! Would take a hundred stormhammers just to dent his hide! Best if we return and let others know what we've seen!"

The other dwarves looked to be in agreement with this, but Vereesa found she could not give up so readily despite the obvious. "Falstad! Rhonin is a wizard! He is likely dead, but if he still lives—if he still floats down there—he could still need our help!"

"You're daft, if you'll pardon me for saying so, my elven lady! No one could've survived a fall like that, even a wizard!"

"Please! Just one sweep of the surface—and then we can depart!" Certainly if they found nothing then, her duty to the mage and his never-to-be-fulfilled mission would be at an end. That her sense of guilt would linger much, much longer was something the ranger could do nothing about.

Falstad frowned. His warriors looked at him as if he would have to be mad to spend any more time in the vicinity of Deathwing.

"Very well!" he growled. "But only for you, only for you!" To the others, Falstad commanded, "Go on back already without us! We should be behind you before long, but if for some reason we don't return, make certain that someone knows of the dark one's reappearance! Go!"

As the other dwarves urged their own mounts west, Falstad had his animal dive. However, as they swiftly headed down to the sea, a pair of savage roars made both elf and dwarf look up in concern.

Deathwing and the red bellowed at one another over and over, each cry louder and harsher than the previous. Both beasts had their talons out and their tails whipping about in a frenzy. Deathwing's crimson streaks gave him a frightening and almost supernatural appearance, as if he were one of the demons of legend.

"The posturing's over," Vereesa's companion explained. "They're about to fight! Wonder what the orc must be thinking?"

Vereesa had no concern for the orc. She again focused her concentration toward the search for Rhonin. As the gryphon soared just a few yards over the water, she surveyed the area in vain for the human. Surely there had to be some trace of him! The desperate ranger could even make out the twisted form of the dead mount not too far from them. Whether dead or alive, the wizard had to be somewhere near—unless he had actually managed after all to magick himself away from the danger?

Falstad grunted, clearly having decided that they were wasting their time. "There's nothing here!"

"Just a little longer!"

Again savage cries drew their attention skyward. The battle had begun in earnest. The red dragon tried to cut around Deathwing, but the larger beast presented too great an obstacle. The membraned wings alone acted as walls that the lesser dragon could not get past. He tried flaming one of them, but Deathwing flapped out of the way, not that the fire would have likely done more than slightly singe him.

In the process of trying to scorch his opponent, Deathwing's foe left himself open. The ebony giant could have easily raked the nearest wing of the red beast, but again the left forepaw remained shut and near to the chest. Instead, he whipped his tail at the other leviathan, sending the crimson dragon scurrying away again.

Deathwing did not look injured, so why would he hold back?

"That's it! We search no longer!" Falstad shouted. "Your wizard's at the bottom of the sea, I'm sorry to say! We've got to leave now before we join him!"

The elf ignored him at first, watching the black dragon and trying to make sense of his peculiar fighting technique. Deathwing utilized tail, wings, and other limbs, everything but the left forepaw. Now and then he moved it enough to reveal its obvious health, but always it returned to the nearness of his body.

"Why?" she murmured. "Why do that?"

Falstad thought that she spoke with him. "Because we gain nothing here but the possibility of death, and while

Falstad never fears death, he prefers it on his own terms, not those of that armored abomination!"

At that moment, Deathwing, even with one paw incapacitated, caught hold of his adversary. The vast wings hemmed in the smaller red dragon, and the lengthy tail wrapped around the lower limbs. With his remaining three paws, the black leviathan tore a series of bloody gaps across the torso of his foe, including one set near the base of the throat.

"Up, blast you!" Falstad demanded of his flagging gryphon. "You'll have to wait a little longer to rest! Get us out of here first!"

As the furred beast pushed skyward as best it could, Vereesa watched as Deathwing cut yet another deep series of wounds across his counterpart's chest. A tiny rain began underneath the crimson dragon, the monster's life fluids showering the sea beneath.

With tremendous effort, the lesser beast managed to free himself. Tottering, he pushed off from Deathwing, then hesitated, as if distracted by something else.

To Vereesa's surprise, the red dragon suddenly turned and flew, in rather haphazard fashion, in the direction of Khaz Modan.

The battle had not lasted more than a minute, perhaps two, but in that short space of time Deathwing had nearly slaughtered his foe.

Curiously, the gargantuan black did not pursue. Instead, he peered at the paw held close to his chest, as if looking over something within the folded digits.

Something . . . or *someone*?

What had Rhonin told Duncan and her about his astonishing rescue from the crumbling tower? *I don't know what it was, but it took me up as if I was a toy and whisked me away from the devastation.* What other creature could so easily take a full grown man and carry him off as if he were no more than a toy? Only the fact that such an astounding act had been unheard of until this time had kept the ranger from seeing the obvious. A dragon had carried the wizard off to safety!

But . . . Deathwing?

The black dragon suddenly flew toward Khaz Modan, but not quite in the direction his crimson counterpart had fled. As he headed away from them, Vereesa noted that he continued to keep the one palm close, as if doing what he could to protect a precious cargo.

"Falstad! We need to follow him!"

The dwarf glanced at her as if she had just asked him to ride into the very maw of the behemoth. "I'm the bravest of warriors, my elven lady, but your suggestion hints at madness!"

"Deathwing has Rhonin! Rhonin is the reason that the dragon did not use his one forepaw!"

"Then clearly the wizard is as good as dead, for what would the dark one want with him other than as a snack?"

"If that was the case, Deathwing would have eaten him before. No. He clearly has some need of Rhonin."

Falstad grimaced. "You ask much! The gryphon's weary and will need to land soon!"

"Please! Just as far as you can! I cannot leave him like this! I have sworn an oath!"

"No oath would take you this far," the gryphon rider muttered, but he nonetheless steered his mount back toward Khaz Modan. The animal made noises of protest, but obeyed.

Vereesa said nothing more, knowing that Falstad had the right of it. Yet, for reasons unclear to her, she could not even now abandon Rhonin to what seemed an obvious fate.

Rather than try to fathom her own mind, the ranger pondered the dwindling form of Deathwing. He had to have Rhonin. It made too much sense in her mind.

But what would Deathwing—who hated all other creatures, who sought the destruction of orc, elf, dwarf, and human—possibly want with the mage?

She remembered Duncan Senturus's opinion of wizards, one shared not only by the other members of the Knights of the Silver Hand, but most other folk as well. *A damned soul,* Duncan had called him. Someone who would just as readily turn to evil as good. Someone who might—make a *pact* with the most sinister of all creatures?

Had the paladin spoken greater truth than even he had realized? Could Vereesa now be attempting to rescue a man who had, in actuality, sold his soul to Deathwing?

"What does he want of you, Rhonin?" she murmured. "What does he want of you?"

Krasus's bones still ached and pain occasionally shot through his system, but he had at least managed to heal himself sufficiently to return to the troubles at hand. However, he dared not tell the rest of the council what had occurred, even though the information would have been relevant to their own tasks. For now, among the Kirin Tor, the knowledge of Deathwing's human guise had to be his and his alone. The success of Krasus's other plans quite possibly depended on it.

The dragon sought to be king of Alterac! On the surface, an absurd, impossible notion; but what Krasus knew of the black dragon indicated that Deathwing had something more complex, more cunning, in mind. Lord Prestor might be pushing to create peace among the members of the Alliance, but Deathwing desired only blood and chaos . . . and that meant that this peace created by his ascension to that minor throne would only be the first step toward formulating even worse disharmony later on. Yes, peace today would mean *war* tomorrow.

If he could not tell the Kirin Tor, there were others to whom Krasus could speak. He had been rejected by them over and over, but perhaps this time one would listen. Perhaps the wizard's mistake had been asking their agents to come to him. Perhaps they would listen if he brought the terror to their very sanctums.

Yes . . . then they might listen.

Standing in the midst of his dark sanctum, his hood pulled forward to the point where his face completely vanished within, Krasus uttered the words to take him to one of those whose aid he most sought. The ill-lit chamber grew hazy, faded. . . .

And suddenly the mage stood in a cavern of ice and snow.

Krasus gazed around him, overawed by the sight despite previous visits here long, long ago. He knew in whose domain he now stood, and knew that of all those whose aid he sought this one might take the greatest umbrage at such a brazen intrusion. Even Deathwing respected the master of this chilling cavern. Few ever came to this sanctum in the heart of cold, inhospitable Northrend, and fewer still departed from it alive.

Great spires that almost appeared to be made of pure crystal hung from the icy ceiling, some twice, even three times, the height of the wizard. Other, rockier formations jutted up through the thick snow that not only blanketed much of the cavern floor, but the walls as well. From some inner passage light entered the chamber, casting glittering ghosts all about. Rainbows danced with each brush of the spires by a slight wind that somehow had managed to find its way inside from the cold, bleak land above this magical place.

Yet, behind the beauty of this winter spectacle lay other, more macabre sights. Within the enchanting blanket of snow, Krasus made out frozen shapes, even the occasional limb. Many, he knew, belonged to the few great animals who thrived in the region, while a couple, especially one marked by a hand curled in grisly death, revealed the fate of those who had dared to trespass.

More unnerving evidence of the finality of any intruder's fate could even be found in the wondrous ice formations, for in several dangled the frozen corpses of past uninvited visitors. Krasus marked among the most common a number of ice trolls—massive, barbaric creatures of pale skin and more than twice the girth of their southern counterparts. Death had not come kind to them, each bearing expressions of agony.

Farther on, the mage noted two of the ferocious beastmen known as wendigos. They, too, had been frozen in death, but where the trolls had revealed their terror at their horrible deaths, the wendigos wore masks of outrage, as if neither could believe they had come to such straits.

Krasus walked through the icy chamber, peering at others in the macabre collection. He discovered an elf and two orcs that had been added since his last sojourn here, signs that the war had spread even to this lonely abode. One of the orcs looked as if he had been frozen without ever having realized what fate had befallen him.

Beyond the orcs Krasus discovered one corpse that startled even him. Upon first glance, it seemed but a giant serpent, a peculiar enough monster to find in such a frozen hell, but the coiled body suddenly altered at the top, shifting from a cylindrical form to a nearly human torso—albeit a human torso covered with a smattering of scales. Two broad arms reached out as if trying to invite the wizard to join the creature's grisly doom.

A face seemingly elven but with a flatter nose, a slit of a mouth, and teeth as sharp as a dragon greeted the newcomer. Shadowy eyes with no pupils glared in outrage. In the dark and with the bottom half of his form hidden, this being would have passed for either elf or man, but Krasus knew him for what he was—or rather, had been. The name began to form on the wizard's tongue unbidden, as if the sinister, icy victim before him somehow drew it forth.

"Na—" Krasus started.

"You are nothing, nothing, nothing, if not audaciousss," interjected a whispering voice that seemed to trail on the very wind.

The faceless wizard turned to see a bit of the ice on one wall pull away—and transform into something nearly akin to a man. Yet the legs were too thin, bent at too awkward an angle, and the body resembled more that of an insect. The head, too, had only a cursory resemblance to that of a human, for although there were eyes, nose, and mouth, they looked as if some artisan had started on a snow sculpture, then abandoned the idea as fruitless once the first marks for the features had been traced.

A shimmering cloak encircled the bizarre figure, one that had no hood, but a collar that rose into great spikes at the back.

"Malygos . . ." Krasus murmured. "How fare you?"

"I am comfortable, comfortable, comfortable—when my privacy isss left to me."

"I would not be here if I had any other choice."

"There isss always one other choice—you can leave, leave, leave! I would be *alone!*"

The wizard, though, would not be daunted by the cavern's master. "And have you forgotten why you dwell so silently, so alone, in this place, Malygos? Have you forgotten so soon? It is, after all, only a few centuries since—"

The icy creature stalked around the perimeter of the cavern, ever keeping what passed for his eyes locked on the newcomer. "I forget nothing, nothing, nothing!" came the harsh wind. "I forget the days of darkness least of all. . . ."

Krasus rotated slowly so as to keep Malygos in front of him at all times. He knew no reason why the other should attack, but at least one of the others had hinted that perhaps Malygos, being eldest of those who still lived, might be more than a bit mad.

The stick-thin legs worked well on the snow and ice, the claws at the ends digging deep. Krasus was reminded of the poles men in the cold climes used to push themselves along on their skis.

Malygos had not always looked so, nor did he even now have to retain such a shape. Malygos wore what he wore because in some deep recess of his mind he preferred this over even the shape to which he had been born.

"Then you remember what he who calls himself *Deathwing* did to you and yours."

The outlandish face twisted, the claws flexed. Something akin to a hiss escaped Malygos.

"I *remember.* . . ."

The cavern suddenly felt much more cramped. Krasus held his ground, knowing that to give in to Malygos's tortured world might very well condemn him.

"*I remember!*"

The ice spires shivered, creating a sound at first like a tiny bell, then quickly rising to a near ear-piercing cry. Malygos poked his way toward the wizard, scratch of a mouth wide and bitter. Pits deepened beneath the pale imitation of a brow.

Snow and ice spread, grew, filling the chamber more and more. Around Krasus, some of the snow swirled, rose, became a spectral giant of mythic proportions, a dragon of winter, a dragon of ghosts.

"I remember the promise," the macabre figure hissed. "I recall the covenant we made! Never death to another! The world guarded forever!"

The wizard nodded, even though not even Malygos could see within the confines of his hood. "Until the betrayal."

The snow dragon now stretched wings. Less than real, more than a phantasm, it moved in reaction to the emotions of the cavern's lord. Even the mighty jaws opened and closed, as if the spectral puppet spoke instead.

"*Until the betrayal, the betrayal, the betrayal* . . ." A blast of ice burst forth from the snow dragon, ice so harsh and deadly that it tore into the rocky walls. "*Until Deathwing!*"

Krasus kept one hand from Malygos's sight, knowing

that at any moment he might have to use it for swift spell-casting.

Yet, the monstrous creature held himself in check. He shook his head—the snow dragon repeating his gesture—and added, in a more reasonable voice, "But the day of the dragon had already passed, and none of us, none of us, *none of us,* saw anything to fear from him! He was but one aspect of the world, its most base and chaotic reflection! Of all, his day had come and gone with the most permanence!"

Krasus leapt back as the ground before him shuddered. He thought at first that Malygos had tried to catch him un-aware, but instead of an attack, the ground simply rose up and formed yet another dragon, this one of earth and rock.

"For the *future,* he said," Malygos went on. "For when the world would have only humans, elves, and dwarves to watch over its life, he said! Let all the factions, all the flights, all the *great dragons*—the *aspects*—come together and re-create, reshape the foul piece, and we would have the key to forever protecting the world even after the last of us had faded away!" He looked up at the two phan-tasms he had created. "And I, I, I . . . I, Malygos, stood with him and convinced the rest!"

The two dragons swirled around one another, became one another, intertwining over and over. Krasus tore his eyes from them, reminding himself that although the one before him clearly despised Deathwing over all other creatures, it did not mean that Malygos would aid him . . . or even let him leave the chill cavern.

"And so," interjected the faceless wizard. "Each dragon, especially the *aspects,* imbued it with a bit of themselves, bound themselves, in a sense, to it—"

"Forever put themselves at its mercy!"

Krasus nodded. "Forever ensured that it would be the one thing that could have power over them, although they did not know it then." He held up one gloved hand and created an illusion of his own, an illusion of the object of which they spoke. "You remember how deceiving it looked? You remember what a simple-looking object it was?"

And at the summoning of the image, Malygos gasped and cringed. The twin dragons collapsed, snow and rock spilling everywhere but not at all touching either the wizard or his host. The rumble echoed through the empty passages, no doubt even out into the vast, empty wilderness above.

"Take it away, take it away, take it away!" Malygos demanded, nearly whimpered. Clawed hands tried to cover the indistinct eyes. "Show it to me no more!"

But Krasus would not be stopped. "Look at it, my friend! Look at the downfall of the eldest of races! Look at what has become known to all as the *Demon Soul!*"

The simple, shining disk spun over the mage's gloved palm. A golden prize so unassuming that it had passed into and out of the possession of many without any of them ever realizing its potential. Only an illusion appeared here now, yet it still put such fear in the heart of Malygos that it took him more than a minute to force his gaze upon it.

"Forged by the magic that was the essence of every dragon, created to first fight the demons of the Burning Legion, then to trap their own magical forces within!" The hooded spellcaster stepped toward Malygos. "And used by Deathwing to betray all other dragons just when the battle was done! Used by him against his very allies—"

"Cease this! The *Demon Soul* is lost, lost, *lost,* and the dark one is dead, slain by human and elven wizards!"

"Is he?" Stepping over what remained of the two phantasms, Krasus dismissed the image of the artifact and instead brought forth another. A human, a man clad in black. A confident young noble with eyes much older than his appearance indicated.

Lord Prestor.

"This man, this mortal, would be the new king of Alterac, Alterac in the heart of the Lordaeron Alliance, Malygos. Do you not find anything familiar about him? You, especially?"

The icy creature moved closer, peering at the rotating image of the false noble. Malygos inspected Prestor carefully, cautiously . . . and with growing horror.

"This is *no* man!"

"Say it, Malygos. Say who you see."

The inhuman eyes met Krasus's own. "You know *very* well! It *is* Deathwing!" A bestial hiss escaped the grotesque being that had once worn the majestic form of a dragon. *"Deathwing . . ."*

"Deathwing, yes," Krasus returned, his own tone almost emotionless. "Deathwing, who has been twice thought dead. Deathwing, who wielded the *Demon Soul* and forever ended any hope of a return to the Age of the Dragon. Deathwing . . . who now seeks to manipulate the younger races into doing his treacherous bidding."

"He will have them at war with one another. . . ."

"Yes, Malygos. He will have them at war with one another until only a few survive . . . at which point Deathwing will finish those. You know what a world he desires. One in which there is only he and his selected followers. Deathwing's *purified* realm ... with no room even for those dragons not of his ilk."

"*Nooo* ..."

Malygos's form suddenly expanded in all directions, and his skin took on a reptilian cast. The coloring of that skin changed, too, from an icy white to a dark and frosty silver-blue. His limbs thickened and his visage grew longer, more draconic. Malygos did not complete the transformation, though, stopping at a point that left him resembling a horrific parody of dragon and insect, a creature of nightmare. "I allied myself with him, and for this my flight saw ruin. I am all that is left of mine! The *Demon Soul* took my *children*, my *mates*. I lived only with the knowledge that he who had betrayed all had perished, and that the cursed disk had been forever expunged—"

"So did we all, Malygos."

"*But he lives! He lives!*"

The dragon's sudden rage left the cavern quivering. Icy spears lanced the snowy floor, creating further tremors that rocked Krasus.

"Yes, he lives, Malygos, he lives despite your sacrifices. ..."

The macabre leviathan eyed him closely. "I lost much— too much! But you, you who call yourself Krasus, you who once also wore the form of *dragon*, you lost all, too!"

Visions of his beloved queen passed quickly through Krasus's mind. Visions of the days when the red flight of Alexstrasza had been ascendant washed over him. ...

He had been the second of her consorts—but the first in loyalty and love.

The wizard shook his head, clearing away painful memories. The yearning to patrol the skies once more had to be quelled. Until things changed, he had to remain human, remain Krasus—not the red dragon *Korialstrasz*.

"Yes . . . I lost much," Krasus finally replied, his control returned to him. "But I hope to regain something . . . something for all of us."

"How?"

"I would free Alexstrasza."

Malygos roared with mad laughter. He roared long and hard, far longer than even his madness warranted. He roared in mockery of all the wizard hoped to achieve. "*That* would serve you well—provided you could achieve such an impossible goal! But what good does that do me? What do you offer *me*, little one?"

"You know what Aspect she is. You know what she may do for you."

The laughter ceased. Malygos hesitated, clearly not wanting to believe, yet desperate to do so. "She could not—*could* she?"

"I believe it may be possible. I believe enough of a chance exists that it would be worth your efforts. Besides, what other future do you have?"

The draconic features intensified, and the wizard's host swelled incredibly. Now at last a beast five, ten, twenty times the size of Krasus stood before him, nearly all vestiges of the macabre creature Malygos had first been, gone. A dragon stood before Krasus, a dragon not seen since the days before humankind.

And with his return to his original form, so, apparently, returned some of Malygos's misgivings, for he asked the one question that Krasus had both dreaded and waited for. "The orcs. How is it that the orcs can hold her? That I have always wondered, wondered, wondered . . ."

"You know the only way they could keep her as prisoner, my friend."

The dragon reared his gleaming silver head back and hissed. "The *Demon Soul?* Those insignificant creatures have the *Demon Soul?* That is why you flashed that foul image before me?"

"Yes, Malygos, they have the *Demon Soul* and although I do not think that they know fully what they wield, they know enough to keep Alexstrasza at bay . . . but that is not the worst of it."

"And what could be worse?"

Krasus knew that he had nearly pulled the elder leviathan close enough to sanity to agree to help in rescuing the Dragonqueen, but that what he told Malygos next might put to ruination those accomplishments. Nonetheless, for the sake of more than simply his beloved mistress, the dragon who masqueraded as one of the wizards of the Kirin Tor had to tell his one possible ally the truth. "I believe Deathwing now knows what I do . . . and will also not stop until the cursed disk—and Alexstrasza—are both *his.*"

TEN

For the second time in the past few days, Rhonin awoke among the trees. This time, however, the face of Vereesa did not greet him, which proved something of a disappointment. Instead, he awoke to a darkening sky and complete silence. No birds sang in the forest, no animals moved among the foliage.

A sense of foreboding touched the wizard. Slowly, cautiously, he lifted his head, glanced around. Rhonin saw trees and bushes, but nothing much more. No dragon, certainly, especially one so imposing and treacherous as—

"Aaah, you are awake at last. . . ."

Deathwing?

Rhonin looked to his left—a place he had already surveyed earlier—and watched with trepidation as a piece of the growing shadows around him detached, then coalesced into a hooded form reminiscent of someone he knew.

"Krasus?" he muttered, a moment later realizing this could not be his faceless patron. What moved before him wore the shadows with pride, lived as part of them.

No, he had been correct the first time. *Deathwing.* The shape might *seem* human, but, if dragons could possibly wear such forms, this could only be the black beast himself.

A face appeared under the hood, a man of dark, handsome, avian features. A noble face . . . at least on the surface. "You are well?"

"I'm in one piece, thank you."

The thin mouth jutted upward slightly at the edges in what almost would have been a smile. "You know me, then, human?"

"You're . . . you're Deathwing the Destroyer."

The shadows around the figure moved, faded a little. The face that almost passed for human, almost passed for elf, grew slightly more distinct. The edges of the mouth jutted up a bit more. "One among many of my titles, mage, and as accurate and inaccurate as any other." He cocked his head to one side. "I knew I chose well; you do not even seem surprised that I appear to you thus."

"Your voice is the same. I could never forget it."

"More astute than some you are, then, my mortal friend. There are those who would not know me even if I transformed before their very eyes!" The figure chuckled. "If you would like proof, I could do that even now!"

"Thank you—but, no." The last vestiges of day began to fade behind the wizard's ominous rescuer. Rhonin wondered how long he had been unconscious—and where Deathwing had brought him. Most of all, he wondered why he still lived.

"What do you want of me?"

"I want nothing of you, Wizard Rhonin. Rather, I wish to help *you* in your quest."

"My quest?" No one but Krasus and the Kirin Tor inner council knew of his true mission, and Rhonin had already begun to wonder if even all of the latter knew. Master wizards could be secretive, with their own hidden agendas set ahead of all others. Certainly, though, his present companion should have been in the dark about such matters.

"Oh, yes, Rhonin, your quest." Deathwing's smile suddenly stretched to a length not at all human, and the teeth revealed in that smile were sharp, pointed. "To free the great Dragonqueen, the wondrous Alexstrasza!"

Rhonin reacted instinctively, uncertain as to how the leviathan had learned of his true mission but still confident that Deathwing had not been meant to discover it. Deathwing despised all beings, and that included those dragons not of his ilk. No past tale in history had ever spoken of any love between this great beast and the crimson queen.

The spell the wary mage suddenly utilized had served him well during the war. It had crushed the life out of a charging orc with the blood of six knights and a fellow wizard on his meaty hands, and in a lesser form had held one of the orc warlocks at bay while Rhonin had cast his ultimate spell. Against dragons, however, Rhonin had no experience. The scrolls had insisted that it worked especially well at binding the ancient behemoths. . . .

Rings of gold formed around Deathwing—

—and the shadowy figure walked right through them.

"Now, was that *really* necessary?" An arm emerged from the cloak. Deathwing pointed.

A rock next to where Rhonin lay *sizzled* madly . . . then melted before his very eyes. The molten stone dribbled into the ground, seeped into every crack, disappearing without a trace as rapidly as it had melted in the first place. All in only scant seconds.

"This is what I could have done to you, wizard, if such had been my choice. Twice now your life is owed to me; must I make it a third and final time?"

Rhonin wisely shook his head.

"Reason at last." Deathwing approached, becoming more solid as he neared. He pointed again, this time at the mage's other side. "Drink. You will find it most refreshing."

Looking down, Rhonin discovered a wine sack sitting in the grass. Despite the fact that it had not been there a few seconds before, he did not hesitate to pick it up, then sip from the spout. Not only had his incredible thirst demanded it of him by this point, but the dragon might take his refusal as yet another act of defiance. For the moment, Rhonin could do nothing but cooperate . . . and hope.

His ebony-clad companion moved again, briefly growing indistinct, almost insubstantial. That Deathwing, let alone *any* dragon, could take on human form distressed the wizard. Who could say what a creature such as this could do among Rhonin's people? For that matter, how did the wizard know that Deathwing had not *already* spread his darkness through this very method?

And, if so, why would he now reveal such a secret to Rhonin—unless he intended to eventually silence the mage?

"You know so little of us."

Rhonin's eyes widened. Did Deathwing's powers include the ability to read another's thoughts?

The dragon settled near the human's left, seeming to sit upon some chair or massive rock that Rhonin could not see behind the flowing robe. Under a widow's peak of pure night, unblinking sable eyes met and defeated Rhonin's own gaze.

As the wizard looked away, Deathwing repeated his previous statement. "You know so little of us."

"There's—there's not much documentation on dragons. Most of the researchers get eaten."

Weak as the wizard's attempt at humor might have seemed to Rhonin, Deathwing found it quite amusing. He laughed. Laughed hard. Laughed with what, in others, would have been an insane edge.

"I had forgotten how amusing your kind can be, my little friend! How amusing!" The too-wide, too-toothsome smile returned in all its sinister glory. "Yes, there might be some truth to that."

No longer complacent in simply lying down before the menacing form, Rhonin sat straight up. He might have continued on to a standing position, but a simple glance from Deathwing seemed to warn that this might not be wise at such a juncture.

"What do you want of me?" Rhonin asked again. "What am I to you?"

"You are a means to an end, a way of achieving a goal long out of reach—a desperate act by a desperate creature. . . ."

At first Rhonin did not comprehend. Then he saw the frustration in the dragon's expression. "You—are *desperate*?"

Deathwing rose again, spreading his arms almost as if he intended to fly off. "What do you see, human?"

"A figure in shadowy black. The dragon Deathwing in another guise."

"The obvious answer, but do you not see more, my little friend? Do you not see the loyal legions of my kind? Do you see the many black dragons—or, for that matter, the crimson ones, who once filled the sky, long before the coming of humans, of even elves?"

Not exactly certain where Deathwing sought to lead him, Rhonin only shook his head. Of one thing he had already become convinced. Sanity had no stable home in the mind of this creature.

"You see them not," the dragon began, growing slightly more reptilian in skin and form. The eyes narrowed and the teeth grew longer, sharper. Even the hooded figure himself grew larger, and it seemed that wings sought to escape the confines of his robe. Deathwing became more shadow than substance, a magical being caught midway in transformation.

"You see them not," he began again, eyes closing briefly. The wings, the eyes, the teeth—all reverted to what they had seemed a moment before. Deathwing regained both substance and humanity, the latter if only on the surface. ". . . because they no longer *exist*."

He seated himself, then held out a hand, palm up. Above that hand, images suddenly leapt into being. Tiny draconic figures flew about a world of green glory. The dragons themselves fluttered about in every color of the rainbow. A sense of overwhelming joy filled the air, touching even Rhonin.

"The world was ours and we kept it well. The magic was ours and we guarded it well. Life was ours . . . and we reveled in it well."

But something new came into the picture. It took a few seconds for the suspicious mage to identify the tiny figures as elves, but not elves like Vereesa. These elves were beautiful in their own way, too, but it was a cold, haughty beauty, one that, in the end, repelled him.

"But others came, lesser forms, minute life spans. Quick to rashness, they plunged into what we knew was too great a risk." Deathwing's voice grew almost as chill as the beauty of the dark elves. "And, in their folly, they brought the *demons* to us."

Rhonin leaned forward without thinking. Every wizard studied the legends of the demon horde, what some called the *Burning Legion*, but if such monstrous beings had ever existed, he himself had found no proof. Most of those who had claimed dealings with them had generally turned out to be of questionable states of mind.

Yet, as the wizard tried to catch even a glimpse of one of the demons, Deathwing abruptly closed his hand, dismissing the images.

"If not for the dragons, this world would no longer be. Even a thousand orc hordes cannot compare to what we faced, to what we sacrificed ourselves against! In that time, we fought as one! Our blood mingled on the battlefield as we drove the demons from our world. . . ." The dark figure closed his eyes for a moment. ". . . and in the process, we lost control of the very thing we sought to save. The age of our kind passed. The elves, then the dwarves, and finally the humans each laid their claims to the future. Our numbers dwindled and, worse, we fought among ourselves. *Slew* one another."

That much, Rhonin knew. *Everyone* knew of the animosity between the five existing dragon flights, especially between the black and crimson. The origins of that animosity lay lost in antiquity, but perhaps now the wizard could learn the awful truth. "But why fight one another after sacrificing so much together?"

"Misguided ideas, miscommunication . . . so many factors that you would not understand them all even if I had the time to explain them." Deathwing sighed. "And because of those factors, we are reduced to so few." His gaze shifted, became more intense again. The eyes seemed to bore into Rhonin's own. "But that is the past! I would make amends for what had to be done . . . for what *I* had to do, human. I would help you free the Dragonqueen *Alexstrasza.*"

Rhonin bit back his first response. Despite the easy manner, despite the guise, he still sat before the most dire of dragons. Deathwing might pretend friendship, camaraderie, but one wrong word could still condemn Rhonin to a grisly end.

"But—" he tried to choose his words carefully, "—you and she are enemies."

"For the same insipid reasons our kind has so long fought. Mistakes were made, human, but I would rectify them now." The eyes pulled the wizard toward them, *into* them. "Alexstrasza and I should not be foes."

Rhonin had to agree with that. "Of course not."

"Once we were the greatest of allies, of friends, and that can happen again, do you not agree?"

The mage could see nothing but those penetrating orbs. "I do."

"And you are on a quest to rescue her yourself."

A sensation stirred within Rhonin, and he suddenly felt uncomfortable under Deathwing's gaze. "How did you—how did you find out about that?"

"That is of no consequence, is it?" The eyes snared the human's again.

The discomfort faded. Everything faded under the intense stare of the dragon. "No, I suppose not."

"On your own, you would fail. There is no doubt of

that. Why you continued as long as you did, even I cannot fathom! Now, though, now, with my aid, you *can* do the impossible, my friend. You *will* rescue the Dragonqueen!"

With that, Deathwing stretched forth a hand, in which lay a small silver medallion. Rhonin's fingers reached out seemingly of their own accord, taking that medallion and bringing it close. He looked down at it, studying the runes etched around the edge, the black crystal in the middle. Some of the runes he knew the meaning of, others he had never seen in his life, though the mage could sense their power.

"You *will* be able to rescue Alexstrasza, my fine little puppet," the too-wide grin stretched to its fullest. "Because with this, I will be there to guide you the entire *way.* . . ."

How did one lose a dragon?

That question had reared its ugly head time and time again, and neither Vereesa nor her companion had a satisfactory answer. Worse, night had begun to settle over Khaz Modan, and the gryphon, already long exhausted, clearly could not go on much farther.

Deathwing had been in sight nearly the entire trek, if only from a great distance. Even the eyes of Falstad, not so nearly as sharp as the elf's, had been able to make out the massive form flying toward the interior. Only whenever Deathwing had flown through the occasional cloud had he vanished, and that for no more than a breath or two.

Until an hour past.

The gargantuan beast and his burden had entered into the latest cloud, just as they had so many others previous. Falstad had kept the gryphon on target and both Vereesa and the dwarf had watched for the reappearance of the leviathan on the other side. The cloud had been alone, the next nearest some miles to the south. The ranger and her companion could see it almost in its entirety. They could not possibly miss when Deathwing exited.

No dragon had emerged.

They had watched and waited, and when they could wait no longer, Falstad had urged his animal to the cloud, clearly risking all if Deathwing hid within. The dark one, however, had been nowhere to be found. The largest and most sinister of dragons had utterly vanished.

" 'Tis no use, my elven lady," the gryphon rider finally called. "We'll have to land! Neither we nor my poor mount can go any farther!"

She had to agree, although a part of her still wanted to continue the hunt. "All right!" The ranger eyed the landscape below. The coast and forests had long given way to a much rockier, less hospitable region that, she knew, eventually built up into the crags of Grim Batol. There were still wooded areas, but overall the coverage looked very sparse. They would have to hide in the hills in order to achieve sufficient cover to avoid detection by orcs atop dragons. "What about that area over there?"

Falstad followed her pointing finger. "Those rough-hewn hills that look like my grandmother, beard and all? Aye, 'tis a good choice! We'll descend toward those!"

The fatigued gryphon gratefully obeyed the signal to descend. Falstad guided him toward the greatest congregation of hills, specifically, what looked like a tiny valley between several. Vereesa held on tight as the animal landed, her eyes already searching for any possible threat. This deep into Khaz Modan, the orcs surely had outposts in the vicinity.

"The Aerie be praised!" the dwarf rumbled as they dismounted. "As much as I enjoy the freedom of the sky, that's far too long to sit on anything!" He rubbed the gryphon's leonine mane. "But a good beast you are, and deserving of water and food!"

"I saw a stream nearby," Vereesa offered. "It may have fish in it, too."

"Then he'll find it if he wants it." Falstad removed the bridle and other gear from his mount. "And find it on his own." He patted the gryphon on the rump and the beast leapt into the air, suddenly once more energetic now that his burdens had been taken from him.

"Is that wise?"

"My dear elven lady, fish don't necessarily make a meal for one like him! Best to let him hunt on his own for something proper. He'll come back when he's satiated, and if anyone sees him . . . well, even Khaz Modan has some wild gryphons left." When she did not look reassured, Falstad added, "He'll only be gone for a short time. Just long enough for us to put together a meal for ourselves."

They carried with them a few provisions, which the dwarf immediately divided. With a stream nearby, both took their fill of what remained in the water sacks. A fire was out of the question this deep into orc-held territory, but fortunately the night did not look to be a cool one.

Sure enough, the gryphon did return promptly, belly full. The animal settled down by Falstad, who dropped one hand lightly on the creature's head as he finished eating.

"I saw nothing from the air," he finally said. "but we can't assume that the orcs aren't near."

"Shall we take turns at watch?"

" 'Tis the best thing to do. Shall I go first or you?"

Too wound up to sleep, Vereesa volunteered. Falstad did not argue and, despite their present circumstances, immediately settled down, falling asleep but a few seconds later. Vereesa admired the dwarf's ability to do so, wishing that she could be like him in that one respect.

The night struck her as too silent compared to the forests of her childhood, but the ranger reminded herself that these rocky lands had been despoiled by the orcs for many years now. True, wildlife still lived here—as evidenced by the gryphon's full stomach—but most creatures in Khaz Modan were much more wary than those back in Quel'Thalas. Both the orcs and their dragons thrived heavily on fresh meat.

A few stars dotted the sky, but if not for her race's exceptional night vision, Vereesa would have nearly been blind. She wondered how Rhonin would have fared in this darkness, assuming that he still lived. Did he also wander the wastelands between here and Grim Batol, or had Deathwing brought him far beyond even there, perhaps to some realm entirely unknown to the ranger?

She refused to believe that he had somehow allied himself with the dark one, but, if not, what did Deathwing do with him? For that matter, could it be that she had sent Falstad and herself on a wild dragon-chase, and that Rhonin had not been the precious cargo the armored leviathan had been carrying?

So many questions and no answers. Frustrated, the ranger stepped away from the dwarf and his mount, daring to survey some of the enshrouded hills and trees. Even with her superior eyesight, most resembled little more than black shapes. That only served to make her surroundings feel more oppressive and dangerous, even though there might not be an orc for miles.

Her sword still sheathed, Vereesa ventured farther. She came upon a pair of gnarled trees, still alive but just barely. Touching each in turn, the elf could feel their weariness, their readiness to die. She could also sense some of their history, going far back before the terror of the Horde. Once, Khaz Modan had been a healthy land, one where, Vereesa knew, the hill dwarves and others had made their homes. The dwarves, however, had fled under the relentless onslaught of the orcs, vowing someday to return.

The trees, of course, could not flee.

For the hill dwarves, the day of return would come soon, the elf felt, but by then it would probably be too late for these trees and many like them. Khaz Modan was a land needing many, many decades to recoup—if it ever could.

"Courage," she whispered to the pair. "A new Spring will come, I promise you." In the language of the trees, of all plants, Spring meant not only a season, but also hope in general, a renewal of life.

As the elf stepped back, both trees looked a little straighter, a little taller. The effect of her words on them made Vereesa smile. The greater plants had methods beyond even the ken of elves through which they communicated with one another. Perhaps her encouragement would be passed on. Perhaps some of them would survive after all. She could only hope.

Her brief rapport with the trees lightened the burden on both her mind and heart. The rocky hills no longer felt so foreboding. The elf moved along more readily now, certain that matters would yet turn out for the best, even in regards to Rhonin.

The end of her watch came far more quickly than she had

assumed it would. Vereesa almost thought of letting Falstad sleep longer—his snoring indicated that he had sunken deep—but she also knew that she would only be a liability if her lack of rest later caused her to falter in battle. With some reluctance, the elf headed back to her companion—

—and stopped as the nearly inaudible sound of a dried branch cracking warned that something or someone drew near.

Not daring to wake Falstad for fear of losing the element of surprise, Vereesa walked straight past the slumbering gryphon-rider and his mount, pretending interest in the dark landscape beyond. She heard more slight movement, again from the same direction. Only one intruder, perhaps? Maybe, maybe not. The sound could have been meant to draw her in that very direction, the better to prevent Vereesa from discovering other foes waiting in silence.

Again came the slight sound of movement—followed by a savage squawk and a huge form leaping from nearby her.

Vereesa had her weapon ready even as she realized that it had been Falstad's gryphon who had reacted, not some monstrous creature in the woods. Like her, the animal had heard the faint noise, but, unlike the elf, the gryphon had not needed to weigh options. He had reacted with the honed instincts of his kind.

"What is it?" snarled Falstad, leaping to his feet quite effortlessly for a dwarf. Already he had his stormhammer drawn and ready for combat.

"Something among those old trees! Something your mount went after!"

"Well, he'd better not eat it until we've the chance to see what it is!"

In the dark, Vereesa could just make out the shadowy form of the gryphon, but not yet its adversary. The ranger could, however, hear another cry over those of the winged beast, a cry that did not sound at all like a challenge.

"No! No! Away! Away! Get off of me! No tidbit am I!"

The pair hurried toward the frantic call. Whatever the gryphon had cornered certainly sounded like no threat. The voice reminded the elf of someone, but who, she could not say.

"Back!" Falstad called to his mount. "Back, I say! Obey!"

The leonine avian seemed disinclined at first to listen, as if what he had captured he felt either belonged to him or could not be trusted free. From the darkness just beyond the beaked head came whimpering. *Much* whimpering.

Had some child managed to wander alone out here in the midst of Khaz Modan? Surely not. The orcs had held this territory for years! Where would such a child have come from?

"Please, oh, please, oh, please! Save this insignificant wretch from this monster— *Pfaugh!* What breath it has!"

The elf froze. No child spoke like that.

"Back, blast you!" Falstad swatted his mount on the rump. The animal stretched his wings once, let out a throaty squawk, then finally backed away from his prey.

A short, wiry figure leapt up and immediately began heading in the opposite direction. However, the ranger moved more swiftly, racing forward and snagging the intruder by what Vereesa realized was one lengthy ear.

"Ow! Please don't hurt! Please don't hurt!"

"What've you got there?" the gryphon-rider muttered, joining her. "Never have I heard something that squealed so! Shut it up or I'll have to run it through! It'll bring every orc in hearing running!"

"You heard what he said," the frustrated elf told the squirming form. "Be silent!"

Their undesired companion quieted.

Falstad reached into a pouch. "I've something here that'll help us bring a little light onto matters, my elven lady, although I'm thinking I already know what sort of scavenger we've caught!"

He pulled out a small object, which, after setting his hammer aside, he rubbed between his thick palms. As he did this, the object began to glow rather faintly. A few more seconds' action, and the glow increased, finally revealing the object to be some sort of crystal.

"A gift from a dead comrade," Falstad explained. He brought the glowing crystal toward their captive. "Now let's see if I was correct—aye, I *thought* so!"

So had Vereesa. She and the dwarf had captured themselves one of the most untrustworthy creatures in existence. A goblin.

"Spying, were you?" The ranger's companion rumbled. "Maybe we should run you through now and be done with it!"

"No! No! Please! This disgraceful one is no spy! No orc-friend am I! I just obeyed orders!"

"Then what are you doing out here?"

"Hiding! Hiding! Saw a dragon like the night! Dragons try to eat goblins, you know!" The ugly, greenish creature stated the last as if anyone should understand that.

A dragon like the night? "A black dragon, you mean?" Vereesa held the goblin nearer. "You saw this? When?"

"Not long! Just before dark!"

"In the sky or on the ground?"

"The ground! He—"

Falstad looked at her. "You can't trust the word of a goblin, my elven lady! They don't know the meaning of truth!"

"I will believe him if he can answer one question. Goblin, was this dragon alone, and, if not, who was with him?"

"Don't want to talk about goblin-eating dragons!" he began, but one prod by Vereesa's blade opened a reservoir of words. "Not alone! Not alone! He had another with him! Maybe to eat, but first to talk! Didn't listen! Just wanted to get away! Don't like dragons and don't like wizards—"

"Wizards?" both the elf and Falstad blurted. Vereesa tried to keep her hopes in check. "He looked well, this wizard? Unharmed?"

"Yes—"

"Describe him."

The goblin squirmed, waving his thin little arms and legs. The ranger did not find herself fooled by the spindly looking limbs. Goblins could be deadly fighters, with strength and cunning their puny forms belied.

"Red-maned and full of arrogance! Tall and clad in dark blue! Know no name! Heard no name!"

Not much of a description, but certainly enough. How many tall, red-haired wizards dressed in dark blue robes could there be, especially in the company of Deathwing?

"That sounds like your friend," Falstad replied with a grunt. "Looks like you were right after all."

"We need to go after him."

"In the dark? First, my elven lady, you've not slept at all, and second, even though the dark gives us cover, it also makes it damn hard to see anything else—even a dragon!"

As much as she desired to go on with the hunt right now, Vereesa knew that the dwarf had a point. Still, she could not wait until morning. Precious time would slip away. "I only need a couple of hours, Falstad. Give me that and then we can be on our way."

"It'll still be dark . . . and, in case you've forgotten, big as he is, Deathwing's as black as—as night!"

"We do not have to go searching for him, though." She smiled. "We already at least know where he landed—or rather, one of us here does."

They both looked at the goblin, who clearly desired to be elsewhere.

"How do we know we can trust him? 'Tis no tall tale that these little green thieves are notorious liars!"

The ranger turned the sharp tip of her sword toward the goblin's throat. "Because he will have two options. Either he shows us where Deathwing and Rhonin landed, or I cut him up for dragon bait."

Falstad chuckled. "You think even Deathwing could stomach the likes of him?"

Their short captive quivered and his unsettling yellow eyes, completely lacking in pupils, widened in outright fear. Despite the close proximity of the sword tip, the goblin began hopping up and down in wild fashion. "Will gladly show you! Gladly indeed! No fear of dragons here! Will guide you and lead you to your friend!"

"Keep it down, you!" The ranger tightened her hold on the devilish creature. "Or will I have to cut out your tongue?"

"Sorry, sorry, sorry . . ." murmured their new companion. The goblin quieted down. "Don't hurt this miserable one. . . ."

"*Pfah!* 'Tis a poor excuse of even a goblin we've got here!"

"So long as he shows us the way."

"This wretch will guide you well, mistress! Very well!"

Vereesa considered. "We will have to bind him for now—"

"I'll tie him to my mount. That'll keep the foul rodent under control."

The goblin looked even more ill at this latest suggestion, so much so that the silver-haired ranger actually felt some sympathy for the emerald creature. "All right, but make certain that your animal will not do him any harm."

"So long as he behaves himself." Falstad eyed the prisoner.

"This poor excuse will behave himself, honest and truly. . . ."

Withdrawing the tip of her blade from his throat, Vereesa tried to mollify the goblin a little. Perhaps with a little courtesy, they could get more out of the hapless being. "Lead us to where we want to go, and we will let you loose before there is any danger of the dragon eating you. You have my word on that." She paused. "You have a name, goblin?"

"Yes, mistress, yes!" The oversized head bobbed up and down. "My name is *Kryll*, mistress, *Kryll!*"

"Well, Kryll, do as I ask and all will go well, understand?"

The goblin fairly bounced up and down. "Oh, yes, yes, I do, mistress! I assure you, this miserable one'll lead you exactly where you need to go!" He gave her a madcap grin. "I promise you. . . ."

ELEVEN

Nekros fingered the *Demon Soul*, trying to decide his next move. The orc commander had been unable to sleep most of the night, Torgus's failure to return from his mission eating at the thoughts of the elder warrior. Had he failed? Had both dragons perished? If so, what sort of force did that mean the humans had sent to rescue Alexstrasza? An army of gryphon-riders with wizards in tow? Surely even the Alliance could not afford to send such might, not with the war to the north and their own internal squabbles. . . .

He had tried to contact Zuluhed with his concerns, but the shaman had not responded to his magical missive. The orc knew what that meant; with matters already so dire elsewhere, Zuluhed had no time for what likely seemed to him his subordinate's fanciful fears. The shaman expected Nekros to act as any orc warrior should, with decisiveness and assurance . . . which left the maimed officer back at square one.

The *Demon Soul* gave him great power to command, but Nekros knew that he did not understand even a fraction of its potential. In fact, understanding the depths of his ignorance made the orc uncertain as to whether he dared even *try* to use the artifact for more than he already had. Zuluhed still did not realize what he had passed to his subordinate. From what little Nekros had discovered on his own, the *Demon Soul* contained such relentless power that, wielded with skill, it could likely wipe out the entire Alliance force the orc officer knew to be massing near the northern regions of Khaz Modan.

The trouble was, if wielded carelessly, the disk could also obliterate all of Grim Batol.

"Give me a good ax and two working legs and I'd throw you into the nearest volcano. . . ." he muttered at the golden artifact.

At that moment, a harried-looking warrior barged into his quarters, ignoring his commander's sudden glare. "Torgus returns!"

Good news at last! The commander exhaled in relief. If Torgus had returned, then at least one threat had been eradicated after all. Nekros fairly leapt from his bench. Hopefully Torgus had been able to take at least one prisoner; Zuluhed would expect it. A little torture and the whining human would no doubt tell them everything they needed to know about the upcoming invasion to the north. "At last! How far?"

"A few minutes. No more." The other orc had an anxious expression on his ugly face, but Nekros ignored it for the moment, eager to welcome back the mighty dragonrider. At least Torgus had not let him down.

He put away the *Demon Soul* and hurried as fast he could to the vast cavern the dragon-riders used for landings and takeoffs. The warrior who had brought word followed close behind, curiously silent. Nekros, however, welcomed the silence this time. The only voice he wanted to hear was that of Torgus, relating his great victory over the outsiders.

Several other orcs, including most of the surviving riders, already awaited Torgus at the wide mouth of the cavern. Nekros frowned at the lack of order, but knew that, like him, they eagerly awaited the champion's triumphant arrival.

"Make way! Make way!" Pushing past the rest, he stared out into the faint light of predawn. At first, he could not spot either leviathan; the sentry who had noted their imminent arrival surely had to have the sharpest eyes of any orc. Then . . . then, gradually, Nekros noted a dark form in the distance, one that swelled in size as it neared.

Only one? The peg-legged orc grunted. Another great loss, but one he could live with now that the threat had been vanquished. Nekros could not tell which dragon returned, but, like the others, he expected it to be Torgus's mount. No one could defeat Grim Batol's greatest champion.

And yet . . . and yet . . . as the dragon coalesced into a defined shape, Nekros noticed that it flew in ragged fashion, that its wings looked torn and the tail hung practically limp. Squinting, he saw that a rider did indeed guide the beast, but that rider sat half-slumped in the saddle, as if barely conscious.

An uncomfortable tingle ran up and down the commander's spine.

"Clear away!" He shouted. "Clear away! He'll need lots of room to land!"

In truth, as Nekros stumped away, he realized that Torgus's mount would need nearly all the free room in the vast chamber. The closer the dragon got, the more his erratic flight pattern revealed itself. For one brief moment, Nekros even thought that the leviathan might crash into the side of the mountain, so badly did he maneuver. Only at the last, perhaps urged on by his handler, did the crimson monster manage to enter.

With a crash, the dragon landed amongst them.

Orcs shouted in surprise and consternation as the wounded beast slid forward, unable to halt his momentum. One warrior went flying as a wing clipped him. The tail swung to and fro, battering the walls and bringing down chunks of rock from the ceiling. Nekros planted himself against one wall and gritted his teeth. Dust rose everywhere.

A silence suddenly filled the chamber, a silence during which the maimed officer and those who had managed to get out of the dragon's path began to realize that the gargantuan creature before them had made it back to the roost . . . only to die.

Not so, however, the rider. A figure arose in the dust, a teetering yet still impressive form that unlashed itself from the giant corpse and slid down the side, nearly falling to his knees when he touched the floor. He spat blood and dirt from his mouth, then peered around as best he could, searching . . . searching . . .

For Nekros.

"We're lost!" bellowed the bravest, the strongest of the dragon-riders. "We're lost, Nekros!"

Torgus's arrogance had now been tempered by something else, something that his commander belatedly recognized as resignation. Torgus, who had always sworn to go down fighting, now looked so very defeated.

No! Not him! The older orc hobbled over to his champion as quickly as he could, his expression darkening. "Silence! I'll have none of that talk! You shame the clans! You shame yourself!"

Torgus leaned as best he could against the remains of his mount. "Shame? I've no shame, old one! I've only seen the truth—and the truth is that we've no hope now! Not here!"

Ignoring the fact that the other orc stood taller and outweighed him, Nekros took hold of the rider by the shoulders and shook him. "Speak! What makes you spout such treason?"

"Look at me, Nekros! Look at my mount! You know what did this? You know what we fought?"

"An armada of gryphons? A legion of wizards?"

Bloodstains covered the once magnificent honors still pinned to Torgus's chest. The dragon-rider tried to laugh, but got caught in a coughing fit. Nekros impatiently waited.

"Would—would've been a fairer fight, if I say so! No, we saw only a handful of gryphons—probably bait! Have to be! Too small for any useful force—"

"Never mind that! What did this to you?"

"What did this?" Torgus looked past his commander, eyeing his fellow warriors. "Death itself——death in the form of a black dragon!"

Consternation broke out among the orcs. Nekros himself stiffened at the words. "Deathwing?"

"And fighting for the humans! Came from the clouds just as I tried for one of the gryphons! We barely escaped!"

It could not be . . . and yet . . . it *had* to be. Torgus would not have made up such a bald lie. If he said that Deathwing had done this—and certainly the rips and tears that decorated the giant corpse added much credence to his words—then Deathwing *had* done this.

"Tell me more! Leave out no detail!"

Despite his own condition, the rider did just that, telling how he and the other orc had come upon the seemingly insignificant band. Scouts, perhaps. Torgus had seen several dwarves, an elf, and at least one wizard. Simple pickings, save for the unexpected sacrifice of a human warrior who had somehow single-handedly slain the other dragon.

Even then, Torgus had expected little more trouble. The wizard had proved some annoyance, but had vanished in the midst of combat, likely having fallen to his death. The orc had moved in on the party, ready to finish them.

That had been when Deathwing had attacked. He had made simple work of Torgus's own beast, who had initially refused his handler's instructions and had sought battle. No coward, Torgus had nonetheless immediately known the futility of battling the armored behemoth. Over and over during the struggle he had shouted for his mount to turn away. Only when the red dragon's wounds had proven too much had the beast finally obeyed and fled.

As the story unfolded, Nekros saw all his worst nightmares coming true. The goblin Kryll had been correct in informing him that the Alliance sought to wrest the Dragonqueen from orc control, but the foul little creature had either not known or had not bothered to tell his master about the forces amassed for that quest. Somehow the humans had managed the unthinkable—a pact with the only creature both sides respected and feared.

"Deathwing . . ." he muttered.

Yet, why would they would waste the armored behemoth on such a mission? Surely Torgus had it right when he said that the band he had discovered had to be scouts or bait. Surely a much vaster force followed close behind.

And suddenly it came to Nekros what was unfolding.

He turned to face the other orcs, fighting to keep his voice from cracking. "The invasion's begun, but the north's not it! The humans and their allies're coming for us first!"

His warriors glanced at one another in dismay, clearly realizing that they faced more threat than any in the Horde could have imagined. It was one thing to die valiantly in battle, another to know one faced certain slaughter.

His conclusions made perfect sense to Nekros. Move in unexpectedly from the west, seize the southern portion of Khaz Modan, free or slay the Dragonqueen—leaving the remnants of the Horde in the north, near Dun Algaz, bereft of their chief support—then move up from Grim Batol. Caught between the attackers from the south and those coming from Dun Modr, the last hopes of the orc race would be crushed, the survivors sent to the guarded enclaves set up by the humans.

Zuluhed had left him in charge of all matters concerning the mountain and the captive dragons. The shaman had not seen fit to respond, therefore he assumed he could trust Nekros to do what he must. Very well, then, Nekros would do just *that*.

"Torgus! Get yourself patched up and get some sleep! I'll be needing you later!"

"Nekros—"

"Obey!"

The fury in his eyes made even the champion back down. Torgus nodded and, with the aid of a comrade, moved off. Nekros turned his attention back to the others. "Gather whatever's most important and get it into the wagons! Move all the eggs in crates padded with hay—and keep them warm!" He paused, going down a mental list. "Be prepared to slay any dragon whelps still too wild to train properly!"

This made Torgus pause. He and the other riders eyed their commander with horror. "*Slay* the whelps? We need—"

"We need whatever can be moved quickly—just in case!"

The taller orc eyed him. "In case of what?"

"In case I don't manage to take care of Deathwing. . . ."

Now he had everyone staring at him as if he had sprouted a second head and turned into an ogre.

"Take care of Deathwing?" growled one of the other riders.

Nekros searched for his chief wrangler, the orc who aided him most in dealing with the Dragonqueen. "You! Come with me! We need to figure out how to move the mother!"

Torgus finally thought he knew what was going on. "You're abandoning Grim Batol! You're taking everything north to the lines!"

"Yes . . ."

"They'll just follow! Deathwing'll follow!"

The peg-legged orc snorted. "You've your orders . . . or am I surrounded now by whining peons instead of mighty warriors?"

The barb struck. Torgus and the others straightened. Nekros might be maimed, but he still commanded. They could do nothing but obey, regardless of how mad they thought his plans.

He pushed past the injured champion, pushed past all

in his path, mind already racing. Yes, it would be essential to have the Dragonqueen out in the open, if only at the mouth of this very cavern. That would serve him best.

He would do as the humans had done. Set the bait—although, just in case he failed, the eggs, at least, had to reach Zuluhed. Even if only *they* survived, it would aid the Horde . . . and if Nekros could achieve victory, no matter if it cost him his life, then the orcs still had a chance.

One beefy hand slipped to the pouch where the *Demon Soul* rested. Nekros Skullcrusher had wondered about the limitations of the mysterious talisman—now he would have a chance to find out.

The dim light of dawn stirred Rhonin from what seemed one of the deepest slumbers he had ever experienced. With effort, the wizard pushed himself up and looked around, trying to get his bearings. A wooded area, not the inn of which he had been dreaming. Not the inn where he and Vereesa had been sitting, speaking of—

You are awake . . . good . . .

The words arose within his mind without any warning, nearly sending him into shock. Rhonin leapt to his feet, spinning around in a circle before finally realizing the source.

He clutched at the small medallion dangling around his throat, the one that had been given to him the night before by Deathwing.

A faint glow emanated from the smoky black crystal in the center, and as Rhonin stared at it, he recalled the entire night's events, including the promise the great leviathan had made. *I will be there to guide you the entire way,* the dragon had said.

"Where are you?" the mage finally asked.

Elsewhere, replied Deathwing. *But I am also with you. . . .*

The thought made Rhonin shudder, and he wondered why he had finally agreed to the dragon's offer. Likely because he really had not had any choice.

"What happens now?"

The sun rises. You must be on your way. . . .

Peering around, the wary mage eyed the landscape toward the east. The woods gave way to a rocky, inhospitable area that he knew from maps would eventually guide him to Grim Batol and the mountain where the orcs kept the Dragonqueen. Rhonin estimated that Deathwing had saved him several days' journey by bringing him this far. Grim Batol had to be only two or three days away, providing Rhonin pushed hard.

He started off in the obvious direction—only to have Deathwing immediately interrupt him.

That is not the way you should go.

"Why not? It leads directly to the mountain."

And into the claws of the orcs, human. Are you such a fool?

Rhonin bridled at the insult, but kept silent his retort. Instead, he asked, "Then where?"

See . . .

And in the human's mind flashed the image of his present surroundings. Rhonin barely had time to digest this astonishing vision before it began *moving*. First slowly, then with greater and greater swiftness, the vision moved along a particular path, racing through the woods and into the rocky regions. From there it twisted and turned, the images continuing to speed up at a dizzying rate. Cliffs and gullies darted by, trees passed in a blur. Rhonin had to hold on to the nearest trunk in order not to become too swept up by the sights within his mind.

Hills grew higher, more menacing, at last becoming the first mountains. Even then, the vision did not slow, not until it suddenly fixed on one peak in particular, one which drew the wizard despite his hesitations.

At the base of that peak, Rhonin's view shifted skyward with such abruptness that he nearly lost all sense of equilibrium. The vision climbed the great peak, always showing areas that the wizard realized contained ledges or handholds. Up and up it went, until at last it reached a narrow cave mouth—

—and ended as abruptly as it had begun, leaving a shaken Rhonin once more standing amidst the foliage.

There is the path, the only path that will enable you to achieve our goal. . . .

"But that route will take longer, and go through more precarious regions!" He did not even want to think of climbing that mountainside. What seemed a simple route for a dragon looked most treacherous to a human, even one gifted with the power of magic.

You will be aided. I did not say you would have to walk the entire way. . . .

"But—"

It is time for you to begin, the voice insisted.

Rhonin started walking . . . or rather, Rhonin's *legs* started walking.

The effect lasted only seconds, but it proved sufficient to urge the wizard on. As his limbs returned to his own use, Rhonin pressed forward, unwilling to suffer through a second lesson. Deathwing had shown him quite easily how powerful the link between them was.

The dragon did not speak again, but Rhonin knew that Deathwing lurked somewhere in the recesses of his mind. Yet for all the black leviathan's power, he seemed not to have total control over Rhonin. At the very least, Rhonin's thoughts appeared to be hidden from his draconic ally's inspection. Otherwise, Deathwing would not have been pleased with the wizard at this very moment, for Rhonin already worked to find a way to extricate himself from the dragon's influence.

Curious. Last night he had been more than willing to believe most of what Deathwing had told him, even the part concerning the black's desire to rescue Alexstrasza. Now, however, a sense of reality had set in. Surely of all creatures Deathwing least desired to see his greatest rival free. Had he not sought the destruction of her kind throughout the war?

Yet he recalled also that Deathwing had answered that question, too, very late in their conversation.

"The children of Alexstrasza have been raised by the orcs, human. They have been turned against all other creatures. Her freedom would not change what they have become. They would still serve their masters. I slay them because there is no other choice—you understand?"

And Rhonin *had* understood at the time. Everything the dragon had told him the night before had rung so true—but in the light of day the wizard now questioned the depths of those truths. Deathwing might have meant all he said, yet that did not mean that he did not have other, darker reasons for what he did.

Rhonin contemplated removing the medallion and

simply throwing it away. However, to do so would certainly draw his unwanted ally's attention, and it would be so very simple for Deathwing to locate him. The dragon had already proven just how swift he could be. Rhonin also doubted that, if Deathwing had to come for him again, the armored behemoth would do so as comrade.

For now, all he could do was continue on along the selected path. It occurred to Rhonin that he carried no supplies, not even a water sack, those items now in the sea along with the hapless Molok and their gryphon. Deathwing had not even seen fit to provide him with anything, the food and drink the dragon had given him last night apparently all the sustenance the wizard would receive.

Unperturbed, Rhonin pushed on. Deathwing wanted him to reach the mountain, and with this the mage agreed. Somehow, Rhonin would make it there.

As he climbed along the ever more treacherous terrain, his thoughts could not help but return to Vereesa. The elf had shown a tenacious dedication to her duty, but surely now she had turned back . . . providing that she, too, had survived the attack. The notion that the ranger might not have survived formed a sudden lump in Rhonin's throat and caused him to stumble. No, surely she had survived, and common sense had dictated that she return to Lordaeron and her own kind.

Surely so . . .

Rhonin paused, suddenly filled with the urge to turn around. He had the great suspicion that Vereesa had not followed common sense, but rather had insisted on going on, possibly even convincing the unconvincible Falstad into flying her toward Grim Batol. Even now, assuming nothing else had befallen her, Vereesa might well be on his trail, slowly closing in on him.

The wizard took a step toward the west—

Human . . .

Rhonin bit back a curse as Deathwing's voice filled his head. How had the dragon known so quickly? Could he read the mage's thoughts after all?

Human . . . it is time you refreshed yourself and ate. . . .

"What—what do you mean?"

You paused. You were looking for water and food, were you not?

"Yes." No sense telling the dragon the truth.

You are but a short distance from such. Turn east again and journey a few minutes more. I will guide you.

His opportunity lost, Rhonin obeyed. Stumbling along the jagged path, he gradually came to a small patch of trees in the middle of nowhere. Amazing how even in the worst stretches of Khaz Modan life thrust forth. For the shade alone Rhonin actually gave thanks to his undesired ally.

In the center of the copse will you find what you desire. . . .

Not *all* he desired, although the wizard could not tell Deathwing that. Nonetheless, he moved with some eagerness. More and more, food and water appealed to him. A few minutes' rest would certainly help, too.

The trees were short for their kind, only twelve feet in height, but they offered good shade. Rhonin entered the copse and immediately looked around. Surely there had to be a brook here and possibly some fruit. What other repast could Deathwing offer from a distance?

A *feast,* apparently. There, in the very center of the wooded area, sat a small display of food and drink such as Rhonin could not have imagined finding. Roasted rabbit, fresh bread, cut fruit, and—he touched the flask with some awe—chilled water.

Eat, murmured the voice of the dragon.

Rhonin obeyed with gusto, digging into the meal. The rabbit had been freshly cooked and seasoned to perfection; the bread retained the pleasant scent of the oven. Foregoing manners, he drank directly from the flask . . . and discovered that, although the container should have been half-empty after that, it remained full. Thereafter, Rhonin drank his fill without concern, knowing that Deathwing wanted him well . . . if only until the wizard reached the mountain.

With his magic he could have conjured something of his own, but that would have drawn strength from him that he might need for more drastic times. In addition, Rhonin doubted that even he could have created such a repast, at least not without much effort.

Sooner than he hoped, Deathwing's voice came again. *You are satiated?*

"Yes . . . yes, I am. Thank you."

It is time to move on. You know the way.

Rhonin did know the way. In fact, he could picture the entire route the dragon had shown him. Deathwing had apparently wanted to make certain that his pawn did not wander off in the wrong direction.

With no other choice, the wizard obeyed. He paused only long enough to take one more glance behind him, hoping against hope that he might see the familiar silver hair even in the distance, and yet also wanting neither Vereesa nor even Falstad to follow him. Duncan and Molok had already perished because of his quest; too many deaths weighed now on Rhonin's shoulders.

The day aged. With the sun having descended nearly

to the horizon, Rhonin began questioning Deathwing's path. Not once had he seen, much less confronted an orc sentry, and surely Grim Batol still had those. In fact, he had not even seen a single dragon. Either they no longer patrolled the skies here or the wizard had wandered so far afield that he had gone outside their range.

The sun sank lower. Even a second meal, apparently magicked into being by Deathwing, did not assuage Rhonin. As the last light of day disappeared, he paused and tried to make out the landscape ahead. So far, the only mountains he could see stood much too far away in the distance. It would take him several days just to reach them, much less the peak where the orcs kept the dragons.

Well, Deathwing had brought him to this point; Deathwing could explain now how he thought the human could possibly reach his destination.

Clutching the medallion, Rhonin, his eyes still on the distant mountains, spoke to the empty air. "I need to talk with you."

Speak . . .

He had not entirely expected the method to work. So far, it had always been the dragon who had contacted him, not the other way around. "You said this path would take me to the mountain, but if so, it'll take far longer than I've time. I don't know how you expected me to reach the peak so quickly on foot."

As I said earlier, you were not meant to travel the entire way by so primitive a method. The vision I sent of the path was so that you would ever remain secure in the knowledge that you had not become lost.

"Then how am I supposed to reach it?"

Patience. They should be with you soon.

They?

Remain where you are. That would be the best.

"But—" Rhonin realized that Deathwing no longer spoke with him. The wizard once again contemplated tearing the medallion from his throat and tossing it among the rocks, but where would that leave him? Rhonin still had to get to the orcs' domain.

Who did Deathwing mean?

And then he heard the sound, a sound like no other he had ever encountered. His initial thought was that it might be a dragon, but, if so, a dragon with a terrible case of indigestion. Rhonin gazed into the darkening sky, initially seeing nothing.

A brief flash of light caught his attention, a flash of light from above.

Rhonin swore, thinking that Deathwing had set him up to be captured by the orcs. Surely the light had been some sort of torch or crystal in the hand of a dragonrider. The wizard summoned up a spell; he would not go without a fight, however futile it might prove.

Then the light flashed again, this time longer. Rhonin briefly found himself illuminated, a perfect target for whatever belching monster lurked in the dark heavens.

"Told you he was here!"

"I knew it all the time! I just wanted to see if you really did!"

"Liar! I knew and you didn't! I knew and you didn't!"

A frown formed on the young spellcaster's lips. What sort of dragon argued with itself in such inane, high-pitched tones?

"Watch that lamp!" cursed one of the voices.

The light suddenly flipped away from Rhonin and

darted up. The beam briefly shone on a huge oval form—
a point at the front—before flickering on to the rear,
where the wizard made out a smoking, belching device
that turned a propeller at the end of the oval.

A balloon! Rhonin realized. *A zeppelin!*

He had actually seen one of the remarkable creations
before, during the height of the war. Astonishing, gas-
filled sacks so massive in size that they could actually lift
an open carriage containing two or three riders. In the
war, they had been utilized for observation of enemy
forces on both land and sea, yet what amazed Rhonin
most about them had not been their existence, but that
they had been powered by resources other than magic—
by oil and water. A machine neither built by nor requiring
spells drove the balloon, a remarkable device that turned
the propeller without the aid of manpower.

The light returned to him, this time fixing on Rhonin
with what seemed determination. The riders in the flying
balloon had him in sight now, and clearly had no intention of losing him again. Only then did the fascinated
mage recall exactly which race had proven to have both
the ingenuity and touch of madness necessary to dream
of such a concept.

Goblins—and goblins served the Horde.

He darted toward the largest rocks, hoping to lose
himself long enough to at least come up with a spell ap-
propriate for flying balloons, but then a familiar voice
echoed in his head.

Stay!

"I can't! There're goblins above! I've been spotted by
their airship! They'll summon the orcs!"

You will not move!

Rhonin's feet refused to obey him any longer. Instead, they turned him back to face the unnerving balloon and its even more unnerving pilots. The zeppelin descended to a point just above the hapless wizard's head. A rope ladder dropped over the side of the observation carriage, barely missing Rhonin.

Your transport has arrived, Deathwing informed him.

TWELVE

L ord Prestor's ascension seems almost inevitable," the shadowy form in the emerald sphere informed Krasus. "He has an almost amazing gift of persuasion. You are correct; he *must* be a wizard."

Seated in the midst of his sanctum, Krasus eyed the globe. "Convincing the monarchs will require much evidence. Their mistrust of the Kirin Tor grows with each day . . . and that can only also be the work of this would-be king."

The other speaker, the elder woman from the inner council, nodded back. "We've begun watching. The only trouble is, this Prestor proves very elusive. He seems able to enter and leave his abode without us knowing."

Krasus pretended slight surprise. "How is that possible?"

"We don't know. Worse, his chateau is surrounded by some very nasty spellwork. We almost lost Drenden to one of those surprises."

That Drenden, the baritoned and bearded mage, had nearly fallen victim to one of Deathwing's traps momentarily dismayed Krasus. Despite the man's bluster, the dragon respected the other mage's abilities. Losing Drenden at a time like this could have proven costly.

"We must move with caution," he urged. "I will speak with you again soon."

"What are you planning, Krasus?"

"A search into this young noble's past."

"You think you'll find anything?"

The hooded wizard shrugged. "We can only hope."

He dismissed her image, then leaned back to consider. Krasus regretted that he had to lead his associates astray, if only for their own good. At least their intrusions into Deathwing's "mortal" affairs would have the result of distracting the black. That would give Krasus a bit more time. He only prayed that no one else would risk themselves as Drenden had done. The Kirin Tor would need their strength intact if the other kingdoms turned on them.

His own excursion to visit Malygos had ended with little sense of satisfaction. Malygos had promised only to consider his request. Krasus suspected that the great dragon believed he could deal with Deathwing in his own sweet time. Little did the silver-blue leviathan realize that time no longer remained for any of the dragons. If Deathwing could not be stopped now, he might never be.

Which left Krasus with one much undesired choice now.

"I must do it. . . ." He had to seek out the other great ones, the other Aspects. Convince one of them, and he might still gain Malygos's sworn aid.

Yet, She of the Dreaming ever proved a most elusive figure . . . which meant that Krasus's best bet lay in contacting the Lord of Time—whose servants had already rejected the wizard's requests more than once.

Still, what else could he do but try again?

Krasus rose, hurrying to a bench upon which many of the items of his calling stood arranged in vials and flasks. He scanned row upon row of jars, eyes quickly passing chemicals and magical items that would have left his counterparts in the Kirin Tor greatly envious, and more than a little curious as to how he could have obtained many of the articles in question. If they ever realized just how long he had been practicing the arts . . .

There! A small flask containing a single withered flower caused him to pause.

The Eon Rose. Found only in one place in all the world. Plucked by Krasus himself to give to his mistress, his love. Saved by Krasus when the orcs stormed the lair and, to his disbelief, took her and the others prisoner.

The Eon Rose. Five petals of astonishingly different hues surrounding a golden sphere in the center. As Krasus lifted the top of the flask, a faint scent that suddenly recalled his adolescence wafted under his nose. With some hesitation, he reached in, took hold of the faded bloom—

—and marveled as it suddenly returned to its legendary brilliance the moment his tapering fingers touched it.

Fiery red. Emerald green. Snowy silver. Deep-sea blue. Midnight black. Each petal radiated such beauty as artists only dreamed of. No other object could surpass its inherent beauty, no other flower could match its wondrous scent.

Holding his breath for a moment, Krasus *crushed* the wondrous bloom.

He let the fragments fall into his other hand. A tingle spread from his palms to his fingers, but the dragon mage ignored it. Holding the remnants up high over his head, the wizard muttered words of power—then threw what was left of the fabled rose to the floor.

But as the crushed pieces touched the stone, they turned suddenly to sand, sand that spread across the chamber floor, overwhelmed the chamber itself, *washed* across the chamber, covering everything, eating away everything . . .

. . . and leaving Krasus abruptly standing in the midst of an endless, swirling desert.

Yet, no desert such as this had any mortal—or even Krasus himself, for that matter—ever witnessed, for here lay scattered, as far as the eye could see, fragments of walls, cracked and scoured statues, rusted weapons, and—the mage gaped—even the half-buried bones of some gargantuan beast that, in life, had dwarfed even dragons. There were buildings, too, and although at first one might have thought they and the relics around them all part of one vast civilization, a closer look revealed that no one structure truly belonged with another. A teetering tower such as might have been built by humans in Lordaeron overshadowed a domed building that surely had come from the dwarves. Some distance farther, an arched temple, its roof caved in, hinted of the lost kingdom of Azeroth. Nearer to Krasus himself stood a more dour domicile, the quarters of some orc chieftain.

A ship large enough to carry a dozen men stood propped on a dune, the latter half of it buried under sand. Armor from the reign of the first king of Stromgarde littered another smaller dune. The leaning statue of an elven cleric seemed to say final prayers over both vessel and armor.

An astonishing, improbable display that gave even Krasus pause. In truth, the sights before the wizard resembled nothing more than some gargantuan deity's macabre collection of antiquities . . . a point not far from fact.

None of these artifacts were native to this realm; in fact, no race, no civilization, had ever been spawned here. All the wonders that stood before the wizard had been gathered quite meticulously and over a period of countless centuries from other points all over the world. Krasus could scarcely believe what he saw, for the effort alone staggered even his imagination. To bring such relics, so many of them so massive or so delicate, to this place . . .

Yet, despite all of it, despite the spectacle before his eyes, an impatience began to build up as Krasus waited. And waited. And waited more, with not even the slightest hint that anyone acknowledged his presence.

His patience, already left ragged by the events of the past weeks, finally snapped.

He fixed his gaze on the stony features of a massive statue part man, part bull, whose left arm thrust forth as if demanding that the newcomer leave, and called out, "I know you are here, Nozdormu! I know it! I would speak with you!"

The moment the dragon mage finished, the wind whipped up, tossing sand all about and obscuring his vision. Krasus stayed his ground as a full-fledged sandstorm suddenly buffeted him. The wind howled around him, so loud that he had to cover his ears. The storm seemed determined to lift him up and throw him far away, but the wizard fought it, using magic as well as physical effort to remain. He would not be turned away, not without the opportunity to speak!

At last, even the sandstorm appeared to realize that he would not be deterred. It swept away from him, now focusing on a dune a short distance away. A funnel of dust arose, pushing higher and higher into the sky.

The funnel took on a shape . . . a dragon's shape. As large as, if not larger than Malygos, this sandy creation moved, stretched dusty brown wings. Sand continued to add to the dimension of the behemoth, but sand seemingly mixed with gold, for more and more the leviathan forming before Krasus glittered in the blazing light of the desert sun.

The wind died, yet not one grain of sand or gold broke from the draconic giant. The wings flapped hard, the neck stretched. Eyelids opened, revealing gleaming gemstones the color of the sun.

"*Korialstraszzzz . . .*" the sandy behemoth practically spat. "You dare disturb my ressst? You dare disssturb my *peace?*"

"I dare because I must, o great Lord of Time!"

"Titles will not appeassse my wrath . . . would be best if you went . . ." The gemstones flared. ". . . and went now!"

"No! Not until I speak to you of a danger to all dragons! To all creatures!"

Nozdormu snorted. A cloud of sand bathed Krasus, but his spells kept it from affecting him. One could never tell what magic might dwell within each and every grain in the domain of Nozdormu. One bit of sand might be enough to ensure that the history of a dragon named Korialstrasz turned out never to have happened. Krasus might simply cease to exist, unremembered even by his beloved mistress.

"Dragonsssss, you say? Of what concern isss that to you? I see only one dragon here, and it isss certainly not the mortal wizard Krasusss—not anymore! Away with you! I would return to my collection! You wassste too much of my precious time already!" One wing swept protectively over the statue of the man-bull. "Ssso much to gather, ssso much to catalog . . ."

It suddenly infuriated Krasus that this, one of the greatest of the five Aspects, he through whom Time itself coursed, this dragon cared not a whit what went on in the present or the future. Only his precious collection of the world's past meant anything to the leviathan. He sent out his servants, his people, to gather whatever they could find—all so that their master could surround himself with what had once been and ignore both what was and what might be.

All so that he, in his own way, could ignore the passing of their kind just as Malygos did.

"Nozdormu!" he shouted, demanding the glittering sand dragon's attention again. "Deathwing lives!"

To his horror, Nozdormu took in this terrible news with little change. The gold and brown behemoth snorted once more, sending a second cloud assailing the tinier figure. "Yesss . . . and ssso?"

Taken aback, Krasus managed to blurt, "You—know?"

"A question not at all worth anssswering. Now, if you've nothing more with which to further bother me, it isss time for you to depart." The dragon reared his head, bejeweled eyes flaring.

"Wait!" Forgoing any sense of dignity, the wizard waved his arms back and forth. To his relief, Nozdormu paused, negating the spell he had been about to use to rid himself of this bothersome mite. "If you know that the dark one lives, you know what he intends! How can you ignore that?"

"Becaussse, asss with all things, even Deathwing will pass into time . . . even he will eventually be part . . . of my collection. . . ."

"But if you joined—"

"You've had your sssay." The glittering sand dragon rose higher and as he did, the desert flew up, adding further to his girth and form. Torn free by the winds, some of the smaller objects in Nozdormu's bizarre collection joined with that sand, becoming, for the moment, a very part of the dragon. "Now leave me be. . . ."

The winds now whipped up around Krasus—and *only* Krasus. Try as he might, this time the dragon wizard could not hold his ground. He stumbled back, shoved hard time and time again by the ferocious gusts.

"I came here for the sake of *all* of us!" Krasus managed to shout.

"You should not have disssturbed my ressst. You should not have come at all. . . ." The glittering gemstones flared. "In fact, that would have been bessst of all. . . ."

A column of sand shot up from the ground, engulfing the helpless wizard. Krasus could see nothing else. It grew stifling, impossible to breathe. He tried to cast a spell in order to save himself, but against the might of one of the Aspects, against the Master of Time, even his substantial powers proved minuscule.

Bereft of air, Krasus finally succumbed. Consciousness fading, he slumped forward—

—and watched, in startlement, as the petals of the Eon Rose dropped to the stone floor of his sanctum without any effect.

The spell should have worked. He should have been transported to the realm of Nozdormu, Lord of the Centuries. Just as Malygos embodied magic itself, so, too, did Nozdormu represent time and timelessness. One of the most powerful of the five Aspects, he would have proven a powerful ally, especially should Malygos suddenly choose to retreat into his madness. Without Nozdormu, Krasus's hopes of success dwindled much.

Kneeling, the mage picked up the petals and repeated the spell. For his troubles, Krasus was rewarded only with a horrendous headache. How could that be, though? He had done everything right! The spell should have worked—unless somehow Nozdormu had caught wind of the wizard's intention to plead with him and had cast a spell preventing Krasus from entering the sandy realm.

He swore. Without a chance to visit Nozdormu, he had no hope, however slight it might have been in the first place, of convincing the powerful dragon to join his plan. That left only She of the Dreaming . . . the most elusive of the Aspects, and the only one he had never, ever, spoken with in all his lengthy life. Krasus did not even know how to contact her, for it had oft been said that Ysera lived not wholly in the real world—that, to her, the dreams were the reality.

The dreams were the reality? A desperate plan occurred to the wizard, one that, had it been suggested to him by any of his counterparts, would have made Krasus break from his accustomed form and laugh loud. How utterly ridiculous! How utterly hopeless!

But, as with Nozdormu, what other choice did he have?

Turning back to his array of potions, artifacts, and powders, Krasus searched for a black vial. He found it quickly, despite not having touched it in more than a century. The last time he had made use of it—it had been to slay what had seemed unslayable. Now, however, he sought to only borrow one of its most vicious traits, and hope that he did not measure wrong.

Three drops on the tip of a single bolt had killed the

Manta, the Behemoth of the Deep. Three drops had slain a creature ten times the size and strength of a dragon. Like Deathwing, nearly all had believed the Manta unstoppable.

Now Krasus intended to take some of the poison for himself.

"The deepest sleep, the deepest dreams . . ." he muttered to himself as he took the vial down. "That is where she must be, where she *has* to be."

From another shelf he removed a cup and a small flask of pure water. Measuring out a single swallow in the cup, the dragon mage then opened the vial. With the greatest caution, he brought the open bottle to the cup of water.

Three drops to slay, in seconds, the Manta. How many drops to assist Krasus on the most treacherous of journeys?

Sleep and death . . . they were so very close in nature, more so than most realized. Surely he would find Ysera there.

The tiniest drop he could measure fell silently into the water. Krasus replaced the top on the vial, then took up the cup.

"A bench," he murmured. "Best to use a bench."

One immediately formed behind him, a well-cushioned bench upon which the king of Lordaeron would have happily slept. Krasus, too, intended to sleep well on it . . . perhaps forever.

He sat upon it, then raised the cup to his lips. Yet, before he could bring himself to drink what might be his last, the dragon in human guise made one last toast.

"To you, my Alexstrasza, *always* to you."

* * *

"There was someone here, all right," Vereesa muttered, studying the ground. "One of them was human . . . the other I can't be certain about."

"Pray tell, how do you know the difference?" asked Falstad, squinting. He could not tell one sign from another. In fact, he could not even *see* half of what the elf saw.

"Look here. This boot print." She indicated a curved mark in the dirt. "These are human-style boots, tight-fitting and uncomfortable."

"I'll take your word. And the other—the one you can't identify?"

The ranger straightened. "Well, clearly there are no signs of a dragon being around, but there are tracks over here that match nothing I know."

She knew that, once again, Falstad could not see what to her sharp eyes screamed out their curious presence. The dwarf did his best, though, studying the peculiar striations in the earth. "You mean these, my elven lady?"

The marks appeared to flow toward where the human—surely *Rhonin*—had at one time or another stood. Yet, they were not footprints, not even pawprints. To her eyes, it looked as if something had floated, dragging something else behind it.

"This gets us no closer than the first spot this little green beast brought us to!" Falstad seized Kryll by the scruff of his neck. The goblin had both hands tied behind him and a rope around his waist, the other end of which had been tied around the neck of the gryphon. Despite that, neither Vereesa nor the wild dwarf trusted that their unwilling companion might not somehow escape. Falstad especially kept his eye on Kryll. "Well? Now what? 'Tis becoming clear to me that you're leading us around! I doubt you've even seen the wizard!"

"I have, I have, yes, I have!" Kryll smiled wide, possibly in the hope of swaying his captors, but a goblin's toothy grin did little to impress those outside of their race. "Described him, didn't I? You know I saw him, don't you?"

Vereesa noticed the gryphon sniffing at something hidden behind a bit of foliage. Using her sword, she prodded at the spot, then dragged out the object in question.

On the tip of her sword hung a small, empty wine sack. The elf brought it to her nose. A heavenly bouquet wafted past. The elf briefly closed her eyes.

Falstad misread her expression. "As bad as all that? Must be dwarven ale!"

"On the contrary, I have not come across such a fabulous aroma even at the table of my lord back in Quel'Thalas! Whatever wine filled this sack far outshone even the best of his stock."

"Which means to my feeble mind—?"

Dropping the sack, Vereesa shook her head. "I do not know, but somehow I cannot help thinking that it means that Rhonin *was* here, if only for a time."

Her companion gave her a skeptical look. "My elven lady, is it possible that you simply wish it to be true?"

"Can you answer me who else might have been in this region, drinking wine fit for kings?"

"Aye! The dark one, after he'd sucked the marrow from the bones of your wizard!"

His words made her shiver, but she remained steadfast in her belief. "No. If Deathwing brought him this far, he had some other reason than as a repast!"

"Possible, I suppose." Still holding onto the goblin,

Falstad glanced up at the darkening sky. "If we hope to get much farther before night, we'd best be getting on our way."

Vereesa touched the tip of her blade against Kryll's throat. "We need to deal with this one first."

"What's to deal with? Either we take him with us, or do the world a favor and leave it with one less goblin to worry about!"

"No. I promised I would release him."

The dwarf's heavy brow furrowed. "I don't think that's wise."

"Nevertheless, I made that promise." She stared hard at him, knowing that if he understood elves as much as he should, Falstad would see the sense in not pursuing this argument.

Sure enough, the gryphon-rider nodded—albeit with much reluctance. "Aye, 'tis as you say. You made a promise and I'll not be the one to try to sway you." Not quite under his breath, he added, "Not with only one life-time to me . . ."

Satisfied, Vereesa expertly cut the bonds around Kryll's wrists, then removed the loop from his waist. The goblin fairly bounced around, so overjoyed did he seem by his release.

"Thank you, my benevolent mistress, thank you!"

The ranger turned the tip of the sword back toward the creature's throat. "Before you go, though, a few last questions. Do you know the path to Grim Batol?"

Falstad did not take this question well. Brow arched, he muttered, "What're you thinking?"

She purposely ignored his question. "Well?"

Kryll's eyes had gone wide the moment she asked. The

goblin looked ashen—or at least a paler shade of green. "No one goes to Grim Batol, benevolent mistress! Orcs there and dragons, too! Dragons eat goblins!"

"Answer my question."

He swallowed, then finally bobbed his oversized head up and down. "Yes, mistress, I know the way—do you think the wizard is there?"

"You can't be serious, Vereesa," Falstad rumbled, so upset he had for once called her by name. "If your Rhonin is in Grim Batol, then he's lost to us!"

"Perhaps . . . perhaps not. Falstad, I think he always *wanted* to reach that place, and not simply to observe the orcs. I think he has some other reason . . . although what it could have to do with Deathwing, I cannot say."

"Maybe he plans on releasing the Dragonqueen single-handedly!" the gryphon-rider returned with a snort of derision. "He's a mage, after all, and everyone knows that they're all *mad*!"

An absolutely absurd notion—but for a moment it gave Vereesa pause. "No . . . it could not be that."

Kryll, meanwhile, seemed to be trying to think really hard about something, something that did not at all look to please him. At last, his face screwed up in an expression of distaste, he muttered, "Mistress wants to go to Grim Batol?"

The ranger considered it. It went even beyond her oath, but she had to push forward. "Yes. Yes, I do."

"Now see here, my—"

"You do not have to come with me if you do not want to, Falstad. I thank you for your aid thus far, but I can proceed from here alone."

The dwarf shook his head vehemently. "And leave you alone in the middle of orc territory with only this untrustworthy little wretch? Nay, my elven lady! Falstad will not leave a fair damsel, however capable a warrior she might also be, on her own! We go together!"

In truth, she appreciated his company here. "You may turn back at any time, though; remember that."

"Only if you're with me."

She glanced again at Kryll. "Well? Can you tell me the way?"

"Cannot tell you, mistress." More and more the spindly creature's expression soured. "Best . . . best if I show you, instead."

This surprised her. "I granted you your freedom, Kryll—"

"For which this poor wretch is so eternally grateful, mistress . . . but only one path to Grim Batol offers certainty, and without me," he dared look slightly egotistical, "neither elf nor dwarf will find it."

"We've got my mount, you little rodent! We'll simply fly over—"

"In a land of dragons?" The goblin chuckled, a hint of madness there. "Best to fly right into their mouths and be done with it, then. . . . No, to enter Grim Batol—if that is truly what mistress desires—you'll have to follow me."

Falstad would not hear of that and immediately protested, but Vereesa saw no choice but to do as the goblin suggested. Kryll had led them true so far, and although she did not, of course, trust him entirely, she felt certain that she would recognize if he tried to lead them astray. Besides, clearly the goblin wanted nothing to do with Grim Batol himself, or else why would he have been where they had found him? Any of his kind who served the orcs would have been in the mountain fortress, not wandering the dangerous wilds of Khaz Modan.

And if he could lead her yet to Rhonin . . .

Having convinced herself that she chose correctly, Vereesa faced the dwarf. "I will go with him, Falstad. It is the best—the only choice—I have."

His broad shoulders slumping, Falstad sighed. " 'Tis against my better judgment, but, aye, I'll go with you—if only to keep an eye on this one, so I can lop off his traitorous head if I prove right!"

"Kryll, must we go on foot the entire way?"

The misshapen little creature mused for a moment, then replied, "No. Can travel some distance with gryphon." He gave her a smile full of teeth. "Know just where beast should land!"

Despite his apparent misgivings, Falstad started for the gryphon. "Just tell us where to go, you little rodent. The sooner we're there, the sooner you can be on your way. . . ."

The goblin's weight added little to the powerful animal's burden, and soon the gryphon was on its way. Falstad, of course, sat in front, the better to control his mount. Kryll sat behind him with Vereesa taking up the rear. The elf had resheathed her sword and now held a dagger ready just in case their undesired companion attempted something.

Yet, although the goblin's directions were not always the clearest, Vereesa saw nothing that hinted of duplicity. He kept them near to the ground and always guided them along paths that steered them from the open areas. In the distance, the mountains of Grim Batol grew nearer. A sense of anxiety spread through the ranger as she realized that she approached her goal, but that anxiousness was tempered by the fact that, even now, she had come across no sign of either Rhonin or the black dragon. Surely this close to the mountain fortress the orcs would have been able to sight such a leviathan.

And as if thinking of dragons allowed one to conjure them up, Falstad suddenly pointed east, where a massive form rose into the sky.

"Big!" he called. "Big and red as fresh blood! Scout from Grim Batol!"

Kryll immediately acted. "Down there!" the goblin pointed at a ravine. "Many places to hide—even for a gryphon!"

With little other choice, the dwarf obeyed, guiding his mount earthward. The dragon's form grew larger and larger, but Vereesa noted that the crimson beast also headed in a more northerly direction, possibly to the very northern border of Khaz Modan, where the last desperate forces of the Horde sought to hold back the Alliance. That made her wonder about the situation there. Had the humans begun their advance at last? Could the Alliance itself even now be halfway to Grim Batol?

If so, it would still be too late for her purposes. Yet, the nearing presence of the Alliance might aid in one way, if it made the orcs here concentrate on matters other than their own immediate defenses.

The gryphon alighted in the ravine, the animal instinctively seeking the shadows. No coward, the gryphon had the sense to know when to choose a battle.

Vereesa and the others leapt off, finding their own places to hide. Kryll pressed himself against one rocky wall, his expression that of open terror. The ranger actually found herself feeling some sympathy for him.

They waited for several minutes, but the dragon did not

fly by. After what seemed far too long a time, the impatient ranger decided to see for herself if the beast had changed direction. Getting a proper grip on the rock, she climbed up.

The elf saw nothing in the darkening sky, not even a speck. In fact, Vereesa suspected that they could have departed this ravine long before, if only one of them had dared look.

"No sign?" whispered Falstad, climbing up beside her. For a dwarf, he proved himself quite nimble crawling up the side.

"We are clear. Very much so."

"Good! Unlike my hill cousins, I've no taste for holes in the ground!" He started down. "All right, Kryll! The danger's done! You can peel yourself—"

The moment his voice cut off, Vereesa jerked her head around. "What is it?"

"That damned spawn of a frog's gone!" He scrambled down the rest of the way. "Vanished like a will-o'-the-wisp!"

Dropping down as safely as she could, the ranger joined Falstad in scanning the immediate area. Sure enough, despite the fact that they should have been able to see the goblin's retreating figure in either direction, not one sign of Kryll existed. Even the gryphon acted baffled, as if it, too, had not even noticed that the spindly creature had run off.

"How could he have just disappeared?"

"Wish I knew that myself, my dear elven lady! A neat trick!"

"Can your gryphon hunt him down?"

"Why not just let him go? We're better off without him!"

"Because I—"

The ground underneath her feet suddenly softened, broke apart. The elf's boots sank deep within seconds.

Thinking that she had walked into mud, she tried to pull free. Instead, Vereesa only sank deeper, and at an alarming rate. It almost felt as if she were being *pulled* down.

"What in the name of the Aerie—?" Falstad, too, had sunk deep, but in the dwarf's case that meant he suddenly stood up to his knees in dirt. Like the ranger, he attempted to extricate himself, only to completely fail.

Vereesa grabbed for the nearest rock face, trying to seize hold. For a moment, she succeeded, managing to slow her progress downward. Then, something powerful seemed to take hold of her ankles, pulling with such force that the ranger could no longer keep her grip.

Above them she heard a panicked squawk. Unlike Vereesa and the dwarf, the gryphon had managed to pull up in time to avoid being dragged under. The animal fluttered above Falstad's head, trying, it seemed, to get a grip on its master. However, as the beast dropped lower, columns of dirt suddenly shot up, trying, Vereesa realized in horror, to seize the mount. The gryphon narrowly escaped, forced now to fly up so high that the animal could not possibly aid either warrior.

Which left Vereesa with no notion as to how to escape.

Already the earth came up to her waist. The thought of being buried alive set even the elf on edge, yet, in comparison to Falstad's predicament, hers seemed slightly less immediate. The dwarf's shorter stature meant that he already had trouble keeping his head above ground. Try as he might, even the mighty strength of the gryphon-rider could not help him. He grabbed furiously at the soft earth, ripping up handfuls that did him no good whatsoever.

In desperation, the ranger reached out. "Falstad! My hand! Reach for it!"

He tried. They both tried. The gap between them had grown too great, however. In growing horror, Vereesa watched as her struggling companion was inevitably pulled under.

"My—" was all he managed before disappearing from sight.

Now buried up to her chest, she froze for a moment, staring at the slight mound of dirt that was all that remained to mark his passage. The ground there did not even stir. No last thrust of a hand, no wild movement underneath.

"Falstad . . ." she murmured.

Renewed force at her ankles tugged her deeper. As the dwarf had done, Vereesa snatched at the earth around her, digging deep valleys with her fingers but doing herself no good. Her shoulders sank in. She lifted her head skyward. Of the gryphon she saw no sign, but another figure, so very familiar, now leaned out from a small crevice that the elf had missed earlier.

Even in the waning light, she could see Kryll's toothy smile.

"Forgive me, my mistress, but the dark one insists that no one interfere, and so he left me the task of seeing to your deaths! A menial bit of work and one undeserving of a clever mind such as mine, but my master does, after all, have very large teeth and so sharp claws! I certainly couldn't refuse him, could I?" His grin stretched wider. "I hope you understand. . . ."

"Damn you—"

The ground swallowed her up. Dirt filled the elf's mouth, then, seemingly, her hungry lungs.

She blacked out.

THIRTEEN

The goblin airship floated among the clouds, now surprisingly silent as it neared its destination.

At the bow of the vessel, Rhonin kept a watchful eye on the two figures guiding him toward his destiny. The goblins darted back and forth, adjusting gauges and muttering among themselves. How such a mad race could have created this wonder had been beyond him. Each moment, the airship seemed destined to destroy itself, yet the goblins ever managed to right matters.

Deathwing had not spoken to Rhonin since telling him to board. Knowing that the dragon would have made him do so whether he desired to or not, the wizard had reluctantly obeyed, climbing up into the airship and trying not to think what would happen if it all came tumbling down.

The goblins were Voyd and Nullyn, and they had built this vessel themselves. They were great inventors, so *they* said, and had offered their services to the wondrous Deathwing. Of course, they had said the last with just a hint of sarcasm in their tones. Sarcasm and fear.

"Where are you taking me?" he had asked.

This question had caused his two pilots to eye him as if

he had lost all sense. "To Grim Batol, of course!" spouted one, who seemed to have twice the teeth of any goblin Rhonin had ever had the misfortune to come across. "To Grim Batol!"

The wizard had known that, of course, but he had wanted the exact location where they intended to drop him. Rhonin did not at all trust the pair not to leave him in the middle of an orc encampment. Unfortunately, before Rhonin could ask, Voyd and his partner had been forced to respond to an emergency, in this case a spout of steam erupting from the main tank. The goblins' airship utilized both oil and water in order to run, and if some component involving one was not breaking down at a critical moment, then something involving the other *was*.

It had made for a fairly sleepless night, even for one such as Rhonin.

The clouds through which they flew had grown so thick that it felt as if the mage journeyed through a dense fog. Had he not known at what altitude he sailed, Rhonin might have imagined that this vessel traversed not the sky, but rather the open sea. In truth, both journeys had much in common, including the danger of crashing on the rocks. More than once, Rhonin had watched as mountains had suddenly materialized on either side of the tiny ship, a few coming perilously close. Yet, while he had prepared for the worst, the goblins had kept on with their tinkering—and even occasionally napping—without so much as a glimpse at the near-disasters around them.

Daylight had long come, but the deeply overcast weather kept it nearly as dark as late dusk. Voyd seemed to be using some sort of magnetic compass to guide them along, but the one time Rhonin had studied it, he had noticed that it had a tendency to shift without warning. In the end, the wizard had concluded that the goblins flew by sheer luck more than any sense of direction.

Early on, he had estimated the length of the trip, but for some reason, even though Rhonin felt that they should have reached the fortress by now, his two companions kept assuring him that they still had quite some time left before arrival. Gradually he came to the suspicion that the airship flew about in circles, either due to the faulty compass or some intention on the goblins' parts.

Although he sought to remain focused on his quest, Rhonin found Vereesa slipping into his thoughts more and more. If she lived, she followed him. He knew her well enough. The knowledge dismayed him as much as it pleased. How could the elf possibly learn about the airship? She might end up wandering Khaz Modan or, even worse, assume rightly and head straight to Grim Batol.

His hand tightened on the rail. "No . . ." he muttered to himself. "No . . . she wouldn't do that . . . she *can't* . . ."

Duncan's ghost already haunted him, just as those of the men from his previous mission did. Even Molok stood with the dead, the wild dwarf glowering in condemnation. Rhonin could already imagine Vereesa and even Falstad joining their ranks, empty eyes demanding to know why the wizard lived after their sacrifices.

It was a question that Rhonin often asked of himself.

"Human?"

He looked up to see Nullyn, the more squat of the pair, standing just beyond arm's length from him. "What?"

"Time to prepare to disembark." The goblin gave him a wide, cheerful smile.

"We're here?" Rhonin dredged himself up from his

dark thoughts and peered into the mist. He saw nothing but more mist, even below. "I don't see anything."

Beyond Nullyn, Voyd, also grinning merrily, took the rope ladder and tossed the unattached end over the side. The slapping of the rope against the hull represented the only sound the wizard heard. Clearly the ladder had not touched bottom anywhere.

"This is it. This is the place, honest and truly, master wizard!" Voyd pointed toward the rail. "Look for yourself!"

Rhonin did . . . with care. It would not have struck him as unlikely that the goblins might use their combined strength to toss him over the side despite Deathwing's desires. "I see nothing."

Nullyn looked apologetic. "It is the clouds, master wizard! They obscure things to your human eyes! We goblins have much sharper vision. Below us is a very soft, very safe ledge! Climb down the ladder and we'll gently drop you off, you'll see!"

The mage hesitated. He wanted nothing more than to be rid of the zeppelin and its crew, but to simply take the goblins' word about whether any land actually lay close below—

Without warning, Rhonin's left hand suddenly reached out, catching Nullyn by surprise. The mage's fingers closed around the goblin's throat, squeezing hard despite Rhonin's attempt to pull back.

A voice not his own, but exceedingly familiar to the human, hissed, *"I gave the command that no tricksss were to be played, no acts of treachery performed, worm."*

"M-mercy, grand and g-glorious m-master!" choked Nullyn. "Only a game! Only a g—" He managed no more, Rhonin's grip having tightened more.

Forcing his gaze down as much as he could, the helpless wizard saw the black stone in the medallion giving off a faint glow. Once more Deathwing had used it to seize control of his human "ally."

"Game?" murmured Rhonin's lips. *"You like games? I have a game for you to play, worm. . . ."*

With little effort, the human's arm shifted, dragging a struggling Nullyn toward the rail.

Voyd let out a squeak and scurried back toward the engine. Rhonin struggled against Deathwing's control, certain that the black leviathan intended to drop Nullyn to his doom. While the wizard had no love for the goblin, neither did he want the creature's blood on his hands—even if the dragon presently made use of them.

"Deathwing!" he snapped, belatedly surprised that his lips were his own for the moment. "Deathwing! Don't do this!"

Would you rather they had led you into their little ploy, human? came the voice in his head. *The drop would not have been at all pleasant for one who cannot fly. . . .*

"I'm not that much of a fool! I'd no intention of climbing over the rail, not on a goblin's word! You wouldn't have bothered saving me in the first place if you thought me that addled!"

True . . .

"And I'm not without power of my own." Rhonin raised his other hand, which Deathwing had not deemed necessary to use. Muttering a few words, the wizard produced a flame above his index finger, a flame which he then directed toward the already panicked face of Nullyn. "There are other ways to teach a goblin lessons in trust."

Barely able to breathe and unable to flee, Nullyn's eyes

widened and the spindly creature tried to shake his head. "B-be good! Only meant to t-tease! Never meant h-harm!"

"But you'll drop me off on a proper place, right? One of which both Deathwing and I would approve?"

Nullyn could only manage a squeak.

"This flame I can make larger." The magical fire sprouted to twice its previous length. "Enough to burn a hull even from below, maybe set off flammable oil . . ."

"N-no tricks! N-no tricks! Promise!"

"You see?" the crimson-tressed mage asked his unseen companion. "No need to drop him over the side. Besides, you might want to make use of him again."

In reply, Rhonin's possessed hand abruptly released its hold on Nullyn, who dropped to the deck with a thud. The goblin lay there for several seconds, trying desperately to gain his breath back.

Your choice . . . wizard.

The human exhaled, then, glancing at Voyd—who still cowered by the engine—called out, "Well? Get us to the mountain!"

Voyd immediately obeyed, frantically turning levers and checking gauges. Nullyn finally recovered enough to join his partner, the beaten goblin not once glancing back.

Extinguishing the magical flame, Rhonin peered over the rail again. Now at last he could make out some sort of formation, hopefully the crags of Grim Batol. He assumed from Deathwing's earlier words and images that the dragon still wanted him set down directly on the peak, preferably somewhere near a gap leading inside. Surely the goblins knew this. Any other choice they made at this point would mean that they had still not learned the folly of crossing either their distant master or the wizard. Rhonin prayed that it would not be so. He doubted that Deathwing would allow the goblins to escape punishment twice.

They began to draw near to one peak in particular, one that Rhonin had vague memories of, even though he had never been to Grim Batol before. With growing eagerness he leaned forward for a better look. Surely this had to be the mountain from the vision that Deathwing had forced upon him. He searched for telltale signs—a recognizable outcropping or a familiar crevice.

There! The very same narrow cave mouth from his dizzying journey of the mind. Barely large enough for a man to stand in, provided he managed the terrifying climb up several hundred feet of sheer rock. Yet, still it would serve. Rhonin could scarcely wait, more than happy to be rid of the mischievous goblins and their outrageous flying machine.

The rope ladder still dangled free, ready for his use. The wary mage waited while Voyd and his partner maneuvered their ship nearer and nearer. Whatever his previous thoughts about the zeppelin, Rhonin had to admit that now the goblins controlled it with a measure of accuracy he found admirable.

The ladder clattered slightly against the rock wall just to the left of the cave.

"Can you keep it steady here?" he called to Nullyn.

A nod was all he received from the still fearful pilot, but it satisfied Rhonin. No more tricks. Even if they did not fear him, they certainly feared the long reach of Deathwing.

Taking a deep breath, Rhonin crawled over the side. The ladder wobbled dangerously, slapping him more than once against the side of the mountain. Ignoring the shock of each strike, the wizard hurried as best he could to the bottom rung.

The slim ledge of the cave stood just a little under him, but although the goblins had the zeppelin positioned as precisely as they could, the high mountain winds kept twisting Rhonin away from safety. Three times he tried to get his footing, and three times the wind dragged him away, leaving his foot dangling hundreds of feet in the air.

Worse, as the current grew stronger, the airship, too, began to shift, sometimes drawing away a few critical inches. The voices of the two goblins rose in frantic argument, although the actual words were lost to the struggling mage.

He would have to risk jumping. With conditions as they were, casting a spell would be too chancy. Rhonin would have to rely on physical skill alone—not his first choice.

The airship veered without warning, slapping him hard against the rock. Rhonin let out a gasp, barely managing to hang on. If he did not abandon the ladder soon, the next collision might just be enough to stun him and cause a fatal loss of grip.

Taking a deep breath, the battered wizard studied the distance between himself and the ledge. The ladder rocked to and fro, threatening again to toss him hard against the rock.

Rhonin waited until it brought him near the ledge— then threw himself toward the cave.

With a painful grunt, he came down on the slim ledge. His feet momentarily slipped, one finding no purchase whatsoever. The wizard scrambled to pull himself forward, finally making progress.

When at last he felt secure enough, Rhonin dropped to

the ground, panting. It took him a few seconds to regain his breath, at which point he rolled onto his back.

Beyond, Voyd and Nullyn had apparently just realized that they had finally rid themselves of their unwanted passenger. The goblin airship began to pull away, the rope ladder still dangling from the side.

Rhonin's hand suddenly shot up, his index finger pointing toward the fleeing vessel.

He opened his mouth to scream, knowing what would happen next. *"Nooo!"*

The same words he had spoken earlier to create the flickering flame over his hand now erupted from his mouth, but this time they were not spoken by the wizard himself.

A stream of pure fire greater than any the horrified spellcaster had ever summoned shot forth—directly toward the airship and the unsuspecting goblins.

The flames engulfed the zeppelin. Rhonin heard screams.

The airship exploded as its stockpile of oil ignited.

As the few remaining fragments plunged from the sky, Rhonin's arm dropped to his side.

Drawing in what breath he had, the mage snapped, "You shouldn't have done that!"

The winds will keep the explosion from being heard, replied the cold voice. *And the pieces will fall to a deep valley little used. Besides, the orcs are used to the goblins destroying themselves in the midst of their experiments. You need not fear discovery . . . my friend.*

Rhonin had not been concerned about his own safety at that moment, only the lives of the two goblins. Death in combat was one thing; punishment such as the black dragon had meted out to his two rebellious servants was another.

You would do yourself better to continue on into the cave, Deathwing continued. *The elements outside are hardly fit for you.*

Not at all mollified by the leviathan's attempt at concern, Rhonin yet obeyed. He had no desire to be swept off the ledge by the ever-increasing winds. For better or worse, the dragon had brought him this close to his goal—one that he could now admit to himself he had suspected he might never reach on his own. Deep down, the wizard had believed all along he would perish—hopefully, at least, *after* he had made amends. Now, perhaps he had a chance. . . .

At that moment a monstrous sound greeted Rhonin, a sound he recognized instantly. A dragon, of course, and one young and fit. Dragons and orcs. They awaited him in the depths of the mountain, awaited the lone mage.

Reminded him that he might yet die, just as he had originally imagined. . . .

The human was strong. Stronger than imagined.

Clad once more in the guise of Lord Prestor, Deathwing considered the pawn he had chosen. Usurping the wizard that the Kirin Tor had sent on this absurdly impossible quest had seemed the simplest thing. He would turn their folly into victory—but *his* victory. This Rhonin would do that for him, although not in the way the mortal expected.

Yet the wizard showed much more defiance than Deathwing had assumed possible. Strong of will, this one. A good thing that he would perish in the course of matters; such strong will bred strong wizards—like

Medivh. Only one name among humans had the black leviathan ever respected, and that had been Medivh's. Mad as a goblin—not to mention as unpredictable as one—he had wielded power unbelievable. Not even Deathwing would have faced him willingly.

But Medivh was dead—and the ebony leviathan believed that to be the case despite the recent rumors to the contrary. No other wizard came anywhere near to having the mad one's skills, and never would, if Deathwing had his way.

Yet if Rhonin would not obey him blindly—as the monarchs of the Alliance did—he would obey out of the knowledge that the dragon watched his every move. The two insipid goblins had made for an object lesson. Perhaps they had only planned to put terror into the heart of their passenger, but Deathwing had not had time for such foolishness. He had warned Kryll to choose a pair who would fulfill their mission without any nonsense. When the chief goblin had completed his own tasks, Deathwing would speak to him about his choices. The black dragon was not at all pleased.

"You had better not fail, little toad," he hissed. "Or your brethren on board the airship will have considered themselves fortunate compared to the fate I will deal you. . . ."

He dropped all thought of the goblin. Lord Prestor had an important meeting with King Terenas . . . about the Princess Calia.

Clad in the finest suit to be found among any of the nobles of the land, Deathwing admired himself in the lengthy mirror in the front corridor of his chateau. Yes, every inch a future king. Had humans carried within them even a shred of the dignity and power that he possessed, the dragon might have thought to spare them. However, what stared back at him represented to Deathwing the perfection that the mortals could never even hope to attain. He did them a favor by ending their miserable existences.

"Ssssoon," he whispered in promise to himself. "Ssssoon."

His carriage took him directly to the palace, where the guards saluted and immediately bid him enter. A servant met Deathwing inside the front hall, begging his pardon for the king not being there personally to greet him. Now fully into his role as the young noble who sought only peace between all parties, the dragon pretended no annoyance, smiling as he asked the human to lead him to where Terenas desired him to wait. He had expected the king not to be ready for him, especially if Terenas still had to explain to his young daughter her chosen future.

With all opposition to his ascension swept aside and the throne only days from his grasp, Deathwing had hit upon what he felt the perfect addition to his plans. How much better to strengthen his hold than to wed the daughter of one of the most powerful of the kingdoms in the Alliance? Of course, not all of the reigning monarchs had had viable choices. In fact, at this moment in time, only Terenas and Daelin Proudmoore had daughters either single or beyond infancy. Jaina Proudmoore, however, was much too young and, from what the dragon had so far researched, possibly already too difficult to control, or else he might have waited for her. No, Terenas's daughter would do just fine.

Calia still remained at least two years away from marriage, but two years hardly mattered to the ageless dragon. By that time not only would the others of his kind be either under his domination or dead, but

Deathwing would have maneuvered himself into a political position in which he could truly begin undermining the foundation of the Alliance. What the brutish orcs had failed to do from without—he would do from within.

The servant opened a door. "If you'll wait within, my lord, I'm sure His Majesty will be with you shortly."

"Thank you." Caught up in his reverie, Deathwing did not notice that he had two new companions awaiting him until just after the door had shut behind him.

The cloaked and hooded figures bowed their shadowed heads slightly in his direction.

"Our greetings, Lord Prestor," rumbled the bearded one.

Deathwing fought back the frown nearly descending upon his mouth. He had expected to confront the Kirin Tor, but not in the palace of Terenas. The enmity the dragon had magically built up among the various rulers toward the wizards of Dalaran should have prevented the latter from daring to visit.

"My greetings to you, sir and madam."

The second mage, old for a female of the race, returned, "We had hoped to meet you sooner than this, my lord. Your reputation has spread throughout the kingdoms of the Alliance . . . especially in Dalaran."

The magic wielded by these wizards kept their features obscured for the most part, and although with but a single action Deathwing could have pierced their veils, the dragon chose not to do so. He already knew this pair, albeit not by name. The bearded one had a familiar feel to his aura, as if Deathwing and the wizard had recently come into contact. The false noble suspected that this mage had been responsible for at least one of the two major attempts to break through the protective spells around the chateau. Considering the potency of those spells, it surprised Deathwing a little that the man still lived, much less confronted him now.

"And the reputation of the Kirin Tor is known to all as well," he replied.

"And becoming more known with each day . . . but not in the way we wish, I must say."

She hinted of his handiwork. Deathwing found no threat there. By this time, they suspected him a rogue wizard—powerful but not nearly the threat he truly presented.

"I had expected to meet His Majesty here alone," he said, turning the conversation to his advantage. "Has Dalaran some business with Lordaeron?"

"Dalaran seeks to keep abreast of situations important to all kingdoms of the Alliance," the woman replied. "Something a bit more difficult of late, due to our not being notified of major summits between members."

Deathwing calmly walked over to the side table, where Terenas always kept a few bottles of his best on hand for waiting guests. Lordaeron wine represented in his mind the only worthwhile export the kingdom offered. He poured a small amount in one of the jeweled goblets nearby. "Yes, I spoke with His Majesty, urging him to request you join in the deliberations over Alterac, but he seemed adamant about leaving you out of them."

"We know the outcome, regardless," huffed the bearded man. "Congratulations are in order for you, Lord Prestor."

Not once had they offered their names, nor had he offered his. Yes, they truly kept an eye on him—as much as Deathwing allowed, that is.

"It came as a surprise to me, I must tell you. All I ever

hoped was to help keep the Alliance from falling apart after Lord Perenolde's unfortunate behavior."

"Yes, a terrible thing that. One would've never thought it of the man. I knew him when he was younger. A bit timid, but didn't seem the traitorous type."

The elder female suddenly spoke up. "Your former homeland is somewhere not too distant from Alterac, is it not, Lord Prestor?"

For the first time, Deathwing felt a twinge of annoyance. This game no longer pleased him. Did she know?

Before he could answer, the grandly decorated door on the opposite side of the entrance opened and King Terenas, his mood clearly not at all pleasant, barged inside. A blond, cherubic boy barely more than a toddler followed behind, clearly trying to get his father's attention. However, Terenas took one look at the two shadowy wizards and the frown on his face deepened further.

He turned to the child. "Run along back to your sister, Arthas, and try to calm her. I'll be with you as soon as I can, I promise."

Arthas nodded and, with a curious glance at his father's visitors, headed back through the door.

Terenas shut the door behind his son, then instantly whirled on the mages. "I thought I told the major-domo to inform you that I've no time for you today! If Dalaran has any claims or protests to make concerning my handling of Alliance matters, they can send a formal writ through our ambassador there! Now, *good day!*"

The pair seemed unmoved. Deathwing held back a triumphant smile. His hold on the king remained strong even when the dragon had to deal with other matters, such as Rhonin.

Thinking of his newest pawn, Deathwing hoped that the wizards would take Terenas's forceful dismissal to heart and leave. The sooner they were gone, the sooner he could get back to checking on their younger counterpart.

"We'll be going, Your Majesty," rumbled the male spellcaster. "But we've been empowered to tell you that the council hopes you'll see reason on this before long. Dalaran has always been a steadfast, loyal ally."

"When it chooses to be."

Both mages ignored the monarch's harsh statement. Turning to Deathwing, the female said, "Lord Prestor, it has been an honor to meet you face-to-face at last. I trust it will not be the final time."

"We shall see." She made no attempt to extend her hand and he did not encourage it. So. They had warned him that they would continue to watch him. No doubt the Kirin Tor believed this would make him more cautious, even uncertain, but the black dragon only found their threats laughable. Let them waste their time crouching over scrying spheres or trying to convince the rulers of the Alliance to see reason. All they would gain by their efforts would be the further enmity of the other humans—which would work just perfectly for Deathwing.

Bowing, the two mages retreated from the chamber. Out of respect for the king, they did not simply vanish, as he knew they could. No, they would wait until back in their own embassy, out of sight of untrusting eyes. Even now, the Kirin Tor took care with appearances around others.

Not that it would matter in the long run.

When the wizards had at last gone, King Terenas began speaking. "My most humble apologies for that scene, Prestor! The very nerve of them! They barge into the palace as if Dalaran and not Lordaeron ruled here! This time they go too far—"

He froze in mid-sentence as Deathwing raised a hand toward him. After glancing at both doors in order to assure himself that no one would come running in and find the king bewitched, the false noble stepped to a window overlooking the palace grounds and the kingdom beyond. Deathwing waited patiently, watching the gates through which all visitors passed in and out of Terenas's royal residence.

The two wizards stepped into sight, heading away. Their heads leaned toward one another as they engaged in urgent yet clearly private conversation with one another.

The dragon touched the expensive glass plate on the window with his index finger, drawing two circles there, circles that glowed deep red. He muttered a single word.

The glass in one of the circles shifted, puckered, shaped itself into a parody of a mouth.

"—nothing at all! He's a blank, Modera! Couldn't sense a thing about him!"

In the other circle, a second, somewhat more delicate, mouth formed. "Perhaps you're still not recovered enough, Drenden. After all, that shock you suffered—"

"I'm over it! Take more than that to kill me! Besides, I know you were probing him, too! Did *you* sense anything?"

A frown formed on the feminine mouth. "No . . . which means he's very, very powerful—possibly almost as powerful as Medivh."

"He must be using some powerful talisman! No one's that powerful, not even Krasus!"

Modera's tone changed. "Do we really know how

powerful Krasus is? He's older than the rest of us. That surely means something."

"It means he's cautious . . . but he is the best of us, even if he isn't master of the council."

"That was his choice—more than once."

Deathwing leaned forward, his once mild curiosity now growing stronger.

"What's he doing, anyway? Why's he keeping so secret?"

"He says he wants to try to find out about Prestor's past, but I think there's more. There's always more with Krasus."

"Well, I hope he finds out something soon, because this situation is—what is it?"

"I feel a tingling on my neck! I wonder if—"

Up in the palace, the dragon quickly waved his hand across the two glass mouths. The pane instantly flattened, leaving no trace. Deathwing backed away.

The female had finally sensed his spellwork, but she would not be able to trace it back to him. He did not fear them, however skilled for humans they were, but Deathwing had no desire at the moment to drag out his confrontation with the pair. A new element had been added to the game, one that, for the first time, made the dragon just a little pensive.

He turned back to Terenas. The king still stood where Deathwing had left him, mouth open and hand out.

The dragon snapped his fingers.

"—and I won't stand for it! I've a mind to cut off all diplomatic relations with them immediately! Who rules in Lordaeron? Not the Kirin Tor, whatever they might think!"

"Yes, probably a wise move, Your Majesty, but draw it out. Let them lodge their protest, then begin closing the gates on them. I'm very certain that the other kingdoms will follow suit."

Terenas gave him a weary smile. "You're a very patient young man, Prestor! Here I've been ranting and you simply stand there, accepting it all! We're supposed to be discussing a future marriage! True, we've more than two years before it can take place, but the betrothal will require extensive planning!" He shrugged. "Such is the way of royalty!"

Deathwing gave him a slight bow. "I understand completely, Your Majesty."

The king of Lordaeron began telling him about the various functions his future son-in-law would need to attend over the next several months. In addition to taking charge of Alterac, young Prestor would have to be present for each occasion in order to strengthen the ties between him and Calia in the eyes of the people and his fellow monarchs. The world would need to see that this match would be the beginning of a great future for the Alliance.

"And once we take Khaz Modan and Grim Batol back from those infernal orcs, we can begin plans for a ceremonial return of the lands to the hill dwarves! A ceremony you shall lead, my dear boy, as you are possibly one of those most responsible for holding this Alliance together long enough for victory. . . ."

Deathwing's attention slipped further and further away from the babblings of Terenas. He knew most of what the old man would say—having placed it into the human's mind earlier. Lord Prestor, the hero—imagined or otherwise—would reap his rewards and slowly, methodically, begin the destruction of the lesser races.

However, what interested the dragon more at the moment was the conversation between the two wizards, and especially their mention of another of the Kirin Tor, one Krasus. Deathwing found him of interest. He knew that there had been earlier attempts to circumnavigate the spells surrounding the chateau, and that one of those attempts had triggered the *Endless Hunger,* one of the oldest and most thorough traps ever devised by a wielder of magic. The dragon also knew that the *Hunger* had failed in its function.

Krasus . . . Was this the name of the wizard who had evaded a spell as ancient as Deathwing himself?

I may have to learn more about you, the dragon thought as he absently nodded in response to Terenas's continued babble. *Yes, I may have to learn more. . . .*

FOURTEEN

Krasus slept, slept deeper than he ever had, even as a small hatchling. He slept the sleep halfway between dreaming and something else, that eternal slumber from which not even the mightiest conqueror could awake. He slept knowing that each hour that passed slid him nearer and nearer to that sweet oblivion.

And while he slept, the dragon mage dreamed.

The first visions were murky ones, simple images from the sleeper's subconscious. However, they were soon followed by more distinct and much starker apparitions. Winged figures both draconic and otherwise fluttered about, seeming to scatter in panic. A looming man in black mocked him from a distance. A child raced along a winding, sun-drenched hill . . . a child who suddenly transformed into a twisted, undead thing of evil.

Troubled by the meanings of these dreams even in the depths of his slumber, the wizard shifted uneasily. As he did, he dropped deeper yet, entering a realm of pure darkness that both smothered and comforted him.

And in that realm, a voice, a soft yet commanding voice, spoke to the desperate dragon mage.

You would sacrifice anything for her, would you not, Korialstrasz?

In his sanctum, Krasus's lips moved as he mouthed a reply. *I would give myself if that is what it takes to free her. . . .*

Poor, loyal Korialstrasz . . . A shape formed in the darkness, a shape that fluctuated with each breath of the sleeping figure. In his dreams, a drifting Krasus tried to reach for that shape, but it vanished just as he almost caught it.

In his mind, it had been Alexstrasza.

You slip quicker and quicker toward the final rest, brave one. Is there something you would ask of me before that happens?

Again his lips moved. *Only that you help her . . .*

Nothing for yourself? Your fading life, perhaps? Those who have the audacity to drink to death should be rewarded with a full goblet of his finest vintage. . . .

The darkness seemed to be pulling him in. Krasus found it hard to breathe, hard to think. The temptation to simply turn over and accept the comforting blanket of oblivion grew stronger.

Yet he forced himself to reply. *Her. All I ask is for her.*

Suddenly he felt himself dragged upward, dragged to a place of color and light, a place where it became possible to breathe again, to think again.

Images assailed him, images not from his own dreams—but from the dreams of others. He saw the wishes and wants of humans, dwarves, elves, and even orcs and goblins. He suffered their nightmares and savored their sweet sensations. The images were legion, yet as each passed him by, Krasus immediately found it impossible to recall them, just as he found it so hard to recall even his own dreams.

In the midst of this flowing landscape, another vision formed. However, while all around it moved as mist, this one retained a shape—more or less—that grew to overwhelm the small figure of the wizard.

A graceful draconic form, half substance, half imagination, spread its wings as if waking. Hints of faded green, such as seen in a forest before the setting of night, spread across the torso of the leviathan. Krasus looked up, prepared to meet the dragon's eyes—and saw that they were closed as if in sleep. However, he had no doubt that the Mistress of Dreams perceived him all too well.

Such a sacrifice will I not demand from you, Korialstrasz, you who have always been a most interesting dreamer. . . . The edges of the dragon's mouth curled up slightly. *A most intriguing dreamer . . .*

Krasus sought to find stable footing, to find *any* footing, but the ground around him remained malleable, almost liquid. He was forced to float, a position that left him feeling wanting. *I thank you, Ysera. . . .*

Ever polite, ever diplomatic, even to my consorts, who have, in my name, rejected your desires more than once.

They did not understand the situation fully, he countered.

You mean I did not understand the situation fully. Ysera drifted back, her neck and wings rippling as if reflected in a suddenly disturbed pool. Ever her eyelids remained shut, but her great visage focused quite distinctly on the intruder to her realm. *It is not so simple a matter to free your beloved Alexstrasza, and even I cannot say if the cost is worth it. Is it not better to let the world run its course, to do as it will? If the Giver of Life is to be freed, will it not happen of its own accord?*

Her apathy—the apathy of *all* three of the Aspects he had visited—set the dragon mage's mind afire with anger. *And is Deathwing truly to be the culmination of the world's* course, then? He certainly will be if none of you do anything but sit back and dream!

The wings folded in. *Mention not that one!*

Krasus pushed. *Why, Lady of Dreams? Does he give you nightmares?*

Although the lids stayed tight, Ysera's eyes surely held some dire emotion. *He is one whose dreams I will never enter—again. He is one who is quite possibly more terrible in his sleep than even waking.*

The beleaguered wizard did not pretend to understand the last. All that concerned him was the fact that none of these great powers could summon up the wherewithal to make a stand. True, thanks to the *Demon Soul* they were not what they once had been, but still they wielded terrible power. Yet, it appeared that all three felt that the Age of the Dragon had passed, and that even if they *could* alter the future, it would not be worth dragging themselves out of their self-imposed stupors.

I know that you and yours still circulate among the younger races, Ysera. I know that you still influence the dreams of the humans, elves, and—

To a point, Korialstrasz! There are limits to even my domain!

But you have not given up entirely on the world then, have you? Unlike Malygos and Nozdormu, you do not hide in madness or the relics of times past! After all, are not dreams also of the future?

As much as they are the past; you would do well to remember that!

The faint image of a human woman holding up a new baby drifted by. The brief glimpse of a young boy doing epic battle with childish monsters of his own imagining flickered into and out of existence. Krasus momentarily surveyed the various dreams forming and dissipating around him. As many dark as there were those of a lighter nature, but that was how it had always been. A balance.

Yet, in his mind, his queen's continued captivity and Deathwing's determination to wrest the world from the younger races upset that balance. There would be no more dreams, no more hopes, if both situations were not rectified.

With or without your help, Ysera, I will go on. I must!

You are certainly welcome to do so. . . . The dream dragon's form wavered.

Krasus turned away from her, ignoring the intangible images that scattered in his wake. *Then either send me back to my sanctum or drop me into the abyss! Perhaps it would be best if I do not live to see the fate of the world—and what becomes of my queen!*

He expected Ysera to send him back to the arms of oblivion, so that he would no longer be able to harp on the subject of his Alexstrasza to either her or any of the other Aspects. Instead, the dragon mage felt a gentle touch on his shoulder, an almost tentative touch.

Turning, Krasus found himself facing a slim, pale woman, beautiful but ethereal. She stood clad in a flowing gown of pale green gossamer, a veil partially obscuring her lower features. In some ways she reminded him of his queen—and yet not.

The eyes of the woman were closed.

Poor, struggling Korialstrasz. Her mouth did not move, but Krasus knew the voice for hers. Ysera's voice. A pensive expression formed on the pale face. *You would do anything for her.*

He did not understand why she bothered to repeat

what they both knew already. Krasus again turned from the Lady of Dreams, searching for some path by which he could escape this unreal domain.

Do not go yet, Korialstrasz.

And why not? he demanded, turning back—

Ysera stared at him, eyes fully open. Krasus froze, unable not to stare back at those eyes. They were the eyes of everyone he had ever known, ever loved. They were eyes that knew him, knew every bit about him. They were blue, green, red, black, golden—every color that eyes could be.

They were even his own.

I will consider what you have said.

He could scarcely believe her. *You will—*

She raised a hand, silencing him. *I will consider what you have said. No more, no less, for now.*

And—and if you find you agree with me?

Then I will endeavor to convince Malygos and Nozdormu of your quest . . . and from them I can promise nothing, even then.

It was more than Krasus had come with, even more than he had hoped for at this point. Perhaps it would come to nothing, but it at least gave him hope to carry into battle.

I—I thank you.

I have done nothing for you yet . . . except kept your dreams alive. The brief smile that crossed Ysera's lips had a regretful tinge to it.

He started to thank her again, wanting her to understand that even this much would give him the strength he needed to go on, but suddenly Ysera seemed to drift away from him. Krasus reached for her, but the distance already proved too great, and when he sought to step forward, she only moved away more swiftly.

Then it occurred to him that She of the Dreaming had not moved; he had.

Sleep well and good, poor Korialstrasz, came her voice. The slim, pale figure wavered, then dissipated completely. *Sleep well, for in the battle you seek to fight you will need all your strength and more. . . .*

He tried to speak, but even his dream voice would not work. Darkness descended upon the dragon mage, the comforting darkness of slumber.

And do not undervalue those you think only pawns. . . .

The mountain fortress of the orcs proved not only to be more immense than even Rhonin had supposed, but more confusing. Tunnels that he expected would bring him toward his goal would suddenly turn off in different directions, even often rising instead of descending. Some ended, for no good reason that he could decipher. One such tunnel forced him to backtrack for more than an hour, not only stealing precious time but depleting his already flagging strength.

It did not help at all that Deathwing had not spoken to him once in all that time. While Rhonin in no way trusted the black dragon, at least he knew that Deathwing would have guided him to the captive leviathan. What could have drawn the attention of the dark one away?

In an unlit corridor, the weary mage finally sat down to rest. He had with him a small water sack given to him by the hapless goblins, and from this Rhonin took a sip. After that, Rhonin leaned back, believing that a few minutes' relaxation would enable him to clear his mind and allow him to better traverse the passages again.

Did he really imagine that he could free the Dragonqueen? The doubts had increased more and more as he tried to wend his way through the mountain. Had he come here just to commit some grand suicide? His life would not bring back those who had died and, in truth, they had all made choices of their own.

How had he ever dreamt of such an insane quest? Thinking back, Rhonin recalled the first time the subject had come up. Forbidden to take part in the activities of the Kirin Tor after the debacle of his last mission, the young wizard had spent his days brooding, seeing no one and eating little. Under the conditions of his probation, no one had been allowed to see him, either, which had made it more surprising when Krasus had materialized before him, offering his support in Rhonin's efforts to return to the ranks.

Rhonin had always thought that he needed no one, but Krasus had convinced him otherwise. The master wizard had discussed his younger counterpart's dire situation in great detail, to the point where Rhonin had openly asked for his aid. Somehow the topic of dragons had arisen, and from there the story of Alexstrasza, the crimson behemoth held captive by the orcs, forced to breed savage beasts for the glory of the Horde. Even though the main element of the Horde itself had been shattered, so long as she remained a prisoner, the orcs in Khaz Modan would continue to wreak havoc on the Alliance, killing countless innocents.

It had been at that juncture that the notion to free the dragon had occurred to Rhonin, a notion so fantastic that he felt only he could have devised it. It had made perfect sense at the time. Redeem himself or die trying in a scheme that would be forever spoken of among his brethren.

Krasus had been so very impressed. In fact, Rhonin

now recalled that the elder mage had spent much time with him, working out details and encouraging the red-haired spellcaster. Rhonin freely admitted to himself now that perhaps he would have dropped the idea if not for his patron's urging. In some ways, it seemed as if the quest had been more Krasus's than his own. Of course, what would the faceless councilor achieve by sending his protégé off on such a mission? If Rhonin succeeded, some credit might go to the one who had believed in him, but if he failed . . . what good would that do Krasus?

Rhonin shook his head. If he kept asking himself questions such as these, soon he would come to believe that his patron had actually been the force behind this quest, that he had somehow used his influence to make the younger wizard *want* to journey to these hostile lands.

Absurd . . .

A sudden noise nearly brought Rhonin to his feet, and he realized that somewhere in the course of his thinking he had drifted off to sleep. The wizard pressed himself against the wall, waiting to see who passed in the darkened corridor. Surely the orcs knew that the tunnel ended. Could they have come here specifically in search of him?

Yet the noise—barely discernible as muttered conversation—slowly faded away. The wizard realized that he had been the victim of the complex acoustics of the cavern system. The orcs he had heard likely were several levels away from him.

Could he follow those sounds, though? With growing hope, Rhonin moved cautiously in the direction from which he believed the conversation had come. Even if it had not exactly originated from that location, at least the echoes might eventually lead him to where he hoped to go.

How long he had slept, Rhonin could not say, but as he journeyed along, he heard more and more sounds, almost as if Grim Batol had just awakened. The orcs seemed to be in the midst of a flurry of activity, which presented the mage with something of a problem. Now there came too many noises from too many directions. Rhonin did not want to accidentally step into the practice quarters of the warriors, or even their mess hall. All he wanted was the chamber where the Dragonqueen lay prisoner.

Then, a draconic roar cut through the sounds, a high roar that died quickly. Rhonin had already heard such cries before, but had not thought about them. Now he cursed himself for a fool; would not all the dragons be kept in the same general region? At the very worst, following the cries would at least get him nearer to *some* beast, and then perhaps he could find the trail to the queen's chamber from there.

For a time he wended his way through the tunnels with little problem, most of the orcs seemingly far away, at work on some great project. Briefly the wizard wondered if Grim Batol planned for battle. By now the Alliance had to be pressing the orc forces in northern Khaz Modan. Grim Batol would need to support their brethren up there if the Horde hoped to drive the humans and their allies back.

If so, the activity would work to Rhonin's advantage. Not only would the orcs' minds be occupied by this, but there would be less of them. Surely every handler with a trained mount would be in the sky soon, on the way to the north.

Encouraged, Rhonin set a more daring pace, a more certain one—which but seconds later nearly sent him stumbling into the very arms of a pair of huge orc warriors.

They were, fortunately, even more stunned to see him than he was them. Rhonin immediately raised his left hand, muttering a spell that he had hoped to save for more dire circumstances.

The nearest of the orcs, his ugly, tusked face twisting into a berserker rage, reached for the ax slung on his back. Rhonin's spell caught him directly in the chest, throwing the massive warrior hard against the nearest rock wall.

As the orc struck the wall, he *melded* into the very rock. Briefly the outline of his form remained behind, mouth still open in rage, but then even that faded into the wall . . . leaving no trace of the creature's savage end.

"Human scum!" roared the second, his ax now in hand. He took a heavy swing at Rhonin, chipping off bits of stone as the wizard managed to duck out of the way. The orc lumbered forward, bulky, dull green form filling the narrow corridor. A necklace of dried, wrinkled fingers— human, elven, and otherwise—dangled before Rhonin's eyes, a collection to which his foe no doubt wished to add him. The orc swung again, this time coming perilously near to severing the mage in two lengthwise.

Rhonin stared at the necklace again, a grim idea in mind. He pointed at the necklace and gestured.

His spell briefly made the orc pause, but when the savage warrior saw no visible effect, he laughed scornfully at the pitiful little human. "Come! I make it quick for you, wizard!"

But as he raised his ax, a scratching sensation forced the orc to look down at his chest.

The fingers on his necklace, more than two dozen strong, had moved to his throat.

He dropped the ax and tried to pull them away, but

they had already dug in tight. The orc began to cough as the fingers formed a macabre hand of sorts, a hand cutting off his air.

Rhonin scrambled back as the orc began to swing about wildly, trying to peel away the avenging digits. The wizard had intended the spell only as a diversion while he came up with something more final, but the severed fingers seemed to have taken the opportunity to heart. Vengeance? Even as a mage, Rhonin could not believe that the spirits of the warriors slain by this orc had somehow urged the fingers to this grand effort. It had to be the potency of the spell itself.

Surely it had to be. . . .

Whether vengeful ghosts or simply magic, the enchanted fingers did their terrible work with seeming eagerness. Blood covered much of the orc's upper chest as nails tore into the softer throat. The monstrous warrior collapsed to his knees, eyes so desperate that Rhonin finally had to look away.

A few seconds later, he heard the orc gasp—then a heavy weight fell to the tunnel floor.

The massive berserker lay in a bloody heap, the fingers still dug deep into his neck. Daring to touch one of the severed digits, Rhonin found no movement, no life. The fingers had performed their task and now had returned to their previous state, just as his spell had intended.

And yet . . .

Shaking off such thoughts, Rhonin hurried past the corpse. He had nowhere to put the body and no time to think about it. Before long someone would discover the truth, but the wizard could not help that. Rhonin had to concern himself only with the Dragonqueen. If he did manage to free her, perhaps she would at least carry him off to safety. In that, truly, lay his only possibility of escape.

He managed to traverse the next few tunnels without interruption, but then found himself heading toward a brightly lit corridor from which the babble of voices grew loud and strong. Moving with more caution, Rhonin edged up to the intersection, peering around the corner.

What he had taken for a corridor had proven to actually be the mouth of a vast cavern that opened up to the right, a cavern in which scores of orcs worked hard at loading up wagons and preparing draft animals, all as if they intended some long journey from which they would not likely soon return.

Had he been correct about the battle north? If so, why did it seem *every* orc intended to depart? Why not simply the dragons and their handlers? It would take far too long for these wagons to reach Dun Algaz.

Two orcs came into sight, the pair carrying some great weight between them. Clearly they would have preferred to put down whatever it was they carried, but for some reason dared not do so. In fact, Rhonin thought that they took special care with their burden, almost as if it were made of gold.

Seeing that no one looked in his direction, the wizard took a step forward in order to better study what the orcs so valued. It was round—no, *oval*—and a bit rough in outer appearance, almost scaly. In fact, it reminded Rhonin of nothing more than an—

An *egg*.

A *dragon's* egg, to be precise.

Quickly his gaze shifted to some of the other wagons. Sure enough, he now realized that several of them bore eggs in some stage of development, from smoother, nearly round ones to others even more scaled than the first, eggs clearly near to hatching.

With the dragons so essential to the orcs' fading hopes, why would they be risking such precious cargo on such a journey?

Human.

The voice in his head nearly made Rhonin shout. He flattened against the wall, then quickly slipped back into the tunnel. Finally certain that none of the orcs could see him, Rhonin seized the medallion around his neck and gazed at the black crystal in the center.

Sure enough, it now glowed slightly.

Human . . . Rhonin . . . where are you?

Did Deathwing not know? "I'm in the very midst of the orc fortress," he whispered. "I was looking for the Dragonqueen's chamber."

You found something else, though. There was a glimpse of it. What was it?

For some reason, Rhonin did not want to tell Deathwing. "It was only the orcs at battle practice. I nearly walked in on them without realizing it."

His response was followed by a lengthy silence, so lengthy, in fact, that he nearly thought Deathwing had broken the link. Then, in a very even tone, the dragon returned, *I wish to see it.*

"It's nothing—"

Before Rhonin could say another word, his body suddenly rebelled against him, turning back toward the cavern and the many, many orcs. The outraged spellcaster tried to protest, but this time even his mouth would not work for him.

Deathwing brought him to the spot where he had last stood, then made the wizard's right hand hold up the medallion. Rhonin guessed that Deathwing observed all through the ebony crystal.

At battle practice . . . I see. . . . And is this how they practice their retreating?

He could not reply to the leviathan's mocking retort, nor did he think that Deathwing really cared if he did. The dragon forced him to stay in the open while the medallion surveyed everything.

Yes, I see. . . . You may return to the tunnel now.

His body suddenly his own again, Rhonin slipped out of sight, thankful that the orcs had been so busy with their task that no one had chanced to look up. He leaned against a wall, breathing heavily and realizing that he had been far more frightened of discovery than he would have thought possible. So, evidently, Rhonin was not as suicidal as he had once imagined.

You follow the wrong path. You must go back to the previous intersection.

Deathwing made no comment about Rhonin's attempt at subterfuge, which worried the wizard more than if the dragon had. Surely Deathwing, too, pondered the orcs' moving of the eggs—unless he knew something about it already? How could that be possible, though? Certainly no one here would relay that information to him. The orcs feared and despised the black dragon at least as much as— if not more than—they did the entire Lordaeron Alliance.

Despite those concerns, he immediately followed Deathwing's instructions, backtracking along the corridor until he came to the intersection in question. Rhonin had ignored it earlier, thinking its narrow appearance and lack of lighting meant it was of little significance. Surely the orcs would have kept any tunnel of importance better lit.

"This way?" he whispered.

Yes.

How the dragon knew so much about the cavern system continued to bother Rhonin. Surely Deathwing had not gone wandering through the tunnels, not even in his human guise. Could he have done so in the form of an orc? Possibly so, and yet that, too, did not seem the answer.

The second tunnel on your left. You will take that one next.

Deathwing's directions appeared flawless. Rhonin waited for one mistake, one error, that would indicate the dragon guessed, at least in part. No such mistake occurred. Deathwing knew his way around the orcs' sanctum as good as, if not better than, the bestial warriors themselves.

Finally, after what felt like hours more of traveling, the voice abruptly commanded, *Cease.*

Rhonin paused, although he had no clue as to what concerned Deathwing enough to demand this stop.

Wait.

A few moments later, voices from down the tunnel carried to the wizard.

"—where you were! I've questions for you, questions!"

"Most sorry, my grand commander, most sorry! It could not be helped! I—"

The voices faded away just as Rhonin strained to hear more. He knew one to be that of an orc, evidently even that of the one in charge of the fortress, but the other speaker had been of quite a different race. A goblin.

Deathwing made use of goblins. Could that be how he knew so much about this vast lair? Had one of the goblins here also been serving the dark one?

He would have liked to have followed and heard more of the conversation, but the dragon suddenly ordered him on again. Rhonin knew that if he did not obey, Deathwing might very well make him march. At least while Rhonin had control of his limbs, he could still feel as if he had some choice in matters.

Crossing the tunnel down which the orc commander and the goblin had gone, Rhonin descended through a deep tunnel toward what seemed the very bowels of the mountain. Surely now he had to be near the Dragon-queen. In fact, he almost swore that he could hear the breathing of a giant, and since there were no true giants in Grim Batol, that left only dragons.

Two corridors ahead. Turn right. Follow until you see the opening to your left.

Deathwing said no more. Rhonin again obeyed his instructions, quickening the pace as much as possible. His nerves were on edge. How much longer would he have to wander through this mountain?

He turned right, followed the next passage on and on. From the dragon's simplistic instructions, Rhonin had expected to come across the opening mentioned in fairly quick time, but even after what had to be half an hour he had seen nothing, not even another intersection. Twice he had asked Deathwing if he would soon arrive, but his unseen guide remained silent.

Then, just as the wizard felt ready to give up—he saw a light. A dim one, to be sure, but definitely a light . . . and on the left side of the corridor.

Hopes renewed, Rhonin hurried toward it as quickly as he could without making much noise. For all he knew, a dozen orcs stood guard around the Dragonqueen. He had spells ready, but hoped they could be preserved for other, more desperate moments.

Halt!

Deathwing's voice reverberated through his head, nearly causing Rhonin to collide with the nearest wall. He flattened against it instead, certain that some sentinel had discovered him.

Nothing. The passage remained empty of any but himself.

"Why did you call out?" he whispered to the medallion.

Your destination lies before you . . . but the way may be guarded by more than flesh.

"Magic?" He had thought of that already, but the dragon had not given him any chance to carefully check for himself.

And sentries of magical origin. There is a quick way to discover the truth. Hold out the medallion before you as you move toward the entrance.

"What about guards of flesh and blood? I still have to worry about them."

He could hear the dark one's growing irritation. *All will be known, human. . . .*

Certain that, at the very least, Deathwing wanted him to reach Alexstrasza, Rhonin held the medallion before him and slowly edged forward.

I detect only minor spells—minor to one such as I, that is, the dragon informed him as he neared. *I will deal with them.*

The black crystal suddenly flared, almost causing the startled mage to lose his hold.

The protective spells have been eradicated. A pause. *There are no sentries inside. They would not need them, even without magical spells. Alexstrasza is thoroughly chained and bolted to* her surroundings. *The orcs have been quite efficient. She is completely secure.*

"I should go in?"

I would be disappointed if you did not.

Rhonin found Deathwing's phrasing slightly curious, but did not think long on it, more concerned with the hope of at last facing the Dragonqueen. He wished Vereesa could have been here now, then wondered why that would so please him. Perhaps—

Even thoughts of the silvery-tressed elf faded as he stepped into the entranceway and beheld for the first time the gargantuan red behemoth *Alexstrasza.*

And found her staring back, an emotion in her reptilian eyes that seemed to him akin to fear—but not for herself.

"No!" she rumbled as best as the brace around her throat enabled her. *"Step back!"*

At the same time, Deathwing's voice, its tone triumphant, uttered, *Perfect!*

A flash of light surrounded the wizard. Every fiber of his being shook as some monstrous force ripped through him. The medallion slipped from his suddenly limp fingers.

As he collapsed, he heard Deathwing repeat the single word, laughing afterward.

Perfect. . . .

FIFTEEN

Vereesa gasped as breathing once more became an option for her. The nightmare of being buried alive slowly receded as she gulped in great lungfuls of air. Gradually, full calm returned to her and she finally opened her eyes—to see that she had traded one nightmare for another.

Three figures hunched about a tiny fire in the midst of what appeared to be a small cave. The flames gave their grotesque forms an additional element of horror, for because of it she could make out the ribs beneath the skin and the mottled, scaly flesh that hung loosely. Worse, she could clearly see the long, cadaverous faces with beaklike noses and elongated chins. The ranger could especially make out the narrow, insidious eyes and the sharp, sharp, teeth.

The three were clad in little more than ragged kilts. Throwing axes sat beside each figure, weapons that Vereesa understood these creatures used with enviable skill.

Despite her attempts to keep silent, some minor movement on her part must have reached the long, pointed ears that so reminded the ranger of goblins, for one of her captors immediately looked her way.

"Supper's awake," he hissed, a patch covering what remained of his left eye.

"Looks more like dessert to me," returned a second, bald where the other two wore long, shaggy mohawks.

"Definitely dessert," grinned the third, who wore a tattered scarf that had once belonged to one of Vereesa's own kind. He seemed lankier than the other two, and spoke as if no one would dare contradict him. The leader, then.

The leader of a trio of hungry-looking trolls.

"Slim pickings lately," the scarf-wearer went on. "But time now for a feast, yes."

Something to the ranger's right suddenly let out what would have been quite a telling epithet if not for the gag that smothered the words. Twisting her head as best as the carefully tied ropes allowed her, Vereesa saw that Falstad, too, still lived, albeit for how long she could not say. Rumors had long persisted, even before the days of the Troll Wars, that these hideous creatures saw anything other than themselves as fair game for food. Even the orcs, who had accepted them as allies, had been said to ever keep one eye on the nimble, cunning fiends.

Fortunately, due to both the Troll Wars and the battle against the Horde, their foul race had dwindled in numbers greatly. Vereesa herself had never seen a troll before, only knew them from drawings and legends. She found she would have much preferred to keep it that way.

"Patience, patience," murmured the scarf-wearer in a mock sympathetic voice. "You'll be first, dwarf! You'll be first!"

"Can't we do it now. Gree?" begged the one-eyed troll. "Why can't we do it now?"

"Because I said so, Shnel!" With one hard fist, Gree

suddenly struck Shnel in the jaw, sending the second creature rolling.

The third troll hopped to his feet, encouraging both of his companions to more blows. Gree glared at him, literally staring the bald troll down. Meanwhile, Shnel crawled back to his place by the tiny fire, looking completely subdued.

"*I* am leader!" Gree slapped a bony, taloned hand against his chest. "Yes, Shnel?"

"Yes, Gree! Yes!"

"Yes, Vorsh?"

The hairless monstrosity bobbed his head over and over. "Yes, oh, yes, Gree! Leader you are! Leader you are!"

As with elves, dwarves, and especially humans, there had existed different types of trolls. Some few spoke with the sophistication of elves—even while they tried to take one's head. Others ranged toward the more savage, especially those who most frequented the barrows and other underground realms. Yet Vereesa doubted that there could be any lower form of troll than the three base creatures who had captured her and Falstad—and clearly had still darker designs for them.

The trio went back to some muffled conversation around the tiny fire. Vereesa again looked to the dwarf, who stared back at her. A raised eyebrow by her was answered by a shake of his head. No, despite his prodigious strength, he could not escape the tight bonds. She shook her head in turn. However barbaric the trolls might be, they were true experts in knot-tying.

Trying to remain undaunted, the ranger peered around at her surroundings—what little there was to see of them. They seemed to be in the midst of a long, crudely hewn tunnel, likely of the trolls' own making.

Vereesa recalled the long, taloned fingers, just perfect for digging through the rock and earth. These trolls had adapted well to their environment.

Despite already knowing the results in advance, the elf nonetheless tried to find some looseness in her ropes. She twisted around as cautiously as she could, rubbed her wrists nearly raw, but to no avail.

A horrific chuckle warned her that the trolls had seen at least her final attempts.

"Dessert's lively," commented Gree. "Should make for good sport!"

"Where's the others?" groused Shnel. "Should've been here by now!"

The leader nodded, adding, "Hulg knows what'll happen if he doesn't obey! Maybe he—" The troll suddenly seized his throwing ax. *"Dwarves!"*

The ax went spinning through the tunnel, passing just a few inches from Vereesa's head.

A guttural cry followed but a moment later.

The walls of the tunnel erupted with short, sturdy forms letting out battle calls and waving short axes and swords.

Gree pulled out another, slightly longer ax, this one evidently for hand-to-hand combat. Shnel and Vorsh, the latter crouched, let loose with throwing axes. The elf saw one squat attacker fall to Shnel's weapon, but Vorsh's went wide. The trolls then followed the example of their leader and readied stronger, bulkier axes as the newcomers surrounded them.

Vereesa counted more than half a dozen dwarves, each clad in ragged furs and rusting breastplates. Their helmets were rounded, form-fitting, and lacking any horns or other unnecessary adornments. As with Falstad, most had beards, although they seemed shorter and better trimmed.

The dwarves wielded their axes and swords with practiced precision. The trolls found themselves pressed closer and closer to one another. Shnel it was who fell first, the one-eyed beast not seeing the warrior who came in on his blind side. Vorsh barked a warning, but it came too late. Shnel took a wild swing at his new foe, missing completely.

The dwarf drove his sword into the lanky troll's gut.

Gree fought the most savagely. He landed one good blow that sent a dwarf tumbling back, then nearly beheaded another. Unfortunately, his ax broke as it collided with the longer, well-built one wielded by his latest opponent. In desperation, he seized the dwarf's weapon by the upper handle and struggled to take it out of the shorter fighter's grip.

The well-honed blade of another ax caught the troll leader in the back.

The elf almost felt some sympathy for the last of her captors. Vorsh, eyes wide with the knowledge of his impending doom, looked ready to whimper. Nonetheless, he continued waving his ax at the nearest of the dwarves, almost landing a bloody strike by sheer luck. However, he could do nothing to stem the tide of foes who now advanced in an ever-tightening circle, swords and axes ready.

In the end, Vorsh's death approached butchery.

Vereesa turned her gaze away. She did not face forward again until a steady voice with a hint of gravel in it commented, "Well, no wonder the trolls fought so hard! Gimmel! Ye see this?"

"Aye, Rom! Much better sight than what I've found over here!"

Thick hands pulled her to a sitting position. "Let's see if we can get these ropes off ye without too much damage to that fine form!"

She looked up into the face of a ruddy dwarf at least six inches shorter than Falstad and built much stockier. Despite first appearances, however, his expert handling of the ropes quickly informed the ranger that she should not take him or any of his companions for clumsy, especially after the manner in which they had dispatched the trolls.

Up close, the garments of the dwarves took on an even more ragged appearance, not surprising if they had been subsisting, as Vereesa suspected, on whatever they could steal from the orcs. A distinctive odor also prevailed, indicating that bathing had also long been at a premium.

"Here ye go!"

Her ropes fell away. Vereesa immediately pulled free the gag, with which the dwarf had not bothered. At the same time, a long string of swearwords from her side indicated that Falstad, too, had now been completely released.

"Shut ye mouth or I'll stuff that gag back in permanent!" Gimmel snarled back.

"It'd take a hand's worth of you hill dwarves to bring one from the Aerie down!"

A rumble of discord indicated that their rescuers could readily become new captors if the gryphon-rider did not quiet. Stumbling to her feet—and recalling at the last moment that the tunnel did not quite match her height in this area—the anxious ranger snapped, "Falstad! Be polite with our companions! They have, after all, saved us from a horrid fate!"

"Aye, ye have the right of it," Rom replied. "The damn trolls, they eat anything of flesh—dead or alive!"

"They mentioned some companions," she suddenly recalled. "Perhaps we had better leave this place before they come—"

Rom raised his hand. His crinkled features reminded Vereesa of a tough old dog. "No need to worry about them. That's how we found this trio." He mused a moment longer. "But ye may be right, nonetheless! It's not the only band of trolls in this region. The orcs, they use 'em almost like hunting hounds! Anything other than an orc that crosses these ruined lands is fair game—and they've even taken one of their own allies from the mountain when they've thought they could!"

Images of the fates that had been planned for them coursed through Vereesa's head. "Disgusting! I thank you wholeheartedly for your timeliness!"

"Had I known it would've been ye we were rescuing, I'd have made this sorry bunch move faster!"

Gimmel, eyes shifting much too often to the elf, joined his leader. "Joj's dead. Still stickin' halfway out the hole. Narn's bad; he'll need fixin' up. The rest of the wounded can travel well enough!"

"Then let's be moving on! That mean's ye, too, butterfly!" The last referred to Falstad, who bristled at what apparently had to be a harsh insult to one of the Aerie dwarves.

Vereesa managed to calm him down with a soft touch on his shoulder, but her friend continued to glower as the party started off. The elf noticed that the hill dwarves stripped not only the trolls of any useful items, but also their dead companion. They made no move to try to bring the body with them, and when Rom noticed her glance, he shrugged in mild shame.

"The war demands some proprieties be left behind, lady elf. Joj would've understood. We'll see that his stuff is divided up to his nearest kin and that they also get an extra share of the trolls' items . . . not that there was much, sorry to say."

"I had no idea that there were any of you left in Khaz Modan. It was said that all the dwarves left when it became clear that they could not hold the land against the Horde."

Rom's canine face turned grim. "Aye, all that *could* leave did! Wasn't possible for all of us, ye know! The Horde, it came like the proverbial plague, cutting off much of us from any route! We were forced to go deeper underground than we'd ever gone before! Many's that died at that time, and many more's that died since!"

She looked over his ragtag band. "How many are you?"

"My clan? Seven and forty, where once we counted hundreds! We've talked with three others, two larger than ourselves. Put that total number at three hundred and a little over, and ye still only got a small fraction of what we once were in this land!"

"Three hundred and more's still quite a number," rumbled Falstad. "Aye, with that many, I'd have gone to take Grim Batol back!"

"And perhaps if we fluttered about in the sky like dizzy bugs, we might confuse them enough to make that seem possible, but on the ground or under it, we're still at a disadvantage! Takes only one dragon to scorch a forest and bake the earth below!"

Old enmities between the Aerie and the hills threatened to explode again. Vereesa quickly tried to breach the gap between the two. "Enough of this! It is the orcs and theirs who are the enemies, am I not correct? If you fight with one another, does that not serve their purpose alone?"

Falstad mumbled an apology to her, as did Rom. However, the elf would not let matters settle at only that. "Not good enough. Turn and face one another, then swear you will fight only for the good of all of us! Swear that you will always remember that it is the orcs who slew your brothers, the orcs who killed what you loved."

She knew no specifics about either of the dwarves' pasts, but could draw upon the common understanding that everyone who fought in the war had lost someone or something dear. Rom had no doubt lost many loved ones, and Falstad, who belonged to a reckless yet daring aerial band, surely had suffered the same.

To his credit, the gryphon-rider held his hand out first. "Aye, 'tis the right of it. I'll shake."

"If ye be doing it, I'll be doing it."

Murmurs arose briefly from the other hill dwarves as the two clasped hands. Likely this sort of quick compromise would have been impossible under any circumstances other than the immediate ones.

The party moved on. This time it was Rom who asked the questions. "Now that the danger of trolls is behind us, lady elf, ye should tell us what brings ye and that one to our wounded land. Is it as we hope—that the war turns back on the orcs, that Khaz Modan will soon be free again?"

"The war is moving against the Horde, that much is true." This brought some gasps and quiet cheers from the dwarves. "The bulk of the Horde was broken a few months back, and Doomhammer has disappeared."

Rom paused in his tracks. "Then why are the orcs still in command of Grim Batol?"

"You've to ask on that?" interjected Falstad. "First of all, the orcs still hold out in the north around Dun Algaz. 'Tis said they're beginning to cave in, but they won't go down without a fight."

"And the second, cousin?"

"You've not noticed that they've dragons?" Falstad asked with mock innocence on his face.

Gimmel snorted. Rom gave his second-in-command a glare, but then nodded in resignation. "Aye, the dragons. The one foe we, earthbound, cannot battle. Caught a young one on the ground once and made short work of it—with the loss of one or two good warriors, sad to say—but for the most part, they stay up there and we're forced to hide down here."

"You've fought the trolls, though," Vereesa pointed out. "And surely the orcs as well."

"The occasional patrol, aye. And the trolls, we've done them some damage, too—but it all means nothing if our home's still under the orc ax!" He stared her in the eye. "Now, I ask again. Tell me who ye are and what ye doing here! If Khaz Modan's still orcish, then ye would have to be suicidal to come to Grim Batol!"

"My name is Vereesa Windrunner, ranger, and this is Falstad of the Aeries. We are here because I search for a human, a wizard, tall of height and young. He has hair of fire, and when last I saw him, he was headed this direction." She decided to omit the black dragon's presence for the moment, and was grateful that Falstad did not choose to add that information himself.

"And as daft as wizards are, especially human ones, what would he be thinking of doing near Grim Batol?" Rom studied the pair with some growing suspicion,

Vereesa's tale no doubt just a bit too far-fetched for his tastes.

"I do not know," she admitted. "but I think it has something to do with the dragons."

At this, the dwarven leader let out a bellowing laugh. "The dragons? What's he plan to do? Rescue the red queen from bondage? She'll be so grateful she'll gobble him right up out of excitement!"

The hill dwarves all found this terribly amusing, but the elf did not. To his credit, Falstad did not join in the merriment, although he, of course, knew about Deathwing, and most likely assumed that Rhonin had already long ago been "gobbled up."

"I swore an oath, and because of it I will go on. I must reach Grim Batol and see if I can find him."

The merriment changed to a mixture of astonishment and disbelief. Gimmel shook his head as if not certain that he had heard right.

"Lady Vereesa, I respect ye calling, but surely ye can see how outrageous such a quest is!"

She carefully studied the hardened band. Even in the near dark, she could see the weariness, the fatalism. They fought and they dreamed of their homeland free, but most likely thought that it would never happen in their lifetime. They admired bravery, as all dwarves did, but even to them the elf's quest bordered on the insane.

"You and your people have saved us, Rom, and for that I thank you all. But if I can ask one boon, it is to show me the nearest tunnel leading to the mountain fortress. I will take it alone from there."

"You'll not be journeying alone, my elven lady," objected Falstad. "I've come too far to turn back now . . .

and I'm of a mind to find a certain goblin and skin his hide for boots!"

"Ye both be daft!" Rom saw that neither would be swayed. Shrugging, he added, "But if it's a way to Grim Batol ye want, then I'll not set that task to another. I'll take ye there myself!"

"Ye cannot go alone, Rom!" snapped Gimmel. "Not with the trolls on the move and the orcs near there! I'll go with ye to watch ye back!"

Suddenly, the rest of the band decided that they, too, needed to go along in order to watch the backs of their leaders. Both Rom and Gimmel tried to argue them down, but as one dwarf was generally as stubborn as another, the leader finally came up with a better notion.

"The wounded must return home, and they need some to watch them, too—and no arguments from ye, Narn, ye can barely stand! The best thing to do is roll the bones; the half with the high numbers comes with! Now, who has a set?"

Vereesa hardly wanted to wait for the band to gamble in order to find out who would be traveling with them, but saw no other choice. She and Falstad watched as various dwarves—Narn and the other wounded excluded—set dice rolls against one another. Most of the hill dwarves used their own sets, Rom's question having been responded to by a veritable sea of raised arms.

The last had made Falstad chuckle. "The Aerie and the hills might have their differences, but you'll find few dwarves of any kind who don't carry the dice!" He patted a pouch on his belt. "Can see what heathens the trolls were; they left mine on me! 'Tis said that even the orcs like to roll the bones, which makes 'em a step up from our late captors, eh?"

After much too long a time for Vereesa's taste, Rom and Gimmel returned with seven other dwarves, each with determined expressions on their faces. Looking at them, the elf could have sworn that they were all brothers—although, in fact, at least two hinted at being sisters. Even female dwarves sported strong beards, a sign of beauty among members of the race.

"Here's ye volunteers, Lady Vereesa! All strong and ready to fight! We'll lead ye to one of the cave mouths in the base of the mountain, then ye are on ye own after that."

"I thank you—but, do you mean that you actually have a path that lets you journey into the mountain itself?"

"Aye, but it's no easy one . . . and the orcs don't patrol it alone."

"What do you mean by that?" burst Falstad.

Rom gave the other dwarf the same innocent smile that Falstad had given him earlier. "Have ye not heard they've dragons?"

The sanctum of Krasus had been built over an ancient grove, one older than even the dragons themselves. It had been built by an elf, later usurped by a human mage, then seized long after its abandonment by Krasus himself. He had sensed the powers lingering underneath it and had managed to draw from them on rare occasions, but even the draconic wizard had been surprised to one day discover the concealed entrance in the most remote part of his citadel, the entrance that led to the glittering pool and the single, golden gemstone set in the midst of the bottom.

Each time he entered the chamber, he felt a sense of awe so rare for one of his kind. The magic here made him feel like a human novice just shown his first incantation. Krasus knew that he had only touched a bare trace of the pool's potential, but that was enough to make him leery of trying to seize more. Those who grew greedy in their need for magical power tended to eventually become consumed by it—literally.

Of course, Deathwing had somehow managed to avoid that fate so far.

Despite being so deep underground, the water was not devoid of life—or something approaching it. Even though no clearer liquid existed in all the world, try as he might, Krasus could never completely focus on the tiny, slim forms that darted around, especially in the vicinity of the gemstone. At times, he had sworn they were nothing but shimmering, silver fish, yet now and then the dragon mage swore that he saw arms, a human torso, even on a rare occasion—legs.

Today, he ignored the inhabitants of the pool. His confrontation with She of the Dreaming had given him some hope of aid, but Krasus knew that he could not plan for it. Time swiftly approached when he would have to commit himself.

And that had been why he had come here now, for among its properties, the pool seemed able to rejuvenate those who drank from it, at least for a time. His use of the poison in order to reach the hidden realms of Ysera had left Krasus drained, and if matters demanded he act quickly, then he wanted to be able to respond.

Bending down, the wizard cupped a hand and gathered a small bit of water. He had tried a mug the first time he had dared sip, only to discover that the pool rejected anything crafted. Krasus leaned over the edge, wanting any drops that escaped his palm to return from whence they had come. His respect for the power within had become that great over the years.

Yet as he drank, a rippling in the surface caught his eye. Krasus glanced down at what should have been the perfect reflection of his human form—but, instead, turned out to be something much different.

Rhonin's youthful visage gazed up at him . . . or so the wizard first thought. Then he realized that his pawn's eyes were closed and the head lolled slightly to the side as if . . . as if dead.

Across Rhonin's face appeared the thick, green hand of an orc.

Krasus reacted instinctively, reaching into the water to pull the foul hand away. Instead, he scattered the image and, when the ripples had finally subsided, saw only his own reflection again.

"By the Great Mother . . ." The pool had never shown this ability before. Why now?

Only then did Krasus recall the parting words of Ysera. *And do not undervalue those you think only pawns . . .*

What had she meant by that, and why had he now seen Rhonin's face? Judging by the glimpse the senior wizard had just had, his young counterpart had either been captured or killed by the orcs. If so, it was too late for Rhonin to be of any more value to Krasus—although having apparently reached the mountain fortress, he had fulfilled the true mission on which his patron had sent him.

Combined with other bits of evidence that Krasus had let the orcs in Grim Batol discover over the past several months, the dragon mage had hoped to stir up the commanders there, make them think that a second invasion, a more subtle one, would be slipping in from the west. While quite a force still remained based in the mountain fortress, its true power lay in the dragons bred and trained there . . . and those grew fewer with each passing week. Worse for the orcs in the mountain, the few they had were more and more being sent north to help the bulk of the Horde, leaving Grim Batol bereft of almost all its defenses. Against a determined army comparable in size to that now fighting in the vicinity of Dun Algaz, even the well-positioned orcs in the mountain would eventually succumb, thereby losing the chance to raise any more dragons for the war effort.

And without more dragons to harry the Alliance forces in the north, the remnants of the Horde would at last crumble under the continual onslaught.

Such a force could have been raised and sent in from the west if not for the general lack of cooperation on the part of the leaders of the Alliance. Most felt that Khaz Modan would fall in its own time; why risk more on such a mission? Krasus could not believe that they would not use a two-pronged assault to finally rid the world of the orc threat, but that proved once again the shortsighted thinking of the younger races. Originally, he had tried to persuade the Kirin Tor to push the course of action to Dalaran's neighbors, but as their influence over King Terenas had begun to slip, his own comrades on the council had turned instead to salvaging what remained of their position in the Alliance.

And so Krasus had decided to play a desperate bluff, counting on the devious thinking and paranoia inherent in the orc command. Let them believe the invasion *was* on its way. Let them even have physical proof to go along with the rumors he and his agents had spread. Surely then they would do the unthinkable.

Surely then they would abandon their mountain fortress and, with Alexstrasza under careful watch, move the dragon breeding operation north.

The plan had started as a wild hope, but to even Krasus's surprise, he noted astonishing results. The orc in command of Grim Batol, one Nekros Skullcrusher, had, of late, grown more and more certain that the mountain's days of use were numbered, and numbered low. The wizard's wild rumors had even taken on a life of their own, growing beyond his expectations.

And now . . . and now the orcs had proof in the person of Rhonin. The young spellcaster had played his part. He had shown Nekros that the seemingly impervious fortress could readily be infiltrated, especially through magic. Surely now the orc commander would give the word to abandon Grim Batol.

Yes, Rhonin had played his part well . . . and Krasus knew that he would never forgive himself for using the human so.

What would his beloved queen even think of him when she found out the truth? Of all the dragons, Alexstrasza most cared for the lesser races. They were the children of the future, she had once said.

"It had to be done," he hissed.

Yet, if the vision in the pool had been meant to remind him of the fate of his pawn, it had also served to incite the wizard. He had to know more.

Bowing before the pool, Krasus closed his eyes and

concentrated. It had been quite some time since he had contacted one of his most useful agents. If that one still lived, then surely he had some knowledge of the activities presently going on in the mountain. The dragon mage pictured the one with whom he sought to speak, then reached out with his thoughts, with all his strength, to open the link the two shared.

"*Hear me now . . . hear my voice . . . it is urgent that we talk . . . the day may be on us at last, my patient friend, the day of freedom and redemption . . . hear me . . . Rom . . .*"

SIXTEEN

L ift him up," grunted the bestial voice.

Sturdy hands harshly seized a dazed Rhonin by the upper arms and dragged him to his feet. Cold water suddenly splashed all over his face, stirring him to consciousness.

"His hand. That one." One of those holding the wizard up lifted Rhonin's left arm. Someone grabbed his hand, took hold of his little finger—

Rhonin screamed as the bone cracked. His eyes flew wide open, and he found himself staring at the brutal visage of an older orc much scarred by years of fighting. The orc's expression showed no sign of pleasure at the human's pain, but rather a slight hint of impatience, as if Rhonin's captor would have preferred to be elsewhere dealing with matters of greater import.

"Human." The word came out sounding like a curse. "You've one chance for life; where's the rest of your party?"

"I don't—" Rhonin coughed. The pain from his broken finger still coursed through him. "I'm alone."

"You take me for a fool?" grunted the leader. "You take Nekros for a fool? How many fingers left, eh?" He tugged on the one next to the broken finger. "Many bones in the body. Many bones to be cracked!"

Rhonin thought as quickly as the pain would allow him. He had already informed his captor that he had come alone and that had not satisfied the orc. What did this Nekros want to hear? That his mountain had been invaded by an army? Would that actually please him?

Of course, it might also help to keep Rhonin alive until he could find some means of escape.

He still did not know what had happened, only that, despite his precautions, he had been fooled by Deathwing. Evidently the dragon had *wanted* the mage discovered. But why? It made as much sense as Nekros's seeming desire to have enemy soldiers wandering through his very fortress!

Rhonin could worry about Deathwing's murky plans later. For now, the ragged wizard's life came first.

"No! No . . . please . . . the others . . . I'm not certain where they are . . . got separated . . ."

"Separated? Don't think so! You came for her, didn't you? You came for the Dragonqueen! That's your mission, wizard! I know it!" Nekros leaned close, his breath threatening to smother Rhonin back into unconsciousness. "My spies heard! You heard, didn't you, Kryll?"

"Oh, yes, oh, yes, Master Nekros! I heard it all!"

Rhonin tried to glance past the orc, but Nekros would not let him see who spoke. Still, the voice itself said much about the spy's identity, especially that this Kryll had to be the goblin he had heard earlier.

"I say again to you, human, that you came for the dragon, isn't that so?"

"I got sep—"

Nekros slapped him across the face, leaving a trail of

blood at the edge of Rhonin's mouth. "Another finger'll be next! You came to free the dragon before your armies reached Grim Batol! You figured the chaos would work for you, didn't you?"

This time, Rhonin learned. "Yes . . . yes, we did."

"You said 'we'! That's twice now!" The lead orc leaned back in triumph. For the first time, the injured mage noticed Nekros's maimed leg. Small wonder this brutal orc commanded the dragon-breeding program instead of a savage war party.

"You see, great Nekros? Grim Batol is no longer safe, my glorious commander!" pitched in the high voice of the goblin. "Who knows how many more enemies still lurk in its countless tunnels? Who knows how long before the Alliance marches on you—with the dark one leading the way? A pity nearly all your remaining dragons are already up near Dun Algaz! You can't possibly defend the mountain with so few! Best if the enemy did not find us here at all rather than waste so much precious—"

"Tell me something I *don't* know, little wretch!" He poked a meaty finger into Rhonin's chest. "Well, this one and his comrades've come too late! You'll not get the dragon or her young, human! Nekros's thought ahead of you all!"

"I don't—"

Another slap. The only benefit of the stinging pain in the beaten wizard's face was that it took away from the agony of his broken finger. "You can have Grim Batol, human, for all the good it's worth! May the whole thing fall down on you!"

"Nekros—you must . . . must stop this insanity!"

Rhonin's head jerked up. He knew that voice, even though he had heard it but once before.

His guards also reacted to the voice, turning enough to enable him to see the gargantuan, scaled form so wickedly bound by chains and clamps. Alexstrasza, the great Dragonqueen, could scarcely move. Her limbs, tail, wings and throat were held firmly in place. She could clearly open her tremendous jaws, but only enough to eat and speak with effort.

Captivity had not treated her well. Rhonin had seen dragons before, crimson ones especially, and those had all had scales that bore a certain metallic sheen. Alexstrasza's, on the other hand, had become dull, faded, and in many places looked loose. She did not seem at all well when he studied her reptilian countenance, either. The eyes had a washed-out look to them, not to mention an incredible weariness.

He could only imagine what her imprisonment had been like. Forced to bear young who would be trained by her captors to serve their murderous cause. Never likely seeing them once the eggs were taken from her. Perhaps she even regretted the lives lost because of her deadly progeny. . . .

"You've no permission to speak, reptile," snarled Nekros. He reached into a pouch at his side and clutched something.

Rhonin's skin tingled as a magical force of astonishing proportions awoke. He did not know what the orc did, yet it made the Dragonqueen cry out with such pain that everyone but Nekros seemed affected by it.

Despite her agony, though, Alexstrasza continued. "You—you waste both energy and—and time, Nekros! You fight for what is—is already—lost!"

With a groan, she finally closed her eyes. Her breathing, so rapid the moment before, briefly grew shallow before returning to a somewhat more normal rate.

"Only Zuluhed commands me, reptile," the one-legged orc muttered. "And he's far from here." His hand slipped free from the pouch. At the same time the magical force that Rhonin had felt abruptly faded away.

The wizard had heard many rumors as to how the Horde could possibly keep such a magnificent creature under their control, but none matched what he had just witnessed. Clearly some artifact or device of tremendous strength lay in that pouch. Did Nekros even truly understand the power he wielded? With such at his beck and call, he could have ruled the Horde himself!

"We need to hunt down the others," the elder warrior turned to a guard standing by the entranceway. "Where'd you find the guard's body?"

"Fifth level, third tunnel."

Nekros's brow furrowed. "Above us?" He studied Rhonin as if looking over a prime piece of beef. "Wizard's work! Start searching everything from fifth level up, then—leave no tunnel alone! Somehow they've come from above!" A slow grin spread across his outlandish, tusked features. "Maybe not magic after all! Torgus saw the gryphons! That's it! The rest of 'em came after Deathwing drove Torgus off!"

"Deathwing—Deathwing s-serves no one—but himself!" Alexstrasza suddenly pronounced, eyes opening wide. She sounded almost fearful, for which Rhonin could not blame her. Who did not fear the black demon?

"But he works now with the humans," insisted her

captor. "Torgus saw him!" His hand slapped the pouch. "Well, maybe we'll be ready for him, too!"

Now Rhonin could not help but stare at the pouch and its contents, which, judging by the vague shape, seemed to be a medallion or disk. What power could it have that Nekros believed would even work against the armored behemoth?

"It's dragons you all want. . . ." Once more Nekros faced the wizard. "And it's dragons you'll get . . . but you and the dark one won't be happy long, human!" He waved toward the exit. "Take him away!"

"Kill him?" grunted one of the guards in what seemed hopeful tones.

"Not yet! More questions later for this one . . . maybe! You know where to put him! I'll come right after to make certain that even his magic won't help him!"

The two massive orcs holding onto Rhonin pulled him forward with such vigorous force that he thought that they would wrench his arms from the shoulder sockets. Through somewhat blurred vision, he caught a glimpse of Nekros turning to another orc.

"Double the work! Get the wagons ready! I'll deal with the queen! I want everything prepared!"

Nekros passed from Rhonin's field of vision—and another figure entered.

The goblin that the orc had called Kryll winked at Rhonin, as if both shared a secret. When the wizard opened his mouth, the malevolent little figure shook his oversized head and smiled. In his hands, the goblin clutched something tight, something that drew the human's attention.

Kryll slid one hand back just long enough for Rhonin to see what he carried.

Deathwing's medallion.

And as the guards dragged him out of the commander's chamber, it came to the worn mage that he now knew how Deathwing had garnered so much information about Grim Batol. He also knew that, whatever Nekros planned, the orc, like Rhonin, did exactly as the black dragon *wanted*.

Although at home in the forests and hills, Vereesa had to admit that, when it came to the underworld, she could not tell one tunnel from another. Her innate sense of direction seemed to fail her—either that or the fact that she had to continually duck distracted her too much. Even though trolls used these tunnels from time to time, most had been hewed out by dwarves in the days when the region around Grim Batol had served as part of a complex mining community. That meant that Rom, Gimmel, and even Falstad had little difficulty navigating them, but the tall elf had to walk bent over much of the time. Her back and legs ached, but she gritted her teeth, unwilling to show any sign of weakness among these hardy warriors. After all, Vereesa had been the one who had insisted on coming here in the first place.

Yet she finally had to ask, "Are we almost near?"

"Soon, very soon," replied Rom. Unfortunately, he had been saying that for some time now.

"This entrance," Falstad mused. "Where's it again?"

"The tunnel comes out in what used to be a transport point for the gold we mined. Ye may even see a few old tracks, if the orcs haven't melted them all down for weaponry."

"And in this way we can get inside?"

"Aye, ye can follow back along the old path even if the tracks're gone. They've some guards there, though, so it won't be easy."

Vereesa thought this over. "You mentioned dragons, too. How far above?"

"Not dragons in the sky, Lady Vereesa, but ones on the ground. That's where it gets tricky, ye might say."

"On the ground?" snorted Falstad.

"Aye, ones with damaged wings or too untrusted to let fly. Should be two on this side of the mountain."

"On the ground . . ." the dwarf from the Aerie muttered. "Be a different sort of battle . . ."

Rom suddenly paused, pointing ahead. "There 'tis, Lady Vereesa! The opening!"

The ranger squinted but even with her exceptional night vision, she could not make out the supposed opening.

Falstad apparently did. "Awful small. Be a tight fit."

"Aye, too tight for orcs and they think too tight for us, but there's a trick to it."

Still unable to see anything, Vereesa had to satisfy herself with following the dwarves. Only when they had nearly reached what seemed a dead end did she begin to notice a little bit of light filtering in from above. Stepping closer, the frustrated elf noticed a slit barely big enough to fit her sword through, much less her body.

She glanced down at the leader of the hill dwarves. "A trick to it, you say?"

"Aye! The trick is that ye must move these rocks here, carefully set by us, in order to open the gap big enough, but ye can't reach them from the outside! From there it looks to be all one rock, and it'd take the orcs powerful more time than they'd like to do the job!"

"They know you are underground, though, do they not?"

Rom's expression grew dour. "Aye, but with the dragons about, they fear little from us. The way ye must go to get inside is a dangerous one. That must be evident to ye. It frustrates us to be so close and yet be unable to rid ourselves of these cursed invaders. . . ."

For some reason she could not fathom, Vereesa sensed that the dwarven leader had not told her everything. What he had said might be true to some extent, but for some other reason his people had not made much use of this route. Had something happened in the past to make them shy away from it, or was it truly that dangerous out there?

If the latter, did the elf really want to take the risk?

She had already committed herself. If not for Rhonin, then for whatever she might do to help end this interminable war—although Vereesa still held out hope that somehow she might find the wizard alive.

"We should get started. Is there a certain pattern needed when removing the rocks from their positions?"

Rom blinked. "Lady elf, ye must wait until dark! Any sooner and ye will be sighted, sure as I stand before ye!"

"But we cannot wait that long!" Vereesa had no idea how many hours had passed since she and Falstad had been captured by the trolls, but surely only a few hours at most.

" 'Tis only an hour and a little more, Lady Vereesa! Surely that's worth ye life!"

That little of a wait? The ranger eyed Falstad.

"You were out for a very long time," he replied to her unspoken question. "For a while, I thought you dead."

The elf tried to calm herself down. "Very well. We can wait until then."

"Good!" The leader of the hill dwarves clapped his hands together. "That'll give us time to eat and rest!"

Although at first Vereesa felt too tense to even consider food, she accepted the simple fare that Gimmel offered her a few minutes later. That these struggling souls would share what little they had spoke of the depths of their compassion and camaraderie. Had the dwarves wanted to, they could have very well slain Falstad and her after having dealt with the trolls. No one outside of their group would have ever been the wiser.

Gimmel took charge of seeing to it that everyone shared equally in the provisions. Rom, after taking his portion, slowly wandered off, saying that he wished to inspect some of the side tunnels they had passed earlier for any sign of troll activity.

Falstad ate with gusto, seemingly enthused by the taste of the dried meat and fruit. Vereesa ate with less enthusiasm, dwarven fare not famous for its succulent taste in either the elven or human realms. She understood that they cured the meat in order to better preserve it, and even marveled that someone had found or grown fruit in this dismal land, but her more sensitive taste buds even now complained to her. However, the food was filling, and the ranger knew that she would need the energy.

After finishing her fare, Vereesa rose and looked around. Falstad and the other dwarves had settled in to relax, but the impatient elf needed to walk. She grimaced, thinking again how her instructor would have called her so human right now. Most elves early on outgrew their tendencies toward impatience, but some retained that trait for the rest of their lives. Those generally ended up either living beyond the homeland or taking on tasks that let them travel extensively in the name of their people. Perhaps, if she lived through this, she might choose one of those paths, maybe even visit Dalaran.

Fortunately for Vereesa, the tunnels here had been carved out somewhat higher than many of those through which she had earlier passed. For the most part, the elf managed to traverse the rocky corridors with minimal bending, even occasionally standing unhindered.

A muffled voice some distance ahead suddenly made her halt. The ranger had journeyed farther than she had intended, enough so that she might have very well dropped herself right into troll territory. With tremendous care so as not to make a sound, Vereesa drew her blade, then inched forward.

The voice did not sound like that of a troll. In fact, the nearer she moved, the more it seemed to her that she knew the speaker—but how?

"—couldn't be helped, great one! Didn't think ye wanted them to know about ye!" A pause. "Aye, an elf ranger fair of face and form, that's her." Another pause. "The other? A wild one from the Aerie. Said his mount escaped when the trolls took 'em."

Try as she might, Vereesa could not hear the other half of the conversation, but she at least knew who presently spoke. A hill dwarf, and one very much familiar to her.

Rom. So his comment about searching the tunnels had not entirely been truth. But who did he speak with and why did the elf not hear that one? Had the dwarf gone mad? Did he talk with himself?

Rom did not speak now save to acknowledge that he understood what his silent companion said. Risking discovery, Vereesa edged toward the corridor from which the dwarf's voice came. She leaned around just enough in order to observe him with one eye.

The dwarf sat on a rock, staring down into his cupped palms, from which a faint, vermilion glow radiated. Vereesa squinted, trying to see what he held.

With some difficulty, she made out a small medallion with what appeared to be a jewel in the center. Vereesa did not have to be a wizard like Rhonin to recognize an object of power, an enchanted talisman created by magic. The great elven lords utilized similar devices in order to communicate with either their counterparts or their servants.

What wizard, though, now spoke with Rom? Dwarves were not known for their fondness for magic nor, for that matter, for their fondness for the ones who wielded it.

If Rom had links to a wizard, one whom the dwarf apparently even served, why did he and his band still wander the tunnels, hoping for the day when they might be free to walk under the heavens? Surely this great spellcaster could have done something for them.

"What?" Rom suddenly blurted. "Where?"

With startling swiftness, he looked up, his gaze focusing directly on her.

Vereesa backed out of sight, but she knew her reaction had been too late. The dwarven leader had spotted her, even despite the darkness.

"Come out where I can see ye!" he called. When she hesitated, Rom added, "I know 'tis ye, Lady Vereesa. . . ."

Seeing no more reason for subterfuge, the ranger

stepped into the open. She made no attempt to sheathe her sword, not at all certain that Rom might not be a traitor to his own people, much less her.

She found him eyeing her in disappointment. "Here I thought I'd gone far away enough to avoid them sharp, elven ears! Why did ye have to come here?"

"My intent was innocent, Rom. I only needed to walk. Your intent, however, leaves many questions. . . ."

"This business is none of ye concern—eh?"

The gemstone in the medallion briefly flared, startling both of them. Rom tipped his head slightly to the side, as if again listening to the unheard speaker. If so, then he clearly did not like what he heard.

"Do ye think it wise—aye, as ye say. . . ."

Vereesa tightened her grip on her sword. "Who do you speak with?"

To her surprise, Rom held out the medallion. "He'll tell ye himself." When she did not take the proffered medallion, he added, "He's a friend, not a foe."

Still wielding the sword, the elf reached out with her free hand and gingerly took hold of the talisman. She waited for a jolt or searing heat, but the medallion actually felt cool, harmless.

My greetings to you, Vereesa Windrunner.

The words echoed in her skull. Vereesa nearly dropped the medallion, not because of the voice, but rather that the speaker knew her name. She glanced at Rom, who seemed to encourage her to converse.

Who are you? the ranger demanded, sending her own thoughts toward the unseen speaker.

Nothing happened. She glanced again at the dwarf.

"Did he say anything to ye?"

"In my mind he did. I replied the same way, but he does not answer back."

"Ye have to talk to the talisman! He'll hear ye voice as thought on his end. The same when he speaks to ye." The canine features looked apologetic. "I've no reason why 'tis so, but that's the way it works. . . ."

Returning her gaze to the medallion, Vereesa tried again. "Who are you?"

You know me through my missives to your superiors. I am Krasus of the Kirin Tor.

Krasus? That had been the name of the wizard who had arranged with the elves for Vereesa to guide Rhonin to the sea in the first place. She knew little more about him than that her masters had reacted with respect when presented with his request. Vereesa knew of few other humans who could command such from any elven lord.

"I know your name. You are also Rhonin's patron."

A pause. An *uneasy* pause if the ranger were any judge. *I am responsible for his journey.*

"You know that he may be a prisoner of the orcs?"

I do. It was not intended.

Not intended? Vereesa felt an unreasonable fury arise within her. Not intended?

His mission was to observe, after all. Nothing more.

The elf had long ago ceased believing that. "Observe from where? The dungeons of Grim Batol? Or was he to meet with the hill dwarves for some reason you have not stated?"

Another pause. Then, *The situation is far more complex than that, young one, and growing more so by the moment. Your presence, for instance, was not part of the plan. You should have turned around at the seaport.*

"I swore an oath. I felt that it extended beyond the shores of Lordaeron."

Near her, Rom wore a befuddled look. Bereft of the means by which to speak to the wizard, he could only guess at Krasus's end of the conversation and to what Vereesa's responses might refer.

Rhonin is . . . fortunate, Krasus finally replied.

"If he still lives," she nearly snapped.

Yet again, the wizard hesitated before answering. Why did he act as he did? Surely he did not care what befell Rhonin. Vereesa knew enough about the ways of the spellcasters, both human and elf, to understand that their kind ever used each other if given the opportunity. It only surprised her that Rhonin, who had seemed more clever, had fallen for this Krasus's trickery.

Yes . . . if he still lives. . . . More hesitation. *. . . then it is up to us to see what can be done to free him.*

His reply completely startled her. She had hardly expected it of him.

Vereesa Windrunner, hear me out. I have made some lapses in judgment—for great concerns—and the fate of Rhonin is one of those lapses. You intend to try to find him, do you not?

"I do."

Even in the mountain fortress of the orcs? A place of dragons, too?

"Yes."

Rhonin is fortunate to have you as a comrade . . . and I hope to be as fortunate now. I will do what I can to aid you in this formidable quest, although the physical danger will be yours, of course.

"Of *course,*" the elf wryly returned.

Please return the talisman to Rom. I would speak with him for a moment.

More than willing to part with the wizard's tool, Vereesa handed the medallion back to the dwarf. Rom took it and stared into the jewel. Occasionally he nodded his head, although clearly whatever Krasus said bothered him much.

Finally, he looked up at Vereesa. "If ye really think it necessary . . ."

She realized his words were for the wizard. A moment later, the glow from the jewel dimmed. Rom, looking not at all happy, extended the talisman to the elf.

"What is this?"

"He wants ye to have it for the journey. Here! He'll tell ye himself!"

Vereesa took the object back. Immediately Krasus's voice filled her head again. *Rom told you that I wished you to carry this?*

"Yes, but I do not want—"

Do you wish to find Rhonin? Do you wish to save him?

"Yes, but—"

I am your only hope.

She would have argued with him, but, in truth, the ranger knew that she needed aid. With only Falstad and herself, the odds already stood stacked against her.

"All right. What do we do?"

Place the talisman around your neck, then return with Rom to the others. I will guide you and your dwarven companion into the mountain . . . and to the most likely place where you might find Rhonin.

He did not offer all she needed, but enough to make her agree. Slipping the chain over her head, Vereesa let the medallion rest upon her chest.

You will be able to hear me whenever I wish it, Vereesa Windrunner.

Rom walked past her, already heading back. "Come! We're wasting time, lady elf."

As she followed, Krasus continued to talk to her. *Make no mention of what this medallion does. Do not even speak around others unless I give permission. Only Rom and Gimmel presently know my role.*

"And what is that?" she could not help muttering.

Trying to preserve a future for us all.

The elf wondered about that, but said nothing. She still did not trust the wizard, but had little other choice.

Perhaps Krasus knew that, for he added, *Hear me now, Vereesa Windrunner. I may tell you to do things you might not think in the best interests of you or those you care about. Trust that they are. There are dangers ahead you do not understand, dangers that alone you cannot face.*

And you understand them all? Vereesa thought, knowing that Krasus would not hear the question.

There is still a short period of time before the sun sets. I must attend to a matter of import. Do not depart from the tunnels until I give you the word. Farewell for now, Vereesa Windrunner.

Before she could protest, his voice had faded away. The ranger cursed under her breath. She had accepted the spellcaster's questionable aid, now she had to obey his commands. Vereesa did not like at all putting her life— not to mention Falstad's—in the hands of a wizard who commanded from the safety of his far-off tower.

Worse, the elf had just put their lives in the hands of the same wizard who had sent Rhonin on this insane journey in the *first* place . . . and seemingly left him to die.

SEVENTEEN

At some point on the journey to where the orcs intended to keep him prisoner, Rhonin had collapsed back into unconsciousness. Admittedly, he had been aided in great part by his guards, who had used every excuse to hit him or twist his arms agonizingly. The pain of his broken finger had seemed little compared to what they had done to him by the time he blacked out.

Yet now, at last, the wizard woke—and woke to the nightmare of a fiery skull with black eye sockets smiling malevolently at him.

Sheer reflex made the startled wizard attempt to pull away from the monstrous visage, but doing so only rewarded Rhonin with more agony and the discovery that his wrists and ankles had been shackled tight. Try as he might, he could not escape the near presence of the demonic horror looming above him.

The fiend, though, did not move. Gradually, Rhonin fought down his horror and studied the motionless creature closer. Far taller and broader than the human, it wore what seemed flaming bone for armor. What he had taken for a sinister smile had actually simply been due to the fact that the demonic sentinel had no flesh covering its visage. Fire surrounded it, but the mage felt no heat. Still, he suspected that if those blazing skeletal hands touched him, the results would be very, very painful indeed.

For lack of any better thought, Rhonin tried to speak to the creature. "What—who are you?"

No reply. Other than the flickering flames, the macabre figure remained motionless.

"Can you hear me?"

Nothing again.

Less fearful and more curious now, the wizard leaned forward as best his chains would let him. Suspicious, he moved one leg back and forth as best he could. Still he received no response, not even a shifting of the head toward his moving limb.

As horrific as the creature looked, it seemed less of a living thing than a statue. Although demonic in appearance, it could be no demon. Rhonin had studied golems, but had never seen one before, certainly not one constantly ablaze. Still, he could think of it as nothing else.

The wizard frowned, wondering at the golem's capabilities. In truth, he had only one way to find out . . . and, after all, the wizard needed to escape.

Trying to ignore his pain, Rhonin started to move his remaining fingers ever so slightly for a spell that would, he prayed, rid himself of the monstrous guard—

With astonishing swiftness, the fiery golem reached forward, seizing Rhonin's already maimed appendage in a grip that completely enveloped it.

A searing fire engulfed the human, but a fire within, one that burned at his very *soul*. Rhonin screamed, then screamed again. He screamed long and hard until he could scream no more.

Barely conscious, his head slumped over, he prayed for the inner fire to either end or consume him utterly.

The golem removed its hand from his.

The flames within dwindled away. Gasping, Rhonin managed to lift his head enough to look at the horrific sentinel. The golem's grotesque mockery of a face stared right back, completely indifferent to the tortures through which it had put its victim.

"Damn—damn you . . ."

Beyond the golem, a familiar chuckle made the hairs on the back of the mage's head stand on end.

"Naughty, naughty!" piped the high voice. "Play with fire, you get burned! Play with fire, you get burned!"

Rhonin tipped his head to the side—cautiously at first, then more when he saw that his monstrous companion did not react. Near the entrance stood the wiry goblin Nekros had called Kryll, the same goblin that Rhonin knew also worked for Deathwing.

In fact, Kryll even now carried the medallion with the black crystal. The wizard marveled at the goblin's arrogance. Surely Nekros would wonder why his minion still held on to Rhonin's talisman.

Kryll noticed the direction of his gaze. "Master Nekros never saw you with it, human—and we goblins are always picking up trinkets!"

There had to be more to it, though. "He's also too busy to notice, isn't he?"

"Clever, human, clever! And if you told him, he wouldn't listen! Poor, poor Master Nekros has much on his mind! Moving dragons and eggs is quite a chore, you know!"

The golem did not react at all to Kryll's presence, which did not surprise Rhonin. Unless the goblin attempted to free the prisoner, it would leave Kryll alone.

"So you serve Deathwing . . ."

A frown momentarily escaped the creature. "His bidding I've done . . . yes. For very, very long . . ."

"Why've you come here? I've served your master's purpose, haven't I? I played his fool well, didn't I?"

This, for some reason, cheered Kryll up again. His toothy smile wider than ever, he replied, "No greater fool could there have been, for you played one for more than the dark lord. Played you one for me, too, human!"

Rhonin could scarce believe him. "How did I do that? In what way did I serve *you*, goblin?"

"In much the same, much the same, as you did the dark lord—who thinks a goblin so low as to serve any master without reason of his own!" A hint of what had to be bitterness escaped Kryll. "But I've served enough, I have!"

Rhonin frowned. Could the mad little creature mean what the wizard thought he meant? "You plan to betray even the dragon? How?"

The grotesque goblin fairly hopped in glee. "Poor, poor Master Nekros is in such a state! Dragons to move, eggs to move, and stinking orcs to march around! Little time to think if that's what others actually want him to do! Might've thought more, but now that the Alliance surely invades from the west, can't be bothered! Has to act! Has to be an orc, you know!"

"You're not making any sense. . . ."

"Fool!" More laughter from the goblin. "You brought me this!" He held up the medallion, then gave Rhonin a false frown. "Broken in fall—so Lord Deathwing thinks!"

As the prisoner watched, Kryll began peeling away at the stone in the center. After a few moments of effort, the gem popped out into the wiry goblin's hand. He held it up for Rhonin to see. "And with it—no more Deathwing. . . ."

Rhonin could scarcely believe him. "No more *Deathwing?* You hope to use that stone to bring him down?"

"Or make him serve Kryll! Yes, perhaps he shall serve me." An exhalation of pure hatred escaped Kryll. ". . . and no more toadying for the reptile! No more being his lackey! I planned long and hard for this, I did, waiting and waiting and watching for when he'll be most vulnerable, yes!"

Fascinated despite himself, the captured spellcaster blurted, "But how?"

Kryll backed toward the entrance. "Nekros will provide the way, not that he knows . . . and this?" He tossed the stone into the air, then caught it again. "It is a *part* of the dark lord, human! A scale turned to stone by his own magic! It must be so for the medallion to work! You know what it means to hold a part of a dragon?"

Rhonin's thoughts raced. What had he once heard? "'To bear some bit of the greatest of the leviathans is to have a hold on their power.' But that's never been done! You need tremendous magic yourself to make it work! Where—"

The golem reacted to his sudden agitation. The ghoulish jaws opened and the skeletal hand started to reach for Rhonin. The wizard immediately froze, not even breathing.

The fiery form paused, but did not withdraw. Rhonin continued to hold his breath, praying that the monstrosity would back away.

Kryll chuckled at his predicament. "But you're busy now, human! So sorry to overstay! Wanted to tell *someone* of my glory—someone who'll be dead soon enough, eh?" The goblin hopped away. "Must go! Nekros will need my guidance again, yes, he will!"

Rhonin could hold his breath no longer. He exhaled, hoping that his hesitation had been enough.

A mistake.

The golem reached for him—and all thought of the traitorous little Kryll vanished as the fires once more consumed Rhonin from within.

Darkness came all too slowly and yet in some ways too quickly for Vereesa. As Krasus had directed, she had told no one about the medallion's purpose and, at further urging from Rom, had secreted it as best she could within her garments. Her travel cloak, well-worn by this point, had managed to obscure it for the most part, although anyone who looked closely would have at least been able to make out the chain.

Shortly after their return to the party, Rom had taken Gimmel aside and spoken with him. The elf had noticed both briefly look her way. Rom evidently wanted his second to also know of Krasus's decision and, judging by the other dwarf's falling expression, Gimmel had not liked it any more than his chieftain.

The moment the light through the hole vanished, the dwarves began to methodically remove the stones. Vereesa saw no reason why this rock or that one had to be taken away before another, but Rom's people were adamant. She finally settled back, trying not to think of all the time wasted.

As the last of the stones were removed, the wizard's voice, sounding oddly haggard at first, echoed in her head.

The way out . . . is it open, Vereesa Windrunner?

She had to turn away and pretend to cough in order to mumble, "Just finished."

Then you may proceed. Once outside, remove the talisman from wherever it is you have hidden it. That will enable me to see what lies ahead. I will speak no more until you and the Aerie dwarf are out of the tunnels.

As she turned back, Falstad came up to her. "You ready, my elven lady? The hill dwarves want to be rid of us quickly, seems to me."

In fact, Rom stood by the entrance even now, his dimly seen form impatiently gesturing for the pair to climb out into the open. Vereesa and Falstad hurried past him, picking their way up to the widened hole as best they could. The ranger's foot slipped once, but she managed to regain her ground. Above her, the wind beckoned her on. She had no love for the underworld and hoped that circumstances would not send her back there soon.

Falstad, who had reached the top first, now extended a strong hand to help her up. With easy effort, he lifted her high, then set her standing next to him.

The instant the two exited, the dwarves began filling up the hole. It dwindled rapidly inside even as Vereesa got her bearings.

"So what do we do now?" asked Falstad. "Climb up that?"

He indicated the base of the mountain, even in the dark of night clearly a sheer rock face for the first several hundred feet up. Try as she might, the elf could not see any immediate opening, which puzzled her. Rom had led her to believe that they would see it almost immediately.

She turned to call down to him, only to discover that barely any sign of the hole remained. Vereesa knelt, then put an ear by the small gap. She could hear nothing at all.

"Forget them, my elven lady. They've gone back into hiding." Falstad's tone revealed a hint of contempt for his hill cousins.

Nodding, the elf finally recalled Krasus's instructions. Pulling her cloak aside, she removed the medallion from hiding, placing it squarely on her chest. Vereesa assumed that the wizard would be able to see in the dark, else he would be of little aid to them now.

"What's that?"

"Help . . . I hope." Krasus might have warned her not to tell anyone, but surely he did not expect her to leave Falstad guessing. The dwarf might think her mad if she started talking to herself.

Everything is quite visible, the wizard announced, causing her to start. *Thank you.*

"What's wrong? Why did you jump?"

"Falstad, you know that the Kirin Tor sent Rhonin on a mission?"

"Aye, and not the foolish one he mentioned, either. Why?"

"This medallion is from the wizard who chose him, who sent him on his true quest—part of which, I think, required Rhonin to enter the mountain."

"For what reason?" He did not sound at all surprised.

"That has not been made completely clear to me so far. As for this medallion, it enables one of those wizards, Krasus, to speak with me."

"But I can't hear anything."

"That, unfortunately, is how it works."

"Typical wizardry," the dwarf remarked, using the same tone of voice he had used when commenting on his hill cousins' deficiencies.

You had best move on, suggested Krasus. *Time is, as they say, of the essence.*

"Did something just happen to you? You jumped again!"

"As I said, you cannot hear him, but I can. He wants us to move on. He says he can guide us!"

"He can see?"

"Through the crystal."

Falstad walked up to the medallion, thrusting a finger at the stone. "I swear by the Aerie that if you play us false, my ghost'll hunt you down, spellcaster! I swear it!"

Tell the dwarf our goals are similar.

Vereesa repeated the statement to Falstad, who grudgingly accepted it. The elf, too, had reservations, ones she kept to herself. Krasus had said that their goals were "similar." That did not mean that they were one and the same.

Despite those thoughts, she passed on Krasus's first instructions to the letter, assuming that he would at least get them inside. His directions seemed peculiar at first, for they forced the pair to circumnavigate part of the mountain in a manner that seemed far too time-consuming. However, the wizard then led them along an easier path that quickly brought them to a tall but narrow cave mouth that Vereesa assumed *had* to be their way in. If not, then she would certainly have a word with their dubious guide.

An old dwarven mine, Krasus said. *The orcs think it leads nowhere.*

Vereesa studied it as best she could in the dark. "Why have Rom and his people not used it if it leads inside?"

Because they have been patiently waiting.

She wanted to ask what they waited for, but suddenly Falstad grabbed at her arm.

"Hear that!" the gryphon-rider whispered. "Something coming!"

They backed behind an outcropping—just in time. A fearsome shape strode purposefully toward the area of the cave, hissing as it came. Vereesa noted a draconic head peering around, red orbs faintly glowing in the night.

"And there's an even better reason why they've not used that way before," Falstad muttered. "Knew it was too good to be true!"

The dragon's head stiffened. The beast turned toward the general direction of the two.

You must remain silent. A dragon's ears can be very sharp.

The elf did not bother to relay that unnecessary knowledge. Gripping her sword, she watched as the behemoth took a few steps toward where they hid. Not nearly so great in size as Deathwing, but nonetheless large enough to dispatch her and Falstad with ease.

Wings suddenly stretched behind the head—wings that, with her night vision, the ranger could see had developed malformed. Small wonder this dragon acted as guard dog for the orcs.

And where was its handler, for that matter? The orcs never left a dragon alone, even one cursed never to fly.

A barked command quickly answered that question. From far behind the beast came a floating torch that gradually revealed itself to be in the hand of a hulking orc. In his other hand he carried a sword nearly as long as Vereesa. The guard yelled something to the dragon, who hissed furiously. The orc repeated his order.

Slowly, the beast began to turn from where the pair hid. Vereesa held her breath, hoping that the warrior and his hound would hurry off.

At that moment, the gem in the medallion suddenly flared so bright it lit up the entire area around the out-cropping.

"Smother that!" Falstad whispered.

The ranger tried, but it was already too late. Not only did the dragon turn back, but this time the orc reacted, too. Torch and blade before him, he started toward their hiding place. The crimson leviathan stalked behind him, ready to move at his command.

Remove the medallion from around your neck, Krasus commanded. *Be prepared to throw it in the direction of the dragon.*

"But—"

Do it.

Quickly removing the talisman, Vereesa readied it in her hand. Falstad glanced at his companion, but held his tongue.

The orc drew nearer. Alone, he represented enough of a challenge, but with the dragon at his side, the ranger and her companion had little hope.

Tell the dwarf to step out, reveal himself.

"He wants you to go out there, Falstad," she muttered, not sure why she even bothered to tell the dwarf such folly.

"Would he prefer I walk into the mouth of the dragon or just lie down in front of the beast and let it gnaw on me at its leisure?"

There is little time.

Again she repeated the wizard's words. Falstad blinked, took a deep breath, and nodded. Stormhammer ready, he slipped around Vereesa and past the protection of the rocks.

The dragon roared. The orc grunted, tusked mouth widening in an anticipatory grin.

"Dwarf!" he growled. "Good! Was gettin' bored out here! You'll make good sport before you're fed to Zarasz here! He's been feelin' hungry!"

" 'Tis you and yours who'll make for good sport, pig-face! I was getting a little cool out here! Crushing in your thick skull will warm my bones up, all right!"

Both orc and beast advanced.

Throw the talisman at the dragon now. Be certain it lands near the vicinity of his mouth.

The command sounded so absurd that at first Vereesa doubted that she had heard correctly. Then it occurred to her that perhaps Krasus could cast a spell through the medallion, one that would at least incapacitate the savage creature.

Throw it now, before your friend loses his life.

Falstad! The ranger leapt out, surprising both sentries. She took one fast glance at the orc—then, with expert aim, threw the medallion at the mouth of the dragon.

The dragon stretched forward with equally amazing accuracy, catching the talisman in his jaws.

Vereesa swore. Surely Krasus had not expected that.

However, a peculiar thing happened, one that caused all three warriors to pause. Instead of either swallowing or tossing aside the medallion, the leviathan stood still, cocking his head. In his mouth, a red aura erupted, but one that seemed to have no ill effect on the dragon.

To everyone's bewilderment, the behemoth *sat down*.

Not at all pleased by this turn, the orc shouted a command. The dragon, however, did not seem to hear him, instead looking as if he listened to another voice far away.

"Your hound's found a toy to play with, orc!" mocked Falstad. "Looks like you'll have to fight your own battles for once!"

In response, the tusked warrior thrust his torch forward, nearly setting the dwarf's beard ablaze. Cursing, Falstad brought his stormhammer into play, coming close to crushing the orc's outstretched arm. That, in turn, enabled the guard to make a jab with his sword.

Vereesa stood undecided. She wanted to help Falstad, but did not know if at any moment the dragon might suddenly break out of his peculiar trance and rejoin his handler. If that happened, someone had to be ready to face the beast.

The dwarf and his adversary traded blows, the torch and sword evening matters against the hammer. The orc tried to drive Falstad back, no doubt hoping that his foe would trip on the highly uneven ground.

The elf took one more look at the dragon. He still had his head cocked to the side. The eyes were open, but they seemed to be staring off.

Steeling herself, Vereesa turned from the leviathan and headed to Falstad's rescue. If the dragon attacked them, so be it. She could not risk letting her comrade die.

The orc sensed her coming, for as she thrust at him, he swung the torch around. Vereesa gasped as the flames came within scant inches of her face.

Yet her coming forced the guard to fight on two fronts, and because of this, his attempt to burn her had left him open. Falstad needed no urging to take advantage of it. The hammer came down.

A guttural cry from the orc nearly smothered the sound of bone cracking. The sword slipped from the tusked warrior's quivering hand. The hammer had shattered the arm at the elbow, leaving the entire arm useless.

Fueled by both pain and fury, the crippled guard shoved the torch into Falstad's chest. The dwarf stumbled back, trying to beat out the fires smoldering on both his beard and chest. His brutish foe tried to advance, but the elf cut him off.

"Little elf!" he snarled. "Burn you, too!"

Between the torch and his own lengthy arm, his reach far exceeded her own. Vereesa ducked twice as the fire came at her. She had to end this quickly, before the orc managed to catch her off guard.

When he swung at her next, she aimed not for him, but rather for the torch. That meant letting the flames come perilously near. The orc's savage face twisted into an expression of anticipation as he thrust.

The tip of her sword dug into the wood, ripping it from the startled sentry's fingers. Her success far better than expected, Vereesa fell forward, pushing the torch with her.

The fire caught the orc full in the face. He roared in pain, brushing the torch away. The damage had been done, though. His eyes, nose, and most of his upper countenance had been seared by the heat. He could no longer see.

Acting with some guilt, but knowing she had to silence him, Vereesa ran the blind orc through, cutting off his pained cries.

"By the Aerie!" snapped Falstad. "Thought I'd never put myself out!"

Still gasping, the elf managed, "Are—are you—all right?"

"Saddened at the loss of so many good years' beard growth, but I'll get over it! What's the matter with our overgrown hound there?"

The dragon had dropped down on all fours now, as if preparing to sleep. The medallion still lay in his mouth, but, as they watched, he gently dropped it to the ground before him—then looked at the pair as if expecting one of them to retrieve it.

"Does he want us to do what I think he wants us to do, my elven lady?"

"I am afraid so . . . and I know by whose suggestion, too." She started toward the expectant behemoth.

"You're not seriously going to try to pick it up, are you?"

"I have no choice."

As the ranger neared, the dragon peered down at her. Dragons were rumored to see very well in the dark, and had an even greater sense of smell. This close, Vereesa would surely not escape.

Using the edge of her cloak, she gingerly picked up the talisman. Left so long in the dragon's mouth, it dripped with saliva. With some disgust, the elf wiped it off as best she could on the ground.

The gem suddenly glowed.

The way is clear, came Krasus's monotone voice. *Best you hurry before others come.*

"What did you do to this monster?" she muttered.

I spoke with him. He understands now. Hurry. Others will eventually come.

The dragon understood? Vereesa wanted to ask the wizard more, but knew by now that he would give her no satisfactory answer. Still, he had somehow done the impossible, and for that she had to thank him.

She replaced the chain around her neck, letting the talisman once more dangle free. To Falstad, the ranger simply said, "We are to move on."

Still shaking his head at the sight of the dragon, the dwarf followed after her.

Krasus remained true to his word. He guided them through the abandoned mine, leading them at last down a passage that Vereesa would have never thought led the way into the mountain fortress. It forced the pair to climb a tight and quite precarious side passage, but at last they entered the upper level of a fairly spacious underground cavern.

A cavern filled with scurrying orcs.

From the ledge on which they crouched, they could see the fearsome warriors packing away material and filling wagons. On one side, a handler put a young dragon through the paces, while a second handler looked to be preparing for imminent departure.

"Looks as if they're all planning to leave!"

It seemed so to her as well. She leaned over for a better look.

It worked . . .

Krasus had spoken, but Vereesa knew immediately from his tone that his words had only been meant for himself. Likely he did not even know that he had said anything out loud. Had he planned somehow to make the orcs depart Grim Batol? Despite her surprise at the wizard's handling of the dragon, the elf doubted that he could have *this* much influence.

The one dragon readied for flight suddenly moved toward the main mouth of the cavern. His handler finished strapping himself in and readied for flight. Unlike in combat, this dragon was laden with supplies.

She leaned back again, thinking. While in many ways the abandoning of Grim Batol meant great things to the Alliance, it left too many questions and more than a few worries. What need would the orcs have for Rhonin if they departed here? Surely they would not bother to bring an enemy wizard along.

And did they really intend to move *all* the dragons?

She had waited for Krasus to give them their next

steps, but the wizard remained eerily silent. Vereesa looked around, trying to decide by which path they might quickest find where Rhonin was being held . . . assuming all along that he had not already been slain.

Falstad put a hand on her shoulder. "Down there! See him?"

She followed his gaze—and saw the goblin. He scurried along another cavern ledge, heading for an opening far to their left.

" 'Tis Kryll! Can be no other!"

The elf, too, felt certain of it. "He knows his way around here well, it seems!"

"Aye! That's why he led us to their allies, the trolls!"

But why had the goblin not let them be captured by the orcs? Why turn them over instead to the murderous trolls? Surely the orcs would have been interested in questioning the pair.

Enough wondering. She had an idea. "Krasus! Can you show us how to get down to where that goblin is heading?"

No voice echoed in her head.

"Krasus?"

"What's wrong?"

"The wizard seems not to be responding."

Falstad snorted. "So we're on our own?"

"For now, it seems." She straightened. "The ledge over there. It should take us where we want to go. The orcs would want the tunnels to be fairly consistent."

"So we go on without the wizard. Good. I like that better."

Vereesa nodded grimly. "Yes, we go on without the wizard—but not our little friend Kryll."

EIGHTEEN

T oo slow. They were much too slow.

Nekros shoved a peon forward with an angry grunt, urging the worthless, lower-caste orc to quicker work. The other orc cringed, then scurried off with his burden.

The lower-caste orcs were useless for anything but menial labor, and right now Nekros found them wanting even in that one skill. As it was, he had been forced to make the warriors work alongside them in order to get everything accomplished by dawn. Nekros had actually considered leaving in the dead of night, but that had no longer been possible and he certainly had not wanted to wait another day. Each day no doubt brought invasion nearer, although his scouts, clearly blind to reality, insisted that they so far had found no more traces of an advance force, much less an army. Never mind that Alliance warriors on gryphons had already been sighted, a wizard had found his way into the mountain, and the most dire of all dragons now served the enemy. Simply because the scouts could not see them did not mean that the humans and their allies were not already nearing Grim Batol.

Still in the midst of trying to get the menials to understand the urgency of their packing, the maimed orc did not at first notice his chief handler come up. Only when he heard an uncomfortable clearing of the throat did Nekros turn.

"Speak, Brogas! Why do you skulk like one of these wretches?"

The slightly stout younger orc grimaced. His tusks tended to turn down at the sides, giving his already frowning face an even more dour look. "The male . . . Nekros, I think he dies soon!"

More bad news and some of the worst possible! "Let's see this!"

They hurried as fast as they could, Brogas carefully maintaining a pace that would not make his superior's handicap more evident. Nekros, however, had greater concerns on his mind. In order to continue the breeding program, he needed a female *and* a male. Without one or the other, he had nothing . . . and Zuluhed would not like that.

They came at last to the cavern in which had been housed the eldest and only surviving consort of Alexstrasza. Tyranastrasz had surely been a most impressive sight when compared to other dragons. Nekros gathered that at one point the old crimson male had even rivaled Deathwing in size and power, although perhaps that had simply been legend. Nonetheless, the consort still filled the massive chamber quite ably, so much so that at first the orc leader could not believe that such a giant could possibly be ill.

Yet the moment he heard the dragon's unsteady breathing, he knew the truth. Tyran, as all called him, had suffered several seizures in the past year. The orc had once assumed that dragons were immortal, only dying when slain in battle; but he had discovered over time that they had other limitations, such as disease. Something within this venerable behemoth had stricken Tyran with a slow but fatal ailment.

"How long's the beast been like that?"

Brogas swallowed. "Since last night, on and off . . . but he looked better a few hours ago!"

Nekros whirled on his handler. "Fool! Should've told me sooner!"

He almost struck the other orc, then considered how useless it would have been to have had the knowledge. He had suspected for some time he would lose the elder dragon, but had just not wanted to admit it.

"What do we do, Nekros? Zuluhed'll be furious! Our skulls'll sit atop poles!"

Nekros frowned. He, too, had conjured up that image in his mind . . . and not liked it one bit, of course. "We've no choice! Get him prepared for moving! He comes, dead or alive! Let Zuluhed do what he will!"

"But, Nekros—"

Now the one-legged orc *did* strike his subordinate. "Simpering fool! Obey orders!"

Subdued, Brogas nodded and rushed off, no doubt to beat the lesser handlers while they worked to fulfill Nekros's commands. Yes, Tyran would be coming with the rest, whether or not he still breathed. At the very least he would serve as a decoy . . . .

Taking a step nearer, Nekros studied the great male in detail. The mottled scales, the inconsistent breathing, the lack of movement . . . no, Alexstrasza's consort did not have long left in the world—

"Nekros . . ." rumbled the Dragonqueen's voice suddenly. "Nekros . . . I smell you near. . . ."

Willing to use any excuse to not think of what Tyran's passing might mean to his own skin, the heavyset orc made his way to the female's chamber. As his usual precaution, he reached into his belt pouch and kept one hand on the *Demon Soul*.

Through slitted eyes, Alexstrasza watched him enter. She, too, had seemed somewhat ill of late, but Nekros refused to believe that he would lose her, too. More likely she knew that her last consort might soon be dead. Nekros wished one of the other two had survived; they had been much younger, more virile, than Tyran.

"What now, o queen?"

"Nekros, why do you persist in this madness?"

He grunted. "Is that all you wanted of me, female? I've more important things to do than answer your silly questions!"

The dragon snorted. "All your efforts will only lead to your death. You have the chance to save yourself and your men, but you will not take it!"

"We're not craven, backstabbing scum like Orgrim Doomhammer! Dragonmaw clan fights to the bloody end, even if it be our own!"

"Trying to flee to the north? That is how you fight?"

Nekros Skullcrusher brought out the *Demon Soul*. "There're things you don't even know, ancient one! There're times when flight leads to fight!"

Alexstrasza sighed. "There is no getting through to you, is there, Nekros?"

"At last you learn."

"Tell me this, then. What were you doing in Tyran's chamber? What ails him now?" Both the dragon's eyes and tone of voice were filled with her concern for her consort.

"Nothing for you to worry your head about, o queen! Better to think of yourself. We'll be moving you soon. Behave, and it'll be much more painless. . . ."

With that said, he pocketed the *Demon Soul* and left her. The Dragonqueen called his name once, no doubt to again implore him to tell her about the health of her mate, but Nekros could no longer spend time worrying about dragons—at least not *red* ones.

Even though the column would likely leave Grim Batol before the Alliance invaders reached it, the orc commander knew with absolute certainty that one creature would still arrive in time to wreak havoc. Deathwing would come. The black leviathan would be there come the morning—if only because of one thing.

Alexstrasza . . . The black dragon would come for his rival.

"Let them all come!" snarled the orc to himself. *"All* of them! All I need is for the dark one to be first. . . ." He patted the pouch where he kept the *Demon Soul*. ". . . and then Deathwing will do the rest!"

Consciousness returned to Rhonin, albeit barely at first. Yet, even as weakened as he felt, the wizard immediately remained still, recalling what had happened to him the last time. He did not want the golem sending him back to oblivion—especially since Rhonin feared that this time he would not come back.

As his strength returned, the imprisoned spellcaster cautiously opened his eyes.

The fiery golem was nowhere to be seen.

Stunned, Rhonin lifted his head, eyes opening wide.

No sooner had he done this when suddenly the very air before him flared and hundreds of minute balls of fire exploded into being. The fiery orbs swirled around, quickly combining, forming a vaguely humanoid shape that sharpened in the space of a breath.

The massive golem re-formed in all its grotesque glory.

Expecting the worst, Rhonin lowered his head, shutting his eyes at the same time. He waited for the magical creature's horrific touch . . . and waited and waited. At last, when curiosity finally got the better of his fear, the wary mage slowly, carefully, opened one eye just enough to see.

The golem had vanished again.

So. Rhonin remained under its watchful gaze even if now he could not see it. Nekros clearly played games with him, although perhaps Kryll had somehow arranged this latest trickery. The wizard's hopes faded.

Perhaps it would be better this way. After all, had he not thought that his death might better serve those who had died because of him? Would that not at last satisfy his own feelings of guilt?

Unable to do anything else, Rhonin hung there, paying no attention to the passage of minutes nor the continual sounds of the orcs finishing their preparations for departure. When he chose to, Nekros would return and either take the wizard with him or, more likely, question Rhonin one last time before executing him.

And Rhonin could do nothing.

At some point after he closed his eyes again, weariness took hold and led him into a more gentle slumber. Rhonin dreamed of many things—dragons, ghouls, dwarves . . . and Vereesa. Dreaming of the elf soothed some of his troubled thoughts. He had known her only a short time, but more and more he found her face popping up in his thoughts. In another time and place, perhaps he could have gotten to know her better.

The elf became the center point of his dreaming, so much so that Rhonin could even hear her voice. She called his name over and over, at first longingly, then, when he did not reply, with more urgency—

"Rhonin!" Her voice grew distant, just a whisper now, yet somehow it also seemed to have more substance to it.

"Rhonin!"

This time her call actually stirred him from his dreams, pulled him from his slumber. Rhonin fought at first, having no desire at all to return to the reality of his cell and his imminent death.

"He doesn't answer. . . ." muttered another voice, not at all as soft and musical as Vereesa's. The wizard vaguely recognized it, and the knowledge brought him further toward a waking state.

"Perhaps that is how they can keep him secure with only chains and no bars," the elf replied. *"It looks as if you told the truth. . . ."*

"I would not lie to you, kind mistress! I would not lie to you!"

And that last, shrill voice did what the other two could not. Rhonin threw aside the last vestiges of sleep . . . and just barely kept himself from shouting out.

"Let's get this done, then," Falstad the dwarf muttered. The footsteps that followed indicated immediately to the wizard that the dwarf and others headed toward him.

He opened his eyes.

Vereesa and Falstad did indeed enter the chamber, the elf's arresting visage full of concern. The ranger had her sword drawn, and around her neck she wore what almost looked like the medallion Deathwing had given Rhonin, save that this one had a stone of crimson where the other had been as black as the soul of the sinister leviathan.

Beside her, the dwarf had his hammer sheathed on his

back. For a weapon, he carried a long dagger—the tip of which presently touched the throat of a snarling *Kryll*.

The sight of the first two, especially Vereesa, filled Rhonin with hope—

Behind the tiny rescue party, the fire golem re-formed in complete silence.

"Look out!" the dismayed wizard shouted, his voice raspy from so many previous screams.

Vereesa and Falstad dropped to opposing sides as the monstrous skeletal figure reached for them. Tossed by the dwarf, Kryll slid toward the very wall where Rhonin had been chained. The goblin swore as he bounced hard against the rock.

Falstad rose first, throwing his dagger at the golem— who completely ignored the blade that clattered against the bony armor—then pulling free his stormhammer. He swung at the inhuman sentinel even as Vereesa leapt to her feet to join in the attack.

Still weak, Rhonin could not do anything at the moment but watch. The ranger and the dwarf came at their fiendish adversary from opposing directions, trying to force the golem into a fatal mistake.

Unfortunately, Rhonin doubted that they could even slay the creature by mortal means.

Falstad's first swing pushed the monster back a step, but on the second one, the golem seized hold of the upper handle. The gryphon-rider became embroiled in a horrible tug-of-war as the golem tried to pull him toward it.

"The *hands!*" the mage gasped. "Watch the hands!"

Burning, fleshless fingers grabbed for Falstad as he came within range. The desperate dwarf let go of his precious hammer, tumbling out of immediate reach of his foe.

Vereesa darted forward, thrusting. Her elven blade did little against the macabre armor, which easily deflected it. The golem turned toward her, then threw the stormhammer in her direction.

The ranger nimbly leapt aside, but now she found herself the only one with any sort of defense against the inhuman guard. Vereesa thrust twice more, nearly losing her blade the second time. The golem, apparently impervious to edged weapons, attempted with each attack to seize the sword by the blade.

His friends were losing . . . and Rhonin had done nothing to help.

It only grew worse. Having regained his balance, Falstad started for his hammer.

The mouth of the ghoulish warrior opened incredibly wide—

A fearsome spout of black fire nearly engulfed Falstad. Only at the last did he manage to roll away, but not before his clothing had been singed.

That left Vereesa alone and in the direct path of the golem. Frustration tore at Rhonin. She would die if he did nothing. They *all* would die if he did nothing.

He had to free himself. Summoning his strength as best he could, the battered spellcaster called up a spell. With the golem occupied, Rhonin had the chance to concentrate on his efforts. All he needed was a moment more. . . .

Success! The shackles holding his limbs burst open, clattering against the rocky wall. Gasping, Rhonin stretched his arms once, then focused on the golem—

A heavy weight struck him on the upper back. An intense pressure on Rhonin's throat cut off all air.

"Naughty, naughty wizard! Don't you know you're supposed to *die?*"

Kryll had a hold around Rhonin's throat that stunned the wizard completely. He had known that goblins were far stronger than they appeared, but Kryll's might bordered on the fantastic.

"That's it, human . . . give in . . . fall to your knees. . . ."

Rhonin almost wanted to do just that. The lack of air had his mind spinning, and that, coupled with the tortures he had suffered at the hands of the golem, nearly did him in. Yet, if he fell, so, too, would Vereesa and Falstad . . . .

Concentrating, he reached a hand back to the murderous goblin.

With a high shriek, Kryll released his hold and dropped to the floor. Rhonin fell against the wall, trying to get his breath back and hoping that Kryll would not take advantage of his weakness.

He need not have worried. Burned on his arm, the goblin hopped away from Rhonin, cursing. "Foul, foul wizard! Damn your magic ways! Will leave you to my friend here, leave you to feel his tender touch!"

Kryll hopped toward the exit, laughing darkly at the intruders' fate.

The golem paused in his struggle with Vereesa and the dwarf, his deathly gaze shifting to the escaping Kryll. His jaws opened—

A burst of ebony fire shot forth from the skeletal maw, completely enveloping the unsuspecting goblin.

With a mercifully short cry, Kryll perished in a ball of flame, so quickly incinerated by the magical fire that only ash drifted to the floor . . . ash and the ruined medallion the goblin had carried in his belt pouch.

"He slew the little wretch!" Falstad marveled.

"And we are certain to be next!" reminded the elf. "Even though I feel no heat, my blade has half turned to slag from the flames surrounding his body, and I doubt I can dodge him much longer!"

"Aye, if I could get my hammer I might be able to do something, but—look out!"

Again the golem unleashed a blast, but this time at the ceiling. The furious column of flame did more than heat the rock, though. As it struck, the flames *shattered* the ceiling, sending massive chunks down on the trio.

One caught Vereesa on the arm, hitting with such violence that the ranger dropped to the floor. The torrent forced Falstad away from her and prevented Rhonin from even trying to make any move in her direction.

The fiery golem focused on the fallen elf. The jaws opened again—

"*No!*" Utilizing raw will, Rhonin countered, throwing up a shield as powerful as any he had ever created.

The dark flames struck the invisible barrier with their full fury . . . and rebounded back at the golem.

Rhonin would not have expected the creature's own weapon to have any effect on it, but the flames not only took hold of their wielder, they coursed over him with hunger. A roar erupted from the golem's fleshless throat, an ungodly, inhuman roar.

The monstrous creature quivered—then exploded, unleashing magical forces of hurricane proportion into the tiny mountain chamber.

Unable to withstand those forces, what remained of the ceiling collapsed atop the defenders.

* * *

In the dark of night, the dragon Deathwing flew east across the sea. Swifter than the wind, he headed toward Khaz Modan and, more significantly, Grim Batol. The dragon actually smiled to himself, a sight that any other creature would have turned from in mortal terror. All went as intended in every venture. His plans for the humans had moved along so very smoothly. Why, just hours ago, he had received a missive from Terenas, outlining how just a week after "Lord Prestor's" coronation, word would go out that the new monarch of Alterac would be wedding the king of Lordaeron's young daughter the day she turned of age. Just a few scant years—the blink of an eye in the life of a dragon—and he would be in place to set about the annihilation of the humans. After them, the elves and dwarves, older and without the vigor of humanity, would fall like the leaves on a dying tree.

He would savor those days well, come the future. Now, however, Deathwing attended to a more immediate and even more gratifying situation. The orcs prepared to abandon their mountain fortress. By dawn, they would be moving the wagons out, heading for the Horde's last stronghold in Dun Algaz.

With them would go the dragons.

The orcs expected an Alliance invasion from the west. At the very least, they expected gryphon-riders and wizards . . . and one black giant. Deathwing had no intention of disappointing Nekros Skullcrusher on that account. From Kryll, he knew that the one-legged orc had something in mind. The dragon looked forward to seeing what folly the puny creature planned. He suspected he knew, but it would be interesting to find out if an orc could have an original thought for a change.

The dim outline of Khaz Modan's shore came up on the horizon. Better equipped to see in the dark, Deathwing banked slightly, heading more to the north. Only a couple of hours remained until sunrise. He would have plenty of time to reach his chosen perch. From there, the dragon would be able to watch and wait, choose just the right moment.

Alter the course of the future.

Another dragon flew, too, a dragon who had not flown in many years. The sensations of unfettered flight thrilled him, yet they also served to remind just how out of practice he had become. What should have been completely natural, what should have been an inherent part of his very being, seemed out of place.

Korialstrasz the dragon had been Krasus the wizard for far too long.

Had it been daylight already, those who would have witnessed his passing would have noted a dragon of great, if not gargantuan, proportions, larger than most, but certainly not one of the five Aspects. A brilliant blood-red and sleek of form, in his youth Korialstrasz had been considered quite handsome for his kind. Certainly he had caught the eye of his queen. Swift, deadly, and quick of thought in battle, the crimson giant had also been among her greatest defenders, protecting the honor of the flight and becoming her foremost servant when it came to dealing with the new, upcoming races.

Even before the capture of his beloved Alexstrasza, he had spent most of his later years in the form of the wizard Krasus, generally only reverting to his true self when secretly visiting her. As one of her younger consorts, he had not held the position of authority that Tyranastrasz had, but Korialstrasz had known that he had yet held a special place in the heart of his queen. That had been why he had volunteered in the first place to be her primary agent among the most promising and diverse of the new races—humanity—helping to guide it to maturity whenever possible.

Alexstrasza no doubt thought him dead. After her capture and the subjugation of the rest of the dragonflight, he had seen his own subterfuge as the only way to continue the struggle. Return fully to the guise of Krasus and aid the Alliance in its war against the orcs. It had disheartened him to have to assist in the death of his own blood, but the young drakes raised by the Horde knew little of their kind's past glory, rarely ever living long enough to grow out of their bloodlust and begin to learn the wisdom that had ever truly been a dragon's legacy. In aiding the elf and dwarf in their bid for entry into the mountain, he had been fortunate enough to speak into the mind of one of those youngsters, calming the drake and explaining what had to be done. That the other dragon had listened had been heartening. Some hope remained for at least one.

But so much still had to be done, enough so that, once more, Korialstrasz had turned his back on the mortals and left them to their own devices. The moment he had viewed the wagons through the medallion, heard the barked order from the orc officers, he had realized that all for which he had struggled was about to come to fruition. The orcs had taken the bait and were departing from Grim Batol. They would be moving his beloved Alexstrasza into the open—where he could at last rescue her.

Even then, it would not be simple. It would require guile, timing, and, of course, pure luck.

That Deathwing lived and clearly plotted the downfall of the Lordaeron Alliance had presented itself as a new and terrible concern, one that had, for a time, threatened the upheaval of everything for which Korialstrasz had planned. Yet, from what he had discovered as Krasus, it seemed that Deathwing had become too immersed in the politics of the Alliance to even concern himself with the distant orcs and what remained of the once proud red flight of dragons. No, Deathwing played his own game of chess, with the various kingdoms as pieces. Left to his own devices, he would surely cause war and devastation among them. Fortunately, such a game required years, and so Korialstrasz felt little concern for the humans back in Lordaeron and beyond. Their situation could wait until he had freed his beloved.

However, if the fleet dragon could ignore the growing threat to the very lands he had taken under his wing, one other matter still gnawed at his thoughts until he could ignore it no longer. Rhonin—and the two who had gone in search of him—had trusted in Krasus the wizard, not knowing that to Korialstrasz the dragon, the rescue of his queen meant more than life itself. The lives of three mortals had seemed of very little consequence in comparison to that—or so he had thought until recently.

Guilt wracked the dragon. Guilt not only for his betrayal of Rhonin, but also his neglect of the elf and the dwarf after promising to guide them inside.

Rhonin had likely been slain some time ago, but perhaps it was not too late to save the other two. The crimson leviathan knew that he would not be able to concentrate on his quest until he had at least satisfied himself with doing what he could for them.

On the very tip of southwestern Khaz Modan, only a few hours from Ironforge, Korialstrasz picked out a secluded peak in the midst of the mountain chain there and alighted. He took a few moments to orient himself, then shut his eyes and focused on the medallion that he had made Rom give to the ranger, Vereesa.

Although she likely thought the stone in the center only a gem, it was, in fact, a very part of the dragon. Fashioned through magic into its present form, it had begun its existence as one of his scales. The ensorcelled scale bore properties that would have astounded any mage—if they had known how to cast dragon magic. Fortunately for Korialstrasz, few did, else he would not have risked creating the medallion in the first place. Both Rom and the elf clearly believed the gem only useful for communication purposes, and the dragon had no intention of correcting their misconceptions.

As the wind howled and snow buffeted the great behemoth, Korialstrasz folded his wings near his head, the better to shield it while he concentrated. He pictured the elf as he had seen her through the talisman. Pleasant to look at for one of her kind, and clearly concerned for Rhonin. A very capable warrior, too. Yes, perhaps she still lived, her and the dwarf from the Aeries.

"Vereesa Windrunner . . ." he quietly called. "Vereesa Windrunner!" Korialstrasz closed his eyes, trying to focus his inner sight. Curiously, he could see nothing. The medallion should have enabled him to see whatever the elf pointed it toward. Had she hidden it from view?

"Vereesa Windrunner . . . make some sound, however slight, to acknowledge that you hear me."

Still nothing.

"Elf!" For the first time, the dragon nearly lost his composure. "Elf!"

And still no reply, no image. Korialstrasz focused his full concentration on the medallion, trying to listen for any sound, even the snarls of an orc.

Nothing.

Too late . . . his sudden act of conscience had come too late to save Rhonin's rescuers, and now they, too, had perished because of the dragon's lack of thought.

As Krasus, he had played on Rhonin's guilt, played on the memories of those companions that the wizard had lost during his previous mission. It had made Rhonin quite malleable. Now, however, he began to understand just how the human had felt. Alexstrasza had always talked of the younger races in tones of caring, of nurturing, as if they, too, were her children. That care she had infected her consort with, and as Krasus he had worked hard to see to it that the humans matured properly. However, his queen's capture by the orcs had shaken his thinking to its very foundations and caused Korialstrasz to forget her teachings . . . until now.

Yet, it had still come much too late for these three.

"But it is not too late for you, my queen," the dragon rumbled. Should he survive this, he would dedicate his life to making up for his failure to Rhonin and the others. For now, though, all that mattered was the rescue of his mate. She would understand . . . he hoped.

Spreading his wings wide, the majestic red dragon took to the air, heading north.

To Grim Batol.

NINETEEN

Nekros Skullcrusher turned from the devastation, grim but determined not to let it lead him astray from his intentions.

"So much for the wizard . . ." he muttered, trying not to think of what spell the human could have possibly cast that had, in the process, also destroyed the seemingly invincible golem. Clearly very powerful, so much so that it had not only cost the wizard his life, but had brought down the mountain on an entire section of tunnels.

"Dig the body out?" asked one of the warriors.

"No. Waste of time." Nekros clutched the pouch with the *Demon Soul*, thinking ahead to the culmination of his desperate plans. "We leave Grim Batol *now*."

The other orcs followed him, most still uneasy about this sudden decision to depart the fortress but not at all enamored with the idea of staying behind—especially if the wizard's spell had weakened the remaining tunnel systems.

An incredible pressure pushed down on Rhonin's head, a pressure so immense he felt as if at any moment his skull would burst open. With some effort, he forced his eyes open, trying to see if he could find out what pressed on him and how he could quickly remove it.

Turning his blurry gaze upward, he gasped.

An avalanche of rock—literally a ton and more—floated just a foot or so above his head. A dim radiance, the only visible sign of the shield he had cast earlier, revealed the one reason why he had not been crushed to pulp.

The pressure in his head, he realized, had been some part of his mind that had managed to keep the spell intact and, thereby, saved his life. The increasing pain, however, served to tell the trapped mage that with each passing second the spell weakened.

He shifted, trying to make himself more comfortable in the hope that it would relieve some of the pressure—and felt something pressing against the bottom of his head. Rhonin carefully reached down to remove it, assuming it to be some pebble. However, the moment his fingers touched it, he felt a slight hint of magic.

Curiosity momentarily shifting his attention from the horror above him, Rhonin pulled the object near enough to see.

A black gemstone. Surely the same stone that had once been set in the center of Deathwing's medallion.

Rhonin frowned. The last time he had seen the medallion had been after Kryll's death. At the time, he had not paid any attention to the stone, his mind more concerned with the danger to Vereesa and—

Vereesa! The elf's face blossomed full into his thoughts. She and the dwarf had been farther away, protected by the initial spell, but—

He shifted, trying to see. However, as he moved, the

pressure in his head multiplied and the stones above dropped a few precious inches more.

At the same time, he heard a deep-voiced curse.

"F-Falstad?" Rhonin gasped.

"Aye . . ." came the somewhat distant reply. "I knew you lived, wizard, since we'd not been flattened, but I was beginnin' to think you'd never wake! About time!"

"Have you—is Vereesa alive?"

"'Tis hard to say. The light from this spell of yours lets me see her a little, but she's too distant for me to check! Not heard anything out of her since I woke!"

Rhonin gritted his teeth. She *had* to be alive. "Falstad! How far above you are the rocks?"

A sardonic laugh escaped his companion. "Near enough to tickle my nose, human, else I'd have slid over to check her sooner! Never thought I'd be alive at my own burial!"

The mage ignored the last, thinking about what the dwarf had said about the nearness of the avalanche. Clearly the farther the spell extended from Rhonin, the less it covered. Both Vereesa and Falstad had been protected from being crushed, but the ranger might possibly have been struck hard on the head—perhaps even slain by the deadly blow.

Yet Rhonin had to hope otherwise.

"Human—if 'tis not too much to ask—can you do *anything* for us?"

Could he rescue them? Did he have either the power or the strength remaining? He pocketed the black stone, now wholly concerned with the more desperate matter. "Give me a few moments. . . ."

"And what else would I be doing, eh?"

The pressure in the wizard's head continued to increase

at a frightening pace. Rhonin doubted his shield could last much longer, and yet he had to maintain it while attempting this second, perhaps even more complex spell.

He had to not only transport all three of them from this precarious position, but send them to a safe place. All this while his battered form cried out for recuperation.

How did the spell go? It pained him to think, but at last Rhonin summoned the words. Attempting this would draw away his concentration from the shield, though. If he took too long . . .

What choice do I have?

"Falstad, I'm going to try now. . . ."

"That would please me to no end, human! I think the rocks're already pressing against my chest!"

Yes, Rhonin, too, had noticed the shift. He definitely had to hurry.

He muttered the words, drew the power. . . .

The rocks above him shifted ominously.

Utilizing his good hand, Rhonin drew a sign.

The shield spell *failed*. Tons of stone dropped upon the trio—

—And suddenly he found himself lying on his back, staring into the cloud-covered heavens.

"Dagath's Hammer!" Falstad roared from his side. "Did you have to cut it so close?"

Despite the pain, Rhonin pushed himself up to a sitting position. The chill wind actually aided, snapping him out of his disoriented state. He looked in the dwarf's direction.

Falstad, too, sat up. The gryphon-rider had a wild look in his eyes that for once had nothing to do with battle. His visage had turned absolutely pale, something Rhonin would never have imagined of the stalwart warrior.

"Never, never, never will I crawl into another tunnel! From now on, 'tis only the sky for me! Dagath's Hammer!"

The wizard might have replied, but a groan from farther on caught his attention. Rising on unsteady feet, he struggled his way toward Vereesa's prone form. At first Rhonin wondered if he had imagined the groan—the ranger looked completely lifeless—but then Vereesa repeated it.

"She's—she's alive, Falstad!"

"Aye, you can tell that from her moaning, I'll bet! Of course she's alive! Quick, though! How does she fare?"

"Hold on . . ." Rhonin cautiously turned the elf over, studying her face, her head, and her body. She had been bruised in some places and her arm bore stains of blood, but otherwise she seemed in as good a shape as either of her companions.

While he cautiously held her head up to study a bruise at the top, Vereesa's eyes fluttered open. "R-Rhon—"

"Yes, it's me. Take it easy. I think you got struck hard on the head."

"Remember . . . remember that—" The ranger closed her eyes for a moment—then suddenly sat up, eyes flaring wide, mouth open in horror. *"The ceiling! The ceiling! It is falling in on us!"*

"No!" He took hold of her. "No, Vereesa! We're safe! We're safe. . . ."

"But the cavern ceiling . . ." The elf's expression relaxed. "No, we are not in the cave any longer . . . but where *are* we, Rhonin? How did we get here? How did we survive in the first place?"

"You remember the shield that saved us from the golem? After the monster destroyed itself, the shield held up, even when the ceiling collapsed. Its sphere of protection shrank, but it still held up enough to keep us from being crushed to death."

"Falstad! Is he—"

The dwarf came up on her other side. "'Tis all of us he's saved, my elven lady. Saved but dropped us off in the middle of nowhere!"

Rhonin blinked. Middle of nowhere? He looked around. The snowy ridge, the chill winds—growing chillier by the moment—and the incredible cloud cover all about them . . . the wizard knew exactly where they were, even despite the darkness surrounding them. "Not nowhere, Falstad. I think I sent us to the very top of the mountain. I think that everything, including the orcs, lies far below us."

"The top of the mountain?" Vereesa repeated.

"Aye, that would make sense."

"And judging by the fact that I can see both of you better and better, I fear that it's nearing dawn." Rhonin grew grim again. "Which means, if Nekros Skullcrusher is an orc of his word, that they'll be leaving the fortress at any moment, eggs and all."

Both Vereesa and the dwarf looked at him. "Now why would they do anything so daft?" asked Falstad. "Why abandon a place so secure?"

"Because of an impending invasion from the west, wizards and dwarves all riding swift, cunning gryphons. Hundreds, perhaps thousands of dwarves and wizards. Maybe even some elves. Against so much, especially magic, Nekros and his men would have no chance even of defending from within the mountain. . . ." The wizard shook his head. The situation might have been different if the commander had realized the true potential of the artifact he carried, but apparently either Nekros did not or his loyalties to his master in Dun Algaz were stronger. The orc had chosen to go north, and north he would go.

Falstad still could not believe it. "An invasion? Where would even an orc get a mad idea like that?"

"From us. From our being here. Especially me. Deathwing wanted me here just to serve as evidence of some forthcoming attack! This Nekros is mad! He already apparently believed that an assault was imminent, and when I showed up in his very midst, he felt certain of it." Rhonin eyed his broken finger, which had grown numb. He would have to deal with it when he could, but for now, so much more was at stake than a single finger.

"But why would the black beast want the orcs to leave?" the ranger asked. "What would he gain?"

"I think I know. . . ." Standing, Rhonin went to the edge of the mountain and peered down, bracing himself so that the wind would not blow him off the edge. He could still see nothing below, but imagined that he heard some sort of noise . . . perhaps of a military column with wagons moving out? "I think that instead of rescuing the red Dragonqueen—as he tried to convince me—he wants to slay her! It was too much of a risk while she was inside, but in the open he can swoop down and kill her with a single blow!"

"Are you sure?" the elf asked, joining him.

"It has to be." He looked up. Even the thick cloud cover up here could not obscure the fact that dawn fast approached. "Nekros wanted to leave by dawn. . . ."

"Is he daft?" muttered Falstad. "Would've made more sense if the blasted orc had tried to leave during the cover of darkness!"

Rhonin shook his head at Falstad. "Deathwing can see

fairly well in the night, maybe even better than any of us! Nekros indicated at one point in the questioning that he was prepared for anything, even Deathwing! In fact, he even seemed eager for the dark one to appear!"

"But that would make the least sense of all!" the ranger returned. "How could a single orc defeat him?"

"How could he keep control of the Dragonqueen— and where did he summon a creature like the golem?" The questions disturbed him more than he let on. Clearly the object that the orc carried had significant abilities, but was it *that* powerful?

Falstad suddenly waved for silence, then pointed northwest, well beyond the mountain.

A vast, dark shape broke momentarily through the higher clouds, then disappeared from sight again as it descended.

" 'Tis Deathwing . . ." the gryphon-rider whispered.

Rhonin nodded. The time for conjecture was over. If Deathwing had come, it meant only one thing. "Whatever is to happen, it's begun."

The lengthy orc caravan moved out as the first light of dawn touched Grim Batol. The wagons were flanked at beginning and end by armed warriors wielding freshly honed axes, swords, or pikes. Escorts rode with the peon drivers, especially on the wagons bearing the precious dragon eggs. Each orc traveled as if prepared to face the enemy at any given second, for word of the supposed invasion from the west had reached even the lowest of the low.

On one of the few horses available to the orcs, Nekros Skullcrusher watched the departure with impatience. He had sent the dragon-riders and their mounts on ahead to Dun Algaz, in order that, even if he failed in what he attempted, a few dragons would still be available to the Horde. A pity that he had dared not use them to transport the eggs, but from one previous attempt the commander had learned the folly of trying that.

Erecting a wagon capable of bearing a dragon would have been impossible, and so it had fallen to Nekros himself to take control of the two senior beasts. Both Alexstrasza and, remarkably, Tyran, followed at the rear of the column, ever aware of the power the *Demon Soul* had over them. For the ill consort, this had to be a harsh situation; Nekros doubted that the male would survive the journey, yet the orc knew there had been no other choice.

They still made for an impressive sight, the two great leviathans. The female more than the male, since she remained in better health. Nekros once caught her glaring at him, her hatred radiating in her eyes. The orc cared not a whit. She would obey him in all things so long as he wielded the one artifact capable of managing *any* dragon.

Thinking of dragons, he looked skyward. The overcast heavens presented any behemoth with ample places to hide, but eventually something had to happen. Even if the Alliance forces were too far away, Deathwing would surely come. Nekros counted on that.

The humans would learn the folly of entrusting victory to the dark one. What ruled one dragon certainly ruled another. With the *Demon Soul*, the orc commander would seize control of the most savage of all beasts. He, Nekros, would be master of Deathwing . . . but only if the damned reptile ever appeared.

"Where're you, you blasted creature?" he muttered. "Where?"

The last row of warriors exited the cavern mouth. Nekros watched them march by. Proud, wild, they hearkened back to the day when the Horde knew no defeat, knew no enemy it could not slaughter. With Deathwing at his command, he would restore that glory to his people. The Horde would rise anew, even those who had surrendered. The orcs would sweep over the Alliance lands, cutting down the humans and the others.

And perhaps there would be a new chieftain of the Horde. For the first time, Nekros dared imagine himself in such a role, with even Zuluhed bowing before him. Yes, he who would bring victory to his people would surely be acclaimed ruler.

War Chief Nekros Skullcrusher . . .

He urged his mount forward, rejoining the column. It would look suspicious if he did not ride with them. Besides, where he positioned himself did not truly matter; the *Demon Soul* gave him control from a distance. No dragon could be released by it unless he willed it—and certainly the grizzled orc had no intention of doing that.

Where was that blasted black beast?

And, as if in answer, an ear-splitting howl arose. However, the howl did not come from the sky, as Nekros had initially believed, but rather from the very earth surrounding the orcs. It caused consternation among the warriors as they turned about, trying to find the enemy.

A breath later—the ground erupted with *dwarves*.

They seemed everywhere, more dwarves than even Nekros could have imagined still remained in all of Khaz

Modan. They burst from the earth, swinging axes and waving swords, charging the column from every side.

Yet, although momentarily stunned, the orcs quickly recovered. Shouting out their own war cries, they turned to meet the attackers. The guards stayed with the wagons, but they, too, readied themselves, and even the peons, pathetic for most things, pulled out clubs. It took little training for an orc to be able to crush something with a piece of wood.

Nekros kicked at a dwarf who tried to pull him down. One of the commander's aides quickly stepped in, and a pitched battle began between the two. Nekros steered the horse nearer to the wagons, needing a moment himself to adjust to the situation. Instead of an invasion, he had been attacked by scavengers, for these looked to be the ragged mob that he had always known existed in the tunnels around the mountains. Judging by the numbers now, the trolls had apparently not done their work well.

But where was Deathwing? He had planned for the dragon. There had to be a dragon!

A thundering roar shook the combatants. A vast form darted half-seen through the thick clouds, then broke free, diving toward the orcs.

"At last! At last you've come, you black—" Nekros Skullcrusher froze, utterly baffled. He clutched the *Demon Soul,* but, at the moment, did not even think about using it as he had planned.

The dragon diving toward him had scales the color of fire, not darkness.

"We need to get down there," muttered Rhonin. "I need to see what's happening!"

"Can't you just do as you did in the chamber?" asked Falstad.

"If I do, I won't have any strength to help us once we land . . . besides, I don't know where to put us. Would you like to end up right in front of an orc swinging an ax?"

Vereesa glanced over the edge. "It does not appear too likely that we can climb down, either."

"Well, we can't stay up here forever!" The dwarf paced for a moment, then suddenly looked as if he had just stepped in something terrible. "Hestra's wings! What a fool! Maybe he's still around!"

Rhonin eyed the dwarf as if he had lost his wits. "What're you talking about? Who?"

Instead of answering, Falstad reached into a pouch. "Those blasted trolls took it earlier, but Gimmel handed it back . . . aah! Here 'tis!"

He pulled out what looked to be a tiny whistle. Both Rhonin and Vereesa watched as the dwarf put the whistle to his lips and blew as hard as he could.

"I don't hear anything," the wizard remarked.

"I'd have wondered about you if you had. Just wait. He's well-trained. Best mount I ever had. Mind you, we weren't taken by the trolls that far from this region. He would've stayed for a while. . . ." Falstad looked a little less certain. " 'Tis not that long since we were separated. . . ."

"You are trying to summon your gryphon?" the ranger asked, her skepticism clear.

"Better trying that than trying to sprout wings, eh?"

They waited. Waited for what seemed like an eternity to Rhonin. He felt his own strength returning—despite the chill conditions—but feared still to drop the trio into a location that might mean their immediate death.

Yet, it appeared he would have to try. The wizard straightened. "I'll do what I can. I recall an area not far from the mountain. I think Deathwing showed it to me in my mind. I may be able to send us there."

Vereesa took him by the arm. "Are you certain? You do not look ready yet." Her eyes filled with concern. "I know what that must have cost you back in the chamber, Rhonin. That was no minor spell you cast, then managed to maintain even for Falstad and myself. . . ."

He very much appreciated her words, but they had no other choice. "If I don't—"

A large winged form suddenly materialized through the clouds. Both Rhonin and the elf reacted, certain that Deathwing attacked.

Only Falstad, who had been watching closely, did not act as if their doom had come. He laughed and raised his hands toward the oncoming shape.

"Knew he'd hear! You see! Knew that he'd hear!"

The gryphon squawked in what the mage could have sworn were tones of glee. The massive beast flew swiftly toward them—or rather, his rider in particular. The animal fairly leapt atop Falstad, only the beating wings keeping the full weight of the gryphon from nearly crushing the dwarf.

"Ha! Good lad! Good lad! Down now!"

Tail wagging back and forth in a fashion more akin to a dog than a part-leonine beast, the gryphon landed before Falstad.

"Well?" the short warrior asked his companions. "Is it not time to go?"

They mounted as quickly as they could. Rhonin, still the weakest, sat between the dwarf and Vereesa. He had doubts about the gryphon's ability to carry them all, but the animal did just fine. On an extended journey, Falstad readily admitted, they would have had more trouble, but for a short trip, the gryphon would have no difficulties.

Moments later, they broke through the clouds—and into a sight they had not at all expected.

Rhonin had supposed that the sounds of battle would be the hill dwarves trying to take advantage of the orcs' cumbersome wagon train, but what he had not thought to see was a dragon other than Deathwing soaring above the battle.

"A red one!" the ranger called. "An older male, too! Not one raised in the mountain, either!"

He recognized that, too. The orcs had not held the queen long enough for such a behemoth to mature. Besides, the Horde also had a habit of slaying the dragons before they grew too old and independent. Only the young could be managed well enough by their orc handlers.

So where had this crimson leviathan come from, and what did he do here now?

"Where do you want us landing?" Falstad shouted, reminding him of a more immediate situation.

Rhonin quickly scanned the area. The battle seemed mostly contained around the column. He caught sight of Nekros Skullcrusher on horseback, the orc holding something in one hand that gleamed bright despite the clouds. The wizard forgot Falstad's question as he tried to make out the object. Nekros appeared to be pointing it toward the new dragon. . . .

"Well?" demanded the dwarf.

Tearing his eyes from the orc, Rhonin concentrated hard. "There!" He pointed at a ridge a short distance from the rear of the orc column. "That'll be best, I think!"

"Looks as good as any!"

Under the gryphon-rider's expert handling, the animal quickly brought them to their destination. Rhonin immediately slipped off, hurrying to the edge of the ridge in order to survey the situation.

What he saw made no sense whatsoever.

The dragon, which had looked ready to attack Nekros, now hovered as best he could in the air, roaring as if in some titanic struggle with an invisible foe. The wizard studied the orc commander again, noting how the glittering shape in Nekros's hand seemed to become brighter with each passing second.

An artifact of some sort, and so powerful that now even he could sense the emanations from it. Rhonin looked from the relic to the crimson giant.

How did the orcs maintain control over the Dragonqueen? It had been a question he had asked himself more than once in the past—and now Rhonin truly saw for himself.

The crimson dragon fought back, fought harder than the human could have imagined any creature doing. The trio could hear his painful roars, know that he suffered as few beings ever had.

And then, with one last rasping cry, the behemoth abruptly grew limp. He seemed to hover for a moment—then plummeted toward the earth some distance from the battle.

"Is he dead?" Vereesa asked.

"I don't know." If the artifact had not slain the dragon, certainly the high fall threatened to do that. He turned from the sight, not wishing to see so determined a creature perish—and suddenly saw yet another massive form dive from the clouds, this one a nightmare in *black*.

"Deathwing!" Rhonin warned the others.

The dark dragon soared toward the column, but not in the direction of either Nekros or the two enslaved dragons. Instead, he flew directly toward an unexpected target—the egg-laden carts.

The orc leader saw him at last. Turning, Nekros raised the artifact in Deathwing's direction, shouting out something at the same time.

Rhonin and the others expected to see even the black fall to this powerful talisman, but, curiously, Deathwing acted as if untouched. He continued his foray toward the wagons—and, clearly, the eggs they carried.

The wizard could not believe his eyes. "He doesn't care about Alexstrasza, dead or alive! He wants her eggs!"

Deathwing seized two of the wagons with surprising gentleness, lifting them up even as the orcs atop leapt away. The animals pulling the wagons shrieked, dangling helplessly as the dragon turned and immediately flew away.

Deathwing wanted the eggs intact, but why? What use were they to the lone dragon?

Then it occurred to Rhonin that he had just answered his own question. Deathwing wanted the eggs for his own. Red the dragons would be that hatched, but, under the dark one's fostering, they would become as sinister a force as he.

Perhaps Nekros realized this, or perhaps he simply reacted to the theft in general, but the orc suddenly turned and shouted toward the rear of the column. He continued to hold the artifact high, but now he pointed with his other hand at the vanishing giant.

One of the two red leviathans, the male, spread his wings rather ponderously and took off in pursuit. Rhonin had never seen a dragon who looked so deathly, so sick. He found himself amazed that the creature had managed to fly as high as he had. Surely Nekros did not think this ailing dragon any match for the younger, more virile Deathwing?

Meanwhile, the orcs and dwarves still fought, but the latter now battled with what seemed desperation, disappointment. It almost seemed as if they had put their hopes in the first red male. If so, Rhonin could understand their loss of hope now.

"I do not understand it," Vereesa said from beside him. "Why does Krasus not help? Surely the wizard should be here! Surely he is the reason the hill dwarves are finally attacking!"

"Krasus!" In all the excitement, Rhonin had forgotten about his patron. In truth, he had some questions for the faceless wizard. "What does he have to do with this?"

She told him. Rhonin listened, first in disbelief, then in growing fury. Yes, as he had begun to suspect, he had been used by the councilor. Not only him, though, but Vereesa, Falstad, and apparently the desperate dwarves below.

"After dealing with the dragon, he led us inside the mountain," she concluded. "Shortly thereafter, he would not speak to me again." The elf removed the medallion, showing it to him.

It looked remarkably like the one that Deathwing had given to Rhonin earlier, even down to the patterns. The bitter mage recalled noticing it when the elf and Falstad had tried rescuing him from the orcs. Had Krasus learned how to make it from the dragons?

At some point, the stone had become misaligned. Rhonin pushed it back into place with one finger, then glared at the gem, imagining that his patron could hear him. "Well, Krasus? Are you there? Anything else you'd like us to do for you? Should we die for you, maybe?"

Useless. Whatever power it had contained had evidently dissipated. Certainly Krasus would not bother to answer even if that had still been possible. Rhonin raised the relic high, ready to throw it off the ridge.

A faint voice in his head gasped, *Rhonin?*

The enraged wizard paused, startled to actually hear a reply.

Rhonin . . . praise . . . praise be . . . there may . . . there may still be . . . hope.

His companions watched him, not at all certain what he did. Rhonin said nothing, trying to think. Krasus sounded ill, almost dying.

"Krasus! Are you—"

Listen! I must conserve . . . energy! I see . . . I see you . . you may be able to salvage something—

Despite misgivings, Rhonin asked, "What do you want?"

First . . . first I must bring you to me.

The medallion suddenly flared, spreading a vermilion light over the astonished spellcaster.

Vereesa reached for him. "Rhonin!"

Her hand went through his arm. He watched in horror as both she and Falstad—and the entire ridge—vanished.

Almost immediately, a different, rocky landscape materialized around him, a barren place that had seen too many battles and now, in the distance, witnessed another. Krasus had transported him west of the mountains, not far from where the orc column fought with the dwarves. He had not realized that the wizard had been so near after all.

Thinking of his traitorous patron, Rhonin turned about. "Krasus! Damn you, show yourself—"

He found himself staring into the eye of a fallen giant, the same red, draconic giant the human had seen plummet from the skies but minutes earlier. The dragon lay on his side, one wing thrust up, his head flat along the ground

"You have my . . . my deepest apologies, Rhonin," the gargantuan creature rumbled with some effort. "For . . . for *everything* painful I have caused you and the others . . ."

TWENTY

So simple. So very simple.

As Deathwing turned to retrieve the next eggs, he wondered if he had overestimated the difficulties of his plan in the first place. He had always assumed that to have entered the mountain either as himself or in disguise would have been more risky, especially if Alexstrasza had noticed his presence. True, there would have been little chance of him being injured, but the eggs he had coveted might have been destroyed. He had feared that happening, especially if one of those eggs proved to be a viable female. Having long decided that Alexstrasza would never be his to control, Deathwing needed every egg he could get his talons on, so as to better his chances. That, in fact, had made him hesitate more than anything else. Now, though, it seemed that he had wasted time waiting, that nothing could have stood in his way then, just as nothing did now.

He corrected himself. Nothing but a sickly, doddering beast well past his prime who even now flew toward his doom.

"Tyran . . ." Deathwing would not dignify the other

dragon by calling him by his full name. "You are not dead yet?"

"Give back the eggs!" the crimson behemoth rasped.

"So that they may be raised as dogs for those orcs? I will at least make them true masters of the world! Once more dragon flights will rule the skies and earth!"

His ailing adversary snorted. "And where is your flight, Deathwing? Aah, my pain makes me forget! They all *died* for your glory!"

The black leviathan hissed, spreading his wings wide. "Come to me, Tyran! I will be happy to send you on your way to oblivion!"

"Whether by the orc's command or not, I would still hunt you down until my last breath!" Tyran snarled. He snapped at the black's throat, barely missing.

"I shall send you back to your masters in bloody little pieces, old fool!"

The two dragons roared at one another, Tyran's cry a pale comparison to Deathwing's own.

They closed for combat.

Rhonin stared. *"Krasus?"*

The crimson dragon raised his head enough to nod once. "That is the name . . . I wear when . . . when human. . . ."

"Krasus . . ." Astonishment turned to bitterness. "You betrayed me and my friends! You arranged all this! Made me your puppet!"

"For which I will always have . . . regrets. . . ."

"You're no better than Deathwing!"

This made the leviathan cringe, but once more he nodded. "I deserve that. Perhaps that is the path . . . the path he took long ago. S-so easy to not see what . . . what one does to others . . ."

The distant sounds of battle reverberated even here, reminding Rhonin of other, more important matters than his pride. "Vereesa and Falstad are still back there—and those dwarves! They could all die because of you! Why did you summon me here, Krasus?"

"B-because there is still hope of seizing v-victory out of the chaos . . . the chaos I have helped to create. . . ." The dragon tried to rise, but managed only a sitting position. "You and I, Rhonin . . . there is a chance. . . ."

The wizard frowned, but said nothing. His only concern now lay in seeing to it that Vereesa, Falstad, and the hill dwarves survived this debacle.

"You . . . you do not reject me out of hand . . . good. I thank you for th-that."

"Just tell me what you intend."

"The orc commander w-wields an artifact . . . the *Demon Soul*. It has p-power over all dragons . . . save Deathwing."

Rhonin recalled how Nekros had tried to use it on the black leviathan with no visible effect. "Why not Deathwing?"

"Because he created it," responded a quiet, feminine voice.

The mage whirled about. He heard a gasp from the dragon.

A beautiful yet ethereal woman wearing a flowing emerald gown stood behind the wizard, a slight smile on her pale lips. Rhonin belatedly realized that her eyes were closed, yet she seemed to have no trouble knowing how best to face either him or the dragon.

"Ysera . . ." the crimson giant whispered reverently.

She did not acknowledge him immediately, though, instead continuing to answer Rhonin's question. "Deathwing it was who created the *Demon Soul,* and for a good cause at the time, so we believed." She strode toward the wizard. "Believed so much that we did as he asked, imparted to it some measure of our power."

"But he didn't impart his own, didn't impart his own!" snapped a male voice, strident and not completely sane. "Tell him, Ysera! Tell him how, after the demons were defeated, he turned on us! Used our own power on us!"

Atop a massive rock perched a skeletal, not-quite-human figure with jagged, blue hair and silver skin. Clad in a high-collared robe of the same two colors as his form, he looked like some mad jester. His eyes gleamed. Daggerlike fingers scratched at the rock upon which the figure squatted, gouging chasms into it.

"He will hear what he needs to hear, Malygos. No more, no less." She smiled slightly again. The longer Rhonin looked at her, the more she reminded him of Vereesa—but of Vereesa as he had once dreamt of her. "Yes, Deathwing neglected to tell us that part, and certainly pretended that he had sacrificed as we had. Only when he decided that he represented the future of our kind did we discover the horrible truth."

It finally occurred to Rhonin that Ysera and Malygos spoke of the black dragon as one of them. He turned his head back to the red leviathan, silently asking the creature he had known as Krasus if his suspicions were true.

"Yes . . ." the injured dragon replied. "They are what you believe them to be. They are two of the five great dragons, known in legend as the Aspects of the world."

The red giant seemed to draw strength from their arrival. "Ysera . . . She of the Dreaming. Malygos . . . the Hand of Magic . . ."

"We are wasssting time here," muttered yet a third voice, another male. "Precioussss time . . ."

"And Nozdormu . . . Master of Time, too!" marveled the red dragon. "You have all come!"

A shrouded figure seemingly made of sand stood near Ysera. Under the hood appeared a face so desiccated it barely had enough dry flesh to cover the bone. Gemstone eyes glared at both the dragon and the wizard in growing impatience. "Yesss, we have come! And if thisss party takesss much longer, perhapss I shall go, too! I've much to gather, much to catalog—"

"Much to babble about, much to babble about!" mocked Malygos from high up.

Nozdormu raised a withered yet strong hand toward the jester, who flashed his daggerlike nails at the hooded figure. The two looked ready to come to blows, both physical and otherwise, but the ghostly woman came between them.

"And this is why Deathwing has nearly triumphed," she murmured.

The two reluctantly backed down. Ysera turned to face everyone, her eyes still closed.

"Deathwing almost had us once, but we joined ranks again and made it so that at least he himself could never wield the *Demon Soul* again. We forced it from his hand and into the bowels of the earth—"

"But someone found it for him," interjected the red dragon, pulling himself together as best he could, now that hope had evidently returned. "I believe that he may even have led the orcs to it, knowing what they would do once they had it. If he cannot use it himself, he can certainly manipulate others into wielding it for his purposes—even if they do not realize it. I—I believe that it suited his plans for Alexstrasza to be captured, for she not only remained the lone power he feared, but it helped the Horde to wreak further havoc in the world without the dark one raising a paw in effort. Now . . . now that it is clear that the Horde has failed him, it better serves his purpose for the orcs to move her."

"Not her," corrected Ysera. "Her eggs."

"Her *eggs*?" the former Krasus blurted. "Not my queen herself?"

"Yes, the eggs. You know that the last of his mates perished in the first days of the war," she replied. "Slain by his own recklessness . . . so now he would raise our sister's get as his own."

"To create a new Age of Dragonssss . . ." spat Nozdormu. "The Age of Deathwing'sss Dragonsss!"

Suddenly Rhonin noticed that the four now stared at him, even Ysera with her closed eyes.

"We cannot touch the *Demon Soul,* human, and out of distrust, we have never tried to make another creature wield it for us. I believe I know what poor Korialstrasz here desired so much of you that he had to drag you from your friends, but while it seems the best way, he will not now be the one who keeps Deathwing occupied."

"It is my duty!" roared the red. "It is my penance!"

"It would be a waste. You are too susceptible to the disk. Besides, you are needed for other reasons. Tyran, who fights now for both his queen and his captor, will not survive. Alexstrasza will have need of you, dear Korial."

"Besides, Deathwing is our *brother,*" mocked Malygos. The talons dug deeper into the rock. "It's only right that *we* should play with him, we should play with him!"

"What do you want me to do?" Rhonin asked, eager yet also anxious. What *he* wanted most was to return to Vereesa.

Ysera faced him—and her eyes opened. For a brief moment, vertigo seized control of the human. The dreamlike eyes that stared back reminded him of everyone he had ever known, hated, or loved. "You, mortal, must take the *Demon Soul* from the orc. Without it, he cannot possibly do to us what he did to our sister and, by taking it, you might be able to free her from his control."

"But that will not deal with Deathwing," Korialstrasz insisted. "And because of the cursed disk, he is stronger than all of you together—"

"A point of fact we know," hissed Nozdormu. "And ssso did you when you came to usss! Well, you have usss now! Be sssatissfied with that!" He looked at his two companions. "Enough babble! Let usss be done with thisss!"

Ysera, her eyes closed again, turned to the dragon. "There is one thing you must do, Korialstrasz, and it does entail risk. This human cannot simply be magicked into the orcs' midst. The *Demon Soul* makes that risky, and there is also always the chance that he will find himself under the ax when he appears. You must instead bear him there—and pray that for the few seconds you are so near, the orc does not bind you to the foul disk this time." She walked up to the stricken dragon, touching the tip of his muzzle. "You are not one of us even if you are her consort, Korialstrasz, yet you fought the *Demon Soul*'s hungry grasp and escaped—"

"I worked hard to build myself up for that, Ysera. I thought I had cast my protective spells better, but in the end I failed."

"We can do this for you." Suddenly, both Malygos and Nozdormu stood beside her. All three had their left hands touching Korialstrasz's muzzle. "So much power the *Demon Soul* took from us, a little more will not matter. . . ."

Auras formed around the raised hands of the trio, the colors reminiscent of each of those contributing. The three auras combined, rapidly spreading from the Aspects to the dragon's muzzle and beyond. In seconds, Korialstrasz's entire immense form lay bathed in magic.

Ysera and the others finally backed away. The crimson behemoth blinked, then rose to his feet. "I feel—renewed!"

"You will need all of it," she remarked. To her two companions, she said, "We must see to our errant brother."

"About *time*, I would sssay!" snapped Nozdormu.

Without another word to either Rhonin or the red dragon, they turned away, facing the distant form of Deathwing. As one, the trio spread their arms wide—and those arms became wings that expanded and expanded. At the same time, their bodies widened, grew greater. Away went the garments, replaced by scale. Their faces lengthened, hardened, all vestiges of humanity shaping into draconic majesty.

The three gargantuan dragons rose high in the air, a sight so impressive that the wizard could only watch.

"I pray that they will be enough," muttered Korialstrasz. "But I fear it will not be so." He looked down at the tiny figure next to him. "What say you, Rhonin? Will you do as they bid?"

For Vereesa alone, he would have agreed. "All right."

The fight had early gone out of Tyran, and now so had the life. Deathwing roared his triumph as he clutched the limp form of the other dragon high. Blood still seeped from a score of deep wounds—most of them in the red's chest—and Tyran's paws were covered with burns, the cost of touching the acidic venom that dripped from the fiery veins coursing along the black's body. No one who touched Deathwing did not suffer in the end.

The dark one roared again, then let the lifeless form drop. In truth, he had done the ill red a favor; would not the other dragon have suffered worse if he had been forced to continue to live with his sickness? At least Deathwing had granted him a warrior's demise, however easy the battle had truly been.

Yet a third time he roared, wanting all to hear of his supremacy—

—and found instead answering roars coming from the west.

"What fool now dares?" he hissed.

Not one fool, Deathwing immediately saw, but *three*. Not *any* three, either.

"Ysssera . . ." he greeted coldly. "And Nozdormu, and my dear friend Malygosss, too . . ."

"It is time to end your madness, brother," the sleek green dragon calmly said.

"I am not your brother in anything, Ysera. Open

your eyes to that fact, and also that nothing will prevent me from creating this new age of our kind!"

"You plan only an age in which you rule, nothing more."

The black dipped his head. "Much the same thing, as I see it. Best you go back to sleep. And you, Nozdormu? Pulled your head out of the sand at last? Do you not recall who is most powerful here? Even the three of you will not be enough!"

"Your time isss over!" spat the glittering brown behemoth. Gemstone eyes flared. "Come! Take your place in my collection of thingsss passst. . . ."

Deathwing snorted. "And you, Malygos? Have you nothing to say to your old comrade?"

In response, the chill-looking, silver-blue beast opened wide his maw. A torrent of ice shot forth, washing over Deathwing with incredible accuracy. However, as soon as the ice touched the fearsome dragon, it *transformed,* turning into a thousand thousand tiny crablike vermin that sought to tear at the scales and flesh of their host.

Deathwing hissed, and from the crimson veins acid poured forth. Malygos's creatures died by the hundreds, until only a few remained.

Expertly using two talons, the black dragon picked one of these off, then swallowed it whole. He smiled at his counterparts, revealing sharp, tearing teeth. "So that is how it is to be, then. . . ."

With an earth-shattering roar, he leapt at them.

"They will not defeat him!" Korialstrasz muttered as Rhonin and he neared the besieged orc column. "They cannot!"

"Then why bother?"

"Because they know that it is time to make a stand, re-gardless of the outcome! Rather would they pass from this world than watch it writhe and die in Deathwing's terrible grip!"

"Is there no way we can help them?"

The dragon's silence answered that.

Rhonin eyed the orcs ahead, thinking of his own mortality. Even if he managed to seize this artifact from Nekros, how long would he maintain hold of it? For that matter, what good would it do him? Could he wield it?

"Kras—Korialstrasz, the disk contains the power of the great dragons?"

"All save Deathwing, which is why he cannot be bound by its power!"

"But he can't wield it himself because of some spell the others cast?"

"So it seems . . ." The dragon banked.

"Do you know what the disk can do?"

"Many things, but none of them able to directly or in-directly affect the dark one."

Rhonin frowned. "How is that possible?"

"How long have you trained in magic, my friend?"

The wizard grimaced. Of all the arts, magic truly had to be one of the most contradictory, guided by laws all its own, laws quite changeable at the worst of times. "Point taken."

"The great ones have made up their minds, Rhonin! By being granted the chance to take the *Demon Soul*, you will not only free my queen—who will, I do not doubt, rise to their aid—but also have the wherewithal for finally crushing the remnants of the Horde! The *Demon Soul* can do that, if you learn to wield it properly, you know!"

He had not even considered that, but of course a relic like this would serve well against the orcs. "But it would take too long to learn how to use it!"

"The orcs did not have willing teachers! I am not one of the Five, Rhonin, but I can show you enough, I think!"

"Providing we both survive . . ." the mage whispered to himself.

"Yes, there is that." Apparently dragons had exceptional hearing. "Aah, there is the orc in question! Be ready!"

Rhonin prepared himself. Korialstrasz dared not get too near Nekros for fear of falling victim to the *Demon Soul,* which meant that, despite the talisman, the wizard had to use magic to reach the orc commander. He had cast many spells in the heat of battle before, but nothing had quite prepared Rhonin for this effort. The dragon might have tried, but around the vicinity of the relic, his magic would have fared worse than the wizard's.

"Get ready . . ."

Korialstrasz dropped lower.

"Now!"

The words came out of Rhonin in a gasp—and suddenly he floated in the air, directly over one of the wagons.

An orc driver looked up, gaped when he saw the wizard.

Rhonin dropped on top of him.

The collision softened his fall, but did nothing good for the orc. Rhonin scrambled to push the unconscious driver to the side, then searched the area for Nekros.

The one-legged commander remained on horseback,

eyes fixed on the turning form of Korialstrasz. He raised the gleaming *Demon Soul* high—

"Nekros!" Rhonin shouted.

The orc looked his way, which had been just as the wizard wanted it. Now the dragon remained out of Nekros's reach.

"Human! Wizard! You're dead!" His heavy brow furrowed and a dark look crossed his hideous features. "Well . . . you will be soon!"

He pointed the artifact toward Rhonin.

The wizard quickly cast a shield, hoping that whatever Nekros threw at him would not be as terrible as the golem's flames. The great dragons had not seen fit to grant him some of the extra strength they had given to Korialstrasz, but then, the red behemoth had been near to total collapse, and they had needed the rest of their power for Deathwing. Rhonin's own hopes all lay in his own flagging capabilities.

A gigantic hand—a hand of flame—reached for him, trying to encircle the mage. However, Rhonin's spell held true, and the hand, rebounding off the faintly visible shield, instead engulfed an orc warrior about to behead his dwarven adversary. The orc let out one short scream before collapsing into a burning heap.

"Your tricks'll not hold you long from death!" growled Nekros.

The ground beneath the wagon began to shake, then crumble. Rhonin threw himself from the sinkhole that formed just as the wagon and the animals pulling it were dragged under. The shield spell dissipated, leaving the desperate mage undefended as he clung to what remained of the path.

Nekros urged his mount nearer. "Whatever happens this day, human, I'll at least be rid of you!"

Rhonin uttered a short, simple spell. A single clump of dirt flew up into the orc's face, lodging there despite his attempts to peel it away. Swearing, Nekros struggled to see.

The wizard pulled himself up, then leapt at the orc.

He came up a bit short, catching the arm that held the *Demon Soul* but unable to pull himself higher. Although still blinded, Nekros seized Rhonin by the collar, trying to get one heavy hand on the mage's throat.

"I'll kill you, human scum!"

Fingers closed around Rhonin's neck. Caught between attempting to pry the talisman free and saving his own life, Rhonin managed to accomplish neither. Nekros began to crush the life out of him, the incredible strength of the orc too much for the mage. Rhonin started a spell—

A winged shape suddenly darted past Nekros. Something landed on the back of the orc, throwing both him and the wizard off the horse and onto the rough ground.

They landed hard. The murderous grip on Rhonin's throat vanished as the two bounced in opposite directions.

Someone seized the dazed mage by the shoulders. "Up, Rhonin, before he recovers!"

"V-Vereesa?" He stared into her striking face, both astonished and pleased to see her.

"We saw the dragon drop you from the sky, then watched as you magicked yourself to safety! Falstad and I came as soon as we could, thinking you might need help!"

"Falstad?" Rhonin looked up, saw the gryphon-rider

and his mount circling back. Falstad had no weapon, yet he howled as if daring every orc in the column to come face him.

"Hurry!" the ranger cried. "We must get out of here!"

"No!" Reluctantly he pulled back. "Not until—look out!"

He pushed her aside just before a massive war-ax would have cut her in two. A beefy orc with ritual scars cut down each cheek raised the ax again, once more focusing on Vereesa, who had fallen to the side.

Rhonin gestured . . . and the ax handle suddenly stretched, weaving about as if some writhing serpent. The orc struggled to control it, only to find his weapon now twisting around him. Suddenly fearful, the warrior released his grip and, after managing to pull free of the living ax, ran off.

The wizard reached out a hand to his companion—

—and fell to the ground as a fist caught him in the back.

"Where is it?" roared Nekros Skullcrusher. "Where's the *Demon Soul*?"

Momentarily stunned, Rhonin did not quite understand the orc. Surely Nekros had the talisman. . . .

A piercing weight pressed down on him from the back. He heard Nekros say, "Stay where you're at, elf! All I need to do is lean a little harder and I'll crush your friend like a piece of fruit!" Rhonin felt cold metal against his cheek. "No tricks, mage! Give me the disk back and I may let you live!"

Nekros gave him just enough movement so that Rhonin could see the orc out of the corner of his eye. The commander had his wooden leg squarely on the wizard's spine, and Rhonin had no doubt that just a bit more pressure would snap the spine completely. "I d-don't have it!" The near-full weight of Nekros's massive body made it nearly impossible to breathe, much less speak. "I don't even know w-where it is!"

"I've no patience for your lies, human!" Nekros pushed a little harder. A hint of desperation colored his otherwise arrogant tone. "I need it now!"

"Nekrosss . . ." interrupted a thundering, hate-filled voice. "You had them ssslay my *children!* My *children!*"

Rhonin felt the orc suddenly shift, as if turning. Nekros let out a gasp, then, "No—!"

A shadow overwhelmed both Rhonin and his adversary. A hot, almost searing wind washed over the mage. He heard Nekros Skullcrusher scream—

—and suddenly the orc's weight vanished from his back.

Rhonin immediately rolled onto his back, certain that whatever had taken his enemy would now take him. Vereesa came to his aid, dragging him to her just as the mage registered what had created the vast shadow and why the voice accompanying it had been familiar.

Scales hanging loose in some areas, her wings bent awkwardly, the Dragonqueen Alexstrasza still presented a most astounding sight. She towered over all else, her head high in the sky as she roared in defiance. Of Nekros, Rhonin saw no sign; the great dragon had either swallowed the orc whole or tossed his body far away.

Alexstrasza roared again, then dipped her head down toward the wizard and elf. Vereesa looked ready to defend them both, but Rhonin signaled her to lower her blade.

"Human, elf, you have my gratitude for finally enabling me to avenge my children! Now, though, there are others who need my aid, however minuscule it might prove!"

She cast her eyes skyward, where four titans fought. Rhonin followed her gaze, watched for a moment as Ysera, Nozdormu, and Malygos battled Deathwing seemingly without result. Again and again the trio dove in, and each time the black monster repelled them easily.

"Three against one and they still can't do anything?"

Alexstrasza, already testing her wings for departure, paused to reply, "Because of the *Demon Soul*, we are more than halved! Only Deathwing remains whole! Would that it could be wielded against him or that we could regain the power lost to it, but neither of those options exists! We can only fight and hope for the best!" A roar from above shook the earth. "I must go now! Forgive me for leaving you thus! Thank you again!"

With that, the Dragonqueen rose into the air, her tail casually sweeping nearby orcs away yet ever avoiding the valiant dwarven attackers.

"There must be something we can do!" Rhonin looked around for the *Demon Soul*. It had to be somewhere.

"Never mind it!" Vereesa called. She deflected the ax of an orc, then ran the warrior through. "We still need to save ourselves!"

Rhonin, however, continued to search despite the pitched battle around him. Suddenly, his gaze alighted on a glittering object half-covered by the arm of a dead dwarf. The wizard raced over to it, hoping against hope.

Sure enough, it proved to be the draconic artifact. Rhonin studied it in open admiration. So simple and elegant, yet containing forces beyond the ability of any wizard, save perhaps the infamous Medivh. So much power.

With it, Nekros could have become War Chief of the Horde. With it, Rhonin could become master of Dalaran, emperor of all the Lordaeron kingdoms. . . .

What was he thinking? Rhonin shook his head, scattering such thoughts. The *Demon Soul* had a seductive touch to it, one of which he had to beware.

Falstad, atop the gryphon, dropped down to join them. Somewhere along the way, he had managed to gain an orc battle-ax, which he had already clearly used well.

"Wizard! What ails you? Rom and his band may have the orcs on the run at last, but here 'tis not the place to stand and gawk at baubles!"

Rhonin ignored him, just as he had Vereesa. Somehow the key to defeating Deathwing had to be in using the *Demon Soul!* What *other* force could possibly do that? Even the four great dragons seemed not enough.

He held up the artifact, sensing its tremendous power and knowing that none of that power would help, at least not in its present form.

Which meant that perhaps nothing, *nothing,* would be able to stop Deathwing from achieving his goals. . . .

TWENTY-ONE

They threw their full might at him—or at least what remained of it. They threw both physical and magical assaults at Deathwing, and he shrugged all off. No matter how hard they fought against him, the fact remained that, diminished by their long-ago contributions to the *Demon Soul*, the other great Aspects might as well have been infants in comparison to the black leviathan.

Nozdormu cast the sand of ages at him, threatening, at least for a moment, to steal Deathwing's very youth. Deathwing felt the weakness spread through him, felt his bones grow stiff and his thoughts slower. Yet, before the change could become permanent, the raw power within the chaotic dragon surged high, burning away the sand, overwhelming the cunning spell.

From Malygos came a more frontal assault, the mad creature's fury almost enabling him to match Deathwing's power, if but for a moment. Icicles of lightning assailed Malygos's hated foe from all directions, intense heat and numbing cold simultaneously beating at Deathwing. Yet the enchanted iron plates embedded in the black's hide deflected nearly all of the raging storm away, readily enabling Deathwing to suffer what little made it through.

Of all of them, though, his most cunning and dangerous foe proved to be Ysera. Initially, she stayed back, seeming content to let her comrades waste their efforts on him. Then Deathwing noticed a complacency in himself, a satisfaction that grew to distraction. Almost too late he realized that he had begun to daydream. Shaking his head, he quickly dislodged the cobwebs that she had cast within his mind—just as all three of his adversaries tried to seize him in their talons.

With several beats of his expansive wings, he pulled out of their grasp, then counterattacked. Between his forepaws formed a vast sphere of pure energy, primal power, that he threw into their very midst.

The sphere exploded as it reached the trio, sending Ysera and the others spiraling backward.

Deathwing roared his defiance. "Fools! Throw what you can at me! The outcome will be no different! I am power incarnate! You are nothing but shadows of the past!"

"Never underestimate what you may learn from the past, dark one. . . ."

A crimson shadow Deathwing had thought never to see aloft again filled his vision, surprising even him for once. "Alexstrasza . . . come to avenge your consort?"

"Come to avenge my consort and my children, Deathwing, for I know all too well that this is all because of you!"

"I?" The black behemoth gave her a toothy grin. "But even I cannot touch the *Demon Soul;* you and yours saw to that!"

"But something led the orcs to a place of which only

dragons knew . . . and something hinted to them of the power of the disk!"

"Does it matter, anyway? Your day is past, Alexstrasza, while mine is about to come!"

The red dragon spread her wings wide and flashed her claws. Despite the deprivations of her captivity, she did not look at all weak at the moment. "It is your day that is over, dark one!"

"I have faced the ravages of time, the curse of nightmares, and the mists of sorcery, thanks to the others! What weapons do you bring?"

Alexstrasza met his sinister gaze with her own determined, unblinking orbs. "Life . . . hope . . . and what they bring with them . . ."

Deathwing took in her words—and laughed loud. "Then you are as good as dead already!"

The two giants charged one another.

"She cannot hope to beat him," Rhonin muttered. "None of them can, because they're all lacking what this damned artifact took from them!"

"If there is nothing we can do, then we should leave, Rhonin."

"I can't, Vereesa! I've got to do something for her—for all of us, actually! If they can't stop Deathwing, who will?"

Falstad eyed the *Demon Soul.* "Can you do nothing with that thing?"

"No. It won't work against Deathwing in any way."

The dwarf rubbed his hairy chin. "Pity 'tis not possible to give back the magic that thing stole! At least then they could fight with him on even terms. . . ."

The wizard shook his head. "That can't be—" He paused, trying to think. With the broken finger, his throbbing head, and the bruises all over his body, it took effort just to keep on his feet. Rhonin concentrated, focusing on what the gryphon-rider had just said. "But, then again, maybe it *can!*"

His companions looked at him in bewilderment. Rhonin quickly glanced around to assure himself that they were safe from orcs for the moment, then located the hardest rock he could find.

"What are you doing?" Vereesa asked, sounding as if she wondered whether he had lost his mind.

"Returning their power to them!" He put the *Demon Soul* on top of another stone, then raised the first high.

"What in blazes do you think—" was as far as Falstad managed.

Rhonin brought the rock down as hard as he could on the disk.

The rock in his hand cracked in two.

The *Demon Soul* glistened, not even blemished by the assault.

"Damn! I should've known!" He looked up at the dwarf. "Can you swing that thing with great accuracy?"

Falstad looked insulted. "It may be inferior orc work, but 'tis still a usable weapon and, as such, I can swing it as good as any!"

"Use it on the disk! Now!"

The ranger put a concerned hand on the wizard's shoulder. "Rhonin, do you really think this will work?"

"I know the spellwork that will return it to them, a variation used by those of my order when trying to draw from other relics, but it demands that the artifact in question be shattered, so that the forces binding the magic within won't exist any longer! I can give back to the dragons what they lost—but only if I can get the *Demon Soul* open!"

"Is that why, then?" Falstad hefted the war-ax. "Stand back, wizard! Would you like it in two neat halves or chopped into little fragments?"

"Just destroy it in whatever way you can!"

"Simple enough . . ." Raising the ax high, the dwarf took a deep breath—then swung so hard that Rhonin could see the intense strain in his companion's arm muscles.

The ax struck true—

Fragments of metal went flying.

"By the Aerie! The head! 'Tis completely ruined!"

A great gap in the blade gave proof of the *Demon Soul*'s hard surface. Falstad threw down the ax in disgust, cursing shoddy orc workmanship.

Rhonin, however, knew that the ax had not been at fault. "This is worse than I would've imagined!"

"Magic must protect it," Vereesa murmured. "Cannot magic also destroy it?"

"It would have to be something powerful. My magic alone wouldn't do it, but if I had another talisman—" He recalled the medallion Krasus—or, rather, Korialstrasz—had given Vereesa, but that had been left behind after the wizard and the red dragon had headed back to the battle. Besides, Rhonin doubted that it would serve well enough. Better if he had something from Deathwing himself, but that medallion had been lost in the mountain—

But he still had the stone! The stone created from one of the black dragon's own scales!

"It has to work!" he cried, reaching into his pouch.

"What've you got?" Falstad asked.

"This!" He pulled out the tiny stone, an object which in no manner impressed the other two. "Deathwing created this from his very being, just as he created the *Demon Soul* through his magic! It may be able to do what nothing else could!"

As they watched, he brought the stone to the disk. Rhonin debated how best to use it, then decided to follow the teachings of his craft—try the simple way first.

The black gem seemed to gleam in his grip. The wizard turned it on the sharpest edge he could find. Rhonin knew very well that his plan might not work, but he had nothing else to try.

With great caution, he ran the stone along the center of the foul talisman.

Deathwing's scale cut into the *Demon Soul*'s hardened gold exterior like a knife through butter.

"Look out!" Vereesa pulled him back just in time, as a plume of sheer light burst from the cut.

Rhonin sensed the intense magical energy escaping from the damaged talisman and knew he had to act fast, lest it be lost forever to those to whom it truly belonged.

He muttered the spell, adjusting it as he thought needed. The weary mage concentrated hard, not wanting to risk failure at so critical a juncture. It *had* to work.

A fantastic, glittering rainbow rose higher and higher, flying up into the heavens. Rhonin repeated his spell, emphasizing as best he could what he wanted as results. . . .

The nearly blinding plume, now hundreds of feet in height, twisted around—heading in the direction of the battling dragons.

"Did you do it?" the ranger breathlessly asked.

Rhonin stared at the distant forms of Alexstrasza, Deathwing, and the others. "I think so—I *hope* so. . . ."

"Have you not been through enough? Will you continue to fight what you cannot defeat?" Deathwing eyed his foes with utter contempt. What little respect had remained for them had long ago died away. The fools continued to bang their heads against the proverbial wall, even though they knew that, together, their power still lacked.

"You have caused too much misery, too much horror, Deathwing," Alexstrasza retorted. "Not just to us, but to the mortal creatures of this world!"

"What are they to me—or, for that matter, even you? I will never understand that!"

She shook her head in what he realized could be pity—for *him*? "No . . . you never will. . . ."

"I have toyed enough with you—all of you! I should have destroyed you four years ago!"

"But you could not! Creating the *Demon Soul* weakened even you for quite some time. . . ."

He snorted. "But now I have recovered my full strength! My plans for this world advance rapidly . . . and after I have slain all of you, I shall take *your* eggs, Alexstrasza, and create my perfect world!"

In response, the crimson dragon attacked again. Deathwing laughed, knowing that her spells would affect him no better than they had before. Between his own power and the enchanted plates grafted to his skin, *nothing* could hurt him—

"Aaargh!!" The fury of her magical attack tore at him

with a force he could not have imagined. His adamantium plates did little to lessen the horrific impact. Deathwing immediately countered with a powerful shield, but the damage had been done. His entire body ached from pain such as he had not known in many centuries.

"What—have you—done to *me*?"

At first Alexstrasza looked surprised herself, but then a knowing—and triumphant—smile crossed her draconic features. "The bare beginnings of what I have these past years dreamed of doing, foul one!"

She looked larger, stronger. In fact, all four of them looked that way. A sensation coursed through the black dragon, the feeling that something had gone terribly wrong with his perfect plan.

"Can you feel it? Can you feel it?" Malygos babbled. "I am me again! What a glorious thing!"

"And it'sss about time!" returned Nozdormu, gemstone eyes uncommonly bright and gleaming. "Yesss, ssso very much about time!"

Ysera opened her arresting eyes, this time *so* arresting that it was all Deathwing could do to pull his gaze from them. "It is the end of the nightmare," she whispered. "Our dream has become truth!"

Alexstrasza nodded. "What was lost has been returned to us. The *Demon Soul* . . . the *Demon Soul* is *no more.*"

"Impossible!" the metallic behemoth roared. "Lies! Lies!"

"No," corrected the crimson figure. "The only lie left to disprove now is that you are invincible."

"Yesss," snapped Nozdormu. "I look forward to disssproving that ridiculousss fallacy. . . ."

And Deathwing found himself under attack by four elemental forces the likes of which he had never faced. No longer did he fight mere shadows of his rivals, but a quartet, each his equal—and he no match for all together.

Malygos brought the very clouds to him, clouds with suffocating holds around the black dragon's jaws and nostrils. Nozdormu turned time forward for Deathwing alone, sapping his adversary of strength by forcing Deathwing to suffer weeks, months, then years without rest. His defenses already crippled by these assaults, Ysera had no trouble invading his mind, turning the armored behemoth's thoughts to his worst nightmares.

Only then did Alexstrasza rise before him, the terrible nemesis. She gazed at Deathwing, still in part with pity, and said, "Life is my Aspect, dark one, and I, like all mothers, know both the pain and wonder that entails! For the past several years, I have watched my children be raised as instruments of war, slaughtered if they proved insufficient or too willful! I have lived knowing that so many died that I could do nothing for!"

"Your words mean nothing to me," Deathwing roared as he futilely struggled to shrug off the others' horrific assaults. *"Nothing!"*

"No, they likely do not . . . which is why I shall let you experience firsthand all that I have suffered. . . ."

And she did just that.

Against any other attack, even the nightmares of Ysera, Deathwing could summon some defense, but against Alexstrasza's he had no weapon upon which to draw. She attacked with pain, but *her* pain. She dealt not with agony as he knew it, but with that of a loving mother who suffered with each child torn from her, with each child turned into something terrible.

With each child who perished.

"You will go through all I have gone through, dark one. Let us see if you fare any better than I did."

But Deathwing had no experience in such suffering. It tore at him where the pain of vicious talons or ripping teeth could not, for it tore at him in his very being.

The most terrible of dragons screamed as none had ever heard a dragon scream before.

That, perhaps, was all that saved him. So startled were the others by it that they faltered in their own spells. Able at last to rip free, Deathwing turned and fled, flying fast and furious. His entire body shook and he continued to scream even as he swiftly dwindled from sight.

"We mussst not let him ssslip away!" Nozdormu suddenly realized.

"Follow him, follow him, indeed!" agreed Malygos.

"I agree," She of the Dreaming quietly added. Ysera looked at Alexstrasza, who hovered, amazed at what she had done. "Sister?"

"Yes," the red dragon replied, nodding. "By all means, go on! I shall join you shortly. . . ."

"I understand . . ."

The other three Aspects veered off, gathering speed as they began their pursuit of the renegade.

Alexstrasza watched them fly off, almost ready to join in the hunt. She did not know if, even with their power returned to them, they could forever end the terror of Deathwing, but he certainly had to be contained. However, there were other matters that she had to deal with first.

The Dragonqueen surveyed both the skies and earth, searching. At last she spotted the one she sought.

"Korialstrasz," she whispered. "You were *not* one of Ysera's dreams after all. . . ."

If they had fought alone, the dwarves might have suffered a different fate. Certainly they could have held their own for a time, but the orcs had not only outnumbered them, they had also been in better condition. Years of skulking underground had hardened Rom's band in some ways, but it had drained them in others.

A fortunate thing, then, that their ranks had been added to by a war wizard, a skilled elven ranger, and one of their mad cousins atop a gryphon with razor-sharp talons and beak. With the *Demon Soul* destroyed, the trio had turned their talents to aiding the trusty hill dwarves and turning the tide.

Of course, the red dragon constantly swooping down on the orcs every time they tried to organize ranks certainly helped.

What remained of Grim Batol's orc forces finally surrendered, so very beaten that they knelt before the victors, certain death would soon follow. Rom, his arm in a sling, might have granted them that, for many of his folk and those of his allies had perished, including Gimmel. However, the dwarven leader followed the commands of another—and who argued with a dragon?

"They will be marched to the west, where Alliance vessels will take them back to the enclaves already set up. There has been enough blood this day, and northern Khaz Modan will certainly cause the shedding of more. . . ." Korialstrasz looked tired, so very tired. "I have seen enough blood today, thank you. . . ."

With Rom's promise to do as the leviathan bid, Korialstrasz turned his attention to Rhonin.

"I won't tell anyone the truth about you, *Krasus*," the young wizard immediately said. "I think I understand why you did what you did."

"But I will never forgive myself for my lapses. I only pray that my queen understands. . . ." The reptilian giant managed an almost human shrug. "As for my place in the Kirin Tor, that will be up for some debate. Not only do I not know if I wish to stay, but the truth about what happened is surely to come out—at least in part. They will realize that I sent you on other than a simple reconnaissance mission."

"What happens now?"

"Many things . . . too many things. The Horde still maintains its hold on Dun Algaz, but that will come to an end soon. After that, this world must rebuild . . . providing it gains the chance." He paused. "In addition, there are some political matters which, after this day's events, will most certainly shift." Korialstrasz eyed the tiny creatures before him somewhat uneasily. "And I will say to you now that my kind is as much to blame for those shifts as anyone else."

Rhonin would have pressed, but he immediately saw that Korialstrasz would not be answering those questions. Having learned of both Deathwing's and the red dragon's ability to masquerade as humans, the wizard did not doubt that the ancient race had interfered much over the history of not only humanity, but the elves and others as well.

"That was quick thinking, what you did, Rhonin," the behemoth remarked. "You were always a good student. . . ."

The conversation came to an abrupt end as a vast shadow swept over the band. For a brief moment, the weary mage feared that Deathwing had somehow escaped his pursuers and had returned to take his vengeance on those who had caused his defeat.

However, the dragon hovering above turned out not to be black, but rather as crimson as Korialstrasz.

"The dark one flees! His evil is, if not stopped, certainly curtailed some!"

Korialstrasz gazed up, longing in his voice. "My queen . . ."

"I had thought you dead," murmured Alexstrasza to her consort. "I mourned you for a long time. . . ."

The male looked guilty. "The subterfuge was necessary, my queen, if only to give me the opportunity to try to win your freedom. I apologize not only for the pain I caused you, but also the inconsideration I displayed by manipulating these mortals. I know how you feel toward their kind. . . ."

She nodded. "If they will forgive you, then so will I." Her tail slipped down, intertwining with his own for a moment. "The others still pursue the dark one, but before I would join them in the hunt, we must gather what remains of our flight and rebuild our home anew. This I think a priority."

"I am your servant," he replied, bowing his massive head. "Now and forever, my love."

Looking at the wizard and his friends, the Dragonqueen added, "For your sacrifices, the least we can do is offer you a ride home—providing you can wait a little while."

Even though, with much effort, Falstad's gryphon could have eventually carried them home, Rhonin gratefully accepted. He found he liked both dragons, despite Korialstrasz's past trickery. Put in the same position, the wizard probably would have acted just as the consort had.

"The hill dwarves will give you food and a place to rest. We will return for you tomorrow after the eggs have all been recovered and safely secreted." A bitter smile crossed her draconic features. "Praise be that our eggs are so very durable, or else even in defeat Deathwing would have struck mine a bitter blow. . . ."

"Do not think about it," urged the male. "Come! The sooner we are done, the better!"

"Yes . . ." Alexstrasza dipped her head toward the trio. "Human Rhonin, elf, and dwarf! I thank all three of you for your parts in this, and know that as long as I am queen, my kind will never be an enemy to yours. . . ."

And with that, both dragons rose high into the air, racing in the direction that Deathwing had gone with the first of the eggs. Those still remaining with the caravan would be under the protection of the jubilant hill dwarves, who could at last claim the mountain fortress and all of Grim Batol as theirs again.

"A glorious sight, them!" rumbled Falstad once the dragons had vanished. He turned to his companions. "My elven lady, you shall always be a part of my dreams!" He took the confused ranger's hand, shook it, then said to Rhonin, "Wizard, I've not dealt much with your kind, but I'll say here that at least one of 'em has the heart of a warrior! Be quite a tale I'll be telling, *the Taking of Grim Batol!* Don't be surprised if you someday find dwarves regaling your story in some tavern, eh?"

"Are you leaving us?" Rhonin asked in complete bewilderment. They had only just won the battle. He still struggled to catch his breath from the entire matter.

"You should not go until at least the morning," Vereesa insisted.

The wild dwarf shrugged as if indicating that, had it been his own choice, he would have gladly stayed. "Sorry I am, but this news must reach the Aerie as soon as possible! As fast as the dragons'll be, I'll get back there before they reach Lordaeron! 'Tis my duty—and I'd like a few particular folk there to know I've not been lost after all. . . ."

Rhonin gratefully took Falstad's powerful hand, thankful that he did not have to use his own injured one to shake. Even tired, the gryphon-rider had a crushing grip. "Thank you for everything!"

"No, human, thank *you!* I'd like to see another rider with a greater song of glory to sing than I've got! Will make the heads of the ladies turn my way, believe you me!"

In a startling display for one so reserved, Vereesa leaned down and kissed the dwarf lightly on the cheek. Underneath his great beard, Falstad blushed furiously. Rhonin felt a twinge of jealousy.

"Take care of yourself," she warned the rider.

"That I will!" He mounted the back of the gryphon with one practiced leap. With a wave to the duo, Falstad tapped lightly on the animal's sides with his heels. "Mayhaps we'll all meet again once this war's truly over!"

The gryphon lifted off into the sky, circling once so that Falstad could bid them farewell again. Then the dwarf's mount steered west, and the short warrior vanished into the distance.

Rhonin waved at the dwindling figure, recalling with some guilt his first impressions of the dwarf. Falstad had proven himself though, in many ways more than the wizard felt that *he* had.

A gentle hand took hold of his crippled one, lifting it slowly up.

"This is long past the need to be dealt with," Vereesa reproved him. "I took an oath to see you safe. This would not look good for me. . . ."

"Didn't your oath end when we reached the shores of Khaz Modan?" he returned, adding a slight smile.

"Perhaps, but it seems that you need to be guarded from yourself every hour of the day! What might you do to yourself next?" However, the elf, too, let a slight smile momentarily escape her.

Rhonin let her fuss over his broken finger, wondering if perhaps there might be a way for him to continue his association with Vereesa after the dragon had brought them both back to Lordaeron. Surely it would be best for those in command if the pair gave their reports together, the better to verify events. He would have to propose that to Vereesa and see how she felt about it.

Curious, he suddenly thought, how one could go from almost seeking death, as he had done in the beginning, to wanting to live to the fullest—and that after nearly having been incinerated, crushed, run through, beheaded, and devoured. He would always have regrets for what had happened on his previous mission, but no longer was he haunted by that time.

"There," Vereesa announced. "Keep it like that until I can find some better material. It should heal well, then."

She had taken a strip of cloth from her cloak and had fashioned a splint of sorts using a piece of wood from a broken war-ax. Rhonin inspected her work, found it exceptional.

He had never bothered to mention that, once recuperated, he would have been able to completely heal the hand himself. She had been very willing to help him.

"Thank you."

He hoped that the dragons would take their time with their task. With nothing to fear from the orcs, Rhonin found himself in no hurry whatsoever to go home.

When news at last spread to the Alliance of Grim Batol's downfall and the loss of the dragons to the Horde's dying cause, celebrations arose among the people. Surely now the war would at last come to an end. Surely now peace was at hand.

Each of the major kingdoms insisted on hearing the words of the wizard and elf for themselves, questioning the pair at great length. Word came down from the Aeries of verification from one of the gryphon-riders, the celebrated hero Falstad

While Rhonin and Vereesa continued their tour of the various kingdoms—and grew closer in the process—he who had worn the guise of the wizard Krasus had made a report of his own in the Chamber of the Air. Initially, he had been greeted with hostility by his fellow councilors, especially those who knew he had outright lied to all. However, no one could argue with the results, and wizards were, if nothing else, pragmatic when it came to results.

Drenden had shaken his shadowed head at the faceless mage. "You could've brought down everything we'd worked for!" he boomed, his words echoed by the storm momentarily raging through the chamber. "Everything!"

"I understand that now. If you like, I will resign from the council, even accept penance or ouster, if that is what you wish."

"There were those who mentioned more than ouster," commented Modera. "Much more than ouster . . ."

"But we've all discussed that and decided that young Rhonin's success has brought Dalaran nothing but good will, even from those of our allies who briefly protested their lack of knowledge of his improbable mission. The elves especially are pleased, as one of their own was also involved." Drenden shrugged. "There seems no reason to continue on with this subject. Consider yourself officially censured, Krasus, but *congratulated* by me personally."

"Drenden!" snapped Modera.

"We're alone here, I can say what I will." He steepled his fingers. "Now, then, if no one else has any other comment, I'd like to bring up the subject of one Lord Prestor, supposed monarch-elect of Alterac—who *seems* to have vanished off the face of the world!"

"The chateau is empty, his servants fled . . ." added Modera, still annoyed at her counterpart's earlier comments concerning Krasus.

One of the other mages, the heavyset one, finally spoke up. "The spells surrounding the place've dissipated, too. And there're signs that there were goblins working for this rogue mage!"

The entire council looked to Korialstrasz.

He spread his hands as if as bewildered as the rest. "Lord Prestor" had clearly had the upper hand in the situation, everything to gain; why, the rest clearly wanted to know, had he abandoned it all now? "It is as much a puzzle to me as it is you. Perhaps he realized that, eventually, our combined might would bring him down. That would be my likely guess. Certainly nothing else would explain why he would give up so much."

This sat well with the other wizards. Like most creatures, Korialstrasz knew, they had their egos to assuage.

"His influence already wanes," he went on. "For surely you have all heard how Genn Greymane has reinstated his protest against Prestor's taking ascension, and even Lord Admiral Proudmoore has joined him on this. King Terenas even announced that a second check into the so-called noble's background left many questions unanswered. The rumors of Prestor's imminent betrothal to the young princess have dwindled away. . . ."

"You were looking into his background," commented Modera.

"It may be that some of that information slipped to His Majesty, yes."

Drenden nodded, quite pleased. "Rhonin's quest has brought us into the good graces of Terenas and the others, and we'll make the best use of that turn. By the end of a fortnight, 'Lord Prestor' will be anathema to the entire Alliance!"

Korialstrasz raised a warning hand. "Best to take a more subtle touch. We have the time. Before long, they will forget he even existed."

"Perhaps you're right." The bearded mage looked at the others, who nodded in agreement. "Unanimous, then. How wonderful." He raised his hand, ready to dismiss the council. "Well, if there's nothing more—"

"Actually, there is," interrupted the dragon mage. A cloud from the fading storm drifted through him.

"What is it?"

"Although you have granted me pardon for my questionable actions, I must tell you now that I must take my leave from council activities for a time."

They looked stunned. None could recall him ever having missed a gathering, much less stepping back from the council altogether.

"How long?" Modera asked.

"I cannot say. She and I have been apart so long, it will take quite some time to regain what we once had."

Korialstrasz could almost see Drenden blink, despite the shadow spell. "*You* have a . . . a *wife*, is she?"

"Yes. Forgive me if I never recalled to tell you. As I said, we were apart for quite some time. . . ." He smiled even though they could not see it. ". . . but now she is returned to me."

The others shared glances. Finally, Drenden replied, "Then . . . by all means . . . we shall not stand in your way. You certainly have the right to do this. . . ."

He bowed. In truth, the dragon hoped to return, for this had been as much a part of his centuries-old life as almost anything else. Yet, compared to being with his Alexstrasza, even it paled in comparison. "My thanks. I hope, of course, to keep abreast of all news of import, I promise you. . . ."

He raised his hand in farewell as the spell he cast transported him away from the Chamber of the Air. Korialstrasz's parting words were truer than even the other wizards might have realized. As one of the Kirin Tor—even one absent from the council—he most definitely planned to watch the political maneuverings.

Despite "Lord Prestor's" disappearance, potentially devastating squabbles remained between the various kingdoms, Alterac again one of the foremost topics. His duties for Dalaran *demanded* Korialstrasz maintain watch.

And for his queen, for his ancient kind, he and others like him would also watch . . . watch and influence, if necessary. Alexstrasza believed in these young races, more so after what Rhonin and the others had done, and because of that Korialstrasz intended to do what he had to in order to steel her belief. He owed that to both her and those who had aided him in his quest.

No one had sighted Deathwing since the black beast's desperate escape. With the others constantly on watch for him now, it seemed unlikely that he would cause much terror for some time to come, if ever. Yet, because of him, the others had taken a renewed interest in life and the future.

The day of the dragon had passed, true, but that did not mean at all that they would not continue to leave their mark in the world . . . even if no one else ever suspected it.

ABOUT THE AUTHOR

RICHARD A. KNAAK is the author of more than twenty fantasy novels and over a dozen short pieces, including the *New York Times* bestseller *THE LEGEND OF HUMA* for the Dragonlance series. Aside from his extensive work in Dragonlance, he is best known for his popular Dragonrealm series, which is now available again in trade paperback. His other works include several contemporary fantasies, including *FROSTWING* and *KING OF THE GREY*, also available again. Besides *DAY OF THE DRAGON* for the Warcraft series, he is writing two novels based on Diablo, first of which will be the upcoming *LEGACY OF BLOOD*. He is also working on a major trilogy for Dragonlance.

Those interested in learning more about his projects should check out his Web site at http://www.sff.net/people/knaak.